THE
LOST CROWN

Atlantic Ocean

Edinburgh

Arctic Ocean

Stockholm

Copenhagen

Helsinki

Berlin

Peterhof • St. Petersburg

Tsarskoe Selo

Warsaw

Mogilev

Moscow

Russi

Tobolsk

Ekaterinburg

Livadia

Black
Sea

Caspian
Sea

Also by Sarah Miller

MISS SPITFIRE

Baghdad • Tehran

Kabul

THE
LOST CROWN

Yakutsk

Pacific Ocean

Sarah Miller

Vladivostok

Tokyo

ATHENEUM BOOKS FOR YOUNG READERS
New York   London   Toronto   Sydney   New Delhi

Seoul

Beijing

ATHENEUM BOOKS FOR YOUNG READERS
An imprint of Simon & Schuster Children's Publishing Division
1230 Avenue of the Americas, New York, New York 10020
ATHENEUM BOOKS FOR YOUNG READERS is a registered trademark of Simon & Schuster, Inc.
For information about special discounts for bulk purchases, please contact Simon & Schuster Special Sales at 1-866-506-1949 or business@simonandschuster.com.
The Simon & Schuster Speakers Bureau can bring authors to your live event. For more information or to book an event, contact the Simon & Schuster Speakers Bureau at 1-866-248-3049 or visit our website at www.simonspeakers.com.
Also available in an Atheneum Books for Young Readers hardcover edition
Book design by Debra Sfetsios-Conover
Interior map art by Drew Willis
The text for this book is set in Adobe Caslon.
Manufactured in the United States of America
First Atheneum Books for Young Readers paperback edition July 2012
10 9 8 7 6 5 4 3 2 1
The Library of Congress has cataloged the hardcover edition as follows:
Miller, Sarah Elizabeth, 1979–
The lost crown / Sarah Miller. — 1st ed.
p. cm.
Summary: In alternating chapters, Grand Duchesses Olga, Tatiana, Maria, and Anastasia tell how their privileged lives as the daughters of the Tsar in early twentieth-century Russia are transformed by World War and revolution.
ISBN 978-1-4169-8340-8 (hc)
1. Nicholas II, Emperor of Russia, 1868–1918—Family—Juvenile fiction. 2. Russia—History—Nicholas II, 1894–1917—Juvenile fiction. [1. Nicholas II, Emperor of Russia, 1868–1918—Family—Fiction. 2. Sisters—Fiction. 3. Kings, queens, rulers, etc.—Fiction. 4. Revolutions—Fiction. 5. World War, 1914–1918—Fiction. 6. Russia—History—Nicholas II, 1894–1917—Fiction.] I. Title.
PZ7.M63443Los 2011
[Fic]—dc22
2010037001
ISBN 978-1-4169-8341-5 (pbk)
ISBN 978-1-4424-2392-3 (eBook)

to Holly

Cast of Characters

THE IMPERIAL FAMILY

Tsar Nicholas II (*Nicky*): last emperor of Russia

Empress Alexandra Feodorovna (*Alix; Sunny*): his wife, a German princess and favorite granddaughter of Queen Victoria

Grand Duchess Olga Nikolaevna (*Olya; Olenka*): eldest daughter of the tsar; born 1895

Grand Duchess Tatiana Nikolaevna (*Tatya; Tatianochka; Governess*): second daughter of the tsar; born 1897

Grand Duchess Maria Nikolaevna (*Mashka*): third daughter of the tsar; born 1899

Grand Duchess Anastasia Nikolaevna (*Nastya; Shvybzik*): youngest daughter of the tsar; born 1901

Tsarevich Aleksei Nikolaevich (*Alyosha; Baby; Sunbeam*): only son of the tsar, heir to the Russian throne; born 1904

FRIENDS

Buxhoeveden, Sophia (*Isa*): lady-in-waiting and friend of the empress

Dehn, Lili: friend of the empress and Anna Vyrubova

Derevenko, Kolya: son of Dr. Derevenko; playmate to Aleksei

Khitrovo, Margarita (*Ritka*): companion of Grand Duchess Olga; former lady-in-waiting to the empress

Rasputin, Grigori (*Otets Grigori*): peasant; friend and spiritual guide to the empress; believed by the imperial family to have healing powers

Vyrubova, Anna (*Anya*): maid of honor and closest friend of the empress

SERVANTS AND MEMBERS OF THE IMPERIAL SUITE

Dr. Evgeni Sergeevich Botkin: personal physician to the empress

Demidova, Anna (*Nyuta*): maid to the empress

Dr. Vladimir Derevenko: physician and surgeon to the tsarevich

Gibbes, Sidney: English tutor of the imperial children

Gilliard, Pierre (*Zhilik*): French tutor of the imperial children

Kharitonov, Ivan: chef

Nagorny, Klementy: *dyadka* (sailor nanny) to the tsarevich

Sednev, Ivan: footman to the grand duchesses; former crew member on the imperial yacht *Standart*

Sednev, Leonid (*Leonka*): kitchen boy; nephew of Ivan Sednev; Aleksei's playmate in Ekaterinburg

Trupp, Aleksei: footman

REVOLUTIONARIES AND GUARDS

Avdeev, Alexander: first commandant of the Ipatiev house

Beloborodov, Alexander: chairman of the Ural Regional Soviet

Glarner: first chief of the Ipatiev house guard; replaced May 13

Goloshchekin, Filipp: military commissar of the Ural Regional Soviet

Kerensky, Alexander Feodorovich: head of the Provisional Government

Khokhryakov, Pavel: Bolshevik responsible for transferring the imperial children from Tobolsk to Ekaterinburg

Kobylinsky, Colonel Evgeni Stepanovich: commandant of Tsarskoe Selo garrison from May 1917; commander of the special detachment guarding the imperial family in Tobolsk until spring 1918

Lenin, Vladimir Ilyich: head of the Bolshevik Party; leader of the October Revolution and later the Soviet Union

Moshkin, Alexander: Avdeev's second deputy commandant (Ukraintsev's replacement)

Nikolsky, Alexander: aide to Commissar Pankratov

Pankratov, Vasili: first commissar in charge of the imperial family in Tobolsk

Rodionov, Nikolai: second commissar in charge of the imperial family in Tobolsk (replaces Kobylinsky)

Skorokhodov, Ivan: guard at the Ipatiev house

Ukraintsev, Konstantin: Avdeev's first deputy commandant; former imperial soldier

Yakovlev, Vasili: Extraordinary commissar, responsible for transferring the tsar from Tobolsk

Yurovsky, Yakov: last commandant of the Ipatiev house

A Note on Nicknames

In Russian culture, doting nicknames are common and plentiful. Unlike English with its clipped, bouncy nicknames, Russians tend to favor longer, smoother sounds. A girl named Anna might be called Anya, Nyuta, Annushka, or Anechka among family and friends, while a boy named Ivan could go by Vanya, Ivanushka, etc. The more elaborate the nickname, the more intimate and familiar the user.

Russian Words & Phrases

arshin - an old Russian measurement; approximately 28 inches

babushka - grandmother

blini - pancakes

bloshki - a game similar to tiddlywinks

borscht - beet soup

Bozhe moi! - My God!

da - yes

dacha - country house

dedushka - grandfather

dokladi - reports

dorogaya - dear, precious

drozhki - a low, four-wheeled open carriage

duma - parliament

dyadka - title given to the sailor nannies entrusted with protecting Aleksei from everyday injury (probably derived from *dyadya*, the Russian word for "uncle")

dushka - darling, dear; literally, "little soul"

fortochka - a small hinged pane (usually 35-45 cm wide) in a larger window, used for ventilation. Also called a Russian window.

galushka - dumpling

gospodin - mister

idiotka - idiot

izvinite - excuse me

khorosho - good

kokoshnik - a traditional Russian headdress, sometimes made of velvet and studded with pearls

konechno - of course

kremlin - a walled citadel or fortress within a city

kvass - a fermented, mildly alcoholic drink made from rye

lazaret - infirmary

Lett - a non-Russian of European descent

matushka - little mother

moi lyubimi drug - my dear friend

muzhik - peasant

nash naslednik - our heir

nelzya - it is forbidden

nyet - no

Obednya - full mass with Holy Communion

Obednitsa - an abbreviated Liturgy without Holy Communion; may be read by lay worshippers when clergy is not present

ochen - very

ochen priyatno - pleased to meet you

otlichno - excellent

Otets - father/priest

Pascha - Easter

polkovnik - colonel

prigoditsya - it may come in useful

prosphora - bread used in Orthodox Liturgy

samovar - a decorative metal urn used to boil water and/or brew tea

sazhen - an old Russian measurement, approximately seven feet

shchi - cabbage soup

slava Bogu - thank God

sobor - cathedral

spasibo - thank you

Stavka - headquarters

sudba - fate

tak i byt - so be it

tarantass - a low horse-drawn carriage mounted on wheels or runners, depending on the season

verst - an old Russian measurement, just over a kilometer

Ya tebya ochen lyublyu - I love you very much

zakuski - appetizers

zdorovo, okhrannik - good day, guard

A Note About Dates

During the reign of Nicholas II, Russia was one of the last countries still recording dates according to the 1,500-year-old Julian calendar. Most of the rest of the world had switched to the Gregorian (New Style) calendar centuries earlier, and by the twentieth century a difference of thirteen days stretched like a giant time zone between the two calendars. For example, Anastasia Nikolaevna was born on June 5, Old Style. When her relatives in England and Germany wanted to send telegrams to wish her a happy birthday, they did not do so when their New Style calendars said June 5—that would have been thirteen days too soon. Instead, for exactly the same reason that I wouldn't dial my phone at noon in the United States if I want to speak to someone in Moscow when it's noon there, they had to wait to send Anastasia's birthday greetings until June 18 according to their Gregorian calendars. June 5 and 18 is the *same moment* in both countries—it's only the label that varies, depending on which calendar is used.

For the sake of simplicity—and also because the Romanovs themselves persisted in observing the Old Style Julian dates in their letters and diaries even after Russia adopted the Gregorian calendar in February 1918—all dates are given in the Old Style.

(To convert events to the modern Western calendar, add thirteen days to the Old Style date.)

MARIA NIKOLAEVNA

1 August 1917
Tsarskoe Selo

Our luggage is packed and we've said our good-byes. The palace is as dark and still as a museum at midnight, but it's been hours and the train still isn't here. No one will tell us when it will come, or where they're taking us. Even Papa doesn't know anything. We can only wait in the semicircular hall with Kerensky's footsteps echoing over the guards' voices as they whisper.

My sisters and I sit together on a pair of suitcases. If we've forgotten to pack anything, it's already too late—our rooms have all been sealed and photographed. Anyway, Tatiana would say it's bad luck to return for something you've forgotten.

Olga and Tatiana hold hands, and Anastasia dozes against my shoulder. Our younger brother, Aleksei, climbs like a bear cub over the piles of bags and crates. Clutching her rose leaf cushion, Mama follows his every step with her eyes. Papa stands against the wall with one hand on her shoulder. His other hand smoothes his beard over and over again.

Even though it's been almost five months since the revolution, sometimes I can't understand how it all happened. I remember Monsieur Gilliard pointing out Russia and all its territories on our classroom map, telling us Papa ruled one-sixth of the world. Now we're prisoners. Papa says we're not prisoners, me and my sisters and Aleksei. If we wanted to go, the guards couldn't stop us. But none of us will ever leave our parents. "We seven," Mama calls us. No matter what else changes, we will always be we seven.

I can't even imagine what else is left to change.

Anastasia shifts against me and yawns. "What time is it?"

"Nearly three o'clock," Tatiana answers.

I screw my eyes shut, nuzzling my shaved head against Anastasia's shoulder. It can't be long now, and I want to remember everything, everything before we go. . . .

June 1914
Imperial yacht Standart

There has never been such a summer! Since sailing from Peterhof, my sisters and I have spent all day on the sunny decks of our dear *Standart*, playing shuffleboard, roller-skating, dancing, and yes, sometimes flirting with the officers. Of course they kissed our hands when we climbed aboard, but only because we're the tsar's daughters. They can't simply wave hello to a flock of grand duchesses. None of the four of us has had a real kiss, unless one of my sisters has started keeping secrets.

The only dark blot on our trip is Aleksei's accident. Three days ago our brother bumped his ankle on a rung of the ship's ladder. Instead of scampering about the decks in his starched sailor suit with his spaniel, the poor darling ended up stranded in bed, the joint twisted and swelling by the minute. Mama's sent three telegrams to *Otets* Grigori, hoping the holy man's prayers will cure our little Sunbeam. In the meantime Anastasia, Tatiana, and I tease our oldest sister, Olga, mercilessly about her matches with Crown Prince Karol of Romania and our cousin David, the prince of Wales. Even the ship's officers join in.

Clearing her throat, Tatiana straightens up, her hands clasped behind her back. "I am requested by the officers of His Majesty's yacht *Standart* to present this card to Her Imperial Highness, the Grand Duchess Olga Nikolaevna," she announces, handing over an envelope with a little curtsy.

I peek at Anastasia. Something's up. We never use our titles among one another, and neither do the officers. Anastasia only shrugs, but you never can tell with her. Our impish little sister could very well be behind this.

Olga pulls a card out of the envelope. "Oh!" she says after hardly a glimpse, her hands flying to her hips. "It was you, wasn't it, Shvybzik?" she demands, shaking the card at Anastasia.

"Not me," Anastasia insists, batting her eyelashes before she ducks under Olga's hand and snatches the card away. She glances at it and snorts with laughter. Behind us, the officers chuckle as Anastasia capers about the deck, waving the card like a banner. Tatiana's dogs, Jemmy and Ortipo, yip and prance along.

"You all are swine!" Olga declares. I catch Anastasia and read over her shoulder.

The joke's a good one: a cutout newspaper photo of cousin David's head pasted on to a picture of Michelangelo's *David*. I can't help hooting right along with Anastasia at the sight of our cousin's face balanced above all that naked marble.

"Oh, Nastya, what a pair they'll make! Him stark naked and Olga in the fifteen-pound silver nightgown of a grand duchess, just like Auntie Ksenia had to wear on her wedding night!"

"Humpf," Olga sniffs at me. "You're just as much a grand duchess as I am, Mashka, and you'll be fitted for your own fifteen-pound nightgown one of these days. If only we can find someone willing to marry our fat little Bow-Wow!"

"Of course I'll marry," I sing out. "I'll marry a soldier and have dozens of children."

"And they'll be prettier than yours, Olga," Anastasia pipes up, "because her babies will all have Mashka's big blue saucer-eyes." I clasp Anastasia around the waist and peck her cheek. She's a *shvybzik*, but she knows my dreams as well as I do.

"Fine," Olga says, "we can set a banquet table with Mashka's saucers."

Tatiana bursts out laughing, and the officers applaud Olga.

At the sound of a sob from Aleksei's rooms belowdecks,

the smile leaves Tatiana's face. Our giggles dissolve in a heartbeat. We all look at one another, thinking the same thing: That time it sounded like Mama. Suddenly somber, the officers shift their eyes to the deck. Tatiana hurries past them all, her skirts fluttering like sails behind her. Olga follows, and Ortipo, too, before Anastasia and I fall into line, hand in hand and a trifle skittish. Stranded at the top of the stairs, Jemmy whines, her little legs too stubby to follow us down the steps.

We find Tatiana with Mama in the passageway outside Aleksei's cabin. Mama's face is pale and her cheeks streaked with tears. As we come closer, she leans her head on Tatiana's shoulder and closes her eyes. Ortipo whines. Beside me, Anastasia stiffens. "What's wrong?" she asks.

Tatiana puts a finger to her lips and motions us toward Aleksei's doorway. "Go in," she whispers. Her eyes flick down to a rumpled telegram in Mama's hand. "No one has told him."

Olga nods and steps inside. I take a breath as Anastasia pulls me along behind her. Nagorny, Aleksei's *dyadka*, nods, then shuts the door silently behind us. Our brother's sailor nanny always makes me relax a little. Having Nagorny nearby is like sitting under a birch tree, he's so tall and steady in his white sailor suit.

Inside the cool, dim cabin, Joy, Aleksei's spaniel, thumps his tail at us but doesn't budge from his place beside our brother's bunk. Only Aleksei's eyes stand out from the bedclothes. His face and hands have begun to turn waxy white. Under the sheet, his ankle bulges, already swollen as big as his knee. The pull of the sheet as Olga sits on the edge of the bed makes him wince. A hollow opens in my chest at the sight of him like that.

"How are you, Sunbeam?" I ask, leaning over to kiss his dear little forehead and slip a candy from my pocket under his pillow.

"Better than yesterday," he says, his voice as small as his face, "but still swelling."

Still swelling! If I'd knocked my ankle on that ladder, I'd have no more to endure than an ugly bruise and my sisters' teasing. Poor Aleksei has lain in bed three days, and the blood is still pooling into the joint.

"Where's Tatiana?" he asks.

Olga and I look uneasily at each other, but Anastasia springs into action.

"Oh, you know the Governess. She's probably discussing your lessons with Monsieur Gilliard this very minute." Anastasia stands on her toes and stretches out her neck to make herself as tall as our regal Tatiana. "Monsieur Gilliard," she says, addressing me with a twinkle in her eyes, "Aleksei is neglecting his studies. Something must be done."

"But Tatiana Nikolaevna," I begin, and as I try to bow, Anastasia takes one of Aleksei's sailor hats from the bed and pushes its long black ribbon against my upper lip to imitate our tutor's wide mustache. Aleksei blinks with amusement, and Anastasia presses on.

"Really, Monsieur, he has lolled about in bed three days now. It is positively disgraceful."

"But surely, Your Highness," I say, bowing again and gesturing to Aleksei's bed. But I forget to keep hold of my mustache, and the sailor hat topples to the floor. Olga shakes her head and rolls her eyes, but Anastasia keeps up the charade.

"My dear monsieur," she huffs, "that will be quite enough. I see I have overestimated you. A man who cannot even keep track of his own mustache simply cannot be capable of educating the next tsar of the Russias. You are dismissed!"

I let my head fall to my chest and make my way to the door.

Anastasia yanks the hat from the carpet and holds it out to me, one ribbon pinched between two fingers with her pinkie sticking out a mile. "And take this with you. I will not have discarded mustaches lying about the tsarevich's bedroom!"

Aleksei smiles, a real smile this time, and bursts into applause. Olga joins in after an instant, while Anastasia and I hold hands and curtsy.

At that very moment, Monsieur Gilliard himself appears in the doorway, his arms full of our brother's favorite storybooks. Aleksei explodes with laughter, and the pinch of happiness inside my chest splits open like a firecracker. Anastasia turns white for a flash, then grabs me by the arm and pulls me straight under Monsieur's mustache and into the corridor, slamming the door on our tutor's bewildered face. Despite Mama's startled glance and Tatiana's glare, I can't help wrapping my arms around my clown of a little sister with a hug that lifts her from her feet. Even though I know something dreadful has happened, for that moment, the only thing I can think of is that I love Anastasia best of all.

2

TATIANA NIKOLAEVNA

July 1914
Gulf of Finland

The news is all bad," Olga whispers, and for once I agree with my melancholy eldest sister. Just a few days ago, a woman stabbed and nearly killed our beloved friend, Mama's confidant, *Otets* Grigori Rasputin. The telegram said she screamed, "I've killed the Antichrist!" then tried to drive the knife into her own abdomen.

"Poor Mama!" I whisper back, nodding toward the deck chair where Mama sits with the French ambassador, a pained expression on her face. "All the powder in the world cannot hide the circles under her eyes. Worrying about Aleksei's accident has wearied her more than anything."

In the midst of everything else the French president is paying us an official state visit. For days we have been wrapped up in ceremonies, receptions, and military reviews. Even here on the president's battleship, away from

St. Petersburg's gossipy socialites, I cannot help hovering nearby. Mama is so anxious for Aleksei, left behind at our *dacha* in Peterhof while his ankle heals, that I pray for Christ to lend His strength to both her and Our Friend. Mama's health depends on *Otets* Grigori's survival almost as much as Aleksei's.

"How has she managed it?" I ask. Olga shakes her head too. "She was frantic with nerves this morning. You know how bad it can be. She nearly cried every time the president's name was mentioned."

Olga squeezes my hand. "You've gotten her this far, Tatya. We'll be back aboard our own *Standart* tonight, after the president's sending-off."

"Thank God for that. I doubt she could take one more banquet or parade." I do not tell Olga, but I know I am not the one who has brought Mama this far. One moment Mama can be frightened as a lamb in the wild, and the next, it is as if Christ himself takes her hand and pulls her above it all.

With a blast of brass and drums, the ship's band breaks into a march, and I startle halfway out of my wicker armchair. Across the deck, Mama's hands go to her ears, her cheeks dark as wine. Before I can recover myself, Olga motions for me to sit, then glides toward Mama just as the ambassador signals the musicians to cease.

My shoulders relax a little as I watch Olga whisper into Mama's ear, then speak to the ambassador. None of my sisters understands our mother the way I do, but they try, God bless them. I only pray Olga's temper will not break loose in all this tension. She comes back smiling, though, and pats my arm as she sits down.

"I asked Monsieur Paléologue to go on talking with Mama."

"What will they talk about?"

She shrugs, her eyes twinkling like Papa's. "I don't know. That's an ambassador's job, isn't it?"

"Anything but war, I hope." Talk of war is everywhere. Two weeks before *Otets* Grigori was stabbed, a Serbian assassin shot the heir to the Austrian throne. The Austrians are furious, and no wonder. All Russia would mourn with us if someone murdered our precious Aleksei. Already Germany has leaped to Austria's defense. The whole world seems to be taking up sides. "At least Papa wants nothing to do with war."

Olga's wide forehead furrows. "I heard Papa tell one of the ministers he's determined to back the Serbians."

I stare at her. "The Serbians? How could we, after what that Serbian beast did?"

"Papa says the Serbs are our Slavic brothers."

My thoughts turn in circles. "If we take the Serbians' side, we have to fight both Austria and Germany. That makes no sense, Olga. Mama is German." So are Auntie Irene in Prussia, Uncle Ernie in Hesse, and their jolly little boys—our cousins. Just four years ago, we played with all of them in the courtyard at Wolfsgarten. "You think Papa would choose the Serbs over our own family?"

"At times like this, he has to be more than just Papa, Tatya."

The certainty in her voice makes me shiver and cross myself in the warm gulf breeze. "Have you told the Little Pair?"

"No."

Thank heaven. "Listen to me, Olga. There is no reason to worry them yet. Or Aleksei. Let them have the rest of their summer." She nods. "What about Mama?"

Olga's face clouds. She coils up her hands, running her thumbs over her fingernails the way she always does when she is nervous or angry. "I haven't heard any more than Mama has. Maybe I've heard less."

"But, Olga," I cry, ready to spring to Mama's side. "What if the ambassador—"

"Shhh!" Olga hisses. "It's not my place. And it's not yours, either," she says, laying a hand on my wrist. She smiles sadly at me. "Even a dutiful Governess like you can't take care of everyone, Tatya."

Peterhof

Olga was right. For days we hardly see Papa at all. Telegrams, ministers, and ambassadors come and go late into the night, while a haze of cigarette smoke creeps outside Papa's study door. In the hall, a tray with a glass of milk and a fresh packet of cigarettes always waits. When he comes out to eat with us, his fingertips are yellowed by the tobacco, his beard flat on one side from the way he strokes it when he thinks.

"I had another telegram from Willi today," Papa says to

Mama at tea. Anastasia wrinkles her nose and rolls her eyes at the kaiser's name, but the look on Olga's face makes me crush the tidbit I've been dangling for Ortipo into crumbs. Papa has hardly spoken about what is happening behind his study doors, and now the kaiser? I watch Mama. Her trembling embroidery needle knots over a simple row of satin stitches.

"Cousin Willi sends his best greetings for our Sunbeam's tenth birthday," Papa says, and reaches over to chuck Aleksei's chin.

"He's almost two weeks early," Anastasia blurts. "Hasn't he figured out how our calendar works yet?"

I pinch her under the table. Surely there was more to Cousin Willi's telegram than birthday wishes. She glares and kicks me back, but she hushes. Papa gives her a tired smile. "He's a very busy man, little Shvybzik." The flash of fear in Mama's eyes fades, but does not go out.

She knows more than Olga realizes.

The next day Papa joins us for evening prayers at the small Alexandria church. We file in the way we always do: Papa and Mama, then Olga, me, Maria, and Anastasia. OTMA, all in a row like the fingers of one hand, with me the tallest and Anastasia the smallest.

In the candlelight, the lines on Mama's face seem deep as the folds of a bishop's robe. She has not looked that way since Aleksei nearly died two years ago on holiday at Spala. Like then, she sends one telegram after another to *Otets* Grigori in Siberia. This time, though, they are not only about

Aleksei. Now she cables him about the possibility of war.

Our parents pray almost feverishly. I watch Mama's chest rise and fall, her jewels flashing in the candlelight with every breath. From where I stand, I can do nothing for her but pray.

Back at the *dacha*, Papa kisses Mama's red cheek. "I'll read the latest *dokladi* and come in to dinner," he tells her. Her breath catches. "Only a few minutes, Sunny," Papa promises. He whispers something in Mama's ear that makes her smile before he walks away down the corridor, rubbing his beard and patting his coat pocket for another cigarette.

In the dining room, we manage to chat a little, but the minutes tick by, and even though she smiles at us, I notice the flush creeping back into Mama's cheeks. My eyes jump from the clock to the door and back to Mama again and again. Olga sits quiet and still, giving me a long look while Maria and Anastasia's talk weaves round us.

Finally Mama puts a hand to her chest and lets out a sharp breath. "Tatiana," she says in a measured voice, "go and fetch your papa before his dinner goes cold." My chair clatters across the floor as I rise, halting the Little Pair's chatter.

The moment my hand touches the knob, it jolts under me. The door swings open. There stands Papa. He blinks at me, then clears his throat and tugs on his dinner jacket. He looks past all of us to the end of the table where Mama stands with her hands braced against the tabletop.

"It's—," Papa begins, then clears his throat again. "It's war."

Mama closes her eyes, trembling as she sinks into her chair. "War," she whispers, and weeps.

All round the table, my sisters begin to cry. Only Anastasia's eyes are dry, but when I see our Shvybzik's sober face and bewildered eyes, I cross myself and cry first for her, and then for Russia.

"*Tak i byt,*" Papa says. *So be it.*

3

ANASTASIA NIKOLAEVNA

July 1914
Peterhof

The whole country has gone mad overnight!" I tell Aleksei. "Everywhere you turn, it's war fever and God-save-the-tsar. Now I have to leave the *dacha* and go to the stinking city for the official declaration of war on Germany? I'd rather go to the beach."

"But, Nastya, the soldiers—" Aleksei's ankle twitches, and his face crimps like he's been pinched from the inside. "The soldiers have to see the tsar before they leave for the front. Papa will give them courage," he says, sadly stroking the red sash of the Legion of Honor the French president gave him just a few days ago.

"Poo. I don't see why *I* have to go. Mama will make us all wear dresses like lace curtains, and those huge hats that make me look like a *galushka* next to our sisters. And whoever felt brave after looking at a boiled dumpling?" I flop Joy's curly ears up over his head. Aleksei smiles a little, at last. "At least if you could go, I wouldn't be the shortest one. I'd rather stay here than go to that musty old Winter Palace."

I know how much Aleksei wants to go to the ceremony. His ankle is still as knobbly as a potato, and the soldiers can't see him all pale and weak like this, no matter what. It's impossible for him to go, and if I can't stay at Peterhof with him, I have to cheer him up as much as I can before I leave.

"I'll be bored to death. They'll snap pictures of us like we're a troupe of caged baboons, and Mama won't even let us bring our Brownie cameras. I'd like to stick my lens in *their* faces for a change." Aleksei doesn't answer, so I arch my eyebrow and say, "They'll sing that same old song again."

"What song?"

He knows perfectly well what song. Our national anthem, "God Save the Tsar." It's a game we play. "Papa's song. I wonder if the band gets as tired of it as I do?"

Aleksei smirks. "I bet they don't have their own words to it like you."

"I bet they do! I bet they're the only people in all of Russia who have to listen to it as much as us." I make my voice deep and trumpety, puff out my belly like a bass drum, and strut around the room, making up a new verse.

> *"Here comes the tsar again!*
> *Strike up the tune, boys.*
> *Why must we play him*
> *that sa-a-ame old song?*

"Surely the tsar could hear
a-a-anything he wants to!
Why don't we pla-a-ay
'Kali-i-inka' instea-a-ad?"

The doorknob clicks, and when I turn around, there's Olga with one fist propped on her hip, grinning like a cat with a canary jammed in its mouth. "Anastasia Nikolaevna, if I told Mama what you were doing instead of getting dressed—"

"But you won't tell. That's Tatiana's job," I say, and flick out my tongue.

She swats at me, but I duck to Aleksei's side, kiss him good-bye, and dart out the door.

St. Petersburg

When we step from the launch onto the streets of the capital, there's already a crowd waiting to gawk as if the six of us were made of gold instead of ordinary leather. I do feel like a *galushka*, wrapped up in a tablecloth of a dress and a hat like a platter of flowers. The people jostle to see Papa, then turn toward Mama, next in line, but by the time they get to the back, they've seen too many lace-encrusted grand duchesses to care about me, the only one still stuck in skirts above the ankle.

Aleksei was right. They want him. Their eyes walk up and down the procession, wondering where the tsarevich is this time. I wonder what kind of ridiculous stories they'll imagine to explain him away. Some of them will be even worse than the truth, I bet.

The crowd elbows and cranes, and I wish I could ogle right back at them. Ahead of us, Papa takes Mama by the hand instead of offering her his elbow, which sends my eyebrows reaching to meet my fringe. Mama is usually so stiff and proper in front of people: Empress with a capital *E*. But today she holds hands with Papa all the way across the red carpet and into the Winter Palace, just like they do at home.

Inside, it's horrible. The halls are stuffy and crowded with overdressed courtiers. The women have red eyes and sloppy handkerchiefs, and the men sweat under their collars as they fiddle with their swords and ribbons. My mouth opens at the sight of nasty old Aunt Miechen standing at the far end of the hall with tears running down her face.

"Anastasia, close your mouth." Maria giggle-snorts. Before I can point out Aunt Miechen, Tatiana gives us both a deadly look over her shoulder, and I promise myself I'll get even with her later.

When the crowd in the Nicholas Hall catches a glimpse of Papa and Mama, a "Hurrah!" rises up that shakes the heavy frowns from all their faces. Papa stops for half a step, then begins nodding his head at them, smiling a little. Mama has her best Empress Face pasted on. She stands tall and nods along with Papa, never letting go of his hand until they reach the altar. I can tell she'll have one of her foul headaches by the time we get back to the *dacha*, especially since no one— not even an empress—can sit down during Liturgy.

Before us stands the seven-hundred-year-old miraculous

Kazan icon of the Mother of God, and the metropolitan and bishops in their best gold mitres sparking with jewels. Satin rustles and swords clink as we kneel on the hard parquet floor, and the Liturgy begins.

I should close my eyes like everyone else, but instead I watch Papa's face turn pale and tight, and see Mama try so hard to hold a calm expression that the rest of her body almost quivers. The service seems to calm the crowd around us, but my skin's creeping. It doesn't make any sense.

When we rise, Papa marches to the altar and announces, "Officers of my guard, here present, I greet my entire army, united as it is, in body and spirit standing firm as a wall of granite, and I give it my blessing. I solemnly swear that I will never make peace so long as the enemy is on the soil of our Holy Motherland. Great is the God of the Russian Land!"

In front of me, Olga lets out a sob just as a cheer rolls up from the crowd. I grab Maria's hand and bite my lip. For ten whole minutes the hall quakes with the sound of the people crying and shouting. As we make our way toward the balcony, everyone rushes us, their voices hoarse and wet, dropping to their knees and stretching out to touch us as we try to pass. Papa's whole face freezes. General Voiekov barks at them all to stay back and make way, but Mama steps forward and puts her hand on his arm.

For once, she looks just like our mama. Her face isn't all tight and blotchy. Tears stand on her cheeks, but she smiles and goes ahead, letting the people kiss her hands and dress. Papa doesn't make a peep as she floats from one person to the next. Some of the women shake and sob, so Mama holds them to her for the length of a hiccup or two before she passes. Behind her, the people bow and make the sign of the cross over us, and suddenly my mouth feels dry as wallpaper.

At the French doors to the balcony, Papa and Mama join hands again and face the crowd along the river Neva. The riverside roars so loud when they see our parents, my sisters and I hang back in a clump, peeking through the curtains at the thousands of upturned faces. I see Papa's mouth move when he tries to speak, but we can't hear his voice even though we're only a few steps behind him. He tries two more times to call out to the people, but the balcony and the windows rattle with the noise from below. Instead Papa bows his head and slowly makes the sign of the cross over them. Like a wave from the water, they fall to their knees on the cobblestones, and for the first time in my life, I see tears streaming down my golden papa's face and into his beard.

From the streets below, five thousand voices break into song, the words washing over us all as my sisters and I kneel too:

God save the tsar!
Mighty and powerful!
May he reign for our glory,
Reign that our foes may quake!
O orthodox tsar!
God save the tsar!

With my face hidden against Olga's shoulder, I cry without knowing why.

4.

OLGA NIKOLAEVNA

September 1914
Tsarskoe Selo

rom the moment Papa leaves for the front, our whole
family throws itself into war work. Hospitals and
sanitary trains in our names open one after another. In
the Catherine Palace across the park from our home, many
of the great halls have been cleared and converted into a
lazaret filled with beds for the wounded. Mama, her best
friend Anya, Tatiana, and I all attend Red Cross classes
so we can nurse the soldiers ourselves. Maria and Anastasia are too young to tend the wounded, but they visit
"their" wards as often as they can to cheer the men with
their childish antics. Tatiana and I each head our own war
relief committees and travel back and forth to the capital—
newly rechristened Petrograd in the spirit of Slavic
patriotism—to collect donations. In our spare moments we
knit socks and mufflers, for Mama never likes our hands to

be idle, and wartime is no time for embroidery.

But when Anya telephones to say that *Otets* Grigori wishes to see us, Mama and I stop everything and hurry to Anya's little yellow house across the corner from our palace—we haven't seen *Otets* Grigori since he was stabbed nearly to death. I take just enough time to slip my volume of Lermontov's poems into an apron pocket.

"Mama," I ask as the motorcar rumbles through our gates and into the streets of Tsarskoe Selo, "that woman who tried to kill *Otets* Grigori—"

"She was insane, darling," Mama interrupts, "a filthy, diseased madwoman. Such people have no reason."

Of all the peasants in all of Siberia, this madwoman happened to stick her knife into the tsaritsa's confidant? If I read it in a novel, I wouldn't believe such a coincidence. "Mama, she called him the Antichrist. Surely she wouldn't have said that to just anyone."

"Our Friend has suffered persecution as all the saints did. It isn't our place to ask why."

A fleck of frustration kindles at the back of my throat. That tone means not only that I shouldn't question God, but that I should stop nagging Mama with questions as well. I stuff my hands into my pockets and finger the pages of my poetry book until we pull up to Anya's front door—right under the three-storied nose of the palace police headquarters. With all its windows facing the streets, Anya's house is private as a curio cabinet. By the time we reach her parlor, news that the empress has visited Grigori Rasputin in the home of Anna Vyrubova will be halfway to the capital.

Inside the tiny foyer, Anya clasps Mama's hands and curt-sies clumsily. "Please forgive me, Madame," she says with the little lisp that always makes her seem a bit like a child. "My leg pains me today." Mama starts to speak, but Anya interrupts her. "It's nothing to worry about," she chirps, shuffling toward the parlor as if her leg were made of wood. I smother a smile. Our Anya is always pleased to have something to complain about. "Come along, dears, Our Friend is waiting."

Otets Grigori sits on the small flowered couch near the fireplace with an afghan tucked over his knees. Beside him on the table stands a photo tree, its branches crammed with Anya's favorite images of Papa and Mama. Seeing *Otets* Grigori like this, it's hard to believe any of the coarse whispers I've begun hearing about him from the nurses at the lazaret.

"Matushka!" he cries, holding out his hands to Mama. He never calls her Imperial Majesty or Empress—always "Little Mother," for every Russian is the child of the tsar and tsaritsa.

Mama kisses both his cheeks and takes up the chair beside him. I sit on the other side of the fireplace, tuck-ing my feet up under me to keep them warm. It's only late September, but already the floors in Anya's house are chilly as the river Neva. Under the handsome blue blouse Mama made for him, *Otets* Grigori's shoulders hunch as though his wound still pains him, but his eyes are bright and deep as water. His dark hair and beard look like he tried to give them a combing, then gave up and matted everything down with greasy tonic.

"Grigori, *moi lyubimi drug.*" Hearing Mama speak Russian makes me smile. At home we speak mostly English with her, but Our Friend speaks only Russian with a Siberian accent and a peasant's vocabulary.

"Matushka, your work pleases God and to make Him happy is as the sun shines. No good will come of war, but the Russian heart will rejoice to see Matushka put her own hands on their wounds." His words run together in a stream. He plays his voice like a harp—one note lingers even as another begins. "Russia bleeds and you will soak their pain from them into your own heart. Is Papa well?"

Quick as that, the conversation flows in another direction before Mama seems to hear what *Otets* Grigori said. Often it happens that way—the sound of his voice alone can rinse away our worries, but this time it flusters me, as though I were listening to a poem with its stanzas out of order. Mama has enough pain of her own without suffering for her country.

As far back as I can remember, Mama's compresses and brown bottles of heart drops have been common as salt shakers in our house. Aleksei's illness is violent and temperamental as a volcano, but sweetheart Mama's eats away bits of every day. To look at her you'd never guess how many hours she spends in the dark on her sofa, miserable with headaches, angina, and shooting pains in her legs. Dr. Botkin visits so often, I feel almost as close to him as my own papa, though his cologne is strong enough to raise a headache out of thin air.

There's something to what *Otets* Grigori says, though. Nursing seems to be good for her. For all Mama used to shun balls and banquets, so far she's rarely missed a day's work at the lazaret. She's never happier than when she's needed.

I'm ashamed to admit it, but the truth is, I miss the days when most of the men I saw in uniform were at Auntie Olga's weekend tea parties, not battered and bedridden in the wards.

Nevertheless, the wounds I've seen don't upset me so much as the thought of those we're sheltered from. No matter how the shattered bones and pulpy flesh turn my stomach, what we see isn't real war. Our lazarets are in the imperial park, the wards surrounded by gilt and marble, and we have cupboards full of bandages and supplies. At the front lines, there are tent hospitals full of mud and panic, where the men arrive brightly bloodied and screaming. Once they've been patched up by field medics, our wounded come in by rail to find themselves pampered with hot cocoa, jigsaw puzzles, chess matches, billiards tables, and concerts. All our luxuries won't keep some men from dying—it can only be a matter of time until I see it happen—but in our lazaret death will creep silently onto the operating table or nestle between clean sheets.

Even during those first weeks of filing instruments and boiling silk in carbolic acid, Tatiana would have told a different story of the lazaret than I. She has such a knack for nursing. The precision that makes her so perfect and dull at the piano serves her well in the wards. It seems to me that she walked into the lazaret on her first day knowing how to keep her face calm and her hands steady. I'm always pressing too hard, or biting my lip, or wincing on some poor soldier's behalf when I should be putting on a brave face.

The way *Otets* Grigori looks at me, perhaps he senses my doubts, as if they rise from me like a scent. I wish his words could rinse away my troubles too. But how can I tell him so with Mama sitting there between us?

The only one I can tell is God.

5

TATIANA NIKOLAEVNA

Autumn 1914
Tsarskoe Selo

*H*er Imperial Highness the Grand Duchess Tatiana Nikolaevna," Dr. Gedroiz announces, presenting my official Red Cross nursing certificate. The scarlet seal stamped beside my name makes me so proud, I do not even blush to hear her read my title in front of so many people. I like to think we are all sisters now, Sisters of Mercy, no matter our rank or station, though I know no reporters or photographers would be at this graduation ceremony if Dr. Gedroiz herself were not a princess, and Mama, Olga, and I among her pupils.

For weeks, my eagerness to get to the lazaret has made me the first of my family to wake and dress each morning. They tease me sometimes for the way I roll the sleeves of my uniform so tightly above my elbows, but I want to be ready to work at a moment's notice. As long as I have my starched nurse's uniform, I can manage not to mind the plain blouses and wartime woolens my sisters and I wear instead of our usual cambrics, linens, and silk-lined cheviots with Orenburg shawls from Tailor Kitaev.

Each night Olga and I write down in our diaries the name, regiment, and wound of every man we bandage.

"How do you keep yourself so composed when you uncover a wound?" she asks. "I can't help bracing myself—I never know what kind of gruesome thing I'll find under the gauze."

"Never look at the whole wound at once," I tell her. "At first I could not look at them any more than you. I had to focus on dressing and sanitizing one stitch at a time. Bit by bit, I learned to work my way through each one."

By the time we graduate to assisting with bone splinters, shrapnel, and bullets, I have trained myself to keep my eyes on the doctor's hands, or the instruments, and no more else than I need to. Olga still stiffens each time an instrument touches a man's skin, but I hold tight to my poise, right down to the moment of an amputation. After the cut is made, I have to turn aside or risk fainting.

"Tatiana Nikolaevna?" Dr. Gedroiz prompted only once, a gangrenous toe pinched in midair between a pair of forceps. My knees had locked. It was all I could do to open my mouth and breathe, much less take it from her. No one but Mama has a stomach strong enough to let her remove the severed digits and limbs from the operating table without going woozy.

Not three weeks after receiving our Red Cross certificates, we see a man die for the first time. At the end of an operation for a terrible chest wound, the blood wells up quickly as a crimson parasol unfurling. It happens so softly I only realize he is gone when Dr. Gedroiz throws down her instruments and crosses herself.

Olga has already backed away. More blood is pooled round the soldier's lung than either of us has seen in our lives. Even Aleksei has never bled so much. The look of it makes me feel as though my stomach has disappeared completely.

"What happened?"

Dr. Gedroiz shakes her head. "I've performed this operation a thousand times and never lost a patient."

Each time a man dies, Olga and I both ask why, but the answers I crave never satisfy my sister. "You want to understand how it happens, not why," she tries to explain as I pore over my notes from Dr. Gedroiz's lectures. I cannot deny it. While I plunge myself into study of the operation or disease, looking for what we might have done differently, Olga broods and storms over the senselessness of war itself. What is the use? Halting this war is not within our power, but learning from our mistakes in the lazaret could save the next man's life.

As seriously as we take ourselves, many of the soldiers still think of us almost as pets. There is no ignoring the way they cluster round us for snapshots and beg us to sign the photographs. But that, too, is a kind of medicine for them, so I forbid myself from complaining. Sometimes Mama lets Aleksei visit the wards for the same reason. *"Nash naslednik,"* they cry when he arrives. *Our heir.*

"Tell me a battle story!" he demands, bouncing on the nearest soldier's bed, and the men are so charmed by our brother's enthusiasm that they never seem to notice his rudeness. Like boys themselves, they stage great conflicts across the hills and valleys of their bedclothes with Aleksei's lead soldiers.

The other nurses sometimes tense when Aleksei arrives, for he can make trouble they are helpless to correct. When one of them, Varvara Afanaseva, caught him in our storeroom looking over the neatly packed rows of cut and rolled bandages, Aleksei asked, "You did all that yourself?"

"Yes," Varvara answered.

He poked the tip of his tongue between his teeth. I held my breath, afraid of what would come next.

"And what if I destroyed it?" he asked, eyeing the shelves again.

Varvara blanched for an instant, then regarded him calmly. "It would remain as our memory of your visit."

Aleksei grimaced, then turned on his heel and marched out of the room.

I let out a sigh. "If you had told him it was forbidden, he would certainly have destroyed it," I told Varvara, and hurried after him.

But if a patient suddenly cries out in pain, our brother abandons his games and silently appears at the man's side, offering his small hand to grip. He has a golden heart, our Aleksei, from knowing so much pain himself.

Often I've seen Olga do the same. As squeamish as she is before an open wound, Olga never shrinks from a patient's suffering. She has a way about her that sometimes calms a man when the skill of Dr. Gedroiz's hands or the power of morphine can no longer reach him, but the effort costs my sister, turning her as pale and drawn as if she is lending our patients the strength from her own body. Each day she sets off early to walk to the Feodorovsky *Sobor*, to pray alone before beginning her work. I miss the mornings when we used to swim or cycle together through the park while the tame deer nibble the grass.

One evening I find her hunched in the chair at the end of her cot, her face buried in her Red Cross apron. When I touch her shoulder, it shakes beneath my hand. "Olya, *dorogaya?*" I whisper, kneeling down beside her. She does not answer, so I take her hands in mine and pull them gently to her lap. Her face is dry. "*Dushka*, what is it? The infection in our grenadier's wound has not spread, has it?"

"I'm just tired, Tatya," she says. "Please don't tell Mama. She'll only worry."

Beneath my fingers, her pulse is regular. I feel no sign of fever, but the rasp in her voice frightens me. "You should go to bed, Olya. I will have Nyuta bring our supper in." She nods and begins slowly to undress. "Mashka can sleep with Mama tonight instead of me," I decide. "I will stay here with you."

Her hands hesitate, poised over her wimple. "No, Tatya.

Please. It's good for me to be alone." She turns away, but I study her a moment longer. Her fingers tremble over the pins.

"I'll be all right, Governess," she says when she feels me watching. "I promise I'll take a warm bath and go straight to bed with a book. Maria and Anastasia are right next door, and if you take Ortipo downstairs I won't have to listen to her snoring like a frog at the end of your cot."

Teasing about my fat French bulldog makes her look less pale all at once, and not so small. "All right," I say. "Let me run the bath for you right now, and set out your tea rose perfume."

"*Spasibo*, Tatya." But her voice does not lift one note, leaving me feeling as though I am doing myself a favor, and not the other way round.

6

MARIA NIKOLAEVNA

Winter 1914
Tsarskoe Selo

Waking up every day and remembering Papa's gone to the front is like biting into a bonbon with nothing in the center. I miss the puffs of cigarettes he shares with my sisters and me on our morning walks through the park, and even the sight of Trupp carrying Papa's glasses of milk down the corridor. When Anastasia and I have our dancing lessons upstairs, my feet blunder more clumsily than ever, knowing Papa isn't downstairs listening to our steps on the ceiling in his study.

While Mama and the Big Pair are at the lazaret, Anastasia takes every chance she has to be a *shvybzik*. She cranks up the gramophone loud enough to shake the picture frames, then dances to ragtime and jazz.

"It's no fun when nobody's down there," she pants.

Mama's always said it's cheerful to hear our footsteps

pattering over her head when she sits reading or sewing in her lilac boudoir, but Anastasia loves even more to dance in our bedroom or the playroom, so guests in the formal rooms below will think Aleksei's elephant has got loose over their heads.

Darling little Jemmy barks and yips and tears around Anastasia's ankles so fast I'm afraid she'll be squashed flatter than *blini*. I scoop her up and press her silky ears against my cheek.

"I wish Mama would let us learn ragtime on the piano," Anastasia grumps when the gramophone runs down.

"Can you imagine Tatiana playing music like this?"

Anastasia snorts. "Yes. I bet she could play every note perfectly. But Tatiana'd manage to turn it into sit-down-and-listen music instead of get-up-and-dance music. I don't know how she does it."

Anastasia always makes me laugh, but she can't make me stop missing Papa. Mama calls Aleksei our Sunbeam, and Papa calls Mama his Sunny, but no one shines brighter for me than my Papa himself.

At least I never feel lonely on the days we visit our own lazaret. My sisters and even our parents will never give up teasing me about my eye for the soldiers. Of course I love seeing all those sweet young men lined up in long rows, but I do more than just look at them. Lots of them are younger than our big sisters, and the poor darlings are so homesick! Anastasia and I go from bed to bed, speaking to each man so they won't be bored or lonesome. I know from his letters how Papa suffers at the front, playing dominoes at night with nothing but a glass of milk for company, and he's not even wounded like our boys at the lazaret.

At first they were awfully shy. Some even pulled their blankets up to their chins when they saw us coming. Anastasia laughed and teased them by hiding behind her hat while I coaxed them out with pastilles and butterscotch toffees from my pockets. One red-haired fellow gasped, "Your Imperial Highness," the first time I sat down at the foot of his bed. I blushed and Anastasia smirked.

"That's just Mashka," she told him, bouncing onto the blankets so close beside him that he blushed darker than the Crimson Drawing Room. "But I am Anastasia Nikolaevna, Chieftain of all Firemen!" The poor man only blinked his pale blue eyes back at her as she grinned wickedly and pinched a sugared Japanese cherry from his nightstand.

"She only says that because she doesn't have her own regiment yet," I whispered to him as Anastasia turned to badger the man in the next bed. "She's only thirteen, and the officers on our yacht tease her about it all the time."

"And you, Grand Duchess? Do you have a regiment?"

"The Ninth Kazansky Dragoons. I'm honorary colonel-in-chief. What regiment are you from?" And simple as that, we were friends.

Now the men gather around us like flocks of seagulls before we can reach the end of a ward. Six or eight of them at a time crowd over and around a single bed for snapshots. Maybe Anastasia and I are too little to be proper nurses, but I know we're doing good, and I love it. There are always new soldiers to win over, though.

One day I hear a new patient ask another man, "Is it true the *Nemka* herself works here?" The others glare at him and make shushing sounds as Anastasia and I come nearer. When I stop at the foot of his bed, he only nods without looking at us, and won't speak. It makes my toes turn toward each other, hesitating. I always make sure to say something to every soldier, but he seems so impatient for us to go, I feel like a disagreeable relative he'd like to shoo off his doorstep.

At supper that night with my sisters, I ask Olga, "Who is the *Nemka*?"

Olga and Tatiana both look as if I've slapped them. "Where did you hear that?" Tatiana asks.

"In the lazaret."

Olga puts down her knife and pushes her plate away. My belly seems to be slinking down to my bottom. "What's wrong?" I ask.

"Do not let Mama hear you say that word," Tatiana says. "Not ever, Maria. Do you understand?"

I nod quickly, even though I don't understand at all. Anastasia's eyes bounce between us like two tennis balls.

"It's an awful name for a German woman," Olga says, looking at the table.

My eyes suddenly swim with tears. "But Mama is Russian now! Isn't she?"

"Of course she is!" Tatiana leans over to wrap her arm around my shoulders and kiss my temple. "She has been Russian longer than some of those boys have been alive. Besides, she was born in Hesse, not Prussia like that beastly kaiser."

"Uncle Henry is Prussian," Olga says to the tines of her fork.

"What has that to do with anything? Uncle Henry did not start the war." Tatiana sighs and squeezes my hand as if to say, *Never mind*. "So it does not matter where a person was born."

"It does matter," Olga says, "if that's all they know about Mama. St. Petersburg had to change its name, and it's been the capital for over two centuries. There's even talk about banning Christmas trees. Why should Mama be immune after only twenty years in Russia?"

Tatiana clucks her tongue and turns back to her plate, but my thoughts are twining like the branches of our family tree. My heart and soul are Russian, but I can't pretend the roots of our family don't reach into Germany, England, and Denmark. If the Russian people believe Mama is German, maybe that makes me only half a Russian in their eyes. My heart beats fast. The next time the Germans win a battle, will people I've never met suddenly decide to hate me, too?

No, I promise myself. I will not give anyone one good reason to hate me.

7

TATIANA NIKOLAEVNA

January 1915
Tsarskoe Selo

When the telephone call comes, Mama does not shake or cry, but the way she grips the receiver tells me something is wrong even before she whispers, *"Bozhe moi,"* and crosses herself. Her answers are short and to the point: "Yes. Where? Is she all right? Yes, we are coming—all of us. Immediately. *Spasibo*, Likhachev."

Mama hangs up and takes a breath. "There has been an accident on the railway line," she tells me, taking hold of my hand. "Anya is gravely hurt. One of Papa's own Cossack guards pulled her from the wreck."

"Christ give her strength."

"Tatianochka," she says in a voice I have not heard since I was a little girl, "not one of the doctors expects her to live. We must go to her." Tears start, threatening to dissolve my composure, but Mama pulls me from my chair and kisses both my cheeks. "Don't cry, Tatianochka, my brave girl. Gather your sisters. I will get word to Papa and call for a motorcar." Her instructions carry me to the doorway. She sounds so sure and strong, both pride and fear seize my heart. "We must be sure Anya's parents have been told, and that the best doctors are there. And *Otets* Grigori, of course. Come now, Tatiana," she says, and I obey.

When we arrive at the station, stretchers pour out of the relief train until the injured lie so thick across the Tsarskoe Selo platform it is all but impossible to avoid stepping over them. Much as it alarms me to see the nurses and orderlies add to their patients' misfortune, there is plainly no time to spare for stepping carefully backward over the victims to avert bad luck.

"Slava Bogu," I murmur at the sight of Dr. Gedroiz. She takes one look at us standing idle in our everyday blouses and coats and waves her hand toward one of the railcars before Mama can even ask after Anya. My cheeks burn over our selfishness, but Mama turns and marches from one stretcher to the next, making her way down the line.

As we move along, Olga wraps her hand round mine, nearly crushing my fingers as she rubs her thumb over her fingernails. "I can't look, Tatya. Please don't make me look at them all."

Behind us, Maria and Anastasia huddle together, their eyes wide. With a jerk of my chin, I motion them to Olga's other side. Over the cries and moans, I hear her murmuring, ". . . give rest also to every servant of Thine in the throes of death, wherever this prayer will be heard. . . ." One by one, we all join in until our lips and feet are moving together down the line of stretchers.

Before we finish our prayer, Mama halts and kneels next to a stretcher. "Darling?" she whispers.

"Bozhe moi," Olga gasps, crossing herself. Maria whimpers and ducks into Olga's arms. Beside them, Anastasia stands frozen, still gripping Maria's hand. I swallow hard and join Mama at Anya's side.

Anya's wounds are terribly fresh, like nothing I have seen in the lazaret. Her face is as swollen as one of Aleksei's bruises, but the bone below one eye socket caves in, making strange slopes across her cheek. Blood rims her lips. Through the thin blanket, Anya's legs lay crushed and still. I never imagined such a large woman could seem so small. Mama tries to smooth Anya's hair, but even the brush of Mama's fingers along her scalp makes Anya shudder. Her hand clutches at Mama's. "I'm dying," Anya rasps.

"An ambulance," Mama demands. Her voice seems to stop everything. Nurses and orderlies snap to attention. Two men abandon other patients and take up Anya's stretcher. "Gently," Mama chides as they elbow their way through the crowd. The patients they left stranded on the rail platform bleed openly before my eyes. Without help, they will soon be as near to death as our Anya.

Mama is busy with Anya, and Maria and Anastasia can manage Olga long enough for me to help—

"Tatiana," Mama calls over her shoulder, "bring your sisters in the motorcar."

For a moment, I hang suspended amid the chaos.

"Tatiana," Mama calls again in that voice that makes heads turn toward her. "The motorcar. You will follow us to the hospital."

At the lazaret, Anya barely sees us through her pain. Her wounds are draped, but still seeping. "God have mercy on you, darling," Olga whispers, then kisses her own fingers and brushes them lightly over Anya's forehead.

I move to Anya's shoulder, positioning myself to block Olga's view of the worst of the wounds. In her pocket, I hear her thumbing the pages of her little book of Lermontov over and over again. Propping my elbows on the bed and lowering my head to my folded hands, I pray for Christ to deliver Anya from her pain.

"Would you like to see the emperor?" Mama's voice startles me. Papa stands at the end of the bed, his beard ruffled and his fingers fidgeting with an unlit cigarette.

Anya's mouth opens, her head trembling with something like a nod.

Papa sits down beside me, slipping his hand under Anya's. She tries to press his hand. The effort leaves her panting.

When Dr. Gedroiz passes by, she hovers a moment, frowning down at all of us. "She can't possibly live until morning," she remarks.

"Is it so hopeless?" Papa asks. "She still has some strength in her hand." The princess sighs and shakes her head, but she does not dare contradict Papa. As Anya slips back into unconsciousness, I fear Dr. Gedroiz is right. Anya's only hope seems to lie with God.

Late in the night, an answer to our prayers arrives: *Otets* Grigori. Anya's mother frowns and turns aside but says nothing as he strides to the bed, pushing at the air though no one blocks his way. Papa goes to stand beside Olga, resting his hands on her shoulders.

Otets Grigori makes the sign of the cross on Anya's forehead and murmurs over her. I wait, wanting to feel something, some sense of his power. Nearly three years ago, *Otets* Grigori's prayers for Aleksei's health reached from Siberia to our hunting lodge in Poland. Now he prays right here beside me. For a moment, I nearly forget about our poor Anya. Maybe God is beside me, too. The thought stills my worries. I want to touch *Otets* Grigori's sleeve, to see if I feel something passing from him to Anya, like water through a pipe.

"Annushka." I jerk my hand back. "Annushka!" Her body shudders. *Otets* Grigori waits a moment, then says again, "Annushka, can you hear me?"

Her eyes quiver back and forth under the lids, then open for an instant. My heart lurches.

"Speak to me," he demands.

"Father Grigori," Anya whispers, and a tear seeps from the corner of her eye. *Otets* Grigori takes her hand, prays once more, then steps away from the bed.

"She will live, but she will always be a cripple."

Anya's parents hold each other and cry. Relief floods through me. "Thanks be to God," I whisper.

8

OLGA NIKOLAEVNA

Summer 1915
Tsarskoe Selo

From the start, the war hasn't gone well. We children don't see many newspapers at home, but I read the headlines plainly enough on the soldiers' bedside tables in the lazaret, and hear the men discussing the battles they've survived. Even on the streets just outside our palace gates in Tsarskoe Selo, the people no longer hide the disappointment and frustration on their faces as we motor past on our way to the lazaret, the train station, or Anya's house. Sometimes it seems their expressions grow darker at the sight of us, especially since Warsaw fell to the Germans.

As I sit trying to write a cheerful-sounding letter to Papa, crashing and shouts from the playroom make me spatter ink across the page. I pick up my skirts and run, only to find Anastasia and Aleksei staging a skirmish. Decked out in his dress uniform of the Twelfth East Siberian Rifle

Regiment, Aleksei careens about the room on his three-wheeled bicycle, slashing at battalions of lead soldiers with his miniature rifle. In the toy guardhouse, Joy lies like a lazy sentry with an officer's hat slouched over his eyes. Anastasia mans the toy cannon.

"Aleksei Nikolaevich, you get out of that uniform this instant! Mama will have your hide if you tear it." Anastasia snorts, and no wonder—it sounds as if Tatiana has commandeered my tongue.

"You can't talk to a second lieutenant like that," Aleksei scoffs, circling me and pulling faces with his chin in the air. "It's my regiment, so you can't make me take it off."

I grab the muzzle of his toy rifle. "As honorary colonel of the Third Elizavetgradsky Hussars, I command you to remove that uniform." That stops him in his tracks. "And if the commander of the Fifth Alexandriisky Hussars has to leave her visitors and climb those stairs to make you behave, you'll be sorry. Now march, little soldier!"

"Mama always takes the lift anyway," he grumbles, but he slides off the bicycle and yanks the rifle from my hands as he slinks off to his bedroom. I turn on Anastasia.

"What's all this about? You know better than to let him romp all over like that. Where's Aleksei's *dyadka*? He should be watching."

"Never mind Nagorny. Haven't you heard? Papa's taken over the high command. He's going to run the army himself from now on."

My jaw drops and my fists tighten. I sink into Mama's cane-backed rocking chair. "What about Great-Uncle Nikolasha?"

"Fired." Anastasia grins. "Well, not exactly. He's been made viceroy of the Caucasus instead. Now Papa can give those Krauts what for!"

A smudge of dread wells up from my chest. "Papa is only a colonel. . . ."

"So what?" Anastasia retorts, rolling her eyes. "Papa is the tsar, and tsar is better than any rank in the army. Besides, he could make himself a general anytime he wants to, so what's the difference?"

"But he won't make himself a general, and you know it." A spark of pride momentarily singes my fears. Our papa was a colonel when he became tsar, and a colonel he stayed, too good a man to promote himself for show. I close my mouth and tug at a stubborn hangnail. Without looking up, I feel Anastasia's eyes dragging over me like a comb.

"What's wrong?" she demands.

"What?"

"You're fussing at your fingernails," she says, jabbing my hand. "Tatiana says you only do that when you're worried."

I smooth my skirt slowly across my lap, forcing my fingers apart. Leave it to Tatiana to unmask me even when she's nowhere in sight. "If Papa is in charge, all the responsibility for the war will fall on his shoulders."

Anastasia gawps at me. "Well of course it will! He's the *tsar*, Olga, that's the way it is. That's the way it's always been."

How can I tell her it's different now? Everything that goes wrong will be Papa's fault, with no one in between to temper the blame. And what about the soldiers? The men love our great-uncle Nikolasha. He's a giant of a man, not bearish like our *dedushka*, Alexander III, was, but tall and proud as an imperial eagle. Papa looks gentle as a thrush beside him.

I take a breath and begin again. "Do you remember when we visited Babushka last month and Papa talked about firing Uncle Nikolasha?"

Anastasia snorts. "*Konechno.* She turned white as a dish of sour cream. Tatiana thought she was having a stroke."

"Babushka isn't the only one who's going to feel that way." Even Papa must have known it—he'd blushed to his collar when our grandmother told him the people would think he was only doing *Otets* Grigori's bidding.

"Oh, poo. What does Babushka know about people? She doesn't even like Mama all that much. All she could talk about was *Otets* Grigori, and I don't see what he has to do with the army anyway."

Frustration vaults me to my feet so fast the empty chair rocks behind me. I'm going to speak with Mama about all this. "Just make sure Aleksei gets out of that uniform."

With Anastasia scowling in my wake, I run downstairs to see if I can talk sense with someone.

"Olga, darling," Mama cries, reaching out for me from her chaise, "have you heard the news? Isn't it glorious?"

"But, Mama—" I begin between kissing both her cheeks.

"That dreadful Nikolasha has been going over your papa's head for months," she interrupts. "And his hatred for our Father Grigori is intense. Now everyone is in his proper place again. God is with us."

I want to believe her. Of course I do. I want to believe my

papa can turn the war around, that the lazaret will stop filling with broken young men. Instead Mama's delight wrings me with shame. I should have more faith in my papa the tsar. God himself has chosen Papa to lead Russia. Who am I to question either of them?

No one wants to blame the person they love best when things go wrong. If Mama had been in the playroom only a few minutes ago, she would have chided me to make my brother behave instead of scolding her Sunbeam herself. Who will she criticize for Russia's next loss, now that "dreadful Nikolasha" has been stripped of his position? For that matter, where will I aim my frustration but at my own papa? But there's no talking to Mama when she's this way, blind with her own rapture.

"Christ be with him," I say into the first gap in her rhapsody. She beams at me, squeezing my hand as if victory is already ours. I want to snatch my fingers back, flee all the way upstairs to my desk, and twist my letter to Papa up in my two fists.

9

ANASTASIA NIKOLAEVNA

September 1915
Tsarskoe Selo

"How do I look?" Aleksei twirls in his new uniform. We all stand back and admire him as if he's a painting.

"Like a ballerina," I tease. "Stand still. Soldiers don't pirouette." He snaps his heels together and stands to attention. "That's better. You look as drab as any army private."

"You've got much fancier uniforms," Maria says. "You're so handsome in the others."

"This is your brother, not an officer, you goose," Tatiana says. "You cannot make eyes at everything in a uniform."

"I like this one best," Aleksei insists, looking a little hurt. "Those others are just for show." As if he doesn't care a whit for all the gold braiding and epaulets on his honorary dress uniforms. "*Stavka* is no place for showing off. At headquarters I'll be a real soldier."

"Not quite a real soldier," Olga reminds him. "But you do look like a proper young man," she says, straightening his cap and brushing off his shoulders to hide the catch in her voice. "You're not a gilded toy soldier in a borrowed uniform anymore."

Tatiana starts in on a lecture. "This will not be easy for Mama, Aleksei—"

"Oh hush, Governess," I scoff. "They don't allow mamas at the front."

Aleksei smirks. "Or sisters," he adds. "Only men."

"And I'll be stuck here with Maria, who'll be too busy scheming up a way to get into *Stavka* to be any fun at all. If you wake up one morning and find someone hanging outside the gates, drooling like a plump puppy dog, that'll be our Mashka!" I clap my hands and dance around her as her rosy cheeks turn darker yet. Everyone says Tatiana's the beauty, but I think Maria's really prettiest, because she doesn't even know it. Olga frowns at me, and I pinch Maria's face like an old auntie so I can get close enough to wink and whisper, "I'll make it up to you, Mashka."

"Report to Mama for inspection, Private Aleksei Nikolaevich," Olga commands.

Aleksei salutes and shoots off down the hallway, his boots clattering on the steps.

"Careful, Aleksei," Tatiana calls after him.

I turn on her. "Why do you do that to him? You're as bad as Mama."

"He has to learn to be careful, Anastasia." She sounds like a wagging finger.

"He's got plenty of people to be careful for him," I fire back. "Nagorny and Dr. Derevenko and Monsieur Gilliard. And Mama. Always Mama! He doesn't need anyone else hovering over him. He's finally getting out, and he shouldn't have to worry about her. Aleksei knows better than any of us that Mama's never been apart from him. Just let him be."

"Getting out of where?" Tatiana demands.

"Of here! Outside! And it won't hurt him a bit to meet some people who can start a sentence with something besides 'don't.' He doesn't have half the freedom we do, and that's not saying much. I'd chop off my hair and dress up in khaki in a heartbeat if it meant I could go with them." My cheeks go hot enough to boil my eyeballs, but I won't cry. *I am Anastasia Nikolaevna, Chieftain of all Firemen*, I tell myself, clenching my fists and stamping a foot.

Tatiana only stares at me. Mashka, too. But Olga smiles sadly, and I can tell that she of all people understands. "You'd make a fine soldier, Shvybzik," she whispers, grinning fiercely through her own watery eyes.

I run into Olga's arms and hug her tight, so tight. She strokes my hair, but after a moment I feel her chest bounce beneath me as she starts to laugh. I blink up at her. "Oh, Shvybs," she says, taking my chin in her hands and kissing my forehead, "can you imagine how terrified our boys in the lazaret would be if they knew what a fighter you are? You're a regular Ivan the Terrible."

Tatiana was right, of course. She always is. At the station, Mama and Tatiana stand twisting their handkerchiefs, trying not to cry. Aleksei leans out of the train's window, smiling and waving so furiously, we ought to feel the breeze from his flapping arms. Mama clutched and petted and squeezed him so much I think he's just happy to be able to move again. As the train pulls away, he runs from window to window, waving and throwing us kisses. Nagorny shadows close as a watchdog, but Mama still flinches every time Aleksei throws himself against another sill.

"Careful, my treasure," she calls. "Don't bump!"

With Mama so distracted, I march along beside the train, calling out, "Hup, hup, hup," so Aleksei won't hear her fussing. The train picks up speed, and I can't keep up without hiking up my skirts and running pell-mell. No matter how worried Mama is over her precious Sunbeam, I know she'd notice that and give me an imperial scolding. I dare to jog a few *sazhens* beyond Aleksei's window, then freeze at attention.

"Ten thousand kisses and a victory salute to Private Aleksei Nikolaevich!" I shout over the clank and roar as the train passes. "And Christ be with you!" I stay rooted to the spot until the caboose disappears, then sigh and trudge back to Mama's end of the platform.

My sisters cluster around her, looking like a pack of weepy white rabbits with their pink-rimmed eyes and wobbly noses. Tatiana's got her arm fastened around Mama's waist like a corset. Honestly, sometimes Tatiana acts as if Mama's no more sturdy than a flap of flowered chintz. I march right up to Mama and throw my arms around her neck, kissing both her cheeks.

"He's so happy, Mama!"

"He is, isn't he?" she says, smiling a little bit. "He didn't even cry, that brave little treasure."

"Bah! Soldiers don't cry."

Mama takes a great breath and squares her shoulders. "Neither do soldiers' mothers," she says. "Come along, my girlies." And away we go.

Back home, we all go our separate ways. Mama settles into her lilac boudoir, and my sisters and I wander to our bedrooms. Maria mopes in an armchair with a box of chocolates and her photo album spread across her lap as if it's been days, not minutes, since we've all been together. Not a sound comes from the Big Pair's room next door. Probably sniveling onto their knitting needles. What a bunch of ninnies we are. But even I can't pretend everything's all right. The place feels dull and hollow as a bread crust with Aleksei and Papa both gone.

Tucking Jemmy under my arm, I wander into the playroom to kick at some of the toys we left scattered about. Nothing looks like any fun. Anyhow, if any of my sisters caught me playing with Aleksei's toys all by myself, they'd think I was a great big baby. Instead I look once over my shoulder, then burrow into the wigwam to sulk until the heavy feeling lets go of my throat.

"You'd better be having great fun, Mr. Private Romanov," I tell the wooden sentry posted beside the doorway to Aleksei's bedroom, and swipe the back of my hand across my nose. Jemmy wriggles free and licks happily at my dirty hand.

I kiss her nose. "Filthy little dear." At the sound of footsteps in the corridor, I scoop Jemmy up and duck behind the flap of the wigwam. Mama's skirts swish through the playroom, past the wooden sentry, and disappear into Aleksei's rooms. I wait a minute, then stuff Jemmy into my sweater and crawl out. The smell of rose oil burning tells me Mama's lit Aleksei's icon lamps. I creep behind on all fours for my own sniff-around.

When I get to the bedroom, I find Mama on her knees in front of the six-paneled iconostasis. There's a quiver in her voice as she prays. The clock chimes, and I realize with a little tickle in my stomach what's happening. Mama always says Aleksei's evening prayers with him. She's saying his prayers as if he were still beside her. The room feels so strange, I squeeze Jemmy against me without realizing it until her little body squirms. I let her go just before she yips, but I can't take my eyes off Mama. When she turns around, she looks as small and worried as I feel myself. As soon as she sees me she tries to paste on a smile.

"Anastasia, darling," she says, dabbing at the corners of her eyes. "I was afraid Baby would forget. All the excitement on the train."

For the first time in my life, I wish for an instant to be Tatiana, just so I'd know what to say.

10

OLGA NIKOLAEVNA

October 1915
Tsarskoe Selo

"Olga, *dushka*?" Tatiana's fingertips brush my shoulder like the starlings that swoop by our bedroom windows. The thought comforts me for a moment, until I remember where those hands were just minutes ago— painted nearly to the wrists with some poor soldier's blood. My stomach convulses, and I clap the towel to my mouth as I retch.

"It was the operation, wasn't it?" Tatiana pulls a fresh towel from the shelves crowding around me. "Did you eat this morning?" I shake my head. There's only a sorry little stain on the towel to show for all my misery. "You have to eat in the morning, Olya," she says, rubbing my back as I shudder. "It makes your stomach even weaker in the operating room if you skip breakfast, and you are so thin anyway." She leads me out of the little linen closet and into the window-lined corridor. "We could arrange it so you do not have to see the operations at all. They always have plenty of work to do in the office. Come now, be brave," she soothes. "God will see you through it."

How can I explain it to her? Yes, the operations leave my hands and stomach quivering, but it isn't only the torn and ragged wounds that fray my nerves. The soldiers' thoughts trouble me as much as their broken bodies. The men are changing before my eyes.

At first the soldiers were our pets. They jostled to be near us, their faces brightening when we spoke with them. With Aleksei away at the front, Mama took a few of the tenderest recruits under her wing, feeding them the attention she usually lavishes on our brother. In their last moments, many of them called for her. It was like a fairy tale, those brave boys dying by their empress's side.

But with the war dragging on and the newspaper headlines turning grim, I've seen the way some of the men have begun looking at Mama. I hear them whisper *Nemka*— German bitch—behind her back. If she heard them, she would weep with shame.

The soldiers who still revere us are even worse, sometimes. When country boys fresh from the front find themselves in a palace tended by a princess, two grand duchesses, and the empress herself, their eyes grow round with awe. Some of them try to bow under their blankets. I could cry at the deference they show me, these young men willing to give their limbs and their lives to Mother Russia, when all I've done is bring them a pillow or a glass of water. But even the plain Red Cross uniforms can't always hide who we are. Our faces are on postcards and placards all across Russia. Many of the soldiers carry images of Papa into battle for protection. We're different in other ways too. With food and fuel shipments becoming erratic in the city, some of the men eye the gold bangles on our wrists with expressions that make my stomach fold with guilt. I wish I could strip mine off and give it away, but it won't fit over my hand.

I wonder if it would make any difference if the men knew we aren't encased in gilt and velvet, that my sisters and brother and I have slept in nickel-plated camp cots with flat pillows and taken cold baths every morning since we were children. What if they knew we have allowances so small we have to scrimp even to give our parents notepaper and cheap perfume for Christmas? But would I also have to tell them that bathtub full of cold water is made of solid silver, engraved with the name of every imperial child who has been bathed in it? Would I have to admit my sisters and I receive one pearl and one diamond every year on our birthday, and even our pets' collars are hand enameled by Fabergé, the imperial court jeweler? Still, we aren't lavish like Cousin Irina's in-laws, the Yusupovs, with bowls of uncut gemstones decorating the end tables.

"You are so pale, *dorogaya*," Tatiana says, breaking into my thoughts. "You look as if you will be sick again." She lays the back of her hand across my forehead, then presses it to my cheek. She means to comfort me, but I know her nurse's mind is also measuring my temperature and pulse. "You have probably become anemic," she reasons, "the way you exhaust yourself here without enough nourishment."

My sister is right in a way, so I let her go on about iron pills, valerian drops, and arsenic shots. Nourishment is exactly what I need, but I don't have the heart to tell Tatiana that I won't find what I crave on my dinner plate or in a medicine vial.

As much as it troubles me, I wouldn't give up my time in the lazaret for nearly anything in the world. Our good friend Ritka Khitrovo, who's been one of Mama's ladies-in-waiting, works the wards with us, and as much as I love my sisters, seeing Ritka and the other nurses is delicious as cracking open a new book every day. The lazaret stands hardly a verst beyond Anya's house, and the security agents always shadow us, but motoring there and back on our own beguiles us with a taste of freedom until I can't resist trying to carve a slice of it for myself.

As we leave the lazaret I eye the waiting motorcar. "Tatya, let's stop in town. We could go to Gostiny Dvor to look at the shops and Mama would never know."

Tatiana doesn't break her stride. "Stop joking. You know we are not allowed to wander the streets."

I snag at her sleeve like a beggar. "It's practically on our way home, barely two blocks from Anya's. We visit there all the time."

She points an eyebrow at me. "*Konechno*, with Mama, and an escort from the Life Guards regiment."

"We won't be in any danger." I nod toward the security agents. "They'll be right behind us, and we're in our Red Cross uniforms, not court dresses and *kokoshniki* with pearls. Please, Tatya. Seeing something new would be like a tonic for me."

Guilt nips my tongue. It isn't fair to beg this way when I know how worried she is over me, even if what I've said is true. Still, I shut my mouth and manage to look my sister in the eye as she weighs the circumstances.

"All right," Tatiana decides. "But not for long. And no place but Gostiny Dvor."

"You're a treasure." I link my elbow through hers, and the two of us walk ahead like a court procession. The security agents' voices scuffle together as Tatya and I stride past the motorcar and across the street with giggles clamped behind our teeth, but the men don't dare stop us.

Out in the streets, people bustle all around us, and we bump among them like a pair of dice. I grin so wide my teeth must show—it's thrilling, being part of a mass of people instead of watching them scatter and bob like a flock of ducks in the wake of the *Standart*.

When we reach the plaza of Gostiny Dvor, the crowd swarms in and out of the yellow and white archways and across the courtyard market. Tatiana steers me into the nearest shop. From her tug on my arm, I'm guessing it will be the only one we visit.

Immediately a display of postcard portraits of my sisters and me halts me just inside the door. "Aren't they lovely?" the shopkeeper says. "They're from right before the war, but they're the latest official portraits of the imperial children, except for the ones of the elder two in their Red Cross uniforms. Grand Duchess Olga has become quite a lady, but

Grand Duchess Tatiana is still the beauty, if you ask me." A blush curtains my cheeks. The woman takes no notice. She hardly even takes time to breathe. "I hope they'll make a new formal set soon. Those dresses they wear are so much more fashionable than nursing habits, don't you think? Besides, I'm eager to see how the younger two are turning out. Lately the children's portraits are selling much better than the tsar and tsaritsa's. All this bad news, if you ask me." Even in my nurse's wimple I don't dare raise my face, though I doubt the woman will be able to see past her own wagging tongue.

"Oh, Olga, look at this scarf!" Tatiana calls, and I rush to her side before the shopkeeper can begin to realize the coincidence. "How beautiful." Tatiana holds up a length of sheer lavender covered with tiny whorls of velvet shaped like lilac blooms. "Mama would love this."

"At least as much as you do," I tease.

She pats her pockets. "Do you have any money?"

"Not a kopek. I dare you to ask the security agents for the loan of a few rubles."

Her hand flies up to capture a giggle. "Olga Nikolaevna, you are absolutely wicked!" she whispers through her fingers. "Those poor men are going to have an apoplexy as it is."

My merriment drains in the space of a heartbeat. In my impulse, I didn't think of what our excursion will mean for the people responsible for us. There's more than a scolding from Mama at stake if we're found out—these men could lose their jobs regardless of whether we get home safe. We've already made all sorts of extra work for them. The moment we leave, they'll be bent over the counter with their notepads, interrogating the shopkeeper who spoke to me. The flush on my cheeks crawls down my neck and across my chest at the thought of it.

"Tatya, let's go home. We can send Nyuta back with our pocket money to fetch the scarf for Mama." I glance at a shelf full of books at the back of the store and press my lips between my teeth.

Tatiana lays the scarf aside at once. "Are you ill again, *dorogaya*? You look feverish."

"No. But those men—it's cruel of us to risk their jobs so we can look at trinkets. We should go back."

Realization douses Tatiana's face. She crosses herself and nods.

No one says a word all the way back. The security agents would never presume to lecture us, but their looks of relief when we leave the shop tamp my spirits down until the guilt smolders like a pipe full of tobacco. Even the driver mops his brow and the back of his neck when we climb into the motorcar. We don't even dare tell the Little Pair about our adventure.

After that I content myself with the inside of the lazaret. So many of the soldiers are kind to us—and good-looking, even in their hospital-issued dressing gowns. We tease Mashka, but Tatiana and I both have our favorites, the way we always pick out officers to flirt with on the *Standart*. But now we aren't just little girls frolicking on holiday with Papa's staff. Many of the young men in the lazaret are only a year or two older than my sister and I, and they know it as well as we do. There's Nikolai Karangozov with his cane and dark mustache, who loves having his picture taken. Tatiana has her sweet Volodya from the Caucasus, and handsome little Dmitri Malama. For me, there is none but dear golden Mitya Shakh-Bagov.

Together we sit and talk, drink cocoa, and play *bloshki*. Sometimes Mama lets my sister and me telephone the lazaret in the evening to talk to our soldiers. From time to time when they're well enough, Anya invites them to tea with the four of us at her house. Volodya and Mitya always humor the Little Pair with their photo albums and chatter, but I know they have a special fondness for Tatiana and me. Even after weeks in the lazaret, sweetheart Mitya's cheeks flush pink when he sees me coming. We both know it isn't fever.

Such a dear boy he is, shy as a little girl, but I can see his feelings painted plainly on his face. And yet we never talk of what we feel for each other, perhaps because we both know nothing can come of it. Even in my Red Cross uniform, even though he calls me simply "Olga Nikolaevna" or "sister," never "Your Imperial Highness," I am still a grand duchess, eldest daughter of the tsar. I am free to say no to the crown prince of Romania, but I can't say yes to an army officer from the Caucasus. Mitya is no freer to ask than I am to answer. I wonder if I were only Citizen Romanova? But what can it possibly matter? My fate is as uncertain as Mitya's, and all the other men we're sending back to the front.

MARIA NIKOLAEVNA

December 1915
Tsarskoe Selo

Poor Mama had only just returned from her dear friend Princess Sonia's funeral when the telegram about Aleksei came. Together we gather in the lilac boudoir, Mama cradled in her chaise with letters and pictures of Papa and Aleksei stacked high on the lemonwood table beside her. Tatiana sits poised in the big armchair with Mama's heart drops at her fingertips, while Olga burrows into the sofa among the built-in bookcases. Anastasia and I toy with Jemmy on the pistachio-colored carpet.

Just being in this room makes me feel better. Mama chose the striped silk on the walls especially to match a favorite sprig of flowers Papa gave her when they were young, and it always smells of lilacs here, no matter the season.

"'Because of his cold Aleksei has had bleeding at the nose at intervals the whole day,'" Mama reads to us.

My heart kicks in my chest. A nosebleed! Mama lays the telegram in her lap and smiles sadly at the photo of Aleksei in his uniform. I can't understand why she seems so calm. One sneeze puts Aleksei in a pickle worse than a cut, as bad as a bruise. You can't tie a bandage around a nosebleed.

"Don't look so grim, girlies." Mama creases the telegram and slides it into her pocket. "Dr. Derevenko will take fine care of our Sunbeam. And Papa wants me to come to *Stavka* on the sixth. Won't that be lovely? Olga, you'll come with me, won't you, dearest?" A little smile blooms on Olga's face, and for a tiny moment I forget about Aleksei. I can't remember the last time I saw Olga smile and mean it. "I'm going to send him a wire this minute," Mama continues. "Come along. We'll stop at Anya's on our way. The air will do you good."

As Olga passes by me, I snatch up her hand in mine and tug it to my cheek. "You'll kiss Papa for me, won't you?"

"*Konechno*, sweetheart Mashka," she says with a good strong squeeze. "A hundred times over."

"Tatya, what's going on?" I ask once they've gone. "Why isn't Mama worried?" Not worrying feels like not breathing when Aleksei is ill.

"She is going to see *Otets* Grigori at Anya's house," she says over her shoulder as she straightens up Mama's chaise and table.

"What makes you so sure?" Anastasia asks. "Mama doesn't even know if he's there."

"I imagine he will be by the time she arrives," Tatiana says. "Anya will see to that. You saw Mama put the telegram

in her pocket. She will show it to *Otets* Grigori, and he will
tell her whether or not she needs to worry. We might as well
do the same. It is all in God's hands."

She sounds just like Papa: *Tak i byt,* he'd say. *So be it.*

"I don't see why Olga gets to go to Anya's *and* to *Stavka,*
and we have to stay here and wait," Anastasia grumps,
slouching onto Olga's empty place on the sofa. "And don't
say it's because she's the oldest."

"She needs it more than we do," Tatiana says, her voice
sharp. I shrink back against the chaise and chew at my lip.
Tatiana glances at me, takes a breath, and begins again. "Seeing Papa and *Otets* Grigori will do her good. Besides, waiting makes Olga nervous, and her nerves have all they can
handle right now."

"Well, I'm not staying in this old room. I'm going to take
Jemmy for a walk," Anastasia says, grabbing up the little dear
and flouncing out, "before she 'does the governor' in here
and *you* have to clean it up."

Tatiana sits down on Mama's chaise, folding her hands
between her knees with a sigh.

"Jemmy is always Nastya's dog, until she makes a mess,"
I say, trying to laugh as I climb up beside Tatiana. "Then she
remembers who Jemmy really belongs to."

Tatiana's lips waver a bit, almost smiling. She puts her
arm around me and squeezes my shoulders. "I would rather
have you, my fat little Bow-Wow, than any dog, no matter
how darling."

I lean in close and hug her back. "She's being a beast," I
admit after a moment. "A jealous little beast."

"She is worried too, Mashka."

"Are you?" I ask quietly, tracing the embroidered edging of the red cross on her uniform. This close, I can smell her jasmine perfume over the iodine and alcohol from the lazaret.

"No. Not for Aleksei. He has Dr. Derevenko, and Papa, Nagorny, and Monsieur Gilliard to look after him." She pauses. "I do worry about Olga, though. She still seems so fragile."

We should have worried about Aleksei. *Otets* Grigori told Mama everything would pass, but the next day we have three more telegrams from Papa, each more frightening than the last. Aleksei had gotten worse, so bad that Dr. Derevenko insisted they should bring him home. It sounds as bad as Spala, when a bruised groin nearly killed him. That time there hadn't been a drop of blood. It all welled up under his tender skin until he couldn't even straighten his leg.

Just like when Anya was hurt, we race to the train station. This time it's so quiet. The station has been emptied so no one can find out that the heir to the throne is ill again. When our own imperial train pulls into the station and the brakes hiss like one giant sigh, I realize I've been holding my breath. Papa steps out, and right then I want to run to him. But he goes straight to Mama's side and hooks his arm around her waist. Tatiana steps back to join my sisters as he speaks softly in Mama's ear.

"Where's Aleksei?" Anastasia whispers. My eyes dart back and forth across the train's windows. All of us huddle closer. Tatiana begins to murmur a prayer. Olga joins her. Finally Papa turns to the train and nods.

Inside, something moves. A stretcher, carried by four big sailors moving slowly as a cloud passing across the sun. Only Aleksei's mouth and sweet blue eyes peep out from the bandages wound around his pale little face, but two scarlet lines mark the place where his nose still bleeds beneath the wrappings. Like part of the stretcher himself, Nagorny braces Aleksei's head and shoulders as the men lower our brother from the train.

"He can't lie down," Papa tells Mama. "We had to stop the train several times during the night to change the plugs in his nostrils. He fainted twice."

Mama moans into Papa's khaki shirt, and I know we're all thinking the same thing: Spala. After days in bed, Mama and Anya took Aleksei for a carriage ride in the fresh air. But the bumpy ride only started the bleeding inside him all over again. The poor darling had nearly passed out from the pain by the time they returned to the hunting lodge. And now we have to get Aleksei from the train station all the way home, in a motorcar.

My sisters and I watch as Aleksei is loaded into one car, then we pile into another with Nagorny and Joy. I've always thought Dr. Derevenko's kind eyes and sable beard are soothing as a teddy bear, but the look on his face as he climbs in behind Papa and Mama makes me want to whimper like Joy. All the way back to the palace we crane our necks around the driver to see the car ahead of us. Even motoring scarcely faster than a walk, the slightest rattle makes every one of us flinch.

Thank heaven for Mama's private lift. Once we get him home, Aleksei glides to the children's floor before we can clatter up the marble steps. Upstairs everyone swarms around Aleksei's narrow army cot while his *dyadka* holds Joy back. My sisters and I kneel before the iconostasis, begging God for mercy.

I've never been this close to my brother in the middle of one of his attacks. In Spala, I heard his screams fade into wails and groans from down the hall, but here, everything is so awfully quiet, like the train station. The doctor hardly speaks louder than our prayers.

A cough from Aleksei makes us all jump, and Dr. Derevenko swears. Beside me, Olga begins to sway. I peek over my shoulder at the crowd around Aleksei's cot. A pile of bright bloody rags is heaped on the floor near the head of the bed. I squeeze my eyes shut, press my folded hands to my chin, and pray harder.

A clatter of metal instruments and a sound like a kitten's mewling interrupts our prayers, and we all look again, even Tatiana. There's a quick whiff in the air of something singed, then it's gone. Dr. Derevenko backs away toward the window, mopping his face. I can't tell if it's sweat or tears sinking into his beard. Mama leans over the cot. She holds Aleksei's limp hand against her lips, stroking the inside of his arm. Papa stands beside her, slowly stroking his beard in the same rhythm as he stares down at our brother. The smell of hot blood fills my nose, suddenly stronger than the rose oil in the icon lamps. Joy barks once, like a sob, before Nagorny can hush him.

"Get Father Grigori," Mama whispers.

"Alix," Papa begins, "the wound has only just been cauterized—"

"Get him, now, before it's too late." The panic rising up in her voice stings my ears. "The doctor has done all he can, Nicky."

Papa closes his eyes and nods at Mama's maid. "Quickly." Nyuta grabs her skirt in two big handfuls and runs off to summon *Otets* Grigori.

When he arrives, *Otets* Grigori staggers across the room like a new fawn, even though it's the middle of the day. Olga lets go of a tiny gasp, then covers her mouth as if nothing's wrong. She shakes her head before I can ask. The air sours sharply as *Otets* Grigori passes. In the corner, Joy seems to calm as he nears.

"Father Grigori," Mama begins, but he doesn't say a word. He holds up a hand and eases himself to his knees beside the narrow cot. Aleksei lies under his blankets and bandages like a small mummy. Points of sweat stand out around his eyes.

Otets Grigori makes the sign of the cross over Aleksei, then bends his head and shuts his eyes. We all do the same. Behind my closed eyes I listen so hard, and hear nothing. None of *Otets* Grigori's sweet pet names for our brother, no soothing talk of finding God in the sea and the sunshine, not even a whisper of scripture or prayer.

I bite my lip and pray with all my heart. But it's as if my words are gone too. All I can do is feel. Everything tumbles inside me, and I think I'll break down and cry. Trying to fight off the terror in my throat, I grope for my sisters' hands. I can't even remember which of my sisters is beside me, but two hands squeeze back, and right then my hopes begin to burn like the flames in the icon lamps. Something clear and bright rises up in my chest, and the lump in my throat breaks apart. I open my mouth and swallow a great breath of air. Tears run down my cheeks, but I don't care. My lips want to smile even as I taste the salt.

"Don't be alarmed," *Otets* Grigori's voice says. "Nothing will happen."

My eyes flutter open. *Otets* Grigori is already walking out of the room. I look at Mama, Papa, and my sisters. I know from their quiet that they've all felt what I did. But where did it come from?

We creep closer to Aleksei's bed and peek down at him. His eyes are closed, the bandages gone. Only a faint crust of blood rims his nostrils.

Mama puts a finger to her lips. Her eyes are bright with tears, and her face glows. "He's asleep." The wonder and tenderness in her voice squeezes my heart and stops my breath once more. It's as if the horrors have melted away, and she's given birth to him all over again.

Oh please, Lord, I pray, someday let me feel the way Mama looks right now.

12

ANASTASIA NIKOLAEVNA

Autumn 1915—Autumn 1916
Stavka

Packing ourselves into our dark blue train and getting away from horrid Petrograd is more fun than ever, now that the war's on. There's nothing better than going to see Papa, but I wish we could all have a real holiday instead of just visiting *Stavka* for a few days at a time. It's gotten so Olga looks like she should be a patient at the lazaret instead of a nurse, and even if Tatiana won't ever admit it, leaving her cotton and carbolic acid behind once in a while doesn't hurt her a bit, either.

Since Papa took over the high command, we can't cruise the Finnish skerries on the *Standart*, or take our train south to Livadia for months in our white marble palace on the Black Sea. It's different now, like pushing the stop lever on my camera until nothing except the war can squeeze through the lens. I don't read the papers like Olga, or trail behind

Mama every minute like Tatiana, but I'm no *idiotka*. I can see Papa getting worried and tired as well as anyone. The Big Pair mopes and frets, but *I* won't give Papa anything more to worry about. Soldiers need to keep up their morale, after all.

I write him cheerful letters sealed with thousands of kisses and clown about just like I always do. Papa always thanks me in his telegrams, writes back cheerful letters of his own whenever he can, and sometimes even sends me cigarettes, too! But the more I see him as the war goes on, the more I hear a little Olga-voice in the back of my own head, wondering if Papa himself is trying just as hard to keep up *our* morale.

Stavka's supposed to be men's quarters, but Mama doesn't care, especially since Aleksei went back to the front to stay with Papa once he recovered from his nosebleed. All of us ladies have to motor back to the rail station every night to sleep on our train, but during the day we march right in. Who would dare look the empress in the eye and say, "No women allowed"?

"What do you men do all day long that's so important?" I ask Aleksei.

"I have breakfast with Papa and all the highest-ranking officers every morning," he says, puffing up like a dinner roll. "Then lessons. In the afternoons we usually drive along the Dneiper, and sometimes the generals eat *zakuski* with us before supper. At night we write letters to you women and then play cards or read out loud together."

Appetizers and river tours? To hear him talk, you'd think it was a camping trip instead of a war. "What about Papa?"

Aleksei shrugs. "He reads the *dokladi* and eats lunch with the commanding officers while I have my lessons."

Why in the world does Papa need to be five hundred miles from home to do any of that? "What about battles?"

"We inspected troops near the front once!" Aleksei rubs his cuff over the medal pinned to his khaki tunic. "If the Germans had fired they could have hit us, but I was brave and got the medal of St. George, fourth class."

Some war.

Whenever Papa can get away, we all motor down the river Dneiper in a launch and picnic on the shores. It's just like Aleksei said, and almost as much fun as our summers in the skerries on the *Standart*.

"Bury me," Aleksei demands, spread out on the sandy bank in his striped bathing costume. Mama won't let us bury him, but we sprinkle shovels full of sand over his back until he looks like a breaded cutlet. Papa pins him to the ground with his boot like a hunter over a stag while they both grin at Mashka and her camera.

"Take off your cap, you idiot!" I yell from the shore when he gets loose and runs down to rinse off. "Soldiers don't wear their hats swimming!" I think the little show-off would wear his cap *and* his medal with his bathing suit if he could get away with it. He's so oafishly proud of that thing.

Farther inland, we tromp through fields and flop down together in heaps to rest in haystacks while Aleksei marches about with his miniature rifle, pretending the tall banks are trenches along the front lines. Mama mostly stays under her parasol, so I sneak smokes from the cigarettes Papa gives us. Tatiana fusses all the time, "Be careful of the ashes! You will fry us to a crisp, Anastasia Nikolaevna!" but she never once tells on me.

"Oh, Mama, please let's stop," Maria begs every night as we motor through the town of Mogilev on the way back to our train. "There's Stephania and Bolyus, and I brought cherry candies especially for Gricha and Lenka." Nobody spots the *muzhik* children who come to gape at our polished black motorcars faster than Mashka. Mama won't order the driver to stop unless we ask, but she almost never refuses, either. At first the children are shy as pill bugs, but once we've romped and cuddled with them and stuffed them full of sweets they swarm us like bees. Even their mamas come out to chat with the Big Pair sometimes, while ours waits in the motor.

At Christmastime, Papa and Aleksei come home to Tsarskoe Selo. While Papa walks in the imperial park, my sisters and I play and wallow in the snow with Aleksei like polar bears, lobbing snowballs at one another and making a warlike rumpus. Once, Aleksei sneaks up behind me and plasters my neck with a great mittenful of snow. I squawk and shiver while he laughs, until we hear Papa's voice.

"Aleksei Nikolaevich!"

Too much roughhousing for the delicate little Sunbeam, I think as Aleksei trots to Papa's side, and just when we were really having fun, too. But I'm wrong. Papa's stern words march over the snow as I fish the slush out of my collar. "You ought to be ashamed of yourself, Aleksei. You're behaving like a German, attacking anyone from behind when they can't defend themselves. Cowardly. Leave that sort of behavior to the enemy."

Poor Aleksei. He hangs his head so I don't even have the heart to pummel him with snowballs the way he deserves. So far, that's the closest thing I've ever seen to Papa commanding a battle.

Almost a whole year goes by, and practically the only thing that changes is the view out the windows as our trains chug to and from headquarters: snow drifts to lilac blooms to haystacks. Even when the seasons change, they're the same. *Stavka*'s no different. By the fall of 1916 everybody knows the war's a mess, but you can't tell by the way people act around us. The place is still crawling with generals and officers who bow and salute and say "Your Majesty" like a battalion of wind-up toys. They treat us like we brought a trainload of gold-plated rifles, even though all we do is stand in front of a row of Cossacks and pose in our new fur-trimmed coats for the cameras: THE TSAR AND HIS HAPPY FAMILY AT HEADQUARTERS, the title cards on the newsreels might say. We *are* happy, but it feels like pretending to make it look like we're pleased with the war instead of just being together again.

"Stop making eyes at that camera and behave yourselves," Tatiana hisses at Maria and me from behind Aleksei's shoulder. "This film is for Russia, not our home movies."

"It doesn't matter what you do, just as long as you move," Aleksei announces. "They took films of me running with Joy and pelting Monsieur Gilliard with snowballs and never complained. And you don't have to whisper," he informs Tatiana. "You know it can't record the sound."

Mama would shush us all anyway, but she's resting in the train. Papa only stands stout and proud as anything in his uniform with the red dolman and tall astrakhan hat and Aleksei like a matching toy soldier beside him.

"How do you think we looked?" I ask my sisters that night on the train.

"*Otlichno*," says Tatiana, petting her fur collar while Ortipo pouts in the corner. "It has been so long since we had new coats. I only wish the film could be in color."

It isn't what I mean, but I don't know how to say it the right way. "Who's in charge of the army when Papa comes cruising the river with us?" I ask instead.

"Papa is," Tatiana answers. "Why should anyone else take over? No one took charge of Russia when we had our holidays on *Standart* or in Livadia."

But this is *war*, not a quiet summer. And if he can leave like that, what does it really mean to be in charge of the army?

Olga looks at me as if she can hear the thoughts linking up inside my head, like a verse to a song we both know. I'm not about to say anything more in front of Tatiana, though.

What would the soldiers at the front think if they knew Papa walks away for a day to picnic with his family and snore in haystacks? Papa and Aleksei sleep in the governor's mansion in Mogilev, while the troops spend their nights camped out in trenches and fields. Has Papa even seen the war, or is it just like always, with everything scrubbed and painted especially for his arrival? I don't know what anyone could do to polish up the front, but I'll bet none of the soldiers scratch or spit or swear while Papa's around. They probably aren't allowed to look tired or discouraged, either.

If we're all of us—Papa, the army, and even my sisters and me—pretending for one another, what good is that to anyone?

13

TATIANA NIKOLAEVNA

December 1916
Tsarskoe Selo

*M*adame," Anya gasps, limping into the lilac boudoir on her two canes. "I've had a call from Father
Grigori's daughter. She saw him get into a motorcar last night
at midnight, and he hasn't come back." She gives Mama and
me no time to answer before rushing on. "It must have been
the Yusupov chauffeur. Father Grigori told me himself he was
invited to meet Princess Irina late last night." She flops down
into Mama's armchair and sighs as if all her energy has flown
straight out of her mouth.

"Irina is in the Crimea, darling." Mama does not even
look up from winding her yarn. "There must be some mistake."

Anya sighs again. "He told me him*self*," she insists. She
sounds so like our Anastasia, I cannot help smiling to myself.

The telephone rings, and we all three look at one another,

pretending none of us jumped in our chairs at the jangle of its bell. Mama listens with a grave face until the wool draped around my hands begins to itch.

"The minister of the interior," she tells us when she hangs up. "He says there was a commotion at the Yusupov palace last night, but I don't believe a word of it. Vladimir Purishkevich answered the door when the policeman rang."

"That dreadful radical from the Duma?" Anya asks.

Mama stares across the room. "Purishkevich told the policeman it was nothing, only that they had just killed Rasputin. He was quite drunk." With such long pauses between her sentences, I know she is dazed by the news, whether she believes it or not. "Purishkevich was drunk," she says again.

I hardly know whether I believe it myself. Purishkevich hates *Otets* Grigori. He denounced Our Friend in front of the whole parliament. *Otets* Grigori never would have gone to the Yusupov palace if he knew Purishkevich would be there, even if our cousin Irina is the most beautiful woman in Russia. Besides, Mama is right; Irina is in the Crimea. Nothing makes sense.

"Father Grigori was very odd yesterday," Anya muses. "I was getting ready to leave, and he looked at me and said, 'What more do you want? Already you have received all.' I didn't have the first notion what he meant. I hadn't asked him for anything at all."

"Anya dear," Mama interrupts, "go and fetch Lili Dehn from the city, will you, please?"

Anya lurches up onto her crutches and hobbles off.

"Now, perhaps we can think," Mama says. "I can hardly string two thoughts together with her gabbing."

I stifle a giggle behind my hand in spite of myself. "Mama, you made her go all that way on crutches just to shut her up?"

"Of course not," she says, but the way she smiles and keeps her eyes fixed on her ball of yarn tells me otherwise. "Lili will help us sort through all this." I nod. Mama always knows what to do.

By the time Lili arrives, all my sisters have drifted into the lilac boudoir. The dogs run straight to her, as if they hope she can explain what is wrong with us. Anya cries on a cushioned stool at Mama's feet. Even Anastasia is subdued. Mama is pale but composed, absently soothing Anya as she talks with Lili.

"You will sleep at Anya's house tonight," Mama tells Lili. She lowers her voice. "There have been threats," she adds.

Cousin Irina's husband Felix has called, and Cousin Dmitri, too, but Mama refused to see either of them. While she talks with Lili and Anya, I nudge my sisters into the cozy-corner. "One of us must sleep in Mama's room tonight. She should not be alone until *Otets* Grigori is found."

"You'd hardly think anything was wrong from looking at her," Maria says. Her fingers wander in and out of Mama's candy dish. "Poor Anya is a wreck."

I know better. Mama will be fine only as long as she has someone in worse shape than herself to take care of. As soon as Anya gets hold of herself, Mama will have nothing but her own fears for company. "Did you see how badly her pen quivered when she wrote the news to Papa? She had to give up and finish in pencil."

"I wish I could stay with Varvara and Marochka Grigorievna," Maria says, putting the last of Mama's chocolates into her mouth. "The poor darlings must be sick with worrying about their papa." Anastasia glances fearfully at Maria and shakes her head. She will never admit it, but I know the idea of sleeping alone in their room tonight frightens her. I am a little frightened myself. I have heard enough of Mama's phone calls to know serious trouble is brewing, even outside our walls. The minister of the interior warned Mama of terrible rumors. Plots to murder her, and Anya too, are circulating, God forbid. I cannot begin to imagine why. The very idea makes me queasy.

"I'll stay with Mama," Olga offers.

"Are you sure, *dushka?*" I ask her.

"*Konechno*, I'll sleep in Papa's bed."

That should settle me, but alone in my room, new worries invade. If *Otets* Grigori has truly been killed, the consequences for us will be almost past bearing. Aleksei has not been seriously ill since his nosebleed at *Stavka* a year ago, but that hardly matters. Hemophilia is not a disease that simply vanishes. *Otets* Grigori once told Mama that Aleksei's health would improve after he turned twelve, but what will become of Mama? She depends so much on *Otets* Grigori, I fear for her most of all. The thought torments me until I steal downstairs and curl up with Ortipo on the couch in Mama's room.

When the truth comes at last, it strikes us all numb. One of *Otets* Grigori's galoshes surfaced on the crusted ice of the river Neva. When the police searched the water, they discovered *Otets* Grigori's body bound in ropes and punctured with bullet holes. Our own cousins, Felix and Dmitri, murdered our dear friend with the help of horrid Purishkevich, then dumped his body into the river. His frozen hand was raised with his thumb and two fingers clenched together, as though his last thought had been to make the sign of the cross.

Olga takes the news so strangely. "It's been brewing for a long time," she says, "though I never thought it would be so brutal. The soldiers aren't always careful with their newspapers, and the servants talk in the halls, you know. The papers have been full of stories about *Otets* Grigori. I've heard there were even dirty cartoons circulating in Petrograd."

My mouth falls open as she tells me some of the rumors. Anastasia's eyes grow nearly as round as Mashka's saucers. If I had known what she was about to say, I would have stopped up the Little Pair's ears with cotton. "Those are filthy lies!"

"Probably," Olga admits. "But it doesn't matter whether they're true. How do you think it looks, having a man like that coming into the palace?"

Across the room, Anya is awash with grief. Olga rubs at her temples as Anya wails. "Mama has ordered Anya to move in with us," I tell my sisters. "Her mail today was full of death threats, God protect her." I shiver.

"Do you get the feeling," Olga begins, then stops with a glance at our younger sisters.

I know what she means, though. Nothing in the room

has changed, yet somehow I feel the way I so often did when *Otets* Grigori was with us. It reminds me of sitting at my desk, writing in my diary with my back to the room. Sometimes I sense something more than furniture and picture frames near me, and look up to find a swallow perched in the windowsill, or that Ortipo has waddled in without a sound.

Right behind it, another thought creeps up the back of my neck. "Have any of you seen a bird at the window?"

"There are always swallows outside our windows," Olga says.

"Chase them away," I demand. "If a bird taps on the window or flies into the glass, it becomes an omen of death. Maybe if I had—"

"Tatya, sweetheart, you couldn't have saved *Otets* Grigori, no matter if a flock of birds came tapping." The steadiness of Olga's fingertips against my elbow startles me; this time, I am the one quivering. "Even with all the rumors I'd heard, I would have thought of Mama, Aleksei, or one of our wounded first. You couldn't have known," she says again.

I nod and force a watery swallow down the pinhole of my throat. "*Konechno*. But with *Otets* Grigori gone, we cannot take chances."

14

OLGA NIKOLAEVNA

January–February 1917
Tsarskoe Selo

Since *Otets* Grigori's murder, I've hardly known how to feel. Mama is nearly crushed with heartbreak, but secretly I wonder if things will begin to improve without *Otets* Grigori stirring up gossip about our family. The few rumors I'd heard about Our Friend were enough to make me blush redder than the cross on my nurse's uniform. So many scandals! And that was what had leaked through the cloistered cracks of our imperial lazaret. The gossip on the streets must have been ten times more poisonous.

But it is said in Russia that a truth is found between two lies, and so I can't help wondering. I've smelled the liquor on *Otets* Grigori myself more than once. My sisters scoff like Mama, but I've told them only a few tidbits about the wine and the gypsy women. They don't know the whispers of stories I've heard circulating about what Our Friend did with

Anya, our own mama, and his grip on the government itself. I even remember one of our nursemaids being dismissed in a flurry of whispers, and suddenly I think I can guess the reason why.

Still, it isn't right, what Cousin Felix and those other men did to *Otets* Grigori. Even in all the ugly fragments of stories I've managed to sweep together, it never seemed that he'd hurt anyone. Drunkenness and lewd rumors are no justification for murder.

It's as if all of Russia is turning its back to us. At the war front, Aleksei writes me, the grand dukes and commanding officers have stopped lunching with Papa. In the lazaret, I don't have to guess anymore which of the new arrivals believe the rumors about *Otets* Grigori.

"'I've sold the horse to pay for our winter fuel. Please don't be angry, Petya dear,'" I read to a soldier from the countryside. In neighboring beds, two men gesture at each other and snigger behind their blankets as Mama passes. I raise my voice over their hissing. "'I'm not sure we could afford his feed much longer. If this war doesn't end and bring you home by spring, the children and I will drag the plow ourselves.'" Almost all the men's letters are choked with dismaying news. Even in the city, bread, flour, and fuel are running short, and the people's tempers aren't far behind.

When I collect the empty water glasses and day-old papers from the men's bedsides, I always skim the headlines for a peek at the outside world before tossing them into the dustbin. That night a newspaper covered in childish doodles

catches my eye. Funny little people pepper the margins, making faces and sly comments about the stories. *Clever fellow,* I
think, and then my smile crumples. Beside a photo of Mama,
one of the figures stands pointing with a word far worse than
Nemka scrawled in the bubble over his head. My hands shake
as I stuff the entire stack of papers into the bin. Just the scent
of newsprint makes the memory sting.

Mama and Tatiana, busy in the operating rooms with
their ether cones and amputees, seem mercifully oblivious—
or else they're keeping secrets too. They speak of nothing but
operations and petty annoyances.

"We removed Konstantin Semyonovich's stitches today,"
Tatiana says as we tidy up the common room the next evening. "His incision is healing beautifully, *slava Bogu.* Oh, for
pity's sake." She stands over the chessboard, her hands on
her hips. "The white queen's bishop has gone missing again.
Keep an eye out, will you, *dushka?* This is at least the third
time since December. Why is it always that same piece?"

I don't tell my sister the bishop isn't missing at all. I
found it myself this morning and flushed it straight down
the lavatory. Someone had scribbled a shaggy beard on to
the white paint, and underneath that the initials "G.R." for
Grigori Rasputin—our *Otets* Grigori—and planted it on
the king's square of the chessboard with a tiny paper crown
on top.

The next morning a crisp new bishop stands in its correct place. One of the nurses must be secretly buying new
chess pieces to replace the defaced ones and shield us from
this small insult, I realize. My gratitude for such a discreet

kindness weakens my knees, yet how can we fix a problem we aren't allowed to see?

Soon enough, my silence doesn't matter. The capital itself rumbles with unrest. The papers show pictures of students marching in the street, waving red banners. Mama is indignant. "Hooligans!" she calls them. "Boys and girls rushing through the streets shouting about no bread."

"Some of the nurses have heard talk that the workers are plotting to strike. There are stories of mobs threatening and jeering at police officers and reserve regiments."

"Malicious gossip," Mama insists. "The people adore us, darling," she soothes, patting my cheek. "The real people, that is. Minister Protopopov has ordered fresh supplies. It will all pass soon enough, like the other strikes."

"But, Mama, how can there be so many stories and none of it true?"

Mama frowns and shakes her head at me, as if to warn, *Now, now, Olga.* "The press can't fool the true Russians—they can't even read, most of them." There is no tender pat this time. She laces her fingers and sets them deliberately in her lap. I run my tongue over my teeth, considering how far to push. When I open my mouth, Mama fixes me with one of her looks. I give up—but she can't stop my thoughts from swirling.

Even if the peasants can't read, talk spreads more quickly than headlines. What will the people believe? The only peasant I've ever known for more than a few minutes was *Otets* Grigori, and he's dead. My head aches to think about it. At night, my eyes and ears throb, as if they're sick of seeing and hearing nothing but bad news.

When Aleksei and I break out in red spots, I have to laugh at the irony of it—"red" is suddenly everywhere, from the streets of Petrograd to the tsar's own children.

At first Mama sits right alongside us, copying our temperatures into her diary every three hours and reading to us from *Aunt Helen's Children*. She's such an angel when we're ill. All three of our sisters are allowed into our rooms, to read to us and fetch cool cloths when our temperatures begin to climb. Papa wrote that it would be much easier if all of us had measles at the same time so we can be done with it once and for all.

In half darkness, I sweat in my camp bed while Mama runs between my room and Aleksei's on the other side of the playroom. His mouth and throat are coated in spots, and his eyes ache terribly. In no time at all, Anya Vyrubova is sick too, moaning and flapping about in a bed on the other side of the palace. Mama drifts in and out, like my thoughts, as my temperature rises. Any little shard of light bites at my eyes, and every sound clumps in my head, as if everything I hear is coated in sour cream. Now and then I taste the cool thermometer in my mouth and know Mama is beside me again. Her voice grows distorted—first sounding too fat, and then too narrow, though I know such thoughts make no sense.

Sounds buzz around me, and I'm sure the painted dragonflies have come loose from the frieze on our walls to flap their wings in my ears, making my skin prickle and crawl as tides of sickness wash me away.

When the first wave of fever breaks, I wake on linens creased with sweat. Beneath my head, the pillow feels as though I've melted a hollow in it. Anastasia sits beside me, leafing violently through one of my books.

"It's about time," she says, dumping the book onto my nightstand. The glasses and medicine bottles squeezed onto it all rattle together. I wince, but my head no longer echoes and throbs with the sound. "All four of you have been roasting like potatoes in a campfire."

My voice only cracks when I try to speak. Anastasia hands me a glass of water. "All four of us?"

Anastasia nods across the room. "Don't you remember? Aleksei was first, and Tatiana's got it too. Her ears have such bad abcesses she can't hear properly. But her fever was so high, even I couldn't tease her about it. Aleksei's was the highest so far, though. Forty point six," she says, as if it's something to be proud of. "And Anya's here. She got sick right after you."

"How long has it been?"

"Five days. And Papa still isn't home."

I struggle to sit up, but I'm weak as a leaf. Anastasia stuffs another pillow behind me and helps haul me up by the elbow. "Why should Papa be coming home?"

Her gaze drops to the floor. For the first time I notice how weary her eyes have become—just like Papa's. Everyone remarks on the size of Mashka's saucers, but Papa and our little imp of a sister both have eyes sweet as cornflowers. "Shvybzik, look at me. What's wrong?"

"Petrograd's a mess," she mumbles. "The people are going mad in the streets. And to top it all off, the water and electricity's been cut. The servants have to break through the ice on the ponds to get water, the lift won't run, and Mama's been climbing up and down the stairs all day long."

A wave of unease sloshes over me like sickness all over again. "Is she all right?"

"She's tired," Anastasia admits. "I think her heart bothers her, but she won't say so. I've been running all over the place for her. Mashka, too. Lili Dehn is coming to help, but Mama's worried about *her* now. She's probably had to leave baby Titi in the city with his nanny."

My heart flops. "Is it that bad in Petrograd, Shvybs?"

"Papa will fix everything," she says, but her face wavers. "The telephone keeps ringing, and the ministers look so grave when they come to report. And Papa's train is late. It's never been so late before. We haven't even had a telegram since last night."

Mama's voice calls out, "Anastasia!" and my little sister jumps from her chair.

"Mashka's stuck with Anya in the sickroom all the way over in the other wing. We can't hardly leave her alone, the great big baby. Mama's with Aleksei."

"How is he?"

She smirks a little. "His legs are so speckled, he looks like he's got a leopard under his sheets. But Mama won't let him scratch. They'll bleed, you know, if you scratch too much. And he sounds like a bear when he coughs." She leans over to kiss my forehead.

"You shouldn't."

She rolls her pink-rimmed eyes at me. "You've all four been coughing and sweating all over the place for days. I'm not sick yet, and I won't be," she insists, and runs out of the room toward Mama's voice.

I fall back on the pillows and try to make my thoughts congeal. What sort of world have I woken to? A city I hardly recognize, and my little Shvybzik acting all grown up.

15

ANASTASIA NIKOLAEVNA

27–28 February 1917
Tsarskoe Selo

For once Olga doesn't know the worst of it," I grumble to myself as the train pulls into the station. The whole world feels like it's tilting and trembling under my feet, and it doesn't stop with the locomotive. I thrust my hand into Maria's coat pocket, pretending to hunt for a candy, and stick close beside her as we search the passengers for Lili. She'll be expecting Mama to meet her, not the two of us all by ourselves.

Lili takes one look at us standing there and for a second her face ripples up as if she might cry. Mashka and I eye each other. We don't look sick, but there's no missing that "poor darlings" expression on Lili's face. Something's up.

"What are you going to do, Lili?" Mama says when we bring Lili into the lilac boudoir. "Titi is in Petrograd. Hadn't you better return to him this evening?"

Mashka and I stand there gaping like two idiots. If the capital's so dangerous, why didn't Lili bring the baby with her? Our guard is the most loyal in all Russia. We know every man by name. Maria probably knows their wives' and mamas' and sisters' and dogs' and cats' names too. I watch Lili look at Mama for a long time. Surely Lili will go back to Titi in Petrograd. But that strange, sad look comes into her face again. "Permit me to remain with you, Madame," she says. Mama only stares at her.

They're so quiet for so long, I want to stamp my foot and shout at them. I know they aren't just not talking. Both of them are working hard not to say something in front of Mashka and me. Mama reaches for Lili and catches her up in a hug. "I cannot ask you to do this," she says, kissing Lili's cheeks as if she's one of my sisters.

"But I must, Madame. Please, please let me stay."

All of a sudden, Mama's expression changes to her Empress Face. "I've tried to phone the emperor," she says, "and I cannot get through. But I have wired him, asking him to return immediately. He'll be here on Wednesday morning." She nods a smart little *that's that* nod, even though we haven't heard a peep out of Papa yet. "Come, let's go see the girls upstairs."

While they go in to see the Big Pair, Mashka and I scuttle around our own room, gathering things to make Lili comfortable for the night. In the Crimson Drawing Room, Mashka and I wrestle with sheets and cushions to make Lili a bed on one of the couches. I lay one of our nightdresses over the coverlet while Mashka finds a lamp and an icon. Together, we dig through our photo albums until we find a picture we took at Anya's house of Mama holding Lili's little Titi. Even though we pry it from the page speck by speck, we manage to rip one whole corner. I sneak into the Big Pair's bedroom and pinch one of Tatiana's enameled frames from her desk. When we slide Titi's picture into it, the torn part hardly shows at all.

Lili's so pleased when she sees the room that for another awful moment I think she wants to cry. Then Mama bustles Maria off to the sickrooms and leaves Lili with me while she goes to see Count So-and-So about whatever it is they won't talk about in front of us children. With nothing to say, Lili and I sit down on the red carpet and work over a jigsaw puzzle.

Mama comes back looking awful, all pale and pasty. I knot up like day-old hair ribbons, thinking about her heart with all this running around, receiving people downstairs and seeing to Anya and Aleksei and the Big Pair upstairs. But when I try to ask Mama how she is, she gives me a thin smile and a kiss and sends me off to bed.

My room feels like a cave. I hate sleeping alone. I'm sure I can hear the Big Pair and Aleksei coughing in their cots, and Lili tossing on the couch. The thought of Mashka, cozied up in Papa's brass bed downstairs with icons all around and Mama beside her, makes me almost jealous enough to forget how worried I am. *Almost*, I think as I scrunch down close to Jemmy and screw my eyes shut.

Mama and Mashka and Lili are in my room by eight thirty the next morning, and we have café au lait together. "I've wired the emperor repeatedly," Mama says, "but there's been no reply." My stomach somersaults. Papa always answers our telegrams within a few hours. "Count Benckendorff suggested the Garde Equipage should stay in the palace, and I've agreed."

Mashka's face lights up like a flashbulb. "It'll be just like being on the *Standart* again," she squeals. Even I feel a little twinge of excitement. It will be almost like our yachting trips, having all the officers' familiar faces around us . . . except no *Standart*, no Papa, and no sea.

The sun shines right through the cold while we run through the halls, meeting one old friend after another as the Mixed Guard and some of the Cossack Konvoi join the ranks indoors and on the grounds just outside our windows.

All day long, our four invalids' fevers climb quicker than sailors up the rigging of the *Standart*. We dash from one bed to the next, trying to keep them cool and comfortable, especially Olga, who turns red as a bowl of borscht. Upstairs reeks of Dr. Botkin's cologne, he stays so late. Everyone wants Mama most, of course, even silly old Anya, and you don't have to be Tatiana to see how tired and worried Mama's getting.

The next day the weather turns foul. I'm tired and achy, and my eyes feel hot all around the edges. My throat itches, but I pretend it's only the extra-strong smell of coffee from the servants' cafeteria in the basement that makes me cough. "I *won't* be ill," I tell myself, and Maria, too, when she gives me her worried eyes.

In the afternoon, there's a clamor downstairs. I pull

Maria away from the windows where she's been waving to the officers and run down the corridor to see what all the fuss is about.

Mama's friend Isa Buxhoeveden is covered in snow and panting like a pug in the sun. "Isa too," Mashka chirps in my ear. "It really will be just like the *Standart*!" I jab her ribs and lean around the corner to listen.

"I must see the empress," Isa gasps to Lili. "I've just come from Tsarskoe Selo. Everything is awful. There's looting and shooting in the streets." Her voice bounces through the long hallway. "They say there is mutiny among the troops."

"Hush, Isa," Lili whispers, sharp as a shout. "The servants will hear, and enough of them have deserted already."

That night we can hear shots in the distance as we visit Olga and Tatiana before bed.

"You look flushed," Tatiana says, reaching out to feel my forehead. Her voice is too loud. Dr. Botkin says it's the abcesses forming in her ears. I hoist Ortipo up to lick Tatiana's fingers before she can touch me.

"Stop your nursing," I tease, loudly enough to turn Mama's head. "You're the ill one. It's only this running back and forth between all of you roasted potatoes and up and down the stairs for Mama that makes me pink in the face."

"You are a good girl. God bless you, *dushka*." Tatiana yawns, and my cheeks turn hotter yet at such a compliment from our hoity-toity sister.

When I turn to Olga, she's whispering something to Lili about the noise.

"Darling, I don't know," Lili half sings. "It's nothing. The hard frost makes everything much louder."

"But are you sure, Lili?" Olga's voice drops even further. "Mama doesn't seem well. We're so worried about her heart."

I shiver as Lili comforts her. Even in their sickbeds, we can hardly keep anything from Olga and Tatiana. Except I don't know what exactly we're keeping from them. If they asked me what's happening, I couldn't tell them. I only know there's more to it than what I've seen and heard.

Outside the Big Pair's room, Mama issues orders like a general. "You, Lili, will sleep with Anastasia, and have Maria's bed." A grin breaks across my face and I grab Lili's hand in both of mine. Then Mama lowers her voice. "Don't take off your corsets. One doesn't know what may happen."

My stomach does a two-step. Don't take off our corsets? I wrinkle up my nose at the thought of wearing the vile old thing all night long. What could possibly happen in the middle of the night that we'd need to be wearing our corsets for? I make a question-face at Mashka, but she only shrugs. Lili looks at Mama in that odd way again, as if she's pointing at Mashka and me with her eyeballs. "The emperor arrives between five and seven o'clock tomorrow morning," Mama insists, as if saying it will make it true. "We must be ready to meet him." And that's that. Mashka helps Mama down the hall to the stairs, leaving Lili and me to undress for bed.

"Have you ever slept in a cot like this, Lili?" I ask as I drag our two camp beds nearer to each other. Lili shakes her head and winces as the legs of her cot furrow a double row of trenches through the thick carpeting. "Don't worry. Maria and I move our beds around all the time, and the screens, too. They're narrow, but it's cozy this way. They're not half so wobbly as they look."

Lili smiles absently at me, standing there working over the buttons on Mashka's nightdress. "Here, let me," I say, pushing away her shaky fingers. "It buttons just like mine." Gunfire crackles far across the snow. "Lili," I ask, looking only at the line of buttons as I work my way up to her chin, "are you scared?"

"No," she says, too quickly.

"I am," I tell her lacy collar. "I wish Papa were here." She doesn't say another word, just pulls me near, rests her cheek on my head, and gently strokes my hair all the way down my back.

"Do you miss Titi?" I ask after a little while. I feel her nod against me, and I think we both cry a little without making a sound to let the other know. When I've had enough, I wipe my eyes on the embroidered cuff of my nightdress and straighten up. "I'll brush your hair if you brush mine," I offer. "Maria and I always do that."

Lili smiles. *"Konechno."*

I drag Mashka's chair over and help Lili climb into her cot. Then she unpins her long dark hair, and I perch on the little wooden chair while we brush and braid each other's hair. Lili's so gentle, not all jerky with the brush like clumsy Mashka, that I nearly fall asleep on the spot. But when I crawl under my own covers, my eyes won't stay closed. The guns boom and crack every so often in the distance, not at all like the regular rifle and cannon salutes the regiments are always doing for Papa. We lie in the dark for ages, whispering about silly things to keep from wondering what's going on outside while I squirm and wriggle against my dratted corset. Sometimes Lili goes quiet. I try and try to let her sleep, but I never last more than a few minutes before I ask, "Lili, are you awake?" She always answers right away, so I know her eyes won't keep shut any better than mine. Once, we creep to the window and look outside. The glass is so cold it burns my forehead when I lean against it to peer out. There on the courtyard sits a great fat cannon, with the sentries dancing around it to keep warm. "Papa will be so astonished," I tell Lili, my breath turning to thick frost on the windowpane. That close to the window, we can hear shouts along with the gunshots, and sometimes a sound like breaking glass. At the sight of smears of firelight flickering just beyond our gates in the streets of Tsarskoe Selo, I abandon Lili and scurry back under my covers. I don't dare open my eyes again all night.

16

MARIA NIKOLAEVNA

28 February-4 March 1917
Tsarskoe Selo

*D*ownstairs, it's impossible for Mama to hide anything from me. The telephone in Papa and Mama's bedroom rings and rings. Every time I try to guess from her questions and answers what Mama's hearing on the other end of the line, my heart dangles from my ribs. First there are rumors in the city that Aleksei has died. Next we hear the strikers have blocked all the railways. Before long, my body braces for the news before Mama even touches the receiver.

At nine o'clock the telephone rings again.

"Rebels?" Mama asks. "Here?" I go weak as broth. "I see. How long?"

Hardly a moment after Mama hangs up, a shot rings out. Not five hundred yards from our walls, a sentry falls. After that, just the jingle of one of the dog's collars stops my breath and jolts my shoulders up to my ears.

That night we don't undress for bed at all. On our way out from seeing my sisters and Aleksei, Isa Buxhoeveden meets us in the corridor with the most horrible look on her face. "Madame," she says, struggling not to wail, "the Tsarskoe Selo garrison has mutinied."

"Bozhe moi," Mama gasps, clutching her chest. "We cannot have fighting here on our account." I'm ready to run for Dr. Botkin to tend to her heart, but Mama recovers in an instant. "I must tell the children not to worry," she says, and nearly runs back to my brother and sisters' rooms to tell them the firing is only from special maneuvers. If they were well, they wouldn't believe her for a second.

"Lili will take care of Anastasia," she decides when everyone is soothed. Everyone but me, that is. Listening to our mama lie to Aleksei and my sisters made me turn all slippery inside. "I'll see to Anya later. Come now, Maria, we are going to speak to the men outside." I follow her like a duckling.

Downstairs, she throws a black fur coat over her Red Cross uniform, then helps me bundle into furs myself. I feel myself shivering even before we go out into the snow. I don't know why I'm so scared. I've known these men all my life, but nothing seems steady anymore. It's like climbing from the *Standart* into a rowboat on choppy seas.

Isa watches from inside, and for a little while I think I see Lili at my bedroom window too. Both of them look awfully frightened. Ahead of us, the men are all arranged for battle, with one row on their knees in the snow and the rest standing behind them with their rifles ready. The light from our windows gleams in thin blue stripes along the barrels of all those guns, but Mama never wavers. She goes straight up to the lines and speaks to each man in turn, calling them by name whenever she can.

"Sergei Vasilievich, I trust your loyalty to the emperor completely. . . . I know you will not fail us, Ivan Petrovich. . . . My good men, don't let the rebels provoke you. . . . Alexander Sergeevich, you are sworn to protect the heir, but I pray no blood will be shed unnecessarily." Across the courtyard and down the entire line we go. Finally feeling useful, I whisper to her the names of the men I recognize, and try to smile and thank every one of them, especially the ones I don't know.

Lots of them are shocked to see their empress outside at this time of night, but they're all polite and bow, even doffing their hats in such fierce cold. Some of the soldiers seem too surprised to do anything but grunt and nod, but some kiss Mama's hand, fur mittens and all.

"They are all our friends," Mama tells Isa when we get back inside. "They are so devoted. I trust them completely." I sink onto Papa's bed, still in my coat and furs, but Mama sets off into the dark corridors to reassure Anya on the other side of the palace. With a big yawn, I force myself up to help her, but Isa says, "Stay here, Maria. I'll walk with your mama on the stairs." Suddenly I'm too tired to argue, or even to be afraid to wait alone in Papa and Mama's bedroom. I curl up under Mama's wall of icons and fall asleep under the flickering rose oil lamp.

All night I drift in and out. Every time I stir, Mama's up too. She fusses with Lili's pillows and blankets on the sofa in her lilac boudoir. "Oh, you Russian ladies," she teases, "my grandmother, Queen Victoria, showed me how to make a bed. I'll teach you." When I roll over again, Mama, nearly silent in her stocking feet, is on her way to the Palisander Room, her arms full of fruit and biscuits for Isa and dear old Countess Benckendorff.

Next thing I know, feet pound on the balcony and fists hammer outside. In the doorway to the lilac boudoir, the countess is struggling to tug Mama inside and shut the tall door all at once. "Your Majesty, the rebels have reached the palace. You and the grand duchess must go upstairs." I gulp back a squeak and scramble to Mama's side. Suddenly the pounding stops. The three of us hold our breath until Isa bursts in, almost laughing with relief.

"It was just a sailor, trying to find his way to the basement to warm up." I want to laugh, but everything feels too jittery and fragile. If I open my mouth I'll only cry instead, and I can't do that in front of Mama.

The next day is awful. By the time I wake, Papa still hasn't come, and Anastasia's sick with measles. When I come down from helping Aleksei mold tin bullets with Monsieur Gilliard, I find Mama with a handful of her unanswered telegrams to Papa.

"Mama?"

She swallows hard and holds the fist full of papers out for me to see. All of them have come back marked in blue pencil: *Address of person mentioned unknown.*

My whole body goes blank, too shocked to think or feel anything at all. I can't imagine what could come after this.

All day long, we sit thinking awful things. It's the anniversary of my great-grandpapa's assassination, when he was blown up by a bomb shaped like an Easter cake. Is Papa, wherever he is, thinking of how he'd watched his *dedushka* die and his own papa become tsar? He was only twelve years old when Alexander II was killed, the same age Aleksei is now.

The telephone blares, and I nearly yelp.

On the other end of the line, Rodzyanko, a hateful man from the Duma, talks so loudly that for once I can hear both sides of the conversation. My heart batters my ribs as I listen in.

"You are in danger and should prepare to leave," he tells Mama, no matter what she says. He can't seem to understand that we can't move my sisters or Aleksei. Both Dr. Derevenko and Dr. Botkin think moving the Big Pair could be fatal. Fatal! Olga's awful fever's broken, but her heart is inflamed, and Tatiana has gone deaf as a marble column.

From across the room I hear the shrug in Rodzyanko's voice. "When a house is burning, the invalids are the first to be taken out." And then he hangs up. Red splotches rush up Mama's cheeks like she's been slapped, and I tuck my chin to my chest, hoping she won't have to see my shock.

The next morning we open the curtains to find the park empty as a blank checkerboard. Only the abandoned cannon and footprints in the snow are left to show the men were there at all. "My sailors, my own sailors," Mama moans. "I can't believe it."

Beside her, I clutch the curtain until the rod above my

head creaks, too frightened to look at Mama's face. My own face is fighting me too hard to be trusted.

How many times have I told my sisters, "I want to marry a soldier and have twenty children!" I've lived alongside these men my whole life. They kept my sisters and me from falling when we roller-skated across the decks of the *Standart*. Aleksei played the balalaika with them, and Anastasia taught some of them to knit. My sisters say I'm boy-crazy, but it was Olga who spent a whole summer falling in love with one of the officers, sweet Pavel Voronov. What's happened to erase all those golden days of tennis, picnics, and mushroom picking? What could make the big gentle men who'd kept Aleksei from toddling over the rails when he was small suddenly desert us in the snow?

I want my sisters. I want my sisters and my papa, because it's only me and Mama and I don't know what to do. I want Tatiana to take care of Mama, Olga to take care of me, Anastasia to make us all laugh, and our papa the tsar to fix everything.

But there's still no news of Papa, only the rumors the servants bring with them as they trudge in from the city: Papa's train is trapped in Pskov and he's given up the throne.

"Ridiculous," Mama says, crumpling up the leaflets. "Such trash! My Nicky would never do such a stupid thing. What on earth would he be doing in Pskov? He's on his way home." I hardly hear what she says. Her feet are awfully swollen and sore from the stairs, and now this. How much more can her poor heart take?

The news arrives with Papa's uncle Pavel Friday night. Upstairs in the Crimson Drawing Room, Mama abandons her letter to Papa and shoos Lili and me into my sisters' classroom so they can talk. Before long, Uncle Pavel's shouting. No one speaks to my darling Mama that way, not ever. Hearing it makes me feel all wrong, like a plucked chicken.

"Don't you think I'd better see what's the matter?" I whisper.

Lili's eyes go terribly wide. "No, no!" she says. "We should remain quietly here."

I can't do it. I just can't, and I know it, not with that storm going on in the next room. Even the owls stenciled along the ceiling seem to be ruffling their feathers at the sound of it. "You can stay here, but I'm going to my room. I can't bear to think that Mama's worried."

I've stopped in the doorway just long enough to touch my fingers to the pencil lines marking my brother and sisters' heights when the Crimson Drawing Room opens. Lili's footsteps rush forward, and I hear her gasp, "Madame!"

I hide myself behind the doorway in time to see Lili grab Mama as she totters toward the writing desk between the windows. *"Abdiqué!"* Mama says. Her voice breaks as she clings to the desk.

Abdiqué. Abdicated. The same word from the leaflets the servants brought from town. My papa, who'd been anointed by God and put the imperial crown on his head with his own hands, is no longer tsar?

Mama's whimpers cut in and out of my own thoughts. "My God . . . the poor darling . . . all alone."

Lili wraps her arms around Mama, and together they walk up and down the long row of bookcases. "Courage," Lili tells her. As they pass near the doorway I clap my hands over my own mouth, pulling my knees up to my chin.

Please God, don't let them hear me cry.

What could make Papa sign away the throne? Poor Aleksei will be so shocked! The two thoughts bang together: My twelve-year-old brother, asleep in his bed, is probably His Imperial Majesty Tsar Aleksei II. Will the people and soldiers rioting in the streets come after our darling Sunbeam now? A sob shakes in my chest, and I push my eyes against my knees to force back the tears.

While I struggle with myself, Lili settles Mama at the desk and convinces her to finish writing to Papa. "Think how pleased he'll be, dear Madame," she says, and Mama obeys as if Lili were the empress. As soon as Mama starts to write, Lili rushes past me. She comes back right away with a little glass of something from Dr. Botkin.

Oh, Papa. My poor golden papa. What is he doing without all of us, far away in Pskov without our loyal Dr. Botkin and kind friends like Lili to comfort him?

Just then old Trupp the footman appears in the doorway. The wispy white hairs at the crown of his head tremble as he bows to Mama. "Dinner is served, Madame," he says in a husky voice. He pauses a moment as he turns to go, looking up from the floor for the first time, and I see his eyes are almost as teary as mine.

Mama gets up from the desk, takes a deep breath, and heads toward the dining room with Lili right behind her, as if she thinks Mama might fall back into her arms at any moment. "Where is Maria?" Mama asks.

"I'll fetch her, Madame."

I'm so ashamed of myself for spying on them, then going to pieces and crying like a baby on the floor, that I can't look at Lili. But she crouches right down in front of me and lets me put my head against her shoulder. I sob harder than ever. When it seems like I won't be able to stop, Lili takes my face in her hands and kisses my cheeks. "Darling," she says, "don't cry. You will make Mama so unhappy. Think of her."

It's like magic—like what *Otets* Grigori used to do for Mama and Aleksei. Just those few calm words make me sit back on my heels and snuffle hard to swallow my tears. I hiccup. "She's been so brave all this time." I scrub at my eyes like a sleepy toddler and wipe my cheeks and chin. My eyes and nose have run like the fountains at Peterhof, and I know I look a fright.

"Come along," Lili says, and offers me her hand. "We can spare a little cold water for your face. Mama won't notice in the candlelight."

I let Lili help me up and pat my face with a cool cloth. Then, together we go in to dinner.

17

TATIANA NIKOLAEVNA

March 1917
Tsarskoe Selo

Mama's lips move again and again, but I hear nothing. All I recognize is "Papa." The room is cold and dim; I cannot even hear myself ask Mama to turn on the light so I might make out what she is saying. Mama shakes her head and her lips move once more, in a different way this time. Sometimes I can hear poor Maria crying out in her fever dreams, but only the wail in her voice, not the words themselves. It seems Mama is telling me Papa will be here soon. I turn to Olga, crying in her bed. Even in the dark, I can tell they are not happy tears. I shake my head to show I still do not understand, and pain flares deep inside my ears.

Mama mimes writing, then taking off a hat and setting it down while her lips repeat, "Papa." Dumbly, I mimic her motions, then close my eyes and wave my hands in front of my face, too tired and confused to try anymore. After a moment, I feel a nudge at my arm. Beside me, Olga stretches across the space between our cots, holding out a pencil and a page torn from the back of her diary:

Abdication, Tatya.

Papa has given up the crown.

He'll be home tomorrow, and we are all under house arrest.

God help us! The news clatters against my deaf ears. Mama moves her hands again, telling me to write. What can I say? There is not enough room on the page to answer my questions. So instead of *How*, *Why*, or *What about Aleksei*, I write only, *When?* and hand the paper to Mama.

Six days ago.

Bozhe moi! I feel nothing then, except for the tears painting my cheeks.

When I find energy to think, I wonder how Mama did it. Even though I could not hear, I saw the muscles pulling against Mama's smile as she tried to comfort us, but I never imagined what an awful strain her heart was truly bearing. "Don't let Mama sleep alone," we had begged Lili the night measles finally caught up with Maria.

And Mashka! Our Mashka is so awfully ill. She has tossed and flailed so much Mama finally moved her into a sturdy brass bed in the sickroom instead of her little cot. Lili and Mama both nurse her round the clock. When double pneumonia sets in, I wish to God I were well enough to put on my Red Cross uniform and help.

"Please, Lili," I plead, still too deaf to know whether I am whispering or shouting.

No, darling, it's too dangerous for you, she writes on a scrap of notepaper. *You haven't fully recovered yet yourself.*

Konechno, she is right, but I can hardly lie still for thinking of all Mama endures while I lay idle in my bed.

The best you can do to ease your mama's worries now is to get well. We'll take good care of Maria. We're even sending for another doctor.

Lili's words send a cold flame of fear through my body. Right then I understand how ill Mashka truly is. Between doctors Derevenko and Botkin, we never had need of another before. When my ears begin to clear at last, I start picking words out of Maria's delirium.

"Crowds of people . . . dreadful people . . . they're coming to kill Mama!"

Her voice pins me to my bed all over again. What must she have been through that makes her dream such dreadful things? When the sounds stop I praise Christ, but only until I learn the doctors are giving Maria oxygen to keep her alive.

When Papa arrives at last, I do not try to speak. There is nothing I could say without crying. Word has already come that not only did Papa abdicate on behalf of Aleksei as well as himself, but Uncle Misha has also refused the throne. Russia has no tsar at all.

At the sight of Papa's dear old face my heart swells like the shining dome of St. Isaac's Cathedral. Beside me, Olga's lips move and the words are like water. Tears streak her cheeks, but I will be brave for my papa. He looks so tired and worn, like the men when they arrive in the lazaret. I wrap my arms round his neck and wish I could whisper to him, *Ya tebya ochen lyublyu*, Papa. *I love you very much.*

Though Olga and I are still too weak to leave our beds, Aleksei is up and about again, so Papa sits between our two cots, holding our hands with our brother at his feet like a puppy. I try not to let Papa see how I study him. Strands of silver streak his red beard. I cannot remember whether they were there the last time I saw him. He seems sad, almost ashamed of himself at first, but not worried. How long has it been since Papa has not looked worried? For the first time in ages, he smokes his cigarettes in long drags, stroking our hands instead of puffing away and fidgeting with his beard and mustache. Soon the smoke calms me as well, and I drift off to sleep.

"Your Majesty," Colonel Kobylinsky, the commandant of the new palace guard, says to Mama the first time I meet him, "I am sorry to have to return this to you." He grips his cap with one hand and holds out a small item in the other. The image of the Holy Virgin that Mama, Anya, and my sisters tucked beside *Otets* Grigori's cheek before sealing his coffin. My head buzzes at the sight of it, so obviously out of place. I cross myself.

"Where did you get this?" Mama demands.

The colonel's knuckles smooth a swatch of white hair at his temple. "The grave has been disturbed, Madame. I retrieved this from the soldiers personally. My orders are to move the remains to a safe place to avoid further distress." Seams of anxiety pull the colonel's face, and I understand from the soft way he says "disturbed" and "distress" that he is trying to spare us. With men capable of such beastly sacrilege under his command, I do not know how Colonel Kobylinsky hopes to keep order.

It turns out that only one of the three regiments assigned to guard us, the tsar's own Fourth Rifles, are good, loyal soldiers. Without a dead man to torment, many of the guards from the First and Second Regiments stoop to needling us with petty indignities.

"When the tsar tried to go outside for his usual walk, the sentries from the Second Regiment jeered and pushed at him with their rifle butts," Anya blubbers into her handkerchief. They have taken to calling him *Gospodin Polkovnik*, or Mr. Colonel. "'You can't go there, *Gospodin Polkovnik*. We don't permit you to walk in that direction, *Gospodin Polkovnik*. Stand back when you are commanded, *Gospodin Polkovnik*.'"

My temper rises like mercury. As if Papa should be ashamed of being "only" a colonel!

"You should have seen him, darlings," she says, swiping fiercely at her nose. "He turned around and walked back into the palace without a word to those filthy pigs. Such dignity! Your papa is the finest man in Russia."

Our Anya may be a silly cow sometimes, but this time I cannot argue with her. Wicked and unchristian as it is, after that I cannot stop a blaze of hatred from running up my throat each time I see a member of the Second Regiment.

On top of their cruelty, the First and Second Regiments are undisciplined and unshaven, with shaggy hair and a loose grip on their rifles. One look at them and I know they have no respect for themselves, much less the dead, the tsar, or the army.

"Look." Isa points to a sentry dragging one of our gilt chairs into the courtyard. He sprawls across it with his rifle slung over his knees, too lazy to stand at his post. It is so ridiculous, I can hardly help laughing at the idle brute. They always want to see Aleksei, but Monsieur Gilliard tells them, "The heir is sick and cannot be seen." What do they think they will see? Our brother is a boy like any other, yet already twice the soldier any of them will ever be.

Worst of all, they shoot the tame deer in our park for sport.

Just when we are starting to become resigned to our situation, Colonel Kobylinsky requests that everyone who is well enough gather in the classroom to meet the revolutionary from the head of the Provisional Government, a man called Alexander Kerensky.

He is clean shaven, with hair like the bristle brushes we use to scrub our hands and nails at the lazaret, and walks with one fist tucked into his blue peasant blouse as if he fancies himself the next Napoleon. He cannot stop moving, and touches everything in sight with his free hand. When he stops pacing for an instant, Papa steps forward to greet him. The edges of Papa's mustache lift and fall the tiniest bit, and I know he wears an uncertain smile.

A strange pause muffles the room. Beside me, Mama stiffens. Papa moves as if to shake hands, then reaches up and touches his beard instead. All five of us know the proper way to greet everyone from the Emir of Bokhara to a turnip farmer, but no one seems to know what to do in a room that holds an ex-tsar and a revolutionary.

Kerensky's eyes dart from Papa to us, and I am sure he senses the same uncertainty.

"Kerensky," he says with a smile, stepping briskly forward with his hand out. Papa shakes it. An uncommon flush blotches Mama's face. Not fear this time, but anger, for her breathing is deadly calm.

"My family," Papa says, leading Kerensky to us. "My son, Aleksei Nikolaevich. My daughters, Olga and Tatiana Nikolaevna." The man bobs at each of us and shakes our hands. Olga and Aleksei are too bewildered to reply, and I know better than to stand next to Mama and answer a revolutionary's greeting with a cordial *Ochen priyatno*. No matter how polite Kerensky seems, I am not pleased to meet him.

"My wife," Papa says when they come to the end of the line. "Alexandra Feodorovna."

Kerensky nods more deeply to Mama, but I know this man of the people will not call her "Your Imperial Majesty." She wears her stoniest expression, the one Anastasia calls her Empress Face. There is no missing it, even meeting her for the first time. Kerensky offers his hand, and Mama slowly raises hers as if someone else is moving it for her.

"The Queen of England has asked for news of the ex-tsaritsa," Kerensky says.

Mama's face flares red as the ribbons on the guards' uniforms. Her hand jerks back. "I am fairly well, though my heart troubles me."

Indeed. Mama's heart troubles her in more ways than this man can imagine.

Kerensky turns to Papa. "How is your health?"

"We are well. My youngest daughters are recovering, *slava Bogu.*" I thank God and cross myself as well. It finally seems that our Mashka will be all right.

"*Otlichno.* I am glad to hear it. Let me also assure you of your safety. You have nothing to fear from the Provisional Government."

I do not like this man, not one bit, but I believe him.

"Thank you," Papa says.

Kerensky glances at us again. "Perhaps there is somewhere we may speak without disturbing your family?"

"Of course." Papa gestures toward the door. Kerensky nods at us and goes out, showing his back to all of us. Aleksei's sharp breath at the sight shoots through me as well. For three hundred years, the tsar has always been first to leave a room. In the space of a heartbeat this man has tromped that courtesy under his black boots without a backward glance.

"Horrid man," Mama says as the door shuts behind them. "No manners whatever."

Later, as I sit reading to the Little Pair, an awful commotion down the corridor sends me hurrying to see what is the matter. I have to push my way into Anya's room. Inside, Anya hobbles on her two crutches, howling to the heavens as she gathers up her things. Lili hovers beside Mama. Olga stands alone, stricken and pale. Although he must be in charge of this, Colonel Kobylinsky does not look much better.

"What is it?" I ask.

"Anya and Lili are under arrest," Mama says.

"But so are we!"

"Not house arrest," Olga says. "The Provisional Government is taking them both away."

My whole body wavers as if my joints have filled with syrup. Our arrest and even the soldiers jeering at Papa are bearable, so long as we are all safe together. Now they would separate us from our dearest friends? What harm is our sweet simple Anya? It is like taking one of our dogs to prison, for all her loyalty and affection. She will be terrified, with no one to pet and soothe her.

"Anya is ill," I insist.

"Dr. Botkin has said Anya may be moved," Mama fumes. "I don't see how he could do such a thing, a man with children of his own!"

My heart falls, leaving a space as though a bullet has torn a path through my chest. *"Bozhe moi,"* I gasp, tasting the scent of the doctor's cologne in the air.

"The children! I must say good-bye to Maria and Anastasia," Lili cries, and runs from the room. Anya howls louder.

We have all of us been so brave, and Christ forgive me, I

cannot do it anymore. I throw my arms round Anya and sob on her soft shoulder. "Anya, my poor *dorogaya*! These beasts have no right to take you away. Trust in God, no matter what happens. I will pray for you. We will all be praying for you."

Mama nods dumbly and takes her turn to say good-bye. As the soldiers try to hurry Anya past me, I catch hold of her arm.

"Anya, *dushka*," I sniffle, "may I have something to remember you by?"

"Of course, darling," she says, patting my hand as if she has changed from an overgrown child into a mother in the space of seconds. She looks round the room. A soldier has already taken her bag. There is nothing. With a glance down at our clasped hands, she shakes free and begins to yank at the gold band cinching her plump finger.

"I cannot take your wedding ring!"

"Yes, you can." She tries to smile as she twists the ring one last time. It pops loose over her fat knuckle, and she pushes it into my palm. "It's no more use to me than the husband who went with it."

My fingers are so much thinner than hers, I have to slip it on over my thumb. I kiss her one more time before the men drag her away.

We manage to be more subdued when they force Lili out, but it does us no good. While Lili weeps in Mama's arms, I finger Anya's ring and cry, still praying God will have mercy on Anya for her selflessness.

And now Lili. She has done so much for us, standing by us even when it meant she could not see her own dear

Titi. For her reward she will be separated from everyone she loves. The thought of her going empty-handed stirs me like smelling salts. I hurry to my bedroom for the little leather frame with Mama and Papa's portraits I have kept beside my bed since I was small. "Lili," I pant, "if Kerensky is going to take you away from us, you shall at least have Mama and Papa to console you." She nods as Mama puts a sacred medal round her neck and blesses her.

When she is gone, Mama, Olga, and I crowd against the nursery windows and peer out onto the drive below. Together, we watch the soldiers put Lili and Anya into the same car; they are two pale faces gazing up at us as they're driven away.

18

MARIA NIKOLAEVNA

April-May 1917
Tsarskoe Selo

By the time I'm well enough to sit up in bed, our lives are an awful jumble. Papa's home at last, but I've been so ill I don't even remember him visiting me. My lungs still feel like two bags of wet sand, and under my nightgown a film of sweat pastes my baptismal cross to my skin if I do much more than reach for a glass of water. When I ask for Papa, Tatiana tells me what happened.

"Kerensky came and said Mama and Papa must be separated in the palace until the Provisional Government questions them. The idiots think Mama is a German spy. Papa spends all day in his rooms on one side of the corridor and Mama in the other. They are allowed to speak to each other only at meals, and only in Russian so the guards can understand them. They cannot even sleep together."

"But I want to see Papa," I whimper. I sound like a baby,

but I can't help it. After all those miserable hours Mama and I worried and prayed for him to come home, now there's only a stairway between us? It's too unreal to think about. "But Mama isn't up here now. Why can't he come?" My wail bends into a gasp, and a thick cough scrapes the bottom of my chest.

"Hush, *dushka*." Tatiana holds a towel for me to spit the gooey clumps that break loose from my lungs. "You are still too weak to come eat at the table with all of us, and Papa is not allowed upstairs. The only reason they let Mama stay in this wing at all is because you were so ill. You almost died, *dorogaya*." Her voice wavers, and she wipes at her eyes.

My own eyes well up, and I work to ease the breaths past the hot lump in my throat. I haven't seen Tatiana cry since *Otets* Grigori's funeral. She looks like she wants to climb right into the bed beside me and hug me like a doll. "I'm sorry I scared you," I whisper, but it doesn't seem to reach her ears.

"It is disgusting," she spits, "the way those brutes could even think about separating a mother from her sick children!" She blows her nose so hard the poor handkerchief flutters. "Never mind. We children are allowed to go anywhere we like. I will tell Papa how much you miss him. We talk together almost every afternoon in his study."

"Did Papa tell you why he did it?"

"To save Russia, Mashka," she says, stroking my hair the way I pet Jemmy's ears. "To keep the disorder from spreading into the army. Putting someone else in charge was like giving the city a good dose of medicine. Now the disease will stop. With God's help, Russia will heal."

"Tatya," I ask, trying not to let the dread creeping through my belly swallow me whole, "what's going to happen to us now?"

"No one knows," Tatiana admits. "Mama heard a British cruiser was waiting in Murmansk to take us all to England, but there has been no further word. There is one good thing about you being so ill—Dr. Botkin is sending a letter to Kerensky, requesting that we be transferred to the Crimea on account of your health."

The room stills all around me, the air suddenly too solid to breathe. "We—we have to leave?"

"There is nothing to worry about, *dushka*," Tatiana promises. "We are all together in God's hands."

When Papa's finally allowed to come upstairs again, it's like the sun itself has climbed into my chest. His hug lifts me out of my bed, and all I can say is, "Oh, Papa!" So long as Papa is beside me, I breathe deeper than I have in weeks. Even the tangy smell of Turkish cigarettes on his clothes and in his beard calms me instead of tickling my cough.

As my strength comes inching back, I begin to realize how dreadfully sick I've been. Even in my kimono, my family clusters around to pose for snapshots with me, as if I'm a ripe piece of fruit they all want to savor. The way Mama pets and fusses over me you'd think I was delicate as Aleksei. I lap it up like a kitten at a bowl of cream.

By the time the congestion in my chest has broken up as much as the ice in the canals, we're allowed to go outside together. Each afternoon we gather in the semicircular hall at the back of the palace and wait for an officer of the guard to come with a key.

Whatever starch kept Mama so strong while Papa was gone and we were all sick must have crumpled when she hung up her Red Cross uniform. Now we have our same brittle Mama back. She sits in a wheelchair with her lap full of embroidery, pulling her threads tighter and tighter as the minutes tick by.

"Zdorovo, okhrannik," Papa says to the loitering soldiers outside the door as he wheels Mama into the park. Mama and Tatiana look past the gaping guards like they're hedge-rows, but Papa makes sure to greet them politely every day as we seven file past the curious faces. Some of them snigger at Papa's manners, and that makes Olga sigh and close up like a locket, so Anastasia bugs her eyes out and twists her neck to mimic them. I never know what to do, so I don't do anything except smile and blush the way I always do when young men in uniforms look at me. Only Aleksei, dressed in his field shirt and cap to match their own, seems to reach beyond their stares.

Outside, we spread a carpet on the ground for Mama's wheelchair. Since I'm still recuperating, I'm almost always the one who stays behind to read aloud or chat with her while Papa and the others exercise in the park. Papa can never be still outdoors. He works at clearing the ice from the canals and the snow from the paths. Sometimes people stand at the gates to watch him shovel.

One day Olga comes rushing back with Tatiana and Anastasia trotting behind. Her face looks like it could melt the snow, she's so angry. I run to meet them. "Those swine!" Olga points past our sisters to the fence. "I've never heard such rude things. I don't care if he abdicated, he was still their tsar! Even the women shouted at Papa from behind the gates." Next thing I know she's crying in my arms. "I don't understand," she wails. "What could have made the people turn against him? Children threw sticks at Papa like some beast in a cage."

I'm overwhelmed as if someone dropped a set of squalling triplets in my lap. All I can do is kiss Olga's tearstained face and wonder to myself whether these things would sting so badly if all of us didn't love one another so, so much.

"Maria, you come with us tomorrow," Tatiana says. "Olga will sit with Mama." My belly crinkles at the thought, but one look at Olga and I know I have to. Anastasia snugs in close and squeezes my arm. "It doesn't always happen," she whispers.

Some do sneer and say rude things, or make gestures I don't dare ask Tatiana about. Papa never flinches, but the people's voices feel like shovels digging at my insides, until I see one quiet little girl who looks at Papa with eyes round as Aleksei's teddy bear's. Her mouth falls open as she tugs at her sister's sleeve. "That isn't a soldier, that's the tsar himself! What's he doing with that shovel?"

"You've got eyes, haven't you, Mila?" her sister answers. "He's clearing the snow from the footpaths."

"But he's *working*, and his trousers are all dirty. He can't be the tsar."

I listen as her sister tries to explain words like "abdication," "revolution," and "house arrest," but I can tell Mila's head is swimming just the way mine does when Monsieur Gilliard tries to explain long division. Watching her try to understand gives me the queerest feeling, like I want to hug her and tell her everything will be all right.

After that, I don't mind the people at the fence so much. But we're all glad once the snow seeps into the ground and Papa gets permission to ride his bicycle instead of shoveling.

"*Otlichno*, Papa!" Olga calls. I snap a picture of him posing along the muddy gravel path as if he's astride a thoroughbred instead of an ordinary black bicycle.

As Papa pedals along the path waving to Olga and me, one of the soldiers slings the point of his bayonet into the spokes. Papa flips like a tiddlywink over the handlebars into the frosty mud. Laughter spatters us.

We watch with tears in our throats as Papa brushes off his coat and trousers, then rights the bicycle and walks it away down the path without a word. Papa's pride bites right through the spring chill to warm my fingers and toes.

"He's the best man in the world," I choke, making a trail across the back of my mitten with my sniffles. "But I'm glad Mama and Tatiana didn't see that."

Olga nods. "Or Aleksei. They get too angry, and it's more dangerous to be angry at these men than to be scared of them. Remember that, Mashka."

Thank goodness, the men aren't always so awful. One warm day, a very young soldier sits down on Mama's carpet, right beside her. He begins talking to her as if they're in the middle of an argument.

"Why do you despise the Russian people?" he demands. "Why didn't you ever travel the country like a tsaritsa should? What kind of tsaritsa doesn't even know her own country?"

I shrink down and peek at him through the spokes of her wheelchair. The fellow doesn't look old enough to shave, much less carry a rifle. Mama edges away just a little. Then she takes a breath and continues sewing on the tapestry in her lap. "My first daughter was born within a year after I became empress," she explains. "I had four more children and nursed them all myself. So you see, I couldn't travel."

The guard blinks at his boots and blushes violently, probably at the thought of Mama's bosom. I stifle a giggle. Mama gives me a stern look over the arm of her chair, then softens and motions for me to go with my sisters. "I'll be fine," she says while the soldier clears his throat and struggles to find his voice.

"Please tell me about your children, Alexandra Feodorovna," the young man says as I go to find Anastasia and tell her what I saw.

"Dr. Botkin has had a reply from Kerensky," Papa says quietly. All six sets of our knives and forks stop their sawing. Nobody's had the nerve to mention Dr. Botkin's request to send us to the Crimea in all these weeks. The thought of our white marble palace on the Black Sea is always warm and sweet as a glass of tea, but just now I feel like I've swallowed a pot of glue instead.

Papa cuts another bite, chews, and swallows. "Kerensky has written that a transfer to the Crimea is quite impossible at the moment."

"Impossible" booms so loud in my head, I can hardly snatch at the puff of hope fluttering behind it. *At the moment,* I tell myself. "At the moment" is different from "never."

Papa looks around the table at our glum faces. "Keep your trust in God, my dears." He lays down his fork to rest his hand for a minute over Olga's. *"Tak i byt."* Olga presses her lips together and nods.

Mama clears her throat. "Speaking of letters," she says in a voice that sounds stiff and rehearsed, "you should see the letter I received from Isa Buxhoeveden today. I couldn't help laughing, it was so ridiculous. The return address says 'Ex-Baroness Buxhoeveden, the Ex-Lady-in-Waiting to the Ex-Empress.'" It feels funny, Mama making a joke just now, but the corners of my mouth hop a little anyway as we chew at our meat.

"This might have been a ham once," Papa decides after a long swallow, "but now it is only an ex-ham."

"How about a surprise to cheer us all up?" Papa rubs his hands together and grins. "If we can't tend our orchards in the Crimea, we'll practice right here. We have permission to put in a kitchen garden," he announces.

It's such fun! I've never done work like this in my life. I have my own shovel, and we haul peat and turn the soil behind the palace ourselves until the long rows fill with hundreds of tender little sprouts. Our fingernails turn black and we all smell of earth and sweat every night, but I don't care. We have a garden bigger than the playroom, bigger even than the Mountain Hall, maybe!

At first I have to rest at the end of every row. While I lean on my spade, Papa sometimes takes a moment to wipe his brow or turn up his cuffs enough to let the tail of his dragon tattoo slither out. When he catches a soldier at the edge of the vegetable bed peeking at the blue scales on his wrist, Papa peels his sleeve to the elbow and offers his forearm for the young man to examine. "A souvenir from my tour of Japan. I must have been about your age. It took seven hours to finish."

The soldier's lips turn down, but not in a frown. It's like Ortipo's backward bulldog smile. The young man nods with his eyebrows high. Even though he doesn't say a word, I can tell he wishes he had one just like it.

"Do you have any tattoos, soldier?" I ask him.

"Only a small one," he admits.

"Can we see it?"

His eyes go awfully wide. "*Nyet.* I'm afraid it's not as . . . well, I suppose you could say 'artful' as . . ." He trails off, pointing to Papa's arm.

"Oh, that doesn't matter," I start to say, and then, "*Oh!*" again as I understand. I gulp back a giggle. "In that case, you can show it to Papa when I've turned my back." He looks at me as if I've spoken Portuguese, but when I glance over my shoulder from partway down the row, the soldier is buttoning up the neck of his tunic while Papa chuckles at whatever he's seen. *Men,* I think, and have a little chuckle myself.

In between all the hoeing and watering my sisters and I are happy to smoke and nap in the sun with Jemmy and Ortipo in our laps just like we used to at *Stavka*. On the other side of the palace, the servants have a garden of their own. We help them dig and weed too. Before long the soldiers themselves pitch in to haul water and wheelbarrows.

"Some of them are not so bad after all," Tatiana admits after an officer of the Fourth Regiment helps her carry a heavy load of peat across to the servants' garden. She swats the smudges from her skirt, then sits down next to Anastasia in the shade of the small wooden toolshed and claps for Ortipo to join us.

"They probably think you're a *muzhik*'s wife in those clothes, with your hands all grimy," Anastasia teases. "I bet they wouldn't have helped if they knew it was the same haughty Grand Duchess Tatiana under that dirty wool skirt."

Tatiana ignores her.

"Do you think maybe Papa would let us share our vegetables with the guards this fall?" I ask, looking over the rows of cabbages plumping up like little green bellies against the brown earth. "We couldn't have kept up such a big garden without them."

Olga peers at me strangely, like I'm a silly little bird twittering away.

"What?" I ask her.

She smiles. "Nothing, Mashka. You're sweet, that's all." She looks aside and pats Jemmy, who's wriggled in between her and Anastasia. "Fall is a long way off."

She sounds sad again, and I can't see why. Things are

almost back to normal. Anastasia and Aleksei and I have lessons like always, except that Papa and Mama teach Russian history and religion alongside Monsieur Gilliard to make up for the tutors who aren't allowed through the gates. We're outside all the time now because of our kitchen garden. There are no more ministers interrupting us at all hours of the day, and Papa has no piles of *dokladi* to read. There are the guards, but like Anastasia says, what's another set of guards? My sisters and I have never been able to come and go as we please. In so many ways, we're freer now than we've ever been.

I could live this way forever.

19

OLGA NIKOLAEVNA

June 1917
Tsarskoe Selo

For most of the spring, we live in our own private world, just as we've always done. We sleep in our own beds, walk in our park, and row in our canals. The memory of Anya and Lili's arrest still throbs, but many of our best people have stayed on—people like our loyal Dr. Botkin, Aleksei's Nagorny, Gilliard, and Dr. Derevenko, and our household servants Nyuta, Trupp, Sednev, and Chef Kharitonov. Meanwhile, the world outside our gates goes about its business. For a while, no one even seems to wonder what will come next.

Something has to come next, of course. The Provisional Government can't keep us forever like this, moving about as if we're figures in a dollhouse with its roof peeled off for everyone to see. Before long, the daily crowd behind the fence dwindles. It's as if we've disappointed them somehow.

Perhaps they expected us to be more interesting, or at least more imperial. Even the Second Regiment's rudeness mellows into indifference as we all grow used to one another.

The news, when it comes at all, keeps changing, yet we tend our garden as if we'll be at Tsarskoe Selo forever as if we can't be uprooted as easily as a row of cabbages. It's been months since I've written in my diary, but I've begun gathering blossoms and leaves from the park to press between the blank pages. Even a sprig from the potted lilacs in Mama's boudoir.

Papa still hopes to go to the Crimea and grow flowers, even though Babushka and Auntie Ksenia and Auntie Olga—pregnant with her first baby—are already under house arrest there. If Kerensky won't transfer us, the Crimeans must not be eager for more Romanov refugees. Papa and Mama's cousin Georgie, the king of England, doesn't want us either, which brings as much relief as disappointment—not one of us wants to leave Russia.

Much as we all crave being out in the fresh air, the evenings, with the guards confined to the corridors, have become my favorite time. Tucked into the Crimson Drawing Room upstairs, my sisters and I knit with Mama while Aleksei toys with his lead soldiers and Papa reads to us. Aleksei and the Little Pair like detective stories best, but Mama, Tatiana, and I all prefer the Bible, especially Psalms.

Alone together, we can be playful and chuckle at the ridiculous things the soldiers do. Papa can be as mischievous as Shvybzik when the mood strikes him. "Give the

Provisional Government thy judgments, O God," Papa reads solemnly from Psalm 72, "and thy righteousness unto the Provisional Government's son."

Tatiana interrupts first. "Papa, what are you reading? It makes no sense."

Glancing up with a twinkle in his eye, Papa says, "'King' has gone so out of fashion these days, I thought I should put in 'Provisional Government' instead."

Even Mama can't pretend that isn't funny, and we seven spend the rest of the night searching for the most ridiculous passages to revolutionize.

The next night it's so stuffy, the joke already feels stale when Shvybs asks Papa to read from 1 Provisional Governments. Too dull-edged to huff, she drifts like a mote of dust over to the windowsill with her sewing. Papa's voice has just barely begun to ease us when old Trupp bursts into the Crimson Drawing Room, trembling all over.

"Your Majesty, the officer on duty requests an immediate interview," he says. The news sends a spurt of cold from my ankles to my toes.

Papa puts down the Bible. "Show him in at once."

"What could it be, Nicky?" Mama asks, straightening up and pulling her feet from his lap.

Papa fingers his beard. "Perhaps a disturbance in Petrograd. The Bolsheviks have been expected to demonstrate."

"Like a parade?" Aleksei asks. Papa doesn't say so, but I know from the papers that the Bolsheviks will probably be armed when they march on Petrograd.

"A sentry outside saw red and green signal lights coming

from this room," the officer says when he strides in with two soldiers from the First Regiment. "What is going on here?"

My sisters make wondering sounds instead of words. Even Papa doesn't know what to say. "Shut the curtains," the officer commands. Nagorny silently moves himself between the men and Aleksei, though our brother peers around his *dyadka* like a fox behind a tree trunk. Anastasia, sitting in the windowsill with her needlework, ducks her head and clutches her embroidery as one of the soldiers snatches the drapes shut above her. He stares at her for a moment while the other men search the room. His look stills the air between them.

"Sir?" the man calls. Anastasia refuses to cower, but I constrict with apprehension as the officer marches to the window.

"Yes, what is it?"

"It's this one here, sir. See those red and green lamps? She's bending down to get her threads and things, and it makes the lights look like signals."

"Very well." The officer motions for the other soldiers to follow him out. At the door, he turns to Papa and Mama. "Thank you for your cooperation. My apologies for the disturbance."

For a moment, we don't know what to do. Then everyone speaks at once and we all laugh. It feels like china breaking.

Not long after that, Papa calls me into his study and closes the door. Behind his desk, the larger-than-life portrait of my *dedushka*, Tsar Alexander III, looms over the room. Looking up at him, it's hard to imagine a revolution ever happening. Following my gaze, Papa sits down beneath the painting and smokes nearly half his cigarette before speaking. His voice is soft as the hazy air.

"I've seen how frightened you are of the soldiers, Olga. I don't know what to make of them myself sometimes," he confesses. He sighs and reaches deep into a drawer. "Mr. Kerensky and Colonel Kobylinksy are honest men, but I do not like to see my children frightened." Down in his lap, his hands turn something over and over. "You are the only one of your sisters I would trust with this, because I know you will do everything under God to avoid using it."

With that, he lays a tiny pearl-handled pistol on the green felt blotter between us.

A queer thrill creeps through me—a mixture of relief and dread—at the sight of that gun. It looks more like a toy or a piece of jewelry than a weapon.

"Keep it hidden," Papa says, "and do not even tell your sisters. It will go badly for all of us if the guards find out about this, especially the men of the Second Regiment. Do you understand?"

I touch the gun before answering. "*Konechno*, Papa." It's cool and smooth as a paperweight in my palm.

"It should fit inside your boot," Papa prompts.

I thread the pistol carefully down the inside of my left boot, snugging it against my ankle. When I stand, the soft wrinkles of leather hide the little bulge. "*Spasibo*, Papa."

"I pray you will never need it, Olenka. But it is worth the

risk if it takes some of the worry from your face." He strokes
my cheek and blesses my forehead. "God's will be done."

For days, any time a soldier so much as glances my way, guilt
slices at me like a bayonet. But the more time passes without
anyone noticing, that gun becomes an anchor. Like Papa, I
pray I'll never need to use it, thanking the Lord nonetheless
for the small measure of assurance it gives me.

In the middle of it all, our hair begins falling out. Great
clumps stick to our brushes and pillows, leaving bare patches
on our scalps. Dr. Botkin says it might have been our fevers,
or perhaps the antibiotics they gave us. When Maria's is
nearly half gone, Mama decides there's nothing to do but
shave our heads. *Bozhe moi!* Poor Tatiana already had her hair
cropped once from typhoid four years ago, and Anastasia is
just turning sixteen this month—she's barely begun wearing
her long hair up.

"It isn't fair," she mumbles, her back to us and her chin
muffled in her elbow.

"It will not be so bad," Tatiana says, "you wait and see. It
grows back. You can put ribbons in it like I did for our 1914
portraits. And we have a few pictures of your hair up from
the last few weeks."

"You're a fine one to talk," Anastasia shoots back. "Who
cares about ribbons? You were ashamed as anything after
you had typhoid, and you weren't even *bald*. You complained
about that itchy bird's nest of a wig all through the tercente-
nary celebrations. It looked like a wreath in the formal portraits. And now I'll be naked as an egg without my fringe,"

she says, tugging a lock of it down over her eyebrows. Tatiana bites her lip.

I would smack Anastasia for that if she wasn't so upset already. She isn't the only one who has to face the barber. I can't imagine how Tatiana feels about losing her hair for the second time. She was only fifteen then, and had to wait an extra two years for her hair to grow long enough to put up. Maria sits watching, weaving the last tendrils of her own curls through her fingers. I don't even want to think about mine. I've always loved to watch in the mirror as Nyuta brushes my hair and pins it in place for me.

"At least your head isn't as big as mine, Shvybs," I offer. "Remember what Great-Grandmama wrote when I was born?" I reach out to smooth the red-gold cascade running down Anastasia's back. It's just the same color as Mama's. She jerks the length of it over her shoulder and snorts.

"'A splendid baby, except for her immense head,'" Anastasia quotes in her Queen Victoria voice as she twists her hair around her fist like a skein of yarn. A smudge of red inches up the back of her neck.

"That's right. I'll look like a melon on a stick."

"I don't care."

Tatiana tries one more time. "Mama will make sure we have the best tonics and shampoos. Do you remember when you poured Miss Eagar's English hair tonic all over that dreadful old bald doll of yours?"

"If I wanted to look like ratty old Vera, I'd tell the barber to chop off an arm and an eye while he's at it."

I shrug at Tatiana. There's no talking to Anastasia when

she's in one of her ugly moods. Just then Aleksei appears in the doorway and peers at Anastasia.

"What's wrong?" he asks.

Tatiana looks queerly at him for a moment while I explain; then she brightens and crouches down beside our cross little sister.

"*Dushka*," she says to Anastasia, "do you remember when Aleksei left for the front and you said you would cut your hair and wear khaki in an instant if it meant you could go with him?"

"So what?" Anastasia grumbles.

Aleksei cocks his head. "You would have cut your hair off to come with me, Nastya?" he asks.

Anastasia looks up over her folded arms. "*Konechno*. Short enough to fit under a soldier's cap, at least."

He looks at all of us, each moping in our own way. "You all have to get your hair cut?"

Suddenly I understand. Clever Governess! I wink at Tatiana. "Shaved," I tell Aleksei. "It's coming out at the scalp."

Aleksei's grins rises like the sun. "Then I'm getting mine shaved too!"

Mashka giggles. Anastasia's eyebrows form two peaks. "Mama will be *furious*," she says, as if the word tastes like chocolate.

Aleksei shrugs. "I don't care."

"You're a pair of *shvybziki*," I tell them. Already their two heads are bent together, conspiring. I thread my arm around Tatiana's waist as Maria abandons her armchair and joins the plot. "And you are a wonder," I whisper to Tatiana.

In spite of my hat and the scarf wrapped around my naked scalp, I'm sure everyone is looking at me when we go outside. Indoors, I'm happy to joke and pose for Monsieur Gilliard's camera with my sisters and Aleksei, but out here I can't look anyone in the eye—not even my own reflection in the canal.

A few *sazhens* downstream, two guards from the Second Regiment point and whisper loudly together. My head feels round and red as a peeled beet. I know it only draws attention, but I can't help reaching to make sure the scarf is still tucked across the tips of my ears.

"They are armed," I hear one man say, and my shame vanishes. The pistol squeezes like a snake against my ankle, seizing up everything except my heart, which rattles my whole body.

"You there!" they shout. Behind me, Aleksei scrambles across the bridge from the Children's Island to Mama's carpet on the grass. I want to run too, but the weight of that small gun rivets my foot to the ground.

Next thing I know, the soldiers stride past me without a glance. They plant their toes on the fringe of Mama's carpet and bark at Aleksei, "Hand over the weapon." Bewilderment melts into relief. It's only my brother's miniature rifle they've seen. He still wears his army khakis and medal of St. George every day, and loves to prowl through the shrubbery like a private at the front lines. Aleksei's eyes go big as silver rubles. He clutches the little rifle and shakes his head.

Quick as a breath of wind, Monsieur Gilliard appears.

"Fellows," he says in a voice smooth and pleasant as ice cream, "it's only a toy."

"We will not have the prisoners carrying weapons."

"Be reasonable," Gilliard insists. "That little gun couldn't kill a rabbit. He doesn't even have cartridges anymore."

"Hand it over," the dark-haired one demands. Aleksei looks helplessly between Mama and Gilliard. Mama closes her eyes and nods. The soldier snatches the rifle from my brother's hands and swaggers off without a glance at the tears spilling over Aleksei's cheeks. In an instant my fear snaps apart and I'm angry enough to imagine my finger on the trigger. Those are the first tears I've seen from our brother—our brother who should have been the next tsar!—in the whole time since Papa abdicated.

Aleksei mourns that little gun for days, looking pale and stricken as if they'd taken two pints of his blood away with it. Putting aside my own self-pity, I do my best to comfort him with stories, card games, and endless parades of lead soldiers. At last, one morning I hear him marching back and forth across the playroom just the way he used to. I freeze in the doorway when I see him, strutting between lines of toy soldiers with his rifle slung over his shoulder.

"Aleksei!" I cry, sick with dread at the thought of what the Second Regiment will do if they catch him. "How did you get that gun?"

He grins like the Cheshire cat and waves me in. "Shhhh!" he says, leaping over the lead battalions to shut the door before handing me the gun. I turn it over and over, making sure it is indeed the same rifle. "Colonel Kobylinsky smuggled it back, one piece at a time," my brother explains. "He said I could keep it as long as I only played with it in my rooms." I shake my head in wonderment. The whirl of kindness and cruelty makes me dizzy.

20

ANASTASIA NIKOLAEVNA

July 1917
Tsarskoe Selo

Out in the kitchen garden, Monsieur Gilliard comes upon the four of us all lined up like paper dolls and raises his camera. With a sweep of her hand, Olga pulls her hat off her bald head and shoots him a more daring grin than even I can manage. Tatiana, Maria, and I follow suit like dominoes.

"Your Highnesses," Gilliard sputters. "Surely I cannot. What will your parents say?"

"Konechno," Olga insists. "Of course you can. What our parents will say is precisely the point."

After that we abandon our hats and scarves and quit skittering about like plucked ducks. I wish we could see that Olga more often. She hasn't been the same since Colonel Kobylinsky started laying hints about the Provisional Government sending us away.

"'Transferred.' So that's what the Provisional Government calls it when they force a family out of its home on four days' notice," Olga says glumly. The colonel clears his throat and shifts in his boots.

"Where are we going?" Mama demands.

"The Crimea?" Maria asks, practically climbing up Kobylinsky's arm. "I know I could bear leaving home if it meant we could go to the Crimea."

"I have not been told," the colonel admits, looking at Papa instead of Mama. "My orders are to request you to prepare for a journey of three to four days."

"Will this be a permanent transfer?" Papa asks. It takes me a second to hear what Papa's asking with his big formal words: Are we ever coming back? I look hard at Kobylinsky, the way Tatiana does, as if the third eyelash on your right eye will tell her everything she wants to know, no matter what comes out of your mouth.

"I'm sorry, Your Majesty, I don't have that information either. Kerensky is somewhat optimistic—perhaps by November—but he makes no promises. A train has been ordered for midnight on the first of August." My arms and legs turn heavy as raw sausages. Four more days and we'll be gone.

"How absurd," Tatiana says. "How do they expect us to pack in that amount of time without knowing the destination or duration?"

"Thank you, Colonel," Papa says. "We will do our best to prepare."

Tatiana huffs and stalls like a train without tracks, for an hour or so, anyhow. Then she goes upstairs and starts packing in a great flurry, for herself and everyone else, whether we need help or not. "Remember your hairpins and ribbons," she insists, even though my hairpins will probably rust before I have enough hair to use them again.

"Think of the Crimea," Mashka gushes. "Babushka and Auntie Ksenia, and all the cousins! I wouldn't care if we're still under arrest. And Auntie Olga—her baby must be due any minute! We could even be there in time for her delivery. I wonder if she'll make us godmothers?" She sighs and leans her dreamy head against her fist. "Can you imagine smelling the sea and the cedars again? And the violets and peach blossoms in the spring?"

Of course I can. "In St. Petersburg we work," Olga likes to say, "but at Livadia, we live." My nose tingles and my chest feels like it's folding up, I want to go so badly, but I'm afraid to hope as brightly as my sister. *I'll pretend,* I tell myself. Pretending is safer than believing.

Even if we don't know where we're going, there's heaps of stuff to pack, especially if we might not be allowed back. Downstairs, Kharitonov and Sednev jam sawdust into crates filled with portraits, lamps, clocks, vases, and statues. Trupp carefully bundles up the gramophone and its discs, the cinema projector, magic lantern, and all the films and pictures that go with them. Nyuta folds tablecloths and bed curtains while others roll up rugs and lug furniture. Even our foot-wiping machine is coming with us. Maids and valets swarm all over the place, carrying things back and forth like ants, but the idea of packing my things leaves me thick and sluggish as a tube of oil paint.

Two days later Colonel Kobylinsky comes back with one hint: "Kerensky advises that you pack warm clothing."

"There goes the Crimea," I tell Mashka.

"What about England?"

"Silly. It's heaps colder in Petrograd than it is in England."

"Then, Siberia?"

"I don't know where else—unless they're going to ship us to Iceland." I didn't think we could sink any lower, but after that all of us mope around as if we're dragging our hearts on strings behind us. That doesn't stop Tatiana from remembering to have our skis, sledges, and skates boxed up, though. Typical.

Once we know we aren't going anywhere familiar, we stop loading up big things and start paying attention to the smaller bits of our lives. Mama leaves most of her Fabergé Easter eggs in their cabinet in the Maple Room but spends hours wrapping the hundreds of icons that hang over her bed, and all the trinkets Aleksei and my sisters and I have given her for Christmas since we were little. Papa's chin-up bar goes into a crate, and he fills another up himself with his diaries, all arranged by year.

Upstairs, I pile up my paints and photo albums and diaries until my lip starts trembling for no good reason. Leaving Mashka behind, I stick my dribbly nose into the Big Pair's room to spy. Tatiana already has a box crammed with fat books labeled RELIGION AND HISTORY in her sideways writing, and her best dresses wrapped in tissue. Olga sits on the carpet in front of her shelves with stacks of books scattered around her, struggling to pick between her old favorites. She's all bent over, like a puppet without a hand inside it.

"*Dushka*, perhaps you will want a few new things to read?" Tatiana suggests.

Olga runs her fingers over an inscription. "We can get new books anywhere. I've had some of these since I was a little girl. Listen: 'For darling Olga, from Aunty Irene, 1903,'" she reads. "It doesn't matter how many times I've read *The Princess and the Goblin*. I can't replace that signature."

Either way they'll both be bored stupid. But with that, I dash to my room and dig my poor old one-armed Vera from the back of our baby cupboard and bury the doll into the middle of one of my trunks.

All day long, Nagorny passes by with great armloads of things from Aleksei's rooms: balalaikas, board games, puzzles, regiments of lead soldiers, a pair of toy boats. The next day our brother turns thirteen.

To give thanks for his birthday, Mama has the icon brought from the Church of Our Lady of Znamenie for Liturgy. The priests come in a procession from Tsarskoe Selo, through the palace, and we follow them into chapel to pray. Everything's so solemn, I can't help remembering the day Russia declared war on Germany. Then the whole country had looked toward Papa. Now it seems like Russia is looking away from us. Prayers are chanted for our safe journey, but they feel like the half-finished sentences in my English exercise books. Our safe journey *where*?

By the time the service is over, everyone, right down to the servants and commandant, is teary-eyed. Some soldiers even step forward to kiss the holy icon as the procession moves past them. We seven follow the icon as far as we're allowed. It isn't the proper hour for us prisoners to be outdoors, but Colonel Kobylinsky looks the other way when we step out on Mama's balcony for the first time in months. The procession winds down the path and disappears into the park.

"I wonder if the icon will ever come back to this place," Tatiana whispers as she crosses herself.

I wonder if we *will ever come back,* I think, and cross myself, too.

In the morning our bedroom screens and cots are folded up, our mattresses, cushions, and satin comforters packed away. Our walls go bald in patches where we take down the last of our favorite picture frames and icons. When I think we're finally done, it's Tatiana who stops for a moment on our way downstairs to reach into a curio cabinet and slip a tiny Fabergé French bulldog figurine into her pocket.

Outside, we walk slowly through the gravel paths of the park and in and out of the rows of our kitchen garden. While Aleksei has one last swim in the pond, Maria and I row to the Children's Island and say good-bye to the playhouse, then wander through the little cemetery where our pets are buried under engraved granite pyramids.

"Should we take a picture?" Maria asks.

I bend over her camera. "Don't spend your last photo on

a bunch of stones. I'll find you something better."

By the time we row back, Aleksei's in his uniform again but still damp, wading along a little plank with his trousers rolled up. Olga lifts her skirt to tiptoe out and linger beside him, gazing forlornly over the pond and park.

"Hey, you two," I call from the shore, lifting up Maria's camera. "Can you still smile?" They both turn around. "We have one picture left on this roll, and I don't want long faces on it." Olga tries her best not to look sad, and Aleksei stands there smirking with one toe dipped into the water while Maria focuses the photo. "He's up to something," I mutter, but we both still gasp when he leaps forward the instant after Maria clicks the shutter button, giving Olga a shove right into the water! She keels backward, her arms rotating like propellors, then rises up dripping and spluttering, drenched through. For a minute she looks like she wants to thrash Aleksei something fierce.

"This is the only summer dress I have that isn't packed up, you know!" she shouts. Maria and I muffle our giggles into each other's shoulders as the water flies off Olga's wagging finger.

Aleksei grins. "I know. But at least you won't have to wait for your hair to dry."

That takes the steam out of her! She reaches up to her gleaming bare scalp and laughs. Then Olga scoops up her hat and bails water onto Aleksei until he dances out of her way. "You're getting my medal wet!"

"Serves you right if it rusts to your shoulder," I tell him. "You're lucky Mama and Tatiana didn't see any of that."

But *now* that I think about it, after being herded into the semicircular hall in the wee hours of the morning, waiting for a train that won't come, to be taken who-knows-where, I wish Tatiana had been there, even if she would've scolded. That was probably the last bit of fun we'll ever have here at home.

I shift against Maria and yawn. "What time is it?"

"Nearly three o'clock," Tatiana answers.

Maria screws her eyes shut, nuzzling her shaved head against my shoulder. Waiting is horrible. I've spent the last four days wishing we didn't have to go, and now? All I want is for the train to come.

TATIANA NIKOLAEVNA

August 1917
Tsarskoe Selo

$\mathcal{M}$otorcar horns blare, their honks sharp as angry geese, and we all startle. My sisters and I rub our eyes and look at our watches. Twenty minutes past five. Time to go. I think of the old Russian custom that says we should sit down for a moment before going on a journey. Even though we have been sitting here all night long, it feels wrong to jump up and leave.

Our legs and feet tingling with sleep, we fumble with our valises of trifles, trying to look at nothing and everything at once. Anastasia juggles Jemmy in her arms; her little legs are too short to climb stairs, much less clamber into a motorcar. Eyeing the door, Joy and Ortipo both whine softly, but not one of us moves until Papa offers Mama his arm.

"Come along, Sunny."

Together they walk past the officers. Papa shakes hands

with every man willing. Mama's face betrays nothing, except for a final flicker of her eyes round the room. With Joy straining at his leash for one last chance at the grass of Tsarskoe Selo, Aleksei follows.

The four of us are left with our noses beginning to run, no matter how stoutly we try not to cry. One of us must take the first step, and I know it will have to be me. My whole body begs me to scoop up Ortipo and go running after Mama, Papa, and Aleksei, yet I cannot make myself move. Beside me, Mashka's eyes have gone brimful enough to drown the last of my composure, so I put my hand gently on her back and ease her forward. Anastasia comes along as if they are stitched together, but they stall after an *arshin* or two. I cannot drag them out any more than I can drag myself. My face threatens to fall; I glance desperately at Olga. She reads my expression as easily as a psalm, and with a nod, we understand each other. Olga and I will wrap ourselves round the Little Pair like a bandage and cushion their leaving. God give us strength!

With a parting caress of the door frame, Olga squares her shoulders and takes the first step out the door. Maria and Anastasia follow like ducklings, God bless them. I cross myself, murmur a quick prayer for our safe journey, and leave our home behind me to join my family on the gravel path.

Outside, we pile into the idling motorcars. Mama, Papa, Aleksei, and Olga in the first; Maria, Anastasia, and I in the second with Nyuta, Sednev, and his nephew Leonka. Behind us, Monsieur Gilliard and Dr. Botkin climb into yet another with more members of the suite and their families. I wish

I could be in the same motor with Mama, but I think the Little Pair is glad to have me beside them. For once, they split in two and sit on either side of me, the three of us meshing together as the line of motorcars pulls away. Maria cries unashamedly on my shoulder while I whisper and pet her cheek, but Anastasia grips my other hand and stares fiercely back at our Alexander Palace with her wet blue eyes until it is no more than a lemon-colored speck against the sunrise.

As we pass through the imperial gate, an armed escort of dragoons falls into place beside our convoy. Through the sleeping streets of Tsarskoe Selo, the horses' hooves clatter over the pavement. Even more guards with loops of bullets ringing their shoulders circle the railway station.

At the platform a strange black train huffs impatiently while we stand bewildered for a moment. I suppose it was stupid to presume we might be allowed to use our familiar imperial train, but this one seems so indifferent. There are not even any steps leading up into the carriages. Mama has to be hoisted aboard by some of the men. Even though they try to be gentle and proper, they have not had the practice of our loyal Cossacks, and it wrings my chest like an inside-out stocking to watch her being jostled by clumsy strangers.

Behind us, another train fills with soldiers. Over three hundred men and officers from three different regiments are coming to guard us. "They must think we are made of dynamite to send so many men," I whisper to Olga.

"We are, Tatya. Think of how the people lined up behind our gates to gawk and shout at Papa after the abdication. You've seen the pictures in the papers of the crowds

demonstrating in Petrograd. It isn't safe here anymore."
It begins to dawn on me why Kerensky paced and fretted
waiting for the train all night long. Christ be with us. I
must pay more attention from now on.

A soldier offers his hands for me to use as a step, and I
swing myself awkwardly up into the carriage. Olga follows,
steady at first; then she lurches as her left ankle gives way,
and sways as if she is about to faint. "*Dushka!* Are you all
right?"

"I'm fine." Such a thin smile cannot convince me, but
suddenly she feels sturdy again. "I only lost my balance for a
moment," she says, and leans on my elbow to adjust the cuff
of her left boot.

Once everything and everyone is aboard, the trains plod
slowly east with the blinds tightly drawn by order of the
Provisional Government. Olga and I close our eyes and grip
each other's hands until we must be outside the borders of
the city. Neither of us moves or says a word, but even without
looking I know from the way she kneads her fingers against
mine that Olga is praying too.

By the time we are well into the countryside, I have to admit
that we are comfortable enough after all, in spite of having
to share a single carriage. We read and embroider to help
pass the time or to keep from wondering where we are going.
All we know is that the trains are pointed east, bearing placards that read, JAPANESE RED CROSS MISSION. How I wish we
were truly on a Red Cross mission! The thought of working
in a hospital again is almost too much to hope for; anyway,

the signs are only to keep the trains from drawing attention.

We always used to travel with two trains, both of them painted dark blue and emblazoned with double-headed imperial eagles between each window. One was a decoy, and I always felt sorry for the people who lined the railroad tracks in hopes of catching a glimpse of us, only to greet the empty carriages instead. Now it is just the opposite. We are our own decoy with our placards and Japanese flags. At every station, the blinds have to be drawn and no one is allowed to look out. Nevertheless, at one stop, Anastasia peeks out of the curtains.

"Get away from there," I tell her.

"Don't be so bossy. The soldiers don't care, so why should you? Besides, there's no station. I can just see a tiny house."

A little voice calls from outside, "Uncle, please give me a newspaper if you have one." I set down the Bible and leave Mama's side. Below the window, a boy looks earnestly up at Anastasia.

"I am not an uncle but an auntie, and I don't have a newspaper," Anastasia says, solemn as a nun. Outside on the platform, the soldiers chuckle. "What are they laughing at?" she demands. "And why did that boy call me 'uncle'?"

Pretending to think, I scratch my own prickly scalp.

Anastasia slaps her forehead. "I forgot. I look like a hedgehog without my hat on, don't I?" Even Mama and Papa laugh at that.

After three days we reach Tyumen, a Siberian town east of the Ural Mountains, and at midnight board a steamer called

Rus to begin twisting our way east again, first up the Tura River, then the Tobol.

Two days upstream, the steamer gets stuck in a sandbar. Mama has been in her cabin all day with her heart drops and rose-leaf cushion, so I get permission from Colonel Kobylinsky for Aleksei and me to go out along the river-bank and gather flowers for her. By the time he calls us back on board, Mama has appeared on deck. With a tender smile she cradles our bouquet in one arm and encircles Aleksei's shoulders with the other.

"Do you know where we are, darlings?" For the first time in months, she looks serene. Her hand rests gently at the back of Aleksei's neck, and her eyes shine as though she has just taken Holy Communion. I look out across the river. In the distance, slanted barn roofs jut toward the spire of a church. "This is Pokrovskoe," Mama says. "Father Grigori's home. He said we would see it ourselves one day."

Pokrovskoe. A shiver swoops out from my spine and along my ribs. "Praise be to God," I whisper as I cross myself. Olga silently takes one of the wildflowers from Mama's bou-quet to press into the pages of her diary. Even in death, *Otets* Grigori brings us comfort. If we had gone to the Crimea, we might never have seen it.

Two days more and we reach the city of Tobolsk, where the steamer finally anchors. From the dock, the city's white-walled kremlin seems to kneel on the embankment above the river. Bells ring out over the riverbanks as Colonel Kobylinsky directs the men to begin unloading our luggage.

"Are the bells ringing for us?" Anastasia asks.

"Of course not. It is the Feast of the Divine Transfiguration," I say, even though the gathering townspeople are already beginning to gawk at us, just as they did at home. Why is everyone suddenly so dumbfounded at the sight of us? Do they think we should be wearing the imperial regalia everywhere we go? If they only knew how many loose gemstones Mama has secretly stowed into our luggage, their jaws would drop even further.

While Colonel Kobylinsky goes ahead to see about our lodgings, I try to keep Mama from becoming flustered with all the staring; I do not think the splotches on her cheeks are from the heat. Before I can think what to do for her, Papa begins to talk soothingly about the town. "I visited Tobolsk twenty-six years ago, on my way home from my tour of the Far East. The stone kremlin is three hundred years old," he tells us, "but the first wooden walls were built in the fifteen hundreds. There are ancient kurgan tombs from the tenth century before Christ. It is a beautiful old city, Alix," he says, stroking Mama's hand.

"I would like to see the relic of St. John of Tobolsk," Mama concedes. I think she would kiss Papa if no one were watching.

"Do you think we'll be allowed to visit the churches, Papa?" Olga asks.

I look over the kremlin wall at the sky blue cathedral domes with their gold crosses flashing in the sun, and my heart dares to thrill.

"I certainly hope so," Papa answers. A tiny smile cracks

Olga's face, just enough for me to see the gap between her front teeth.

"I wonder if there is a hospital here?" Being able to work as a nurse again would be such a blessing.

"Mashka wants to know if there's a candy shop," Anastasia declares, but before Papa can answer either of us the colonel comes back, looking disgusted.

"My apologies, Your Majesties, but the governor's house is not prepared."

Not prepared? We seven gape at one another like the townspeople. We have traveled for days on end over thousands of miles, and the house where we are to stay is not ready for us?

"It's dingy and unpleasant inside, Your Majesty. The paint and wallpaper are peeling, and there is virtually no furniture."

The younger ones burst out laughing. Mama and I speak at the same time. "No furniture!"

"Is this what we should expect from the new government— disrespect and disorder? It's an embarrassment."

Colonel Kobylinsky turns pink as a filet of salmon and mops his brow as he apologizes to Mama once again. "Poor man," Olga murmurs.

God help him. Mama is rarely easy to please, but the colonel is stranded between us and the Provisional Government, and three regiments of soldiers, too. How can he possibly satisfy everyone?

"When I was a young man," Papa says, "I stayed in that very house on my return trip. We will be comfortable here," he assures us. But for another full week, we must live on board the *Rus* while the house is cleaned, decorated, and furnished.

Our aimless cruise drifts dully by: Mama spends most of the long, hot days in her cabin. Maria catches a summer cold. Joy kills a poisonous snake.

"It feels like we are nowhere at all, only drifting along the border between two places," I tell Olga and Anastasia up on deck one afternoon.

"Like the River Styx," Olga says.

"Huh?" Anastasia grunts.

"The ancient Greeks believed the River Styx was the boundary between earth and the underworld," Olga explains. "When someone died, a coin was placed in his mouth to pay the ferryman Charon to guide his soul across the river."

My stomach always feels as if it has been lined with lead when Olga talks this way. I can never be sure when she is putting more meaning behind her words than the story they tell. With nothing to say myself, I watch Anastasia and Olga look across to the Siberian bank of the Tobol. Their thoughts are murky as the river to me.

"Open your mouth," Anastasia says suddenly. "You too, Tatya." She peers at us like our dentist Kotstrisky, then smirks. "That explains it—not a kopek in there. It's all your fault, both of you."

"Oh, Shvybs!" One side of Olga's mouth curves up like a festoon of lace, and she swats at Anastasia. Watching my sisters like this swings my heart between melancholy and gratitude.

"I'm going to tease Mashka and Aleksei, too," Anastasia says, and off she dashes to the cabins.

With the deck to ourselves, I take my turn to gaze over the rail. "Remember how different it was four years ago?"

Olga nods and covers my hand with hers. I do not even have to explain. What a year 1913 was. As part of the twelve-month celebration of three centuries of our family's rule, we seven spent a week cruising down the Volga on board the steamship *Mezhen*. Our carpets, furniture, and paintings from home furnished the vessel. When we cast off, bell towers rang out and peasants sang "God Save the Tsar" and "Down the Mother Volga" in the torchlight. Their cheers rocked the entire boat. All along the riverbanks that whole week long, crowds of them waded over their waists in the water to get near Papa. Some even fell to their knees and kissed his shadow as we steamed by. *Slava Bogu*, no one could tell from the shore that Aleksei's leg was still too bent from his hemorrhage at Spala to walk. When we reached Kostroma, a public holiday had been declared. Cannons boomed and the bells in the town's kremlin pealed overhead. The entire city gleamed with paint and polish.

"It was like arriving in heaven itself," Olga says, as if she has been watching the scenes inside my mind this whole time.

I close my eyes to return to my memories, but the images blur and dissolve into the tears trapped under my eyelids.

22

OLGA NIKOLAEVNA

August–September 1917
Tobolsk

For the length of the walk from the dock to the governor's house, my arms and legs tingle as if someone has poured a bottle of fermented mint *kvass* through my veins. Even the soldiers marching alongside us can't stop the little bubbles of cheer from rising up in me at being able to stride ahead without a boundary in sight. I jostle along the wooden sidewalks with the Little Pair, remembering the rare thrill we used to feel at being part of the bustle of a town on our holidays in Sweden or Germany, and feeling sorry for Tatiana, who follows by motor with Mama.

The signpost on our street, freshly repainted FREEDOM STREET, makes my heart stumble for a moment, but watching the people along the sidewalks take off their hats and cross themselves as we pass smoothes my nerves.

Far too soon, the governor's house rises up in front of us

like a block of snow bounded by a sharp picket fence.

"What a snug, sturdy-looking place! Is this a big house, Papa?" Maria wants to know.

I'm glad Maria asked instead of me. The soldiers can snort all they like at our ignorance, but except for Anya's dear cottage in Tsarskoe Selo, what do my sisters and I know about houses?

"It is. In fact, it's a mansion," Papa corrects her.

It's likely the largest house in Tobolsk, and just looking at it makes me feel cramped. Extravagance never seemed like part of my life before, but now shame curls my toes until the gun in my boot pinches against my ankle.

"If we live here now, where will the governor stay?" Sweetheart Mashka, always thinking of everyone but herself.

"Where will the servants stay?" Anastasia interrupts. "This place could fit inside the courtyard of our palace back home."

My cheeks flare. What must the soldiers think, listening to us balk? "Hush, you two! We haven't even seen the inside."

Papa is right—the house is comfortable enough. On the ground floor, every space but the dining room gets divided up for bedrooms and filled with our best servants as neatly as the compartments in Mama's traveling jewelry chest. Dr. Botkin's family and the rest of our people will have to board across the street in the Kornilov house, or take rooms in town.

Right away, Papa hangs his chin-up bar upstairs in the front corner study while we convert the ballroom next door into a chapel with one of Mama's handmade bedcovers on the altar.

"What about services?" Mama wants to know. "We cannot celebrate the full *Obednya* service without a consecrated altar. We must go to church in town for *Obednyu.*"

Colonel Kobylinsky dodges the question. "For now I will arrange for nuns and a priest to celebrate *Obednitsa*." Only the abbreviated service without Communion? My spirits droop. "And of course there will be no objections to daily prayer services without clergy."

The ballroom opens into Mama's sitting room, which we sisters arrange before Mama sets foot in it. Tatiana directs while the Little Pair and I put Mama's own crocheted coverlet on the sofa, and her favorite portraits of Papa, Aleksei, and ourselves on the walls and tabletops.

Next to that comes Papa and Mama's bedroom, and finally the adjoining corner room my sisters and I share. "Four big windows," Mashka says, cheerful as a canary in a new cage. "One for each of us." Aleksei will sleep in the pink room just across the hall, with his *dyadka* bunking in an adjoining scrap of space not much larger than a closet.

Together, my sisters and I fix our bedroom as much like home as we can. We line up our nightstands and striped camp cots along two walls as snugly as books on a shelf—any one of us can lie in bed and reach across the space between to hold hands with our neighboring sister. At the foot of our cots we each place a white wooden chair to drape our clothes over at night, just like always. Icons and identical portraits of *Otets* Grigori watch over us from our nightstands. For furniture we have only a couch and a single writing table to share, but Maria is right—it's cozy with all four of us together.

"Did you ever see such bare walls?" Tatiana asks. It's true. Fresh wallpaper and curtains decorate the rest of the house, but our room is awash in nothing but a seasick shade of blue. "What will we do without our chintz screens and all our picture frames?"

"Thumbtacks," Anastasia says, and within an hour after Nyuta arrives from town with a box of them, we've blotted out whole stretches of the queasy paint with colorful shawls and tacked masses of our favorite photos and drawings over our beds.

Once we've unpacked, we seven walk across the street to see the Kornilov house. The moment we return, Colonel Kobylinksy informs us this is not allowed. "The soldiers of the Second Regiment have protested. For the time being you must stay inside the yard."

"We had hopes of seeing the town," Papa says.

"And attending services," Mama reminds him.

"I will take it up with the new commandant when he arrives. Please, for the time being, bear with me, Your Majesties."

His request seems reasonable enough, but before we know it another fence is going up outside the first one, enclosing the governor's garden, poultry coops, greenhouse, and a portion of the side street with pointed gray boards. For days, the sounds of hammers and saws stamp their prints on our hours.

While my sisters study their lessons, I have nothing to

do but watch the soldiers work outside our windows. I ought to be grateful they're expanding our yard, but it's still shorter than the deck of the *Standart*. "The gates at Tsarskoe Selo never felt this way."

"We should be used to it," Tatiana reasons. "There have always been lines separating us from the rest of the world, whether they were satin ribbons or iron rails." She wrinkles her nose at the workmen's progress. "Though at least the fence back home was attractive."

"This is the first one built especially to keep us *in*," Anastasia adds.

"That's true," says Maria. "It's queer being shut in this way."

"What are you talking about?" Anastasia scoffs. "Maybe Papa and Mama could come and go before the revolution, but not us, and even they couldn't go anywhere without at least half an hour's notice and a pack of security agents."

"It's the first fence we can't see through," I realize.

When the palisade is finished, it's as if someone has put a lid over the yard. *"Tak i byt,"* is all Papa has to say. *So be it.* He surveys the serrated row of planks, then tries to shake one of the crosspieces. "Well made."

Leaving Tsarskoe Selo was like tearing a page from my heart, but even penned in like this, Tobolsk isn't so bad. Right away Maria and Anastasia take to leaning out of our bedroom window to wave at passersby. "You should see how they look at us." Mashka beams. "You'd think they'd seen a shooting star in broad daylight. Until Nastya pulls a face and sends them scurrying, at least."

Already we've had daily gifts of fresh eggs and milk from local farmers, and nuns from a convent nearby deliver enough sugar and cakes to plump Maria up like a ripe strawberry again. When Mama sits on the balcony, passersby take off their hats and bow or cross themselves.

Could this be how Aleksei's pet elephant felt, penned up far from home but lavished with treats and curiosity? And yet if the people are so proud to have us in their city, who rechristened this block Freedom Street?

Inside the house, everything carries on as usual. It's like being part of the scenes in Mama's Fabergé Easter eggs: the morning prayer service egg, the garden stroll egg, the tea-time egg. Papa and Mama take up nightly games of bezique or dominoes with Dr. Botkin. Tatiana often joins them, while Aleksei plays endless hands of *nain jaune* with Monsieur Gilliard and Nagorny. Those nights, surrounded by our furniture, our people, and our familiar routine, I can close my eyes and almost forget we left home at all. Almost.

"Olga, girlies," Mama gasps from our doorway, "can you guess who has come to Tobolsk?" My sisters and I gape at one another and shake our heads. It's enough of a surprise to see Mama outside her drawing room—we can hardly imagine such a thing as a visitor. "Margarita Khitrovo. All by herself!"

I jump from the writing table and pull Mama into the room by both her hands. "Ritka? All the way from Petrograd?" My heart beats in my ears, my throat, the tips of my fingers. Ritka, our dear friend, all the way from the lazaret at

Tsarskoe Selo! It's like something from a fairy tale—a devoted maid following her lady over mountains and across rivers. A hundred questions swarm inside my head: Why did she leave the lazaret? How did she get here alone? What about her mother and sisters and brothers? My voice shakes as I ask the most important question of all. "Where is she now, Mama?"

"At the Kornilov house, with Countess Hendrikova. She arrived this morning and walked right in."

Right across the street. And yet she might as well be on the other side of the Ural Mountains. It feels as if there's a fish flopping under my ribs. How I wish we could leave this house and go to her! Instead I lean out our bedroom window like the Little Pair, hoping to catch a glimpse of my dear Ritka until dark.

The next morning I perch in the windowsill again, then run downstairs to pounce on Dr. Botkin the moment he crosses the street. "Where's Ritka?" I ask him. "When will they let her come see me?"

"I'm sorry, Olga Nikolaevna." He sighs and pinches the rim of his glasses. "Your friend has been put on a steamship back to Petrograd."

It's as if a carpet has been yanked out from under my heart. The excitement that danced inside me all night and day flashes out like a shattered lightbulb. "Why?"

"Miss Khitrovo brought a packet of letters with her from Petrograd. I'm afraid she was quite indiscreet about it. The soldiers searched Countess Hendrikova's room, confiscated the letters, and sent the young lady home."

"It's that awful Second Regiment again, isn't it?" I blaze. "Will they even let us have our letters?"

"I have my doubts. There was talk of confining us all to the Kornilov house, but Colonel Kobylinsky persuaded the soldiers to compromise: servants and members of the suite may go into town accompanied by an armed guard."

Disappointment stiffens me like chunks of ice clogging a river, and I mope for days, not caring in the least what anyone thinks of my mood. I'm almost glad when an earache confines me to bed, where I can toss and sigh while Mama pets my hands and hums my favorite hymns.

When the pain clears, I can hardly believe my ears—it sounds as if I'm hearing double voices from Aleksei's bedroom. Across the corridor, I discover my brother and young Kolya Derevenko sprawled across the floor with Aleksei's model boats.

"Dr. Derevenko and his family arrived in town Friday," Tatiana explains. She can't even look at me. "Kolya has permission to come play with Aleksei once a week."

If I could go to church, I think I could stand it, but every Sunday when Kolya arrives, jealousy licks at me like the rough tongue of a cat, even when I hear them arguing together over some trifle. Surely Ritka and her letters weren't any more dangerous than Aleksei's miniature army.

By September, two new men arrive to take charge of us. Their names are Nikolsky and Pankratov.

On the first day, Papa meets with Pankratov in his study while we wait in our rooms. None of us can hear a thing, but I imagine Papa speaking politely to the commissar, asking to be allowed to walk in the town, to go to church, and to receive foreign newspapers. My stomach mumbles to itself as I wonder how this new man will react. Could he be nervous, the way Kerensky was? Will he be courteous like our Colonel Kobylinsky, or surly as the men of the Second Regiment?

Before my questions settle, Papa appears at our door. "The commissar has asked to meet us. Please come into the corridor." Outside, Papa organizes us into a neat row, just as we stood when we met Kerensky in our classroom at home—Mama, Aleksei, then me and my sisters arranged from oldest to youngest. Papa steps back and gazes down the line at us. A smile lifts his beard, crinkling the corners of his eyes. *"Otlichno,"* he says. "Now wait right here."

He strides down the hallway, his back straight as a soldier's, and disappears into his study. When Papa reappears, a man both smaller and older than himself accompanies him. For an instant, the older fellow looks panicked, as if he's facing an execution squad instead of a line of captive women and children. "This way, Mr. Commissar," Papa calls amiably. "May I present my wife and my children. Now you see why you have no reason to fear my running off. How could I leave such a family?"

Pankratov recovers himself and begins to greet us. "How is your health, Aleksei Nikolaevich?"

"Khorosho, spasibo," Aleksei answers.

Pankratov turns to my sisters and me. "Have you ever been to Siberia before?" Something about his expectant look makes me think of a schoolteacher. He smiles and holds his eyebrows high, as if to say, *Come along now, children, you know the answer.* We only shake our heads shyly.

"It's not as terrible as many people say," Papa interrupts. "The climate here is good, and the weather is marvelous." They talk agreeably for a minute about Siberia, with its sunny days unlike gray Petrograd, and how severe the temperature might be in the winter.

Their interlude done, Pankratov returns to the four of us. "Do you have books?"

Puzzlement tickles my mouth. What a funny little man, chatting with his prisoners about the weather and books! A giggle squeaks like a pinched balloon from the Little Pair's end of the line.

"We brought our library," Tatiana answers over them.

Pankratov seems genuinely pleased. "If you need anything, I ask that you let me know." With a smart nod, away he goes down the corridor.

After that, the days unfold one like another, until I feel as if I'm caught in a book with its pages glued together. Each morning Papa and I take tea alone at nine o'clock, but for the rest of the day I'm adrift. Tatiana busies herself with Mama. The Little Pair have their passersby. There are the governor's turkeys and chickens for Aleksei to feed. Papa helps Aleksei dig a shallow pond for the ducks, then retires to puttering over the plants in the greenhouse. Even the dogs have the rubbish pile to nose through.

Just as in Tsarskoe Selo, the world exists around us, but

we aren't a part of it, and it's no longer concerned with us, except to wonder at our sheared heads when we sun ourselves on the balcony. For the longest time, the only break in our languor is a telegram from the Crimea—sweetheart Aunt Olga has had her baby, a little boy called Tikhon. We cheer and offer up prayers for the little one's health, until our excitement swallows itself. Perhaps the same question has dawned on us all at once: When will we ever see Tikhon ourselves?

"I have a treat for you children," Dr. Botkin says one Saturday afternoon, leaning so close my forkful of fish tastes like cologne. His keeps his voice low, as if the words might run over the edge of the table and into the ears of the guards in their barracks. "Come into the heir's bedroom when luncheon is done and you shall have it." I know he's talking to Aleksei and the Little Pair when he says "children," but I'm already so weary with tedium I find myself trailing them up the steps.

Upstairs, Dr. Botkin eases the door shut and reaches into his coat. "With compliments from my son, Gleb," he says, handing Aleksei a black album. Inside is a painting of a white teddy bear in a blue uniform tearing the tail from an awful red dragon.

Aleksei reads the lettering along the dragon's tail. "*The Sacred Truth of the History of the Times of the Monkey Revolution.*" A grin parts his face. "It's a new Mishka story, isn't it, Dr. Botkin?" The doctor folds his hands behind his waistcoat and smiles as he rocks forward and back on his heels, just once. It's as if his whole body is nodding. Gleb is only a little older than Anastasia, but he has a talent with watercolors and words. Back home, he invented a storybook world of teddy bears and monkeys just for us. We all crowd around the album as if it's a beckoning campfire. Even the Little Pair is really too old for such fancies, but in this dull place Gleb's stories are refreshing as peaches. The glow from their smiles warms my own cheeks. Tatiana quietly thanks our good doctor, and I know he is proud of his boy.

From time to time, Dr. Botkin pats his coat pocket when he arrives in the morning, and we know there is a fresh chapter in the Monkey Revolution from Gleb inside. When I don't have my own letters to read or write, I linger in Aleksei's doorway, listening as they untangle the latest twist in the Mishkoslavian plot to overthrow the monkeys and pore over the pictures with their detailed military uniforms. Gleb is a kind young man to go to such trouble for my brother and sisters. I wish I could thank him somehow.

One afternoon Dr. Botkin takes me aside and reaches again into his coat pocket. "My son asks if you will take a look at this for him, Olga Nikolaevna." He hands me a small exercise book. Inside are a few poems in Gleb's careful lettering. Has Gleb dashed off these poems just to fill my time—a grown-up version of the Mishka stories? I'm not sure if I should be grateful or insulted by the idea. My teeth grab hold of my lower lip and tuck it over the tip of my tongue as I try to consider my feelings.

"Gleb tells me he is having trouble with some of the rhymes," Dr. Botkin continues. "I told him you might be

willing to give your opinion on the verses and rhythm."
This time there is no proprietary nod or smile. The doctor
looks almost as anxious for my reaction as if he'd written the
poems himself.

"My opinion?"

"And your suggestions, if you have any."

My lips unfold. A strange sense of relief sweeps over me.
I wrap my fingers around Gleb's exercise book as though it's
the rung of a ladder. "*Konechno*, Dr. Botkin. *Spasibo*."

23

MARIA NIKOLAEVNA

September 1917
Tobolsk

ou will have your photos taken and carry identification cards at all times," Pankratov's assistant declares. The two of them are as different as salted cucumbers and ice cream. Nikolsky's hardly spoken to us before this, and now he's giving orders like a sergeant.

"What?" Mama bursts out. Papa puts his hand on her arm but doesn't say anything.

"It was forced on us in the old days, so now it's your turn," Nikolsky barks at her. He smiles when he speaks to Mama, but his eyes are hard, and his teeth show too much, like a dog when it growls.

"Why is Mama so angry?" I ask the Big Pair while we freshen up for the photo session. I can hear Mama's sharp voice poking through their bedroom wall like a needle through an embroidery hoop.

"It is absolutely insulting," Tatiana huffs. "Why should the tsar and tsaritsa of Russia have to carry identification cards inside their own house? I have never heard of anything so ridiculous."

"He's nursing a grudge, Mashka," Olga explains. "To be ridiculous and make us angry. And anyway, it isn't our house," she adds.

I don't like the sound of that. And I don't feel angry at all. I suddenly feel small as a kitten in a basket.

"Anything that brute says is insulting," Tatiana goes on. "He barges right in without knocking and never takes his cap off when he speaks to Mama and Papa."

"The whole thing is silly," Anastasia answers. "With our hair cut they can hardly tell us apart in the first place. They might as well take the dogs' pictures instead. Besides, it's not as if we can go anywhere. What are they going to do, check our photos at the dining room door?"

She picks up an envelope from the writing table and holds it at arm's length beside Tatiana's face like an artist considering a painting. "Ah yes, you there beside the empress, you must be Daughter Number Two. And the noisy one, isn't she Daughter Number Four?"

Tatiana snatches the paper from her hand. "Stop that. This is nothing to joke about."

"I should pull a face for the camera so they'll be able to tell me apart from the rest of you baldies."

Olga looks horrified, all pale and awful.

"Anastasia Nikolaevna, don't you dare!" Tatiana scolds. Anastasia flares so quickly I can feel her temper rising beside me like a hot Crimean wind before the blotches show on her neck and cheeks.

"Please, Shvybs," Olga says gently. A little tremor in her voice goes through me like a pinprick. She tries to take Anastasia's hand, but Anastasia brushes Olga away—she hates being babied almost as much as being told what to do.

I hate watching my sisters fight. When something I say sets their tempers flinging back and forth, I'm helpless as a tennis net in the middle of it all. Before Anastasia can answer back, I throw myself between them. "Don't worry, Tatya," I say with a big grin I don't mean, "nobody's better at getting pictures taken than we are!"

I don't know if it's what I said or the tears brimming just above my smile, but Tatiana takes one look at me and backs down. "You are right, Mashka." Her voice has gone haughty, almost like Anastasia's when she's being fresh, but harder. "We have looked into more cameras than that Nikolsky has seen in his entire life. If he wants to insult us, he will have to find something better than a photograph to do it."

Olga hooks her hand through my elbow without saying a word, and I know she's proud of me.

The photos are nothing like the formal portraits we used to have. Nikolsky's curtained off one end of the corridor and set up a wooden chair with a sheet draped behind it. A black camera stares its wide empty eye at the wall. One by one, we're marched to the bare seat and told to hold still and look straight ahead, then to the side. Olga was right. There's something about Nikolsky's smirk as the photos are snapped that makes me squirm inside. Every time the flashbulb flares, I flinch. When Aleksei peeks around the other side of the curtain before his turn, Nikolsky bellows at him like cannon fire. Aleksei skitters away, probably to Mama. Not one of us smiles after that.

Things settle down again once that's all over. Olga keeps herself buried in books, or the poems by Gleb that Dr. Botkin carries across the street in his pockets. Mama holes up in her drawing room with her Bible and embroidery and hardly ever comes downstairs, even for dinner. Every day we take turns sitting and reading with her, and I'm glad that when the sun shines she'll sit out on the balcony so I can peep over the pages and watch my people in the streets. Except for our Anya, I don't have friends from the Red Cross like Mama and the Big Pair, so instead of writing stacks of letters to Petrograd I imagine stories for the townspeople. My favorite is a young lady in a blue coat who walks by almost every afternoon at three o'clock. She always has two small boys by the hand, and I call her Natalya. In my head, she has a black-haired baby girl at home, and a husband named Andrei away at war. Natalya never lets go of the boys' hands, but she smiles up at my window when the little ones stop to wave.

"Is there anything you require?" Pankratov asks each morning.

"We would like to be allowed to walk in town," Papa says, like always. "You can't be afraid that I might run away?"

If he knew my papa, Pankratov might be able to hear

the annoyance hiding behind the joke in his voice. Listening to them feels like swallowing an aspirin tablet without any water.

"Of course I believe you, Nikolai Alexandrovich. And anyway, an attempt to escape would only make things worse for you and your family."

"Then what is your objection, sir? I visited Tobolsk as a young man. I remember it as a beautiful city. I would like to see it again, with my family. My wife and daughters are especially keen to visit the churches, and I know my son would enjoy the kremlin."

The commissar looks at us. I try to smile as much with my eyes as my lips. All of us would love to go to church, but I know it would fill Mama, Olga, and Tatiana like a thick cut of beefsteak.

"In the best interests of your safety, I cannot permit it. Have you any letters to post today?"

We always have letters to send, but Pankratov has to read them before they're posted. It makes Mama so mad, she won't even look at him. When we get letters in return, she won't take them from his hand, either. She glares at her knitting needles until he puts the opened envelopes on the table and leaves the room. I don't know how she can stand it. I'm so eager to hear from the outside—especially for any word of Auntie Olga's precious baby—that I want to ask Pankratov himself for the news instead of waiting to open them.

"Maria darling," Mama says, tucking a thick envelope into my pocket, "see if an officer of the Fourth Regiment will post this one letter to Anya for me. I won't tolerate that man reading my private correspondence." My insides flip over like hot *blini* in a pan whenever Mama asks me to do this. I'm proud that she trusts me, but I'm a dreadful sneak.

Out in the corridor, I find Commissar Pankratov speaking to Aleksei.

"Since you can't go into town yourself, I thought perhaps you would like to look at this." Pankratov hands over a little blue notebook with a government seal printed on the cover.

"'1916 Souvenir,'" Aleksei reads. Pictures of the city fan by as he pages through it.

"It isn't new, but Tobolsk hasn't changed so much in the meantime. You may keep it in your room until you're finished with it."

Aleksei says, *"Spasibo,"* and carries the booklet away like it's a silver tray.

"God bless you, Mr. Commissar," I tell Pankratov, coming up beside him. He jumps as if I've poked him.

"It's nothing," he says, but I think it is something. It's as if the commissar's trying to make up for all the times he has to say no, and it makes Mama's letter sizzle like a hot stone in my pocket. I ought to turn it over to Commissar Pankratov right then and there, but I don't. He may be responsible for us, but the thought of disobeying Mama puts a bigger quiver in my belly than going behind the commissar's back.

Anytime our favorite section of the Fourth Regiment is on duty, Papa and Aleksei slip off to play cards with the men in their barracks. Whenever I can get away without Mama noticing, I follow them, and today is a perfect chance. It's all right for me to smuggle her letters to the guards in the yard, but she tells me it isn't proper for a young lady to consort with all those men in their barracks. I don't care. Mama doesn't know the Fourth Regiment the way I do, and they're never anything but perfectly proper. The men still call out, *"Nash naslednik"* whenever Aleksei visits, even though he isn't heir to anything at all anymore, and they call me Imperial Highness, even though I turn eighteen shades of red and tell them they don't have to anytime our parents aren't listening. Sometimes the three of us even share a bit of supper with them.

"Why is the Second Regiment still such a surly bunch?" I ask the officers around the table.

"They're young, and eager to fight," one of the older men says. "Maybe things would have been better if they'd seen the front instead of being reserves. Since they were stationed in Petrograd, the revolution broke out and went straight to their heads like a round of drinks. Besides, lately Commissar Nikolsky has been lecturing them about their so-called rights."

"Nikolsky might as well drop a lit match into a bottle of vodka as pass out those pamphlets of his," another officer mutters.

"Is that why we hardly see him in the house? I'm glad. He's awfully rude to us, especially Mama."

"Missing out on a war seems to turn young men into bullies," another tells me. "We old fellows have fought at the front, and we have families of our own. We've seen enough fighting."

"That sounds backward," I say, turning it over in my

head. "You've gone to war and come back more decent. They stayed behind and turned sour."

Aleksei interrupts. "But why won't Commissar Pankratov let us visit the town, or go to church for *Obednya*? He's in charge, and the men are supposed to do what he says. But those soldiers boss him and Colonel Kobylinsky around like new recruits."

Before anyone can answer, the door swings open and Commissar Pankratov himself walks into the barracks. At the sight of us, he stops and blinks at our plates of food.

"Come join us, Mr. Commissar," Papa says, sounding jolly as Father Christmas. "There's plenty more to share."

Pankratov looks for a moment as if he's swallowed a live oyster, then turns and leaves.

In cold weather, Papa saws and chops wood for hours at a time. I snap photos of them: Papa and Gilliard, Papa and Aleksei, Papa and Olga. On top of all the chin-ups he does each morning, nobody can outlast Papa with a saw or an ax, and soon there are stout birch logs piled up higher than the little white picket fence. Next thing we know, he's mounted a rough platform along the roof of the greenhouse where we can all sit in a row to catch the afternoon sunshine. Some of the soldiers even help him build a catwalk up the side of the building. With three big round lengths of wood, the men rig a frame in the yard to hold a swing for us children. When it begins to snow, all three of my sisters and I bundle up in our gray capes and red and black angora caps to take turns pushing one another and jumping into the drifts. Soon there'll be enough snow to toboggan, but it's flat as a pond inside our fence.

While we play, Aleksei noses through the sheds and out-buildings, collecting all sorts of rubbish. "You're just like the dogs, pawing through the trash. What are you going to do with a bunch of bent nails and bits of string and glass?" I ask him.

"*Prigoditsya*," he says. *It may come in useful.*

"Useful for what?" Anastasia pesters. Aleksei only shrugs and goes back to his foraging. How like a boy!

Just then, one of the Fourth Regiment nudges his way into our little triangle. "*Izvenite* for interrupting, but would these be of interest to a young man like yourself?" His name is Oleg Sergeevich. He holds out two tarnished brass buttons and a belt buckle to Aleksei.

"*Da, spasibo!*" Aleksei salutes, then runs off to show Papa his newest treasures.

"You have a boy yourself, don't you, soldier?" I ask.

"Indeed I do, Your Highness. My little Vanya is younger than the heir, but boys are very much alike. I'm sorry there isn't much here to interest young ladies." Anastasia giggles. I kick at her boot heel to hush her.

"It is awfully muddy and ugly in here," I admit. It's like living inside a cardboard box. Every time we circle the yard, it seems smaller and duller. "I miss the trees and paths in the park back home."

"I miss keeping up with the latest fashions," says Tatiana, coming up behind us, "but I would trade all my best dresses for an afternoon by the sea."

"Parts of Siberia are quite beautiful," Oleg Sergeevich tells us. "You should ask Commissar Pankratov to tell you about it. He's been all over this part of the country."

Tatiana doesn't answer. It's one thing to chat with the officers from Petrograd, but striking up a conversation with Pankratov seems odd, even to me.

I am the clumsiest thing!

"I don't know how she managed it," Anastasia tells Dr. Botkin as they help me up the stairs. "There isn't a thing out there to trip on. Even the ducks know to waddle out of the way when they see Mashka coming." Under my cupped hand, my eye throbs and waters. My whole face feels like it's twisted up tight around my eye socket.

Upstairs, Dr. Botkin and Mama and Tatiana bustle around me.

"I'm afraid it will bruise, but I don't think any real harm's been done," Dr. Botkin decides.

Mama crosses herself. "Thank God it wasn't Aleksei."

My feelings trip and spill all over each other. *Konechno*, I'd take Aleksei's place in a heartbeat rather than see him suffer for days over such a silly bump as this, but hearing the words the way Mama says them leaves me feeling like more than my face is bruised.

"Try not to look so glum, *dushka*," Tatiana whispers. "Remember, tripping over your left foot is a good omen."

I end up on the couch, tucked under a blanket with a nasty headache and a bag full of chipped ice to keep down the swelling. Tatiana sits at the other end, tatting a lace collar.

Natalya's little boys will be disappointed if I'm not there to wave at three o'clock, but I know better than to ask Tatiana if I can go to the window like this.

Every chance she gets, Anastasia peeks under the ice bag to see if my skin's turning colors yet. "One of Mashka's saucers will have a black-and-blue rim by tomorrow," she sing-songs.

Tatiana starts to scold, but a knock and then boots on the floor interrupt. I squint out from under the frosty cloth. Commissar Pankratov stands over our couch. "I'm sorry to hear you are hurt, Maria Nikolaevna. Are you in much pain?"

My try at smiling turns into a wince. "Not too much. Dr. Botkin says I should rest my eye for a day or two."

"One of the officers mentioned you might be interested in Siberia." Pankratov hands me a book, smaller than the one he gave Aleksei, and thicker, too. The print inside swims, but I make out his own name in the larger letters on the cover.

"You wrote this yourself?"

He nods. His head looks like a bearded cloud. I shut my eyes before my stomach moves too. "My memories and travels in Siberia," he says. "Perhaps one of your sisters could read it to you while you recover."

This time when I smile, it doesn't hurt a bit. "*Spasibo*, Mr. Commissar." His face colors, and I don't know why, but I blush a little too. The heat of it makes my sore eye pulse all over again. When I open them back up, he's gone.

"Probably a lot of propaganda," Tatiana says without looking up from her lace. "He was a criminal, after all."

Anastasia claps her hands. "*Otlichno!* That only makes it better."

"Anastasia Nikolaevna—"

"Oh stop, you two," Olga says from the writing table. "It won't hurt us to see what he thinks."

If I didn't know better, I'd swear I can hear Tatiana frowning. "Please read it to me, Tatya," I beg. "It was awfully kind of him to visit me. We can stop if it's terrible."

"Oh, all right." She spreads her tatting carefully across the arm of the couch. "But keep that ice over your face." I grin and slosh the soggy bag back into place.

All afternoon my sisters' voices paint pictures in my mind with the commissar's words. When Tatiana's throat gives out, Olga and Anastasia take turns reading so we don't have to stop. It's so romantic—it turns out our Commissar Pankratov was punished for killing a police officer in defense of a woman in Kiev years and years ago!

"Sentenced to solitary confinement in Schlusselburg Fortress for fourteen years," Olga says, "and another twenty-seven in Siberian exile. Can you imagine? It's a wonder he's civil to us, much less thoughtful."

I spread it all out in my head: The Fourth Regiment went to war and came back better men. The Second Regiment stayed home and turned into a pack of angry dogs, like Nikolsky. Pankratov spent almost my whole life in prison under Papa's government, and he's so kind to us.

"What will we be like when this is all over?" I ask my sisters. "Better, worse, or just the same?"

"Why should we change at all?" Tatiana asks. "Our faith may grow stronger with these trials, but we are still Romanovs, no matter what the revolution brings." She snaps the book shut like a period on the end of her sentence. "There. I am going to see Mama about my tatting." She kisses my cheek and tucks a damp string of hair behind my ear. "And I will send Nyuta with more ice, so stay put."

"*Spasibo*, Tatya."

"She sounds just like Mama," Anastasia says after Tatiana's gone. "Anyway, I'm tired of sitting. I'll run downstairs and get your ice. Nyuta's got enough to do keeping Mama happy."

The room is quiet except for the rustle of Olga turning the pages in Commissar Pankratov's book. "Olga? Do you still feel like the same person?"

"No," Olga admits. Her voice is so soft. "Not for a long time, Mashka. Do you?"

I have to think a long time too, but I still don't know what to say.

24

TATIANA NIKOLAEVNA

October 1917
Tobolsk

*E*very day when Papa is done with the newspapers, I read them over myself. They are almost always late, especially the foreign papers, but even old news is better than none at all. Olga hardly bothers with them, sometimes even leaving the room as soon as Papa spreads them open. I scour the pages like a doctor working over a wound, fishing out dirty fragments of rumor and stitching the rest back into something more or less useful. Of course, Papa beats me to the most interesting stories and reads them aloud to us over tea in Mama's drawing room.

"Tatiana, my dear," Papa says, his beard twitching, "why haven't you told us you're engaged to be married?"

My toe drops from scratching under Ortipo's chin so quickly she nearly topples over. "What?"

"It's all here in the Petrograd *Evening Post*." He holds the newspaper up like a poster and reads, "'London telegraphs that there is a rumor circulating that the former tsar Nicholas Romanov's second daughter escaped from Tobolsk and has now arrived in America. It appears that Tatiana Nikolaevna plans to give lectures on Russian events and to open a school in the United States. According to these same rumors, Tatiana Nikolaevna is said to have married Count Fredericks, son of the former minister of the court.'"

Papa lowers the paper and raises one eyebrow. My mouth gapes like a sturgeon's. The Little Pair hoot and snort while Mama shakes her head at her tea.

"What rubbish!" I sputter. "The Frederickses do not even have a son. Besides, I would much rather open a hospital right here in Siberia than a school in America."

"But you could teach manners, comportment, and etiquette, Your Imperial Highness," Anastasia says in a high voice with her lips pursed. "Or, 'How to maintain your poise during a revolution.'"

She finishes with a curtsy. Papa chuckles with Aleksei, Mama's lips wriggle, and I blush to the earlobes, trying to decide if I should I be flattered or embarrassed. Anastasia's remarks always seem to be a soup of insult and compliment. Only Olga remains subdued. She smiles, but her thumb worries back and forth over her fingernails.

"Why do you ignore the papers?" I ask Olga later. "You used to read them even more than I do. I would never be able to stand not knowing what happens outside."

"'For in much wisdom is much grief, and he who increases knowledge increases sorrow,'" she quotes.

"Ecclesiastes 1:18," I reply automatically.

She nods. "There's so little good news." Her words burst out like steam from a samovar, then almost evaporate. "But I'm not happy not knowing, either! I imagine awful things—things probably worse than the truth."

"Maybe it would help if you only read the headlines?"

She sighs. "I don't know what to do. So much of it is lies and rumors anyway, like today."

"That was just nonsense. Why should such a silly rumor bother you?"

"Because it shows how much they don't understand us, Tatya, and how little they care. How could you ever give lectures on Russian events, the way you've been cooped up since February? No one bothered to find out if the Frederickses even have a son for you to marry. And how could anyone who knows you think for even an instant that you'd leave us and run off to America? If they can print trash like that, how do we know what's true and what isn't about what's happening outside?"

"Some truth must find its way into the papers," I insist.

Olga nods, but something rumples her eyebrows. Even if I cannot guess her thoughts, I can tell she is thinking. "Tatya," she says after a pause, "do you want to marry?"

My answer should come quickly. This is something a young woman ought to know about herself. "I know what you think. To leave Mama would be . . ." I trail off. What would it be? Thinking about it is almost too much.

"You're her favorite, but—"

"No, Olga! Mama loves all of us." Even as I protest I know Olga is right, and she knows it as well as I do.

"Listen, Tatiana. You are her favorite, except for Aleksei, and you're so sweet with her that not one of us minds. But Mama has all of us, and Aleksei, and Papa to take care of her. There's no shame in wanting something for yourself."

I flatten my lips to keep my chin from quivering. "There is more to it than Mama," I explain when I can speak again. "Who would we marry, now that Papa has abdicated? Which of our foreign cousins would accept a deposed bride?"

"You're right. If the king of England wouldn't offer asylum to his own cousins, or even send a ship to rescue us, he'd never stoop to let one of his sons marry an ex–grand duchess."

"To think, *dushka*, if you had accepted the crown prince of Romania, you could have been a queen someday instead of a captive. Are you ever sorry?"

Her eyes flash like Mama's, and her snub nose tilts toward the ceiling. "*Nyet*. I am a Russian and I intend to remain in Russia, no matter what the revolutionaries think of us. Tobolsk may be hundreds of miles from anything, but at least it is still in Russia." The flare of passion subsides, easing her expression. "Tatya, never mind what we can or can't have—what do you want?"

"Without being practical, you mean?"

She nods.

I feel a little like I should kneel beside her, the way we do for confession. Once I begin, the words follow one another like notes in a hymn. "I wish I could be like Princess Gedroiz at the lazaret. Think of being a doctor! Even if I could not do that, I would thank God every day if I could manage a children's hospital, or a school for nurses."

"Oh, my dear Governess," Olga says, shaking her head. "You're practical even when you aren't, and I can't help loving you for it! You talk about antibiotics and your cheeks glow like Mashka's when she moons over an officer. Besides, you'd be so much more pleasant than Princess Gedroiz."

"I have to admit, she could give a better scolding than even Mama." We giggle and snort in the most undignified way until I ask, "Olga, what do you want?"

Her spirits drain like a cup of Communion wine. "I want to feel like Russia isn't shaking underneath us every time we open a newspaper."

"Oh, Olya." I wrap my arms round her shoulders and cradle her head against my cheek. "Hold on to me," I tell her, and we lean into each other until her ragged breathing smoothes like satin.

"Olga, *dushka*, we are going to church!"

"In a real church, outside the fence?"

"*Konechno.* And there will be Communion, too." My own chest warms as her cheeks turn rosy as Mashka's.

"Full *Obednya!*" She presses her clasped hands to her chin and beams. "*Slava Bogu.*"

Outside the fence, two rows of soldiers line the street all the way to the church.

Inside, where nearly every word and gesture has remained

unchanged for centuries, I know exactly what to expect, and how to respond. The moment the priest begins to intone the Divine Liturgy, I feel myself letting go of the world outside, allowing the holy ritual to carry me. Here, there is nothing to adjust for, or anticipate. I surrender Mama and Olga to the grace of God, and let the familiar words drape over me: "Blessed is the kingdom of the Father, and of the Son, and of the Holy Spirit, now and forever, and to the ages of ages."

When I swallow my portion of the wine-soaked *prosphora*, it is as if that tiny bit of sacred bread reawakens the strength of Christ in my own body.

The feeling lasts nearly two weeks, until the day before Olga's birthday, when news comes that makes every one of us cringe at the sound of rustling newsprint. Papa looks ill as he reads, "'With the collapse of the Provisional Government, Alexander Kerensky has fled Petrograd, and the Bolshevik Party, headed by V. I. Lenin, has seized power.'" Mama's knitting needles freeze, then vibrate rigidly as Papa's eyes skim the article. "The mob looted the wine cellars of the Winter Palace," he tells us, slapping the paper aside. "Such gluttony. It's nauseating to read about!"

"*Bozhe moi*. When did it happen, Nicky?" Mama asks with a sympathetic squeeze to Papa's forearm.

Olga fingers the chain round her neck, the one that holds a St. Nicholas medal and a tiny portrait of *Otets* Grigori. We all wear a matching set, even Aleksei.

"Over a week ago, and we have to find out from an old newspaper. I would never have abdicated if I'd known it would come to this!" Papa shoves back his chair and shoots to his feet like a bullet from a rifle. Too agitated to smoke his cigarette, the ash grows longer and longer as he paces the floor. "I can't understand it. Kerensky was a man of the people, a favorite of the soldiers. How could they have overthrown him?"

"It's a disgrace," Mama agrees. Her needles clack furiously again. "They're behaving like a lot of spoiled children."

From across the room, Olga's thoughts fuse with mine. This is not only about Russia and the government, it is about our family. We both stood in the classroom back home when Kerensky guaranteed our safety. We both know he is the one who arranged our secure departure from Petrograd and appointed Colonel Kobylinsky and Commissars Nikolsky and Pankratov. With Lenin in charge, everything could change all over again. God help us.

Olga comforts herself reading psalms late into the night, but even after she turns off her bedside lamp, neither of us can sleep. "This Lenin isn't good for us, is he?" Her voice drifts across the darkness between our cots like smoke from a censer. "I saw your face when Papa read his name, and I've overheard enough about the Bolsheviks to know Russia is never going to be the same."

"No. Lenin has been in exile for years, printing his newspaper and stirring up the Jews with his Bolshie nonsense about Communism. He grew up in the same town as Kerensky." I pause, wondering how much to worry her, even though I know she will worry no matter how much I say.

"You can tell me, Tatya."

I sigh over Mashka's soft snoring. "His older brother was hanged for trying to assassinate Dedushka in 1887."

"He hates us, then."

"I think so." I hear the swish of her short hair against the pillow as she nods, then nothing. "Please try not to worry, *dushka*. God will watch over us."

"*Konechno*, Tatya. But now Lenin is watching too."

What can I say to that? Alone in the dark, I rub my St. Nicholas medal on its chain and drift off to sleep with Olga's words buffeting my prayers like waves against the *Standart*.

25

ANASTASIA NIKOLAEVNA

November 1917
Tobolsk

My diary looks like a big white yawn every time I open it," I gripe at Maria. "Listen to this week so far:

"'Monday: Morning prayers. Breakfast. Lessons in the hall with M and A. Walked in the garden with Papa. Olga sat with Mama. Lunch. Walked in the garden. Tea. Lessons. Painted an ugly portrait of Jemmy. Supper. Coffee and bezique in the hall. To bed at ten o'clock.

"'Tuesday: Morning prayers. Breakfast. Lessons in the hall with M and A. Walked in the garden with Papa. Maria sat with Mama. Lunch. Chopped and sawed in the garden. Tea. Lessons. Bible readings. Supper. The others played cards in the hall again while I wrote letters. To bed at ten o'clock.

"'Wednesday: Morning prayers. Breakfast. Lessons in Aleksei's room with M and A. The usual walk. I sat with

Mama and looked at photo albums. Lunch. Walked in the garden while Papa sawed. Tea. More lessons. Papa read psalms out loud. Supper. Coffee and dominoes(!) in the drawing room(!) To bed at ten o'clock.

"'Thursday: Morning prayers. Breakfast. Lessons in Aleksei's room with M and A. Walked. Tatiana sat with Mama and patched our underwear (again). Lunch. Sawed with Papa. Tea. Lessons again. Knitted up a hole in my sock while Papa read. Supper. Coffee and bezique in the hall. To bed at ten o'clock.'"

I whap the book shut and give it an extra shove for good measure. "How utterly boring! Who would ever want to read this? *I* don't, and it's my own life. I can't wait for Sunday, so I can write 'singing' instead of 'lessons.'"

Maria looks at me like I'm pitiful as a three-legged kitten. "I think it's cozy, the way we seven are finally all together all day long with nobody bothering us," she gushes. "We have Papa all to ourselves, Mama can rest as much as she likes, Aleksei's been healthy for months and months. . . ."

I must be making quite a face if it's enough to derail one of Mashka's fancies of hearth and home. "The world is bigger than the inside of a house, you know." I twiddle my pencil a minute, then reach for my diary again. "Maybe I'll do it this way instead: Papa chopped a stack of wood three *arshins* high, walked eighteen circles around the garden, then spent forty minutes in the loo—hemorrhoids again?! Mama wrote seventeen pages of letters and humphed at Nikolsky and Pankratov twice. Olga read so much, I can't even pretend to count how many words. Tatiana sewed eight hundred fifty-six stitches (maybe more) and read one hundred eighty-seven Bible verses. Maria sighed and batted her eyes at four soldiers. Aleksei collected two greenish stones and one bent nail, and played with seventy-five toy soldiers. The dogs made two messes each in the garden, except for Ortipo, who 'did the governor' three times. All us girls took a bath, so the place reeks of perfume. I was too busy counting to do anything except fit six pieces into Aleksei's jigsaw puzzle."

"You can't do that!" Mashka's saucers go so wide, you'd think I've been drawing filthy pictures or something.

"I don't see why not. Who cares what the youngest ex–grand duchess puts in her own diary?" With a harrumph, I scoop Jemmy up and head out for a run in the yard.

"Hurry up." I fumble my mittens at Maria's sleeve and tug her along the frozen path. "I don't care how cold it is. If I have to go back in that house I'll howl 'God Save the Tsar,' and if we stand still we'll freeze." We stumble and shiver over the rutted mud as if our legs aren't any longer than Jemmy's. Our hair is finally long enough to brush, but no matter how many scarves or hats we wrap around our heads, the cold always marches right up our necks to our ears. At least the fence cuts the wind. "Besides, I'm getting fat as an elephant, lazing around in this place."

"You'll grow out of it," Maria pants, her breath huffing out in clouds ahead of us. "I did. My waist was thick as a bowl of cream for our formal portraits in 1914. Maybe you should chop wood with Papa, or pull Aleksei on the sled like Olga."

"If we had nothing but news to eat, I'd be thinner than a

rifle barrel," I grumble. Since the river Irtysh froze, only tele-grams and horsecarts can get through. "Meanwhile Lenin and his men are strutting all over Petrograd and Moscow, those Red Bolshie pigs."

"Where did you hear that?"

"What, 'Red Bolshie pigs'? From Tatiana."

"Tatiana said that?"

"They aren't bad words, you know. Not like swearing. Anyway, she ought to know. She reads those old newspapers so much."

Maria glances at a sentry standing along the fence, thumbing his frosty earlobe as if it's a balalaika string. "You'd better not let the Second Regiment hear you talk like that. Or Commissar Nikolsky."

"Now *you* sound like Tatiana. What kind of an *idiotka* do you think I am?" I drop Maria's elbow and stomp ahead, suddenly warm enough to yank the scarf away from my neck. We tramp silently around the whole yard—silently except for the sound of Maria tripping over our own frozen foot-prints, anyway—before I cool down enough to turn around and ask, "Mashka, do you still want to marry a soldier?"

"*Konechno.* Why shouldn't I? Auntie Olga did, and now she's got a darling little baby of her own."

How obstinate! And they think I'm the dope. "Who says he's darling? We haven't even seen a picture of Tikhon. He could be ugly as a monkey for all you know." Her face starts to twist, but I'm so sick of her dreamy nonsense I can't shut up. "Soldiers aren't the same as they used to be, you know."

She doesn't even shout back, and that makes me so mad

I stab at her with the only thing I've got: "You think any man in the army will want to settle down with the ex-tsar's daughter and have your twenty children now that Lenin's in charge?"

It's worse than kicking a puppy. A whimper rises up in Maria's big blue eyes, but she doesn't make a sound. Instead she wraps her arms around herself and dashes into the house. Jemmy follows without even looking behind. Alone in the yard, the wind slaps the blaze from my cheeks, but not half as hard as I deserve.

"What's wrong, Shvybs? Your turn with 'Madame Bekker'?" Olga asks when I stalk into our bedroom without Maria and burrow into a corner of our couch.

"Mind your own business." As if the whole household doesn't know when one of us is into the sanitary napkins. Stuffing my nose into a book is enough to keep Olga off my back, but there's no hiding from Tatiana when she comes swishing through the door.

"Out with it," she demands.

I don't know how anyone so thin can manage to look bigger than a Cossack standing over me. "What?" I ask, trying not to squirm. I don't look up, either.

"Anastasia Nikolaevna, if you want me to believe you are reading that book, at least have the sense to move your eyes back and forth. Mashka is curled up on the sofa in Mama's drawing room looking like the Second Regiment has drowned all our dogs, and here you sit playing innocent. What is going on?"

Oh, for the love of borscht. There's no getting around Tatiana when she's like this. "She's being ridiculous, that's what. Still blabbering about marrying a soldier and having her dozens of babies as if nothing's happened."

Olga covers her mouth with her hands. "Oh, Shvybs. How could you?"

I'd like to smash my face into the pages and scream. "You're not going to tell me that's ever going to happen, are you? Everything we can't do is because we're the tsar's daughters, and Papa isn't even tsar anymore."

Tatiana quivers so hard, I'm sure she's going to smack me until I spin.

"She's right, Tatya," Olga says. "In more than one way." Tatiana sinks to the couch beside me and nods. "You might as well let our Mashka dream, Shvybs."

"Remember when Maria had her tonsils removed?" Tatiana asks.

My lip rumples and I squint at her. It's like she's swapped scripts in the middle of a play. "*Konechno*. She laid in bed and ate ice cream for a week. I wished someone would take *my* tonsils out."

"She almost died. She hemorrhaged so badly the doctor panicked and ran out of the room."

"What does *that* have to do with anything, Nurse Romanova?"

"Think of how easily Aleksei bleeds and bruises. Great-Uncle Leopold was the same way. Mama's brother Frittie died of it when he was a little boy. Two of Auntie Irene's boys had it, and Heinrich was dead before Aleksei was born.

Hemophilia spreads through our family from mothers to daughters, from Queen Victoria all the way to Mama. . . ." Tatiana trails off. She can't even look at me.

Everything in me goes still. "And probably to us?"

"Yes. Sons bleed, but daughters carry the disease. Any one of us might have it, Mashka most of all, Christ be with her. You know what it does to Mama, having just one son with hemophilia. Now think of our poor Mashka with her twenty children. See, Nastya? Who she marries is beside the point. Even if God is merciful enough to give her healthy babies, it does not change the fact that giving birth to any one of them could kill her if she hemorrhages like that again."

For a moment I wonder if it's crueler to let Maria dream for nothing, or to tell her the truth. But only for a moment. Olga's right. Without her fancies, our sweet Mashka'd be as forlorn as a flagpole without the imperial colors, and life here is dull enough already.

Before I know it I'm snuffling against Tatiana's shoulder. I never wanted a soldier of my own, or twenty children, but I feel like it's my own dream that's been yanked out from under me, not Mashka's.

What is my dream, anyway? Ever since I was a little girl I've been straining on tiptoe to see what's behind the gates and railings and fences between me and the world. But I haven't ever once thought about what I'd do if I actually got to the other side.

Even though I know it'll only mean more lessons, I'm glad when one of our other tutors, Mr. Gibbes, arrives. If we can't leave the yard, at least it's nice to see a new face once in a while. Maria is so excited, her hug lifts him right off the floor. Mashka's never one to nurse a grudge, but I wonder if she'd be doting on our tutor this way if I hadn't been such a brat out in the yard. I still haven't told her I'm sorry.

Anyhow, it's funny to see Mr. Gibbes's face when Maria hoists him up, like he's a fancy vase worried about getting himself broken. He's such an odd little fellow, I'll bet he's looked serious as an old man ever since he was five years old. Instead of squeezing in with Monsieur Gilliard or boarding in town, he sets up housekeeping for himself and his toothless maid, Anfisa, in one of the sheds in our yard. "Do you think she's his girlfriend?" Maria whispers.

I shrug. "If she isn't, she's going to get awfully cold out there."

He's supposed to be improving our English, but every time Mr. Gibbes overhears an exciting episode from one of Aleksei's history lessons, he comes across the corridor eager to tell us the story. Anything that smacks of drama stokes him up like a chimney fire. From Mr. Gibbes we learn about Princess Tarakanova, who claimed to be the daughter of Empress Elizabeth but died of tuberculosis as a prisoner in the Petropavlovskaya Fortress, and the three false Dmitris, who pretended to be the dead son of Ivan the Terrible. "How stupid. How could three different people pretend to be one dead boy? Didn't anyone recognize him?" I ask.

"Perhaps his personality was not as . . . vivid as yours, Anastasia," Tatiana chimes in. Mr. Gibbes's eyebrow goes up, and he leans back to watch us like we're actresses in a play.

A smirk slices across my face. "No one could pretend to be me and get away with it. I am Anastasia Nikolaevna, Chief—"

"Chieftain of All Firemen," Tatiana finishes. "We know."

I ignore her and fan through the pages of my own history book. It ends with Tsar Alexander III, our *dedushka*, who died before any of us were born. "What do you suppose they'll write about Papa in the history books when this is all over?" I ask.

"That depends on who does the writing," Olga says.

"What's that supposed to mean? Facts are facts."

"Think about it, Shvybs. If Mama wrote the chapter on the revolution, it wouldn't be anything like what someone like Nikolsky would say, would it?"

"Brava, Olga Nikolaevna," Mr. Gibbes says, and claps.

I flip to the front of the book and look at the author's name. I've never heard of him. Maybe to some people history is just history, but this is my own family. I'd like to know how anyone can write the truth about us if we've never met.

In the evenings, when it's too stinking cold in this house to do anything but clump down the hall in our felt boots and pack ourselves around the tile stove in Mama's drawing room, Monsieur Gilliard begins reading us long poems by a writer called Nekrasov. The first is "Red-Nosed Frost," but our favorite is called "Russian Women," and it's about two princesses who follow their husbands into exile all the way to Siberia. "It's like they were written all about people like us," I say from the very first night.

"Why didn't anyone ever tell us we had such a wonderful poet?" Olga wants to know. She looks so absolutely scandalized I think she'd thump someone if she had the chance.

"They're so romantic," Maria says. Her chin nests in her hand, and her eyes have gone all starry.

"Commissar Pankratov suggested them," Monsieur Gilliard says.

"May I borrow the book, monsieur?" Olga asks.

Every time I look, Olga's got her nose crammed into the pages, copying down verses into her poetry notebook. "What's so great about them?" I want to know.

"Didn't you like them?"

"*Konechno*, but not over and over again. What's the use once you know what happens in the end?"

"A poet has more to say than the story he tells, Shvybs. For Maria, it's about romance, but Mama and Tatiana love the princesses' faith. For Papa there's the women's loyalty to their husbands. You and Aleksei like the adventure best, I'll bet."

"What about you?"

"Many things." Her voice drops. I lean in, hoping for something juicy. "Right now, I think it's terribly ironic that we all loved a poem about criminals."

"Criminals?"

"You'd forgotten by the end of the poem, hadn't you?" She gives me a know-it-all smile. "Troubetzkoy and Volkhonsky were revolutionaries, plotting against Tsar Nicholas I."

"Fine, but they weren't like the Bolshies."

"Weren't they? They incited three thousand soldiers in

St. Petersburg to revolt and tried to overthrow the tsar's government. Sound familiar?"

My eyes start to roll before she's finished. "How can you stand seeing everything from seventeen angles all at once?" I demand. But what I'd really like to know is, if I ever do have the chance to get a good look at the world, will I really *see* it?

26

MARIA NIKOLAEVNA

Christmas 1917
Tobolsk

"A parcel, a parcel!" Aleksei whoops, dancing around the tea table.

"From Anya," Mama says, and the five of us children crane and bob up and down like little birds in the nest. There've been letters from Anya ever since she was released from prison, but nothing like this.

"On the feast day of the Virgin of Unexpected Joy," Tatiana points out. She crosses herself and kisses the gold ring Anya gave her the day she was arrested. Mama's smile reaches all the way across the table at that. I wish I could remember feast dates like my sister.

Papa sets the box in front of Mama, and we lean in so close you could snap a picture and get every one of us in the frame, parcel and all. *Konechno*, it's been inspected already, but Commissar Pankratov was kind enough to wrap it all back up again so we can pretend to open it ourselves.

Mama unties the dirty string, and Aleksei stuffs it into his pocket. Olga reaches out to trace Anya's handwriting on the brown paper wrapping.

"Stop petting the thing and open it up," Anastasia begs.

Mama lifts out a silk bed jacket, blue like Papa's eyes. My sisters and I all coo, "Oooh!" and stroke the quilted sleeves. Aleksei wrinkles up his nose, wriggles his hand into the box, and comes up with a plump packet of fruit pastilles.

"Candy!"

All of us, even Papa, put out our hands for a piece. Mine is like summer on my tongue. We stand there grinning for a minute as we suck. Last of all, Mama brings up a darling little pink perfume bottle, all cushioned in tissue paper. She pulls the stopper out, takes a sniff, and her eyes puddle with tears.

"Sunny?" Papa asks. She shakes her head and hands him the bottle. One by one, we all smell it and go quiet, even Anastasia and Aleksei. It's Anya's perfume. The scent makes me feel like a ghost has floated into the room—a sweet fat ghost I'd like to wrap my arms around and squeeze like a giant warm dinner roll.

"Don't smell it too much," Olga says. "We'll wear it out."

"Wear it out?" Anastasia scoffs. "We haven't touched a drop."

"If we sniff at it all the time, soon it won't remind us of Anya anymore. Before long, it'll only make us think of sitting around a tea table in this house."

Mama takes the bottle from under Anastasia's nose and corks it. "We'll save it until Christmas, darlings. From then on, only when we're lonely. We won't waste the Lord's kindnesses."

After that, Christmas puts us in a frenzy. How are we supposed to give presents if no one is allowed in or out to buy and deliver them? Even if Commissar Pankratov would let us visit the stores in town, I wouldn't have the first notion where to go or what anything costs. Back home, merchants from the city used to bring displays of gifts right to the palace for us to choose from.

"We still must have gifts for all our people," Mama insists. "If we cannot buy anything, I'll knit and paint their gifts. Every last one of them deserves a token of their loyalty and service, so far from home." She lifts an eyebrow at us. "And you must keep it secret, my treasures. Christmas is so much nicer with secrets, don't you think?"

It's true, but it's awfully hard to keep our secrets from bumping into one another in this house, especially with the way we bunch together in the evenings to keep the chill and boredom from creeping too close. We all have our orders to keep different members of the household distracted while Mama works on their presents. Olga and Tatiana take turns sleeping late and chattering with Nyuta to slow her down at stripping our beds and putting on fresh sheets every morning. Meanwhile Anastasia and Aleksei and I are supposed to take extra long with our lessons so Mama can knit a little bit every day on the waistcoats for Mr. Gibbes and Monsieur Gilliard.

For once, we argue over who gets to stay inside with

Mama during our daily walks in the yard. It's just about the only time we can snatch to work on our gifts for one another. Poor Tatiana hardly gets five minutes in a row to work on her present for Mama, a blank exercise book to use as a journal, with a purple cover sewn over it and a little swastika, Mama's lucky symbol, embroidered on the corner. I stroke the smooth yellow threads when she's finished the first arm of the bent cross.

"It'll be perfect," I tell her, "just like always. Like you worked on it for hours at a stretch instead of three stitches at a time."

Tatiana turns pink around the edges. "*Spasibo*, Mashka."

Any time she thinks no one's paying attention, Olga spends ages paging through the little book of Nekrasov's poems Monsieur Gilliard lent her. "I bet she's copying out bits of verse for each of us," I tell Anastasia.

"I hope mine's not too brainy." She giggles. "I don't want to *think* on Christmas."

"Oh, Nastya." We may get terrifically bored here, but nothing will make Anastasia any less lazy. She won't shirk Christmas, though. At least I hope not! The idea of thinking up presents for everyone all by myself makes me cringe. "What are we going to give for gifts?"

"Bookmarks for the Big Pair," she says as if we've arranged all this weeks ago. "Like the ones Mama's painting for the ladies. Those two always read such fat books."

The little worries clutching at my shoulders fizz away. "Maybe with prayers copied out on them? I think Olga and Tatiana would like that."

"All right, but I'll fill in the prayers," she decides. "My handwriting's neater than yours. You paint flowers better than I do, anyway. What about for Mama? We can't copycat what she's giving away—she'll be sick of the sight of book-marks by Christmas Eve."

I think of Anya's sweet little parcel and Mama's favorite pillow stuffed with rose leaves, and an idea comes at me like a breath of air. "We could make her a set of sachets and scent them with our perfume, one for each of us! Tea roses for Olga, jasmine for Tatiana . . ."

"We'll maybe have to sneak it. The Big Pair doesn't have much perfume left."

"I'll take care of that," I promise her. "They'll give up a few drops for Mama. What about Papa and Aleksei?"

That leaves us with our chins in our hands for ages.

"Nastya," I ask, perking up, "you're the best sneak of all of us, aren't you?"

"*Konechno.* Why?"

"Aleksei's lead soldiers have gotten so dull and chipped. What if we snitched them a few at a time and brightened up their uniforms with our paints?"

"I bet if we asked Papa or Monsieur Gilliard to teach Aleksei a new card game or something to distract him, it might work."

For Papa, we decide to make a little photo album. All five of us work together on it. I develop pictures of my sisters and Aleksei on the swing, of Papa chopping wood with Mon-sieur Gilliard, of Olga and Anastasia in the yard, and the six of us perched up on the roof of the greenhouse. There's even one of Papa and Aleksei feeding the flock of turkeys. It's funny to think we've been here long enough that these photos bring back memories.

Olga pastes them all onto squares of cardboard without smearing a drop of glue, and Anastasia decorates the borders with her paints. After Tatiana sews all the pages together, Aleksei draws a double-headed eagle for the cover.

"It's not as good as the crest on our big leather albums," Aleksei worries.

"He'll love it," I promise.

We have the most heavenly tree in Mama's drawing room. Pankratov says it's called a balsam fir, and when it isn't too cold, the scent reaches all the way into our bedroom at the corner of the house. By the time we get it all decorated with candles and snowflakes, it looks bright and jolly as a snowman.

On Christmas Eve we walk into the ballroom, and there's a priest for vespers! Monsieur Gilliard is there, and Mr. Gibbes, doctors Botkin and Derevenko, Nyuta, Colonel Kobylinsky, Trupp, Chef Kharitonov with his black hair slicked back, and Sednev and his nephew Leonka from the kitchen. I wish the Botkin children, Gleb and Tanya, and Isa Buxhoeveden could be here too, but it's still almost like a party. It doesn't feel like home, but it still feels like Christmas, and it gives me the queerest feeling, like I want to dance and cry all at once. Mama lets us children pass out the gifts just as we always do, making me wish I could give something to my window-friend Natalya and her boys.

Anastasia and I both have new wooden pencil boxes from the Big Pair, all decorated with flower patterns burnt into the lids, and a verse of Nekrasov tucked inside. On mine, Olga changed the first line and wrote in my name instead:

"Dear Mashka, our love and our youth will prevail,
Don't cry," I implored as I kissed her.
"Our destinies link us together from now,
To both of us Fate was deceiving,
The tides which your happiness wrecked in their flow
Have swept away mine past retrieving.
We'll walk hand in hand through this desert, my dear,
As once through green fields we went straying,
Our crosses we'll lift and courageously bear,
Each strength to the other conveying."

"It's perfect," I tell them, but I look at Olga when I say it. Her smile is so soft, I think she knows I mean the poem most of all.

"Papa helped me build the boxes," Tatiana explains, "and Olga did everything else while I had lessons."

"In Papa's study," Olga adds, "so his cigarettes covered the smell of the wood scorching. And when did the two of you find time to paint?"

Anastasia claps her hands and bounces on her toes like one of the dogs begging for a scrap. "While you thought *we* were having lessons! Mr. Gibbes and Monsieur Gilliard let us dodge a little every day."

"Why, they were playing double agents." Tatiana laughs.

"Monsieur Gilliard let me off early to help Olga with your presents."

The Big Pair scurry off to tease our tutors for fooling all four of us, but Anastasia holds me back. "Here," she says, shoving a flat package tied up with gold embroidery floss at me. "Open it." Anyone else might think she was angry if they heard her barking orders this way, but I know my Nastya better than that, and pull carefully at the tissue.

Inside the wrapping I find a watercolor painting of a baby pasted in a cardboard frame. The little cherub has a tuft of blond hair, a round forehead almost as broad as Olga's, and teardrop-shaped eyes like Tatiana's set wide apart in his flat face.

"What a darling picture!"

"It's Tikhon," Anastasia says, more to my knees than my face. "Or anyway, what I think Auntie's baby might look like."

My breath blooms up from my chest. "Oh, Nastya—" But I can't say a single thing more. Instead I clamp my sister in a hug that leaves her toes sweeping the floor until we're both gasping.

I wipe at my eyes, careful not to smudge Tikhon's portrait. "I can't give you your present now," I tell her, almost wailing like a baby myself. "It's just too stupid."

"Hand it over."

It's my turn to look at the floor as I take the tissue-wrapped packet out of my pocket. "It's only my share of the pastilles from Anya's package, and a few extras I begged from the others."

"You saved them all for me?" I nod, and she grins. "That's like Olga giving away every last one of her books!" Happiness warms me to my toes, and we don't let go of each other's hands until we have to cross ourselves at prayers.

Christmas morning, we're allowed to go to church in the town! It's been so long—since we took Holy Communion in October. Guards line both sides of the path through the public garden to the church. Behind them, the local people bow and doff their caps. Some even kneel in the snow. Clouds of their breath slip between the soldiers' shoulders, like hands reaching out to greet us. Papa and Mama and the Big Pair are so happy, their faces shine like icons of the baby Jesus, and I'm lighthearted as a swallow, being outside that dull fence with new faces clustered all around me. I don't care how old I am, I'd like to skip and run all the way to the church. I don't dare peek at Anastasia and Aleksei, though. One look at my face and they'd whoop and run right along with me, and then we'd be in a vat of trouble.

Inside, the church is practically empty except for some soldiers who follow us in. Our private chapel at home was always empty too, but now that I've seen all those people outside, I wonder why they can't come in to worship with us. It's terribly cold out, and it's Christmas.

As soon as the priest and deacon begin the Great Litany, I forget about the world outside. Everything about *Obednya* in a church is better than our ballroom *Obednitsa* and prayer services back at the governor's house. Here the light is gentle and golden, and I can smell the wax and smoke of hundreds of candles, the incense in the censers and the rose oil in the icon lamps. Our voices ring off the stone walls and domed ceiling just the way they're supposed to. It sounds so much holier this way. Everything, the words and the songs and the prayers, are just like they've been since I was a little girl. I wish I could drink the air right out of this place, or bottle it up and carry it back with us. Church always feels like home, more than any other place.

When the service ends and we file back across the square through the bright morning, everyone looks so awfully sober, I can't understand it. Even Olga, who usually leaves church as contented as if she's swallowed the sun, looks like something's burning her from the inside.

"What's wrong with everyone?" I whisper to Anastasia.

She squints at me. "Didn't you hear? The priest used our titles in the Liturgy. He sang the *mnogoletie* prayer for the long life of the House of Romanov and called Papa 'His Imperial Majesty' right in front of all those soldiers. The Second Regiment's going to throw a fit."

My stomach shrivels like a dried-out mushroom. I can't help feeling like maybe it was all my fault for daydreaming about how everything used to be. No wonder I didn't notice the mistake.

"The poor priest! He's been saying Liturgy the same way his whole life. Even on Christmas Day, with all of us standing right there in front of him, they can't excuse an honest slip?" Suddenly my head is so full of unchristian thoughts I can't look at the soldiers lining our path or swallow past the burn in my throat.

27

OLGA NIKOLAEVNA

January 1918
Tobolsk

"Citizen Romanov, you and your son will remove the epaulets from your uniforms immediately if you know what's good for you," Commissar Nikolsky announces. The glint in his eye matches the shine on his boots. He works his mouth as though he's savoring Papa's reaction.

Papa sets down his glass of tea. "Our epaulets? Why?"

My heart feels like it's beating sideways as Aleksei reaches up to finger the narrow colored strips on his own shoulders where Papa's initials are embroidered. What harm can there be in epaulets? Do they even mean anything, now that the army answers to Lenin?

"My apologies, Nikolai Alexandrovich," Pankratov adds, "but the men of the rifle detachment have voted one hundred to eighty-five in favor of the guards and officers removing imperial epaulets from their uniforms. We request that you and your suite do so as well to avoid provocation. It's for your own safety. We fear insults and attacks in the town."

Nikolsky stalks off, his face curled up as if this whiff of courtesy makes him ill.

"This is absurd," Papa says. "We aren't even allowed into town."

"My apologies," Pankratov says again, and excuses himself.

"Incomprehensible," Papa says, sipping his tea. "This little man thinks he can order us about?"

"Papa," Aleksei asks, "are we going to do it?"

Papa takes another swallow of his tea, considering. I don't breathe until he answers. "*Nyet, konechno*, son. Pankratov may be in charge of this house, but he is not an enlisted man, and I will not take such orders from a civilian."

Pride and anxiety storm hot and cold inside me. In ten months under arrest we have never defied our captors.

"Such childishness," Mama sputters over her sewing. All the others have gone outside for their afternoon walk. I wish I were with them—I'd trade my whole poetry notebook for one of Papa's cigarettes right now. "It's all that horrid Nikolsky's doing, filling the men's heads with Bolshevik nonsense. They're testing us. Your papa won't stand for this kind of disrespect."

Her words needle at me, drawing questions through my mind like an itchy woolen thread. Part of me wants to laugh at myself for worrying so over shoulder boards, but I know what epaulets mean to Papa. One look at the shoulders of his uniform and anyone can see he's honorary colonel-in-chief of the Fourth Guards Rifle Regiment, and was adjutant to tsars Alexander II and Alexander III. His epaulets are like no one else's in all of Russia, and he wears them buttoned on every military shirt and coat he owns. They're as much a part of my papa as his beard and cigarettes.

"Maybe Lenin's government will issue new epaulets," I offer. As soon as I say it, I know it's a stupid idea. Papa would never wear Bolshevik insignia, and Lenin certainly won't commission a set of epaulets for the ex-tsar. It doesn't matter, though—Mama hasn't even heard me.

"Russia needs authority, not equality. How do they expect to lead a country if every soldier is on equal footing?" She sighs, making it sound as if expelling air is an irksome chore. "It's such a trial, being the mother of an undisciplined country. They have no sense of perspective. Isa Buxhoeveden arrived at the Kornilov house over a week ago, and they still refuse to let her in. What threat is a lady's maid, I'd like to know? Everything is the same to them."

My fingers knot around my own mending. That's exactly what I'm afraid of, that something as small as strips of cardboard will set them off. God help us if the soldiers are as agitated as I am—my nerves have flared so, I could light a candle from my own fingertips. As I watch Mama serenely darning Papa's socks, I wish for a moment that I had the same unchallenging faith that comforts her, and Tatiana, too. Leaving me with Mama on a day like this is like trying to dowse a grease fire with water.

"But, Mama, what will they do if Papa and Aleksei don't take off their epaulets?"

Her answer bounces back so quickly, I'm sure the possibilities haven't pricked her consciousness. "Do? Their duty is to protect us, darling. And if they don't, God will."

Even as I cross myself, I'm thinking that may have been true before, especially back in Petrograd, but it isn't so now. Something has shifted since Lenin seized power, and I don't have the energy anymore to be angry with Mama for not seeing it.

"Papa, why do they do such things to us?"

"The Lord gives us our crosses to bear, Olga. It is not our place to question His will. *Sudba*."

Konechno. It's what I knew he would say, and there's a measure of comfort in that. Papa at least doesn't dismiss the danger—*sudba* is about submitting to fate, not ignoring it. "If this is God's cross to bear, why do you still wear your epaulets?" It's the closest I can come to asking him why he's willing to risk the soldiers' anger. He's been meek as a lamb in every other way.

"Being born on the feast day of St. Job the Sufferer means I must bear the insult, but for dignity's sake I will not bow to their demands. Aleksei wears my initials on his epaulets, as I wear my father's and grandfather's. The Bolsheviks have no right to erase our heritage."

Papa's convictions douse me with humility, but my worries still moil like the steam rising from my tea. "It's nothing but spite, evil spite." I run my finger round and round the hot rim of my glass. "I'd like to show them how it feels to be pried from their homes and subjected to these petty insults."

Papa reaches across his desk to still my hand. "The evil in the world now will be stronger still before this is all over, my Olga," he says. "But remember, it is not evil that conquers evil, but love."

He's lost so much already, and borne it with the patience of Job. Weaker men would have crumbled. I don't have the heart to ask him to give up one more thing, no matter how small. *Tak i byt.*

"*Izvinite.* May I have a moment?" The sight of Colonel Kobylinsky wearing a suit and tie instead of his uniform pulls my stomach taut. What can it mean if the colonel would rather wear civilian clothes before Papa than wear his epaulets in front of the very men he commands? Without a cap, the colonel's streak of white hair stands out like a flag of surrender. His eyes skitter over Papa and Aleksei's epaulets, and he holds his hands so still at his sides I think he must be quaking inside.

"Your Majesty." Each word is a carefully mapped step. "Power is slipping out of my hands. They've taken away our epaulets. I can no longer be of any use to you. With your permission, I would like to leave. My nerves are completely shot. I can't take it anymore."

There must be more going on inside the guardhouse than debate about epaulets. The thought shrinks my skin like a coat of paint.

Papa puts his arm around the colonel's shoulders.

Suddenly I can barely swallow—I've never seen Papa embrace anyone outside our own family this way. "Evgeni Stepanovich," he says in his gentle way, "on my own behalf, and on behalf of my wife and children, I beg you to stay. You see how we're all forced to endure this. You, too, will have to endure."

Bozhe moi. I will never leave my family or my country, but what it would be like, even for an instant, to have to ponder the choice to stay or go? I'm not sure I envy the colonel, standing alone with seven pairs of eyes appealing to him. Our choice was so much easier.

Tears rise in Kobylinsky's eyes. He nods just as my own sight blurs.

After that, nothing but sawing and chopping wood in the garden calms my nerves. Inside the house my heart rushes like a stream of water, but driving the ax forces it to pump with vigor and purpose. As long as my muscles tingle with exertion, my mind rests.

Out in the pale sunshine, we climb to Papa's homemade platform on the greenhouse roof to sit with our backs to the warm boards and our feet dangling over the glass. It's almost like the way we used to lie in the haystacks at *Stavka*. But when the sun glints off the gold braid on Papa and Aleksei's epaulets, my fears slosh loose all over again. What must the soldiers and the people in the streets think of us, sitting up here like vain little eagles with our imperial plumage out for all to see?

"Gentlemen, please sit," Papa calls from the card table. "Your tea will take a chill. Do you prefer bezique or bridge this evening?"

We seven have settled in our usual spots for teatime, but Dr. Botkin and Monsieur Gilliard stand in the doorway of Mama's sitting room, looking as apprehensive as if they've been struck with stage fright.

"I had hoped, Your Majesty, that we might have a chat instead."

Papa lays aside the worn deck of cards. "As you wish, monsieur."

"May we speak frankly, Your Majesty?"

"Certainly. You are among friends."

The way the doctor and the tutor look frantically at each other, I have the feeling they've plotted out a script, yet forgotten to discuss who will take the first line. Silence stretches tight between them and Papa. When Monsieur and the doctor both clear their throats, it startles all nine of us so, we chuckle sheepishly together.

"Sire," Dr. Botkin begins with a smile and a nervous pinch to his spectacles, "Colonel Kobylinsky is losing his authority. As you know, Kerensky appointed him, and Kerensky has fled the country since Lenin came to power."

The doctor pauses, and Monsieur Gilliard takes his cue. "The colonel is an honorable man, but the guards know there's no government behind Kobylinsky anymore."

"Tobolsk itself remains loyal," Dr. Botkin assures us, "but the larger political climate is such that if the soldiers of the guard take it into their heads to protest, there will be no stopping them, Your Majesty."

Our tutor sneers, drawing up his goatee. "Perhaps on their own they would not protest, but with Commissar Nikolsky playing schoolmaster in the guardhouse with his Bolshevik tracts—"

"Protest what?" Papa asks.

Neither replies, but their eyes, like mine, trail to Papa's shoulders.

"The epaulets?"

The hurt on Papa's face wilts Monsieur Gilliard's mustache. "Yes, Your Majesty."

Papa reaches up to stroke his left shoulder, the way he usually smoothes his beard. "Then you agree with the soldiers' demands?"

Both men shake their heads. "No."

"*Nyet,*" Dr. Botkin repeats. "But in the interest of your safety, it seems wiser not to burden so many weak men with undue temptation."

The pressure in the room eases. I've always thought Dr. Botkin a deep well of profound ideas, and now he's found a way to make Papa the better man by giving in.

Papa considers all of us children, then turns to Mama. The air around me thickens to clay, waiting. Mama sighs down at her mending, then nods at last.

Papa reaches for the straps on his epaulets. "*Tak i byt.* We will not wear them in view of the soldiers."

I cross myself, knowing I cannot ask for more than this from my papa.

On Monday we begin building a snow mountain in the garden. Even some of the better guards help. Monsieur Gilliard
and Nagorny carry thirty buckets of water from the kitchen
to pour down the side of the mountain. It's so cold, the slope
steams like an upturned bowl of soup, and some of the buckets freeze halfway across the yard. By the time they're done,
the hill is tall enough that we can see over the fence when
we climb to the top.

Immediately the Little Pair begin scheming to see Isa
Buxhoeveden and Gleb and Tanya Botkin from the peak.
When I climb to the top, I gaze at the houses with their
chimneys ribboning smoke all across the town and wonder
what sort of people live inside them all. How many are good
loyal citizens, and how many have called my papa Bloody
Nikolashka behind his back?

Anastasia drives her finger into the side of my coat.
"Bzzzzzzz! Telegram for Citizen Olga Nikolaevna Romanova!" she says, and salutes. "Snow mountain complete.
Stop. Tobogganing to commence immediately. Stop. Brood-
ing on this hill will not be tolerated. Stop. Procure a sled or
vacate the premises. Stop." With a wicked grin, she lunges
as though she's about to push me down the hill. The look in
her eyes sparks me into action.

"Toboggan? I'll show you who knows a thing or two
about tobogganing, my little *shvybzik*." I grab her wrists,
swing her into a piggyback, and poise myself over the edge
like a skier with Anastasia draped over my shoulders.

"You wouldn't dare!" she squeals as she flails.

"Wouldn't I?" I flop onto my belly, and the two of us slip like a pair of eels down the icy slope. Tatiana's gasps and Maria's laughter trail behind us. At the bottom we roll apart and lie panting in the snow.

"I . . . may be . . . a *shvybzik*," Anastasia puffs, "but you're crazy." She scrambles to her knees and tugs at me until I sit up. "Let's do it again."

"Not without a real sled, we won't. I'm not that crazy."

"Oh, fine. Come on, you two!" Anastasia shouts up at our sisters.

"I will not," Tatiana says.

"Show her how it's done, Mashka!" Anastasia yells. We watch Maria mince back and forth across the top of the hill with Tatiana chiding her like a jaybird. "I don't know why she's thinking about it so hard," Anastasia says to me. "She's going to fall anyway."

On cue, Maria totters and sails down, landing at our feet with her arms and legs splayed like tent poles. Anastasia hauls Maria up by an elbow and brushes the snow from her coat. "Honestly, if you blush any harder you'll melt the snow. Now you, Governess! If you don't hurry up, the guards will come see what all the yelling is about!"

We screech and tease and clap until Tatiana gives in. She sits fussily in the snow, tucks her skirt around her boots, points her toes, and nudges herself down the slope. I hold out my hand and Tatiana rises as gracefully as though she's stepping out of a carriage.

"Perfectly proper," Anastasia says, rewarding her with a curtsy. "You should write a book in your spare time. *The*

Grand Duchess's Guide to Winter Amusements: How to Have Fun in the Snow Without Showing Your Petticoats."

"You are the most vulgar little thing," Tatiana proclaims, and out of nowhere splatters Anastasia point-blank with a snowball.

Maria and I split into gales of laughter. For a moment, Anastasia can only blink and tremble. Her eyes are like two blue ice-holes in her face full of snow. "Where did you get that snowball?" she whispers.

"I carried it down the hill in my lap."

"If you write that book," she tells Tatiana, "I'll be first in line to buy a copy."

For days we sled and tumble until we're stamped black and blue as postmarks. Joy skitters, barking, alongside us, while Jemmy and Ortipo yip from the mountain's base. Once, Anastasia manages to coax a chicken onto the sled with her, and the pair of them squawk their way down as if the butcher's waiting at the bottom of the hill. It's wonderful, being able to trample the tedium under screams and jostles. Even when I fall it's invigorating to be shaken by something real and solid instead of letting my worries jitter and jangle me from the inside out. I don't think I've breathed—really breathed—like this in months. It's as if I've thrown open a window inside my head and the crisp Siberian air is pouring in. The sky above me is so wide and blue it makes my eyes water. Maybe between this hill and Gleb's poems, I can keep myself from eroding any further.

28.

ANASTASIA NIKOLAEVNA

February—March 1918
Tobolsk

Just when things begin to seem decent again, Lenin's Bolshies muscle in and start bossing us around. First it's by telegram. Before we know it, our whole family is on soldiers' rations.

"No butter or coffee?" Maria asks.

"And only half a pound of sugar each," Papa adds.

"Neither one of us needs more butter," I tell Maria, crossing my arms over what's supposed to be my waist, "and we don't even drink coffee."

"No, but it smells like home," Maria says. "Don't you remember how the servants' cafeteria always had coffee brewing? I could smell it all through the corridors downstairs."

It's like Maria's popped a little pinhole right in my side. I *had* forgotten.

"They're also limiting our expenses to six hundred rubles a month, per person," Papa says. "We'll have to dismiss ten of our people."

"Nicky!" Mama cries. "After they've followed us all this way? Some of them have brought their families here."

"We simply can't afford them, Sunny."

While Mama laments and Papa consoles, Tatiana sits down and starts drawing up a list of all our people, and who they've brought with them. I keep out of it. She'll probably have everything figured out by the time Mama stops huffing about the unfairness of it all, so what's the use of sticking my nose in?

Next thing we know, the Fourth Regiment gets sent back home. All our best officers and guards, gone, just like that. Our whole family, even Mama, troops out to the snow mountain to wave good-bye as they march away. Inside, it's gloomier than ever just knowing we're stuck with the First and Second Regiments.

"I wish they didn't have to go," Maria sighs at the windowpane. I plop down beside her and drop my chin onto my fists.

"It's only fair," Olga says. "They have homes and families of their own too."

"Must be nice," I mutter.

"What do you mean?" Tatiana asks. Without even turning around I know she's bristling. "I thank God every day for keeping all of us safe and together. Aleksei is well and Mama has not needed her heart drops for weeks. What more would you ask for?"

I guess I'm too dreary to bother getting angry. But that doesn't keep me from being jealous that Tatiana can always make do with any little scrap of good. "Be grateful all you want, but wouldn't you rather be back at Tsarskoe, even if we were still under arrest? The Fourth Regiment gets to go back to their regular lives. We don't *have* regular lives anymore."

"I could live here forever if we could only go for a real walk," Maria says.

"You could be happy anywhere, sweetheart Mashka," Olga tells her, "and our pious Tatiana could always manage to at least be content. But Shvybs and I are different, aren't we?" She comes to stand beside me and holds out her hand. I take it, and look a long time out the window. Maria hardly waves when her window-family walks by.

"We can't go back home anymore, can we?" I ask.

"Where do you go when home isn't home anymore? We're refugees in our own country."

Tatiana sniffles behind us, and that makes me sadder than anything else so far. I let go of Olga's hand. She kisses me before she goes to Tatiana. When I look, Olga's draped herself around Tatiana, their heads leaning against each other like two pearls on a string.

"Hey! All of you, come here and look at this!" I yell. Along the corridor, heads pop out of the doorways. Mama's not the only one still in her dressing gown.

Olga gets there first. "What is it, Shvybs?"

Tatiana rushes down the hall, shushing me with every step. "Anastasia Nikolaevna, you know better than to shout like that! And what do you think you are doing in Papa's study before he has exercised?"

"Shut up a minute and look," I tell her, pointing down at the yard.

"Our snow mountain!" Maria wails.

Outside, soldiers with pickaxes hack at our tobogganing hill. Chunks of snow clutter the yard like cottage cheese. I could cry just watching them, and I'm not even ashamed of myself.

All Olga says is, "Oh," and then she sinks into the chair behind Papa's desk. She can't even watch.

"Those spiteful beasts!" Tatiana hisses. "What do they have against us having a little fun? Papa will see about this!"

"I'm sorry, my dears," Papa says when he comes in. "Your mama and I, we shouldn't have climbed your snow mountain to wave good-bye to the Fourth Regiment yesterday morning. Colonel Kobylinsky says the soldiers' committee protested."

"All those soldiers ever do is protest," I say, so angry I can't even shout. "Why don't they just tell us what they want instead of being so mean?"

I wish I wasn't an imperial highness or an ex–grand duchess. I'm sick of people doing things to me because of what I am. *Girl-in-white-dress. Short-one-with-fringe. Daughter-of-the-tsar. Child-of-the-ex-tyrant.* I want people to look and see *me*, Anastasia Nikolaevna Romanova, not the caboose on a train of grand duchesses. Someday, I promise myself, no one will be able to hear my name or look at my picture and suppose they know all about me. Someday I will do something bigger than what I am.

"That's what you meant, isn't it?" I ask Olga later. "About that poem Monsieur Gilliard read to us about the revolutionaries' wives. We don't look at the Bolsheviks any more fairly than they look at us, do we?"

She nods. "How can we expect them to see beyond our titles if we won't look beyond their politics? Underneath we're all Russians, but we refuse to admit it."

This kind of talk makes my head hurt, even if I'm the one who brought it up. "You think they're good people?"

"Not all of them. But I think some of them have good intentions. For Russia, at least."

Another one of Olga's half answers. For all the times she lets her opinions run away with her, if there's something she doesn't want us to know, we'd need a whole regiment to pry it out of her. "Does it make you feel any better, seeing so many sides of everything?"

"No. Not when I'm the only one. I'd rather know nothing than too much."

My stomach wrinkles. There she goes again.

Without the snow mountain our boredom grows thick as the frost, until one night Mr. Gibbes announces, "Ladies and gentlemen, I propose we introduce a bit of drama into our Sunday evenings." He's got whole booklets of little farces in English, Russian, and French, and once we've agreed to take turns acting, he doles out the parts every week like Mama used to pick out our dresses: This-one's-for-you-and-no-buts.

From January all the way into March we rehearse through

the frigid evenings until we're ready to perform on Sunday. Mostly it's us children, but Mr. Gibbes takes plenty of parts for himself, and acts as stage manager. Even Mama helps out, drawing up official programs with all our names and roles.

The plays are funny enough all by themselves, but the way Mr. Gibbes casts them makes us snort and quiver with laughter. First, Tatiana gets the part of a fussy young wife, pouting over the household account books. It's too perfect. Next, Olga and Papa do one from Chekhov, with a dusty old widow and this boorish fellow who comes to collect on a debt. By the end they've fallen in love and have to fake the most revolting kiss.

But Mashka and I have the best play of all, about a husband and wife packing up for a trip. My very first line is "Damn!" and I get to wear Mr. Gibbes's dressing gown and bellow through the whole thing while Mashka does what she does best, playing a cheerful little wifey who finally gets fed up and bawls me out: "You're an idiot! Do you hear? A blithering, blustering idiot! You came home tipsy last night and have bullied me all day, and I'm going to kick." She's got to practice for ages until she can do it without giggling.

I've got the finale, though. After I've strutted around for ten solid minutes complaining about how my silly wife takes much too long to pack and dress, and the porter (Aleksei) has carried our trunk away to the cab, Maria says, "Come on, dear, quick—are you ready?"

"Yes dear, quite ready," I tell her, putting a silk hat on.

"You can't go like that—take off your dressing gown."

I grab my lapels and stop dead. "Mary, dear, we can't go."

"Yes, we can—come on, hurry up!"

"We *cannot* go!"

"Cannot go? Why?"

"Because because—"

"Because what?"

I turn my back, open my dressing gown as if I'm about to strip, and announce in my best husband-voice, "Because I've packed up my trousers!"

Silence, then laughter blasts from behind me. For a second I stand there, blinking at the wall, then I spin around and the draft hits me. It seems like something only Mashka could manage, but somehow I've pulled Mr. Gibbes's dressing gown all the way up to my waist in back. Everybody—Papa, Mama, Dr. Botkin, and the tutors and all our people—is howling at the sight of my legs and backside, jammed into Papa's suit of woolen Jaeger underwear. Even Mama has to fan herself with her hands to batten down her chortles. I don't think I've seen her laugh like that in my whole life.

Of course, they're merciless after that. For days afterward, my sisters chant, "Encore!" and "Brava!" when I dress in the morning and undress at night. My backside is all anyone can talk about, until news of the Treaty of Brest-Litovsk hits.

Leave it to nasty old Cousin Willi, the German kaiser, to make peace with the Bolsheviks! After that, the grown-ups go on about treason and insult and disgrace for hours at a time. All my sisters and I can do is mope around our icehouse of a bedroom if we don't want to hear it.

"I've never seen Papa look so low," I say, "even after the abdication. I thought his beard might drop right into his soup at lunch."

Olga paces the floor with her fists clamped under her arms. "He abdicated to keep the army from splintering and falling to the Germans. A separate peace is like spitting in Papa's face after all these years of war."

"Papa is right," Tatiana adds. "This is suicide for Russia. How can the kaiser even speak to those Bolshie traitors?"

"Do you really think the treaty says the Bolsheviks have to transfer us safely to Germany?" Maria asks. "Imagine seeing Auntie Irene and Uncle Ernie and all the cousins again!"

"Don't believe everything you read in the papers, Mashka," Olga answers.

"What difference does it make?" I ask. "Didn't you hear what Mama said? After what they've done to Papa, she'd rather die in Russia than be saved by the Germans." I flip over in my cot and look across the room at Olga and Tatiana. "Which would you rather do?"

"Die in Russia," the Big Pair says together, without even looking up. Mashka's saucers go wide. Olga and Tatiana really mean it. They didn't have to *think* about it. I'd rather not die anywhere at all, thank you very much.

"Girlies, come look!"

Mama shouting? That brings us all running. My sisters crowd the windows in her drawing room. Outside, troika bells jingle and horses' hooves slop in the snow. "It's a detachment of Red Guards," Olga says as I drag Mama's footstool over to stand on. "Probably a hundred men."

"Bolshies?" I practically climb over my sisters' shoulders. "Let me see." No epaulets, of course, but except for that I can't even tell they're Reds. "Poo. I thought they'd at least have beards, or dress in red uniforms or something. They look like plain old soldiers."

"That's because they're good Russian men," Mama says. "Papa and I have heard there are sympathetic officers from Omsk enlisted in this detachment. Wait and see. God is looking out for us."

If this is God's idea, He must know something we don't about the Reds, because soon more jostle into town through Tyumen, then another heap turns up from Ekaterinburg. These actually look how I think Bolshies should look— scruffy ruffians who loiter in the street outside our fence and badger our guards and the men from Omsk. Guns stick out like porcupine quills all over them.

After our lessons, Maria and I pile on sweaters and shawls and perch in the frosty sills of the corner ballroom windows to watch. All we hear about are committees and demands and orders from Moscow.

"I don't know how you two can look at that all day long," Olga says from the altar when she comes in to pray. "Dr. Botkin says the entire town is nervous."

I'm not going to tell her that Mashka's lady in the blue coat has only been by twice this week. She turned those little boys right around the second she saw the Bolshies, and the next time she came alone.

Maria surprises me. "We're probably the safest people

in Tobolsk, way up here," she says. "There's a fence and two whole regiments of guards between us and them."

Ha! Smart Mashka. *Konechno,* I put in. "The First and Second Regiments aren't the politest, but they've never let anyone *else* bother us. Besides, it's better than sitting in the corridor all day wondering what's happening."

It's fun while it lasts, but before we know it, Mama's Omsk detachment runs the other bandits out of town, fifteen troikas full, jangling all the way while the Omsk men whoop behind them! It's like watching one of Aleksei's adventure films right outside our windows. Even Papa comes to look.

It doesn't matter, though. Just when we've had time to get bored again, more Reds pour in from Omsk, right behind the spring thaw, then another two hundred back from Ekaterinburg, and the whole thing starts all over again.

Olga won't even come out on the balcony with us if there are soldiers in the street. She'll only hover by the door to take the air, looking like a rubber band about to snap.

"Is it good or bad for us if the Reds are arguing with each other?" I ask her.

"More fighting can't be good, especially if it's Bolsheviks."

I wrinkle my nose. After all her talk about the Bolshies maybe being halfway decent?

The Ekaterinburg Reds have demanded to be allowed to inspect the house, but Colonel Kobylinsky and our soldiers refuse to let their commissary in.

"If the situation is not resolved, we may have to transfer you to the archbishop's house on the hill," Kobylinsky informs us. "And I must request that you not sit on the balcony for at least the next three days." I deserve an I-told-you-so from Olga, but she's too busy crossing herself to be smug.

That night the Omsk guards join up with our men to make a double set of sentries and patrols to keep watch over the house. I don't expect to sleep any more than they do, but I must have dozed off, because a sound by our bedroom door pops my eyes wide open in the dark. At first I think I dreamed it up, then there's the soft flop of a boot falling over, and Olga swears under her breath. I peek over the edge of my cot in time to see her scoop something small and glinty from the floor and slip it under her pillow. For a long time, the edges of her breaths are sharp like mine, like we both have to remind ourselves to let each lungful go. If I were one of the dogs, I'd crawl in under the covers right beside her.

"It's safe to go to sleep now, Shvybs," she whispers. "Don't worry."

Since it's Olga's voice, I know this isn't jabber meant to humor me. It's like a vow. And just like that, I do exactly as she says.

"Girlies," Mama says the next day, "I'm going to need your help with some sewing." She won't say another word until we're inside her drawing room with the doors shut tight. Then she tells us, "Colonel Kobylinsky has let the Red commissary from Omsk inside. Papa saw him inspecting the guards' quarters this morning." A spurt of alarm zings from my gut right up the back of my neck. Red sentries on the street are one thing, but inside the fence? "It's time to hide our jewelry, darlings," Mama goes on. "I won't have those Bolsheviks getting their hands on our fortune."

My thoughts snap like popping corn inside my head. First they were "good Russian men," and now they're "*those* Bolsheviks"?

"We must keep some jewelry on, or the soldiers will be suspicious." Mama pulls out a little satchel and pours a stream of diamonds onto the table. They sparkle like the broken chunks of our snow mountain. "The guards don't know about our loose gems. I want all of them hidden in our clothes, to keep them out of sight and make sure we are all protected."

I don't see how walking around with diamonds in our hems will protect us, but at least it's another way to keep busy. All day long, we sew jewels into all sorts of clothes and pillows. We pull apart cloth buttons, throw away the hard little knobs inside, and replace them with pearls and precious stones wrapped in cotton wadding. Sashes and hatbands get stuffed like roast chickens. Every time I think we're done, Mama comes up with a new stash. Some of the pearls are big as cherries, which makes them a hateful bother to hide inside anything without making us look like walking sacks of marbles.

"We must be ready to flee if the White Army occupies Tobolsk," Mama says if I even sigh at my sewing.

"Reds and Whites," Maria half sings. "It's just like Alice in *Through the Looking Glass*. Ouch!" She sucks at her finger and pouts at the bent needle in her lap. I shake my head.

Maria can't manage anything sharper than a spoon. That's the third needle she's ruined, jabbing it into a diamond. Without a word, Tatiana takes over Maria's hemming and gives her a pile of buttons to pull apart instead.

"It isn't a game of chess, or a storybook," Olga says. "It's a civil war." Mama frowns, but since when does that stop Olga? "And they're not all imperial knights on white horses. I've never heard of such a mix—monarchists, Constitutional Democrats, republicans—they wouldn't have a thing to say to one another under ordinary circumstances. Half of them probably wouldn't even speak to us. The only thing the Whites have in common is hating the Bolsheviks."

"That's good enough for me," I pipe up, and Olga buttons her lip. I'm glad. Listening to her is like drinking a glass of vinegar sometimes.

"The Whites are on their way," Mama insists, "and the people of Tobolsk are sympathetic. Look at all the food and gifts they've brought us. We must be ready when they come to our rescue."

As if to prove Mama right, a merchant from town brings Aleksei a wooden sledge and boat. He's awfully pleased with them. "Fat lot of good they'll do you, without our snow mountain or a canal to play in," I tell him.

"You just watch and see," he says.

So while I'm stuck wrapping up jewels like cotton-covered bonbons, he and Kolya Derevenko spend the whole day careening down the stairs on their makeshift sleds, shrieking and shouting like hoodlums.

Aleksei shouts so much, he coughs all night. Serves him right. For the next two days after that, he plays outside with Kolya, swinging and practicing at archery and breaking up pools of ice for the ducks in the yard. I don't know why the soldiers don't have fits about his arrows and ax. Meanwhile, I stitch and sew and whisper in Mama's drawing room. We've got more diamonds than guards, and *that's* saying something around here lately.

And then, *blam!* Like a smack in the face, Aleksei is sick again.

29

TATIANA NIKOLAEVNA

April 1918
Tobolsk

T his is his worst attack since Spala," I whisper to Olga
in our doorway as Dr. Derevenko examines Aleksei.
"Cramps every half hour, and the poor darling was sick four
times in the night. The pain is so bad, neither of them slept
more than twenty minutes. Mama will make herself ill if she
keeps on this way, God help her." Even Joy will not leave our
brother's side, forcing Nagorny to carry him down to "do the
governor" in the garden twice a day.

"Why does everything happen all at once?" Olga presses
at her temples. "I don't know how you can stand it. Aleksei crying up here, the workmen installing partitions downstairs, and those Bolsheviks swarming all over the streets.
It won't be long before the Reds have their way and search
the house. If the extraordinary commissar everyone's talking about shows up from Moscow, I don't see how Colonel

Kobylinsky will be able to refuse. I hope Mama has the rest of the jewels hidden well enough."

"'Medicines,'" I correct her with my eyebrows raised. "You heard what Mama said. As long as Aleksei is ill, we can talk about 'arranging medicines' and no one will be suspicious."

"That's the only good thing to come out of all this. We're lucky the doctors are still allowed in and out. It's going to be crowded as a bird's nest downstairs with all our people and their maids moving in."

"Hush a minute. I want to see Dr. Derevenko's face when he comes out of Aleksei's bedroom." Perhaps he notices the two of us peeking round the door jamb. He keeps his back to us as he speaks to Mama in the corridor, but even with his thick beard muffling his words I see Mama cross herself, and that is all I need to know.

"What will she do without *Otets* Grigori?" Olga whispers.

I shake my head. It hardly bears thinking about. "We have to do the best we can without him, for both Mama and Aleksei."

There is nothing I can do about the Bolsheviks, nor the order from Moscow for all our people but the doctors to move out of the Kornilov house and submit to house arrest with us. What I can do is relieve Mama and Nagorny at Aleksei's bedside. I can hold his hand when he cries, and the basin when he retches.

In spite of what Olga must think, doing these things does not empty my mind of the troubles outside Aleksei's bedroom, especially the talk we have all heard about this so-called extraordinary commissar, a man named Yakovlev who is expected to arrive in town with orders from Moscow. Rumor has it he can have anyone who disobeys him executed without trial. *Bozhe moi*, not even Papa could do that! But I must not burn energy Aleksei and Mama need today on worrying over tomorrow. There is nothing I can do about Yakovlev until he arrives.

"I thought Baby would like it if I read to him," Olga says, a blanket and a book clutched in her arms. She wears a sweater fastened to the neck over her black and gray tricot blouse, the one with the amethysts hidden in the buttons, and her face tightens when she tries to smile at Aleksei.

I go to the door and touch her hand. Cold, though her face is flushed. "*Dushka*, are you all right?"

"Colonel Kobylinsky has let four men inside to inspect the house," she whispers. "I don't think they'll come in here. So if you don't mind company . . . ?"

"*Konechno*, come in. The pains stopped last night, *slava Bogu*, but he has not slept. Maybe reading will relax him." I watch her perch on a chair beside Aleksei's cot and tuck the blanket tightly round her legs, down to the toes of her tall leather boots.

"My feet won't get warm today," she says when she catches me looking at them. Our jewels are hidden in our buttons and sashes, not our shoes, but the way Olga's eyes leap to the door and back makes me think she is covering up more than her boots. When Joy crawls out from under

Aleksei's cot to lay his head in her lap, I'm certain something is wrong.

"The medicines are all in order," I reassure her. She nods, but not one centimeter of her relaxes until Papa comes in to tell us the men have gone.

"Are the men satisfied now?" Olga asks, her fingers combing nervously through Joy's ears.

"I certainly hope so. Mama said no one bothered the medicines, but they've confiscated the dagger from my Cossack uniform."

Aleksei's face darkens. Olga's goes white. "Your dagger," Aleksei mourns. "Why?"

Papa pats Aleksei's hand, but he looks at Olga when he answers. "To calm the riflemen, the colonel says. They aren't keen on the idea of us keeping weapons."

My voice flashes out before my thoughts. "How absurd! They call themselves soldiers, yet they cannot tell the difference between a common weapon and a ceremonial dagger?" One look at Olga and Aleksei and I regain myself. Carrying on this way is no help to anyone, least of all my delicate brother and sister.

Within the week the extraordinary commissar himself arrives, taking tea with our parents that same evening. "Polite," Mama says afterward, "and he spoke to Monsieur Gilliard in French. Tomorrow when he returns I'll make arrangements for walking to church during Passion Week." She sounds satisfied with this Yakovlev, but that night, instead of their usual card game, Mama and Papa begin feeding their latest letters from

Anya and our family into the tile stoves in Mama's drawing room. Without a word, my sisters and I fetch our bundles of letters and do the same. Maria and Anastasia even burn their diaries.

As we suspected, Yakovlev arrives to inspect the house early the next morning. So early, in fact, that Mama is not ready to receive him and shuts herself into her room with Olga. The Little Pair and I join Papa in the corridor to greet the extraordinary commissar, just as we did for Commissar Pankratov's arrival in September. I plant my feet and hold my chin perfectly parallel to the floor when I see the three men with him. I will not face Reds looking anything less than imperial, no matter how shabby my clothes have become.

"You remember Commissar Yakovlev," Colonel Kobylinsky says to Papa, "and these are his comrades Rodionov, Avdeev, and Khokhryakov."

When he smiles, Yakovlev's bare cheeks gleam with embarrassment. His hair is as black as Chef Kharitonov's. Although they are not large, his ears seem to flare out at the bottom. Now and then, he fiddles with the lobes as if he wants to tuck them back like a stray lock of hair. Yakovlev speaks as if he and Papa have not met before.

"Are you satisfied with your guard and accommodations?" he asks. "Do you have any complaints? I understand your son is ill. May I be permitted to look in on him?" He reminds me of Kerensky, always moving and rushing from one thing to the next, but this man seems more deliberate. "It is extremely important that I see him," Yakovlev insists.

Papa turns to me. Aside from Mama, I have spent more

time at Aleksei's bedside than anyone during this crisis. In
the last week the hemorrhage has eased, but he is still bedridden, weak from blood loss and crippled by the pressure
the hematoma puts on his hip. For now, our Sunbeam can
do nothing but wait for his body to reabsorb all the blood
accumulated in the joint. None of this seems reason enough
to deny the commissar's request, though. As long as Aleksei
remains quiet, he is in no danger. I nod, once.

"All right, but only you alone," Papa agrees. Yakovlev fairly runs down the hall to our brother's room, leaving
Maria, Anastasia, and me awkwardly in front of Kobylinsky
and the three other Bolshies. After a few moments, Yakovlev
reappears at the end of the corridor and hurries in and out of
each room in turn.

"He looks like a cuckoo bird, poking his head in and
out," Anastasia snuffles. A snap of my fingers behind my
skirt hushes her just in time.

"Thank you for your cooperation," Yakovlev tells us. "My
apologies for the interruption."

"The empress would like to speak to Commissar Yakovlev about attending Easter services in town," I remind Papa.

"Very well. I will return the day after tomorrow." Yakovlev adds after a pause, "To make the necessary arrangements.
What time will be most convenient?"

"After luncheon," I tell Papa. "The empress will be ready
then."

"Are you able to come after luncheon?" Papa asks.

"Konechno." Yakovlev pulls out a small datebook to make
a note. "Thank you again for your cooperation. Do you have

much luggage?" he asks, stuffing the booklet back into his shirt pocket. Papa shakes his head absently, but Yakovlev's parting question ruffles my brow. The two sides of this conversation seem not to match, as if he and Papa are passing two different threads through the same needle.

Before Mama has a chance to say the words "Passion Week," Yakovlev announces, "Nikolai Alexandrovich, I have been assigned by the Council of People's Commissars to remove you from Tobolsk. Departure is set for four o'clock tomorrow morning. Please be ready by that time."

Across from me, Mama cries out as if she has been slapped, but I cannot break loose from my own shock to go to her. Even Papa's mouth moves blankly before any words emerge. "And where am I being transferred?"

"I do not know myself. My orders will come when we are on the road. I should have liked to transport your whole family at once, but Aleksei Nikolaevich is obviously too ill to travel by carriage."

Papa looks at Mama and strokes his beard. "I will not go."

Mama's voice surges up. "What are you doing with him? You want to tear him away from his family. How can you? He has an ill son. He can't go, he must stay with us!"

The sound of Mama's frenzy pries me from my seat, but my voice still sits trapped in my throat, as if I have swallowed one of our cotton-wrapped jewels.

"If you persist in this refusal, I will have to use force," Yakovlev says, disregarding Mama's tone. I watch his eyes, and they neither shift nor narrow as he speaks. Despite what he is saying, his steady tone reassures me. "I am responsible for your safety with my own life. You may bring any of your family and people that you choose," he continues, gesturing round the room with both palms open. "The rest will follow by ship when the boy is well enough and the rivers have thawed. *Izvinite.*" He sneezes. "You have my word."

My sisters would call me silly, but that sudden sneeze lends me another morsel of reassurance. Sneezing in the middle of a conversation means someone is telling the truth.

Papa replies as though he has heard not one word. "I have an ill son! How can I be separated from my family? I can't go."

"The departure is scheduled for four a.m.," Yakovlev repeats. "Everyone who is going must be ready by that time."

"This is too cruel," Mama insists. Her voice is ragged with oncoming tears. I press my hand on her shoulder to steady both of us. "I don't believe that you'll do this."

Yakovlev leaves without a word of argument.

Papa storms to the window. "They want to get me to Moscow to sign that Treaty of Brest. I would sooner have my hand cut off than do that," he vows, slamming his fist into his open palm. Mama and I both jerk at the sound. Papa halts, looks a long time at us, and slowly unclenches his fingers. *"Sudba,"* he murmurs, and crosses himself. "The man gave his word," he tells Mama. "You may come with me or stay with Aleksei. The decision is yours, Alix."

Christ have mercy.

"Tatiana, run and fetch Monsieur Gilliard," Mama says.

I dash down the corridor to Aleksei's room, aware for the first time of the tears streaking my cheeks. By the time we return Mama is alone, pacing and wringing her hands.

"Madame?" Monsieur Gilliard says.

Mama cannot even pause to explain. "The commissary says that no harm will come to the tsar, and that if anyone wishes to accompany him there will be no objection. I can't let the tsar go alone. They want to separate him from his family as they did before."

She talks in quick little gasps, the way a dog pants, leaving no space for us to answer her. Every time a thought seizes her, her hands flutter and she turns on a new path across the carpet. Too large for the room to contain, her anxiety vibrates through my own body like a tuning fork.

"They're going to try to force his hand by making him anxious about his family. The tsar is necessary to them, they feel that he alone represents Russia. Together we shall be in a better position to resist them. I ought to be at his side in the time of trial. But Baby is still so ill—suppose some complication sets in? Oh, God, what ghastly torture!" She turns to us, and the look on her face makes me want to shut my eyes and fold my shoulders in like a shield over my heart. "For the first time in my life I don't know what I ought to do," she cries. "I've always felt inspired whenever I've had to make a decision, and now I can't think!"

I have never in my life seen Mama like this—not at Spala, not when *Otets* Grigori was killed, not even when Papa abdicated. Sometimes her duty has frightened her, but she has always known what she must do. I step into her path,

taking her by the hands. "Mama, you cannot go on torment-
ing yourself this way. If Papa has to go no matter what, then
something must be decided."

She blinks at me, suddenly still. "I'm going," she says.
"Without me there they'll force him to *do* something
again—that's exactly what they've done already. Monsieur,
please break the news to Aleksei. I must pack. Tatiana, tell
your sisters."

A wave crashes over me. Oh, my darling Mamochka,
how can I? But I do not ask. I go and do it.

"One of us must go along to console her," I tell them. "No
matter how set her mind is, she will be completely worried and miserable without Aleksei." My sisters look at me
through tears and handkerchiefs. They know as well as I do
that I am the best one of us at looking after Mama. But
what about Aleksei? Someone must take care of him. I consider my three sisters, think of them left here alone without
Mama, Papa, or me to watch over them, and my head swims.
God help us.

Olga will be no good for Mama. The melancholy pair
of them would only wallow and worry together. Anastasia
would be a cheerful distraction, but Mama needs more than
a *shvybzik*. Besides, Aleksei will be glad for Anastasia's company. That leaves Maria and me to choose from.

Unlike Mama's, my choice is painfully clear: We cannot
both leave Aleksei behind. These last days, I am the only one
Mama will allow to sit with him while she sleeps, and then
only for a few hours. I will have to trust Mama to Dr. Botkin

and Maria. Dear, sweet Mashka! How will we manage here without our fat little Bow-Wow?

"Mashka, *dorogaya*, you must go with Mama and Papa," I tell her as I smooth her hair from her face and straighten her collar. Behind me, Anastasia bites back a sob. My chest twists. I have no choice but to be the knife that splits the Little Pair in two.

"Alone?" Maria whispers, looking first at Anastasia and then all of us with her wide, wide eyes. I can see her heart in them.

I nod, take a deep breath, and pray God will make me brave for Maria's sake. "You are our good, cheerful, sturdy girl," I tell her, squeezing her hands with each word, "and Mama needs you."

"Not . . . not you, Tatya?"

My throat collapses, crushing what little I'd planned to say. I pull her into a bracing hug before she sees my chin quiver.

Like an angel of the Lord, Olga swoops in and saves me. "You are stronger than a Russian bear, sweetheart Mashka," Olga says as I retreat to Anastasia's side, "and more cheerful than Siberian sunshine. Remember what the princess in Nekrasov's poem said? 'Their lot by our presence we'll brighten / By mildness we'll soften their jailers, you'll see / By patience their burdens we'll lighten.' Not one of us can do that as well as you. You'll be better medicine for Mama than anything in Dr. Botkin's black bag."

With my hands on Anastasia's trembling shoulders, I beg God to help keep her from falling to pieces.

"What about all of you?" Maria asks.

"I'll nurse Aleksei," Olga says. "Tatiana will run the whole household, top to bottom, and Anastasia will cheer everyone up. When Aleksei is well, we'll be together again. Yakovlev gave his word."

"We will be fine," I tell her. I give Anastasia a nudge, and she nods along with me like a marionette. I wonder if they are all thinking what I am thinking: Yakovlev made no promises about our safety here in Tobolsk.

30

MARIA NIKOLAEVNA

April 1918
Tobolsk

All that dreadful night long, we seven sit up together in Aleksei's room. Anastasia barely makes a sound. She clings to me like a forlorn little puppy. I could hardly pack without bumping into her. Now we grip each other's hands until I don't know whose fingers are whose anymore.

Everything is so awfully quiet. We don't talk, and we don't cry. None of us can cry anymore, not really. The sadness only burns at the back of our throats. I can't even feel the time passing. All around me hands crisscross and cheeks press against shoulders. We are all of us memorizing one another, already trying to mend the holes our leaving has begun to tear. When I've gone, I want to be able to close my eyes and pull this feeling tight around me.

At three thirty a pair of ugly black tarantasses pull up in front of the governor's house. Out in the hall come grunts, scrapes, and the sounds of feet scuffling as the servants see to our trunks and baggage. I'd cover my ears if it didn't mean letting go of Anastasia's hands. Somewhere near me, I hear a tiny sob, like a bird caught in Mama's throat, then nothing.

When the windowpanes start to turn from black to gray, my sisters cradle themselves around me, rocking me like the sea until I can taste the salt of our tears.

I wish I was brave, like Tatiana. I could never tell my sisters, especially Anastasia, but when I think about them being left behind, part of me is glad I'm going with Papa and Mama. Staying here without our parents, even with my sisters and so many of our best people to help look after us, would frighten me to death.

But leaving will make me different, and I don't want to be. I wish I were a person who'd never felt like this. We're still together, and the cracks are already so deep.

By the time Monsieur Gilliard taps at the door, we're all crying, but without any fuss at all. The tears just drain out of us, like breathing. Papa's boots creak as he stands, and we all rise after him—all but Mama, who stays hunched over Aleksei's bedside.

I could kiss Aleksei's dear face and hands a thousand times and still not be ready to leave, but I force myself to say good-bye after only a dozen so Mama can have a few more seconds with her Sunbeam. I back away from his cot and face my sisters, all of us clutching handkerchiefs limp as lettuce leaves. First Tatiana kisses both my cheeks and whispers, "God go with you, *dushka*," then passes me to Olga. My big sister holds me close as a newborn, pressing my cheek to her chest and resting her own cheek against my hair. We don't say one word. I just breathe in her tea rose perfume. I don't believe how thin she's gotten. Her spine feels like a string of pearls under her blouse.

Olga lets me go, and there's only Anastasia left. How can I say good-bye to my Nastya? Instead we nestle our faces against each other's shoulders and hold tight together until my arms ache. I never knew I could hurt like this, not when Aleksei was ill, not when Papa abdicated, not even when we left home. All of those things wore us both thin as tissue, but this could shatter us. I don't know how I'll hold myself together, much less Mama.

Beside us, Papa blesses the Big Pair and Aleksei. Anastasia and I hardly even breathe until it's her turn to say good-bye to him. It's too soon to let go, but I won't make our Papa peel us away from each other.

There's so much I want to say, but all I can quaver into her collar is, "Christ be with you, precious Nastya."

"You too, my Mashka."

"Here." I let go enough to hand her the little sachet scented with my Lilas perfume we made together for Mama's Christmas present. The other three are packed into Mama's valise. For now, Anastasia needs mine more than Mama does.

She sniffs it, but her nose sounds too runny to smell anything. With a gulp, she locks her hands behind my neck once more, and then we're apart, the cool air of the room rushing to replace my sister's arms around me. Thank God, Mama has already separated herself from Aleksei, and Nagorny has rooted himself to her place next to Aleksei's bed. It's hard enough watching Papa bless my darling Nastya, and see her step away from me into a space between the Big Pair. The thread between our hearts is stretched so thin already, but the way Olga and Tatiana have made room for her there makes me brave enough to move to Mama's side. Tatiana's lips press tight together and she nods, proud of me through her tears. There's a tiny snap in my chest, and even though we seven still stand in the same room, I know we are truly apart now.

Someone, Nyuta maybe, helps me into my coat. Papa takes Mama's arm, just the way he did when we left Tsarskoe Selo, and walks us through the door. Yakovlev is there to meet us, his scarf wrapped up over his ears.

In the corridor, Papa shakes hands with all our people. At the stairs, two guards of the First Regiment step in front of my sisters. "That's far enough."

Papa and Mama and I pause for a moment, stricken. The look on my sisters' faces make me close my eyes. Then Papa makes the sign of the cross over Olga, Tatiana, and Anastasia. "Watch over them," he says to our footman, Trupp.

The tarantasses harnessed to the horses waiting in the courtyard are hardly more than big wicker baskets strung on poles between the wheels. Only one of them is covered, and there aren't any seats, just a little bit of straw on the floor. Monsieur Gilliard pushes a mattress from the shed into one of them. The men lift Mama in, and she motions for Papa to join her.

"You must ride with me," Yakovev tells Papa. I scramble up next to Mama before they can order me aside too. This is my job. I must comfort Mama and make my sisters proud of me. Ahead of us, Papa and Yakovlev get into the other basket. Yakovlev's men ride on their horses all around us, and some of our own rifle guards come too.

We bounce and jootle all over the road. I'm exhausted after staying up all night long, and there isn't a chance for sleeping now. Mama groans and gasps so quietly I can barely hear her, but I'm sure she's only trying to be brave for me. I don't feel at all cheerful or sturdy, or useful. If Tatiana were here, she'd know just what to do for Mama, but all I can think to do is brace myself through the ruts and puddles and try not to whimper. I can hardly think at all, or even feel sad.

All day long it's perfectly awful. Linchpins break, and wheels smash on the ice. Sometimes where the rivers have begun to thaw the snow and water comes up to the horses' stomachs! It stinks of animals and straw, and the cold musty mattress underneath us. We rattle against that tarantass like two marbles in a wooden box. If we try to open Mama's heart medicine, the glass dropper will shatter against the bottle, so she has to do without.

When we finally stop to sleep in a house that used to be a shop, our luggage is late. By the time we crawl into our beds, I don't care the least little bit that I'm sleeping on a mattress on the floor. Both Mama and Dr. Botkin are miserable. The poor doctor's kidneys hurt him so badly he can't even tend to Mama. I'm so achy and shaky, the dropper clinks against Mama's teeth as I squeeze the medicine under her tongue.

Yakovlev scurries around telegraphing in the morning, but won't say a word to us about what he's up to. "Fidgety,"

Mama says as we bundle up, padding ourselves against the jostling cart as much as the cold. When I pull my mittens from my coat pocket, something crinkles. Out comes a strip of paper with two lines from one of Nekrasov's poems in Olga's handwriting:

> *Our path may be stony but we shall not fall,*
> *Our passage is sure and protected.*

Clutching the little scrap tight, I wrap my muffler across my face before Mama can see me cry.

On the second day, we arrive in Pokrovskoe around noon and stop right beside *Otets* Grigori's house to change horses. His wife and children peek out the window at us. "Oh, Mama," I whisper, and point. "It's Marochka in the window!" I wave shyly, and they make the sign of the cross over us. It makes me shiver, the way they look at us.

At midnight on Palm Sunday, we finish with the awful tarantasses and move to a train. Near Tyumen, a squadron on horseback makes a chain around us, all the way to the station. For three more days, we travel by rail. The plain dingy cars feel posh as the Winter Palace after those horse carts. Nyuta and I get one car, and Papa and Mama have another. In between are Yakovlev and Avdeev. Without his chin-up bar and daily walks, Papa does sit-ups on the floor three times a day to keep from pacing. There's nothing else to do except watch the names of the stations and guess where we're headed.

"Toward Omsk, so far," Papa says. "And then where, do you suppose?"

"West to Moscow," Mama says.

"Or east to Vladivostok?" I ask. Imagine seeing the Pacific Ocean! But in the morning the sun's on the wrong side of the train. We've been turned around again. "Now where?"

"Maria, go to the next car and ask Yakovlev himself," Mama says.

Would Tatiana choke on her own breath the way I do?

I make my way along the swaying corridor, trying to remember the lines of Nekrasov Olga slipped into my coat pocket the night we left. *Our passage is sure and protected.* I'm not sure I've gotten them right, but the thought of her voice in my ear helps me knock at Yakovlev's door.

"Yes?"

"Please, Mr. Commissar, my mother would like to know where you're taking us?" I sound like a little girl. Tatiana would have said "the empress," not "my mother," and it wouldn't have come out at all like a question.

For a moment, I wonder if he knows the answer himself. He swallows, tweaks an earlobe, then says, "I'm sorry, Citizen Romanova, that is classified information."

Mama doesn't answer when I tell her what Yakovlev said. Papa shrugs and lights a cigarette. "I would go anywhere at all, except the Urals."

That's exactly where we end up. A mining town in the Ural Mountains. Before we've even stopped, I understand why Papa didn't want to come here.

"Lock the windows and pull the curtains," Yakovlev orders as the train pulls into the station at Ekaterinburg. It doesn't do a bit of good. The most horrible shouts blare through the panes. It sounds like my measles dreams all over again, but this time it's real.

"Finally they're in our hands!"

"Let me spit in his dirty face!"

"We ought to throttle them!"

For ages, we sit in the train while Yakovlev speaks to the soviet deputies. Even though we can't see the mob, their voices crowd closer and closer. Papa smokes and strokes his beard, but Mama's fingers shake under my sweaty hands. At three o'clock we're ordered out. Yakovlev hands us over to the chairman of the Ural Regional Soviet, a young man called Beloborodov. They pile us into an open motorcar, and a truck loaded with armed soldiers follows. I'm sure I can hear their rifles clanking as we drive through the streets. Mama sits tall and stiff as anything, but my stomach bumps worse than the road from Tobolsk.

"Where are they taking us?" I whisper to Papa, even though he can't have any more idea than I do.

I know as soon as I see it. On the corner across from a square, the ugliest fence of gray pilings juts onto the sidewalk, reaching from a canopied doorway all the way across the front of the building and around the block. The house behind it is yellowed plaster, but all we can see is the gate to the courtyard and the trim along the roofline that makes it look like a big stale wedding cake.

Before we can even go inside, a new officer and guard

inspect our hand baggage. One of them yanks Mama's valise right out of her hand.

"I see no reason for such rough treatment," Papa says, so calmly I wonder if they know how angry he is.

Another Red soldier stands at the door. The whiskers of his black mustache almost prick his lower lip. He gestures inside like he's welcoming us, but he smiles in a way that doesn't make me feel welcome at all. "Citizen Romanov, you may enter the House of Special Purpose."

31

TATIANA NIKOLAEVNA

Holy Week 1918
Tobolsk

t first we have news almost every day. Maria even thinks to send a note back with the man who drove the first leg of the journey: *Travel dreadful, we were terribly shaken on roads barely usable.*

It makes me absolutely ill to think of Mama with her weak heart and sciatica in that wretched tarantass. If only I had time before they left to tell Maria how to watch Mama for signs of pain, when to give her drops, and how to comfort her without medicine! But they are all safe, *slava Bogu*, I remind myself.

The next day there are two telegrams from Tyumen, and the day after that a letter from Mama herself. The sight of her handwriting soothes me like a hot glass of tea, but the words themselves send me to my handkerchief again: *My soul has been shaken out.*

Then for days, my worries fester as the hours limp by with no news at all. At least Aleksei is a distraction. If I cannot be with Mama, I must make sure her precious Sunbeam gets well.

"Is there a letter from Mama today?" he asks, his teeth clinking against the thermometer.

I put my finger to my lips. "You know better than to talk while I take your temperature. The last thing you need is a mouth full of broken glass." Aleksei cushions the thermometer with a guilty smile and sinks into his stack of pillows. From his nightstand, he takes the round watch Papa left him and watches the seconds tick by. When the time is up, he points the thermometer at me and raises his eyebrows to ask again. "No, Alyosha. Only a letter to Mama from one of her friends at the lazaret." His body slumps further, but his knees tent the blankets into uneven pyramids. His hips are still too inflamed to let him relax his legs.

I lower my hand over one of them. "Does it hurt today?"

His face shifts as he tries not to grimace. "Not as much."

"Would you like to put your feet up to rest your knees?"

Aleksei nods, and with hardly a rustle his *dyadka* unfurls from the corner to help me ease my brother down onto his back and transfer the pillows to brace up his aching joints. Aleksei's muscles tense under our hands, but he keeps his eyes fixed on the hands of his watch. "Anastasia will have breakfast with you," I tell him as we work. "Then Olga for luncheon, and dinner with me. If you eat well and your temperature stays steady, I will have Nagorny and Monsieur Gilliard carry your cot into Papa's study for tea with all of us. *Khorosho?*"

A small smile. "*Spasibo*, Tatya. Will you ask Zhilik to come read to me?"

"*Konechno.*" I kiss his forehead and start off to fetch Monsieur Gilliard.

"Tatya?"

"Yes?"

"You'll tell me if a telegram comes?"

The question snatches my voice. "The very instant, Alyosha," I choke.

Christ give me strength. There is no reason I should not be able to handle this. Every day I tell myself I have done the right thing by staying behind, yet the responsibility is a heavier weight than the gemstones tugging constantly at my sashes and buttons. I look out our bedroom window at the slush-rutted street. This would be almost bearable if I could only see the sea, even with just one eye.

We have been apart before, and I have Nagorny, Monsieur Gilliard, Mr. Gibbes, Dr. Derevenko, and so many of our people to help me, but managing an entire ward of wounded soldiers would be a comfort compared to having charge of my own sorrowful family. Anastasia smiles and clowns, but she keeps herself rolled up tight as a bandage. It pains me to think of what must be aching behind her brittle grin. And Olga, the poor darling! I do not even know the name for what she needs, but I think only God can give it

to her. It is all she can do to write letters to Mama and pray
with Aleksei.

Just then Olga emerges from the adjoining doorway to
our parents' bedroom.

"You have not started packing Mama and Papa's room
already?" I ask. "Disturbing their things before we know they
have arrived safely is bad luck."

"*Nyet, konechno.* Not even a button. Sitting at Mama's
desk makes me feel closer to them when I write," she
explains, then peeks across the corridor to Aleksei's room.
Anastasia is putting on a pantomime with the dogs for our
brother. Shutting the hallway door, Olga says, "Tatiana, you
can talk to me about what's troubling you."

I shake my head. "You have enough to worry about,
dushka." Her eyes flicker. I think she would be angry with
me if she only had the energy. Instead she seems to be using
every muscle in her body to stand upright instead of folding into herself like a well-creased letter. Her fingertips have
gone ragged from the way she bites and picks at them.

"We all do," she says. "And that's why we don't need to
worry about each other. You can't hide it from me—I can
see you're fretting. Don't make me imagine what's causing it,
Tatya. It's too much for me."

Confessing my troubles to Olga feels backward, even
humbling. My head is knotted with threads of anxiety, but
Olga's worries are always like whole bolts of cloth in comparison. What I say surprises both of us.

"Every time I think of Gleb and Tanya Botkin, all alone
without their father, it makes me sick with guilt! Our papa

stood before Commissar Yakovlev and refused to leave his family behind. What on earth can it be like for Gleb and Tanya, knowing their papa had a choice, and that he chose to follow the tsar? Such a good, loyal doctor is a treasure, and I thank God every day that he is with Mama now, but Olga?" My fists have clamped together, just the way my sister's do when she tries to hold in her fears. I unlock my knuckles and let the last thought go. "Can there be such a thing as too much loyalty?"

So much happens on Olga's face, I cannot read it all. I see only the beginning and the end: the tenderest smile, and then such sadness that it pulls her whole body to the couch. "I don't know, Tatya."

My voice pinches tighter and higher. "There is not one single thing I can do for them, corked up in this house like aspirin tablets in a bottle."

"I wish we could invite them for Easter, but I don't dare ask Colonel Kobylinsky to press the men to tolerate anything extra."

"What's going on in here?" Anastasia asks, popping in from the corridor with Jemmy tucked into her elbow and Ortipo waddling behind. Both dogs have scarves tied over their heads like *babushki*, and Ortipo drags a cape made from an embroidered dinner napkin.

In an instant I shed my distress and step between my sisters to give Olga an extra moment to recover herself. "We are deciding what to do for Gleb and Tanya for Easter," I tell Anastasia as I scoop up Ortipo and strip the make-believe finery from her. "And you should knock before barging in."

Anastasia's fingers tighten over the doorknob. Her face flushes like Mama's. "*Knock?* It's my room just as much as yours to barge into, isn't it? And don't scowl at Ortipo like that," she tells me, though she studies Olga as she says so. "That brown butterball may be fat and ugly, but she likes frilling up just as much as you do." Her voice trails off. Again she looks from me to Olga, still silent on the couch. "Fine. Why don't I go paint some eggs for the Botkins and you two can go back to your . . . *chat?*" Off she trounces, yanking the door shut behind her.

"I'm sorry, but I cannot arrange for you to attend Easter services in town," Colonel Kobylinsky says. "The soldiers' committee will not allow it."

Olga and I cry out like a pair of mourning doves. "Easter is the most High Holy Day! We have always been allowed to go to church on High Holy Days."

"Surely they won't deprive us?" Olga begs. "It's too cruel."

One look at the colonel, and I think he would sit down and cry himself if he could. "I'm sorry," he says again. "I know what a comfort real Easter services would be to all of you, especially with your parents away. But the men know I don't have the backing of Lenin's government. I can't even pay them regularly anymore. All I have to appeal to them is common decency, and that is in shorter supply than butter and sugar these days. In the interest of your safety I don't dare press the matter, but you have my word that there will be a priest here to perform the full Divine Liturgy, both for the Paschal Vigil on Holy Saturday and vespers on Easter Sunday."

Instead of complaining, I should thank God we have such a good man looking after us. "Thank you, Colonel. We will be grateful for whatever arrangements you can make."

"Easter's going to be so dreary, stuck in here," Anastasia mopes. "We don't even have flowers for the altar."

My temper shoots past the disappointment lodged in my chest. I could spank my little sister like a baby for bringing up something so petty, but to my surprise, the colonel brightens. "I understand the custom here is to use spruce boughs," he says. "I will see to it that you have plenty to decorate your altar." Purposeful once more, he goes away down the corridor with something like a spring back in his step. It makes me smile, but a second later my temper crests again.

"I wish I were a man!"

"What?" Anastasia's mouth drops open as though I have cut her off in the middle of singing a hymn.

"Look at us, with our cropped hair and patched stockings! Everyone is either gentle or rough with us. Those guards would treat us differently if I were a man in uniform."

"Some of them do look at us differently, ever since Papa and Mama left," Olga says, picking at the loose threads in her skirt.

Her plucking makes my skin itch under my old blouse. "Everything is so dingy and dull! What I would give for a new dress in layers of fresh pink lawn, and a picture hat with flowers for Easter . . ." Anastasia and Olga both raise their eyebrows. "Stop your grinning, you two. The Governess can daydream, even if it smacks of vanity. Anyway, I could make do just as well with my Red Cross uniform. That would be some kind of dignity at least."

"You'd put on your velvet court dress and pearled *koko-shnik* every night for dinner if we let you," Olga teases.

I smirk at myself. "And you would be happy in a *muzhik*'s smock and felt boots."

"You're both crazy," Anastasia says, rolling her eyes as always.

"Am I the only one who misses the imperial processions?" I ask, turning to Olga. "Remember descending the Red Staircase in Moscow with the music and the crowd cheering? They roared so loudly sometimes, the lace on my hat brim trembled. I was so proud to be Russian then, and a Romanov. I know it sounds stuck-up, but I never felt like their cheers were for me, or any of us, really. At moments like that, we were more than ourselves. It was the pride of the people that thrilled me, their pride in our country." My voice catches. "We belonged to everyone then."

Olga nods, and the tears slip from her chin to melt in her collar. When I turn back to Anastasia, she is swiping her cheeks with her fists. "I don't know why you couldn't have told us that when I still had a chance to feel it for myself," she hiccups. "Now we don't belong to anyone."

I offer her my arms, and she tucks herself like a sash round my waist. "We still belong to each other," I tell her.

By the eighteenth of April we still have no news, but Aleksei's joints have relaxed enough that I ask his *dyadka* to lift him out of bed and into the wheelchair. In the sunshine of the balcony, our brother looks pale and fragile as a Communion wafer.

"Why don't they write, or send another wire?" Aleksei asks. "They could have been in Moscow days ago." He holds up his watch, as if he has been marking every minute of our separation.

"The roads are bad, Alyosha. Plenty of villages in Siberia probably do not even have telegraph offices," I tell him. If I try to be any braver, my face will split in two. *Slava Bogu*, he is not screaming in agony the way he did in Spala, but it troubles me that his questions are harder to manage than his pain. There is nothing I can do to ease his worry, and I never seem to know the right thing to say.

"Yakovlev himself didn't know where they were going," Olga assures him. "Maybe no one at all is allowed to know until they get there. That's the safest way."

"But aren't they traveling by train? Don't stations have telegraphs?"

"Remember when we came here? We couldn't even look out the windows at the station. They can't be spreading news all across the telegraph wires if everything is secret." Our Olga is so smart.

But even Olga doesn't know what to say when we get a short telegram marked EKATERINBURG from one of the officers on Good Friday. "Ekaterinburg?" Anastasia asks. "That isn't anywhere *near* Moscow."

"It's in the Ural Mountains," Olga says. "Over sixteen hundred miles from Lenin's capital."

All these days we have been desperate for news, and now? I cannot even find my thoughts. I want to believe all is well, as the telegram says, but it makes no sense for them to be passing through Ekaterinburg. We all believed Yakovlev was taking Papa to Moscow. Why move us at all if not to the new capital?

True to his word, Colonel Kobylinsky delivers two entire spruce trees for us to decorate our ballroom chapel for Easter. "You may use anything you please in the greenhouse as well," he tells us, and with the tutors' help Anastasia carries up armloads of pots from the garden. She takes all afternoon to trim the branches and position them across the altar, taking care not to snag Mama's handmade cloth, and even convinces Mr. Gibbes to climb up on a stool to suspend two branches over the iconostasis.

"*Otlichno*, Nastya," I tell her when she finally steps away. "Maria would say it smells like Christmas."

The two of us breathe deep lungfuls through our noses. It helps to mask our sniffles at the thought of our Mashka. I wish it were Christmas. Perhaps none of us realized it, but we were content then. Only one thing will resurrect our spirits, and I do not know how much longer any of us can bear waiting.

Finally, two days after Easter, God smiles on us at last. "A letter from Maria, with a note from darling Mamochka!" I pick up my skirts and run straight to Aleksei's bedside, with my sisters' heels pounding behind me. Aleksei cheers and kisses the envelope. "It's addressed to you, Olga," he says, and hands it over so gallantly. The sight of her name in Mashka's sloppy writing on the envelope is enough to make

Olga glow. I manage only to cross myself before I sink to the floor and weep with relief.

When I look up, Anastasia is on her knees before me. "You've been just as scared as the rest of us, haven't you?" she asks.

I can do nothing but nod.

"Poor Tatya!" she cries, and plants a big kiss on my cheek. My baby sister, comforting me! I wrap my arms round her, and together we laugh like church bells.

"Read it, Olga," Anastasia demands.

"'In my thoughts I kiss you thrice, my dear Olga, and greet you on this joyous holiday.'" Tears brighten Olga's cheeks at Maria's description of the sleeping arrangements and the birds chirping outside the window. It sounds almost like any ordinary letter. Then Olga's voice skids the slightest bit. "'We live on the upper floor; around us is a wooden fence; we can see only the crosses on the cupolas of the churches on the square. We unpacked our things in the evening because all the baggage was searched, as well as the medicines and candies.'" She glances at me. That last part is the code Mama and I arranged to signal that my sisters and I must hide the rest of our jewels. "Down at the bottom Mama says, 'It's not clear how things will be here.'"

With that one line, it feels as if everything Maria's letter had begun to set free inside of me has come back to roost.

"What does that mean?" the little ones ask. "Can they be staying in Ekaterinburg?"

My mouth opens, but I have no words to answer them.

32

OLGA NIKOLAEVNA

April–May 1918
Tobolsk

"The train was rerouted at Omsk," Officer Matveev explains. He has come all the way back from Ekaterinburg to tell us the news about Papa, Mama, and Maria. "I believe Yakovlev intended to deliver them to Moscow, but your family is now under the jurisdiction of the Ural Regional Soviet."

My mind won't let me think about what any of this means until I know one thing: "But they're all right?"

"Konechno," Matveev assures us. "I saw them safely to their new lodgings. They are under house arrest, much as you are here."

Like a puff of wind, some small part of the fear I have been carrying these last two weeks rises off my skin.

"Slava Bogu," Tatiana murmurs as we all cross ourselves,

seeping with relief. "Are they expected to remain in Ekaterin-burg?" she asks.

"It seems that way. The owner of the house, a well-to-do merchant by the name of Ipatiev, has been relocated, and there was a stockade and sentry box outside the house. It did not look like a temporary arrangement. None of the stops along the way had such provisions for security."

"They made Papa leave while Aleksei was sick just so they could fence him into another house? Why even bother if they didn't take him to Moscow?" Anastasia wants to know.

At least I'm not the only one thinking it. Yakovlev can't have split us apart for nothing, but if the Bolsheviks didn't transfer Papa for political reasons, it makes no sense to move him from one house to another, not across so many hundreds of miles.

"God bless you for coming all the way back to explain the situation," Tatiana says.

"When I thought of how my own mother and sisters wait for news of me, there was no question," Matveev answers.

They go on a moment more, but I barely hear them. My mind grinds like a pair of mismatched gears, trying to force Matveev's news into a shape that makes some kind of sense.

"*Dushka*, you hardly thanked him," Tatiana chides.

"I'm sorry, Tatya. I didn't know how to ask Matveev, but I was thinking, if they didn't move Papa to anything, I'd like to know what they moved him from."

Tatiana's eyes dart to Anastasia. I've left her no delicate way to answer. "You think we are in danger here?"

Anastasia scoffs. "Just because the Bolsheviks are nervous doesn't mean we should be. We're not even on the same side."

Click, click, click—my thoughts line up like jumps across a checkerboard. "You're right, Shvybs. Maybe Mama was right all along. Perhaps the Whites truly are in range of Tobolsk."

"We'll never know for sure unless they get here," Anastasia says.

"If there is a chance it is true, we have no time to waste with the medicines," Tatiana decides. "I will check Aleksei's temperature and ask Monsieur Gilliard to read with him, then meet you two in Mama's drawing room."

For all the jewels we've already hidden, there are hundreds more, pounds of them, locked up in Papa and Mama's bedroom. We don't have enough buttons in our entire wardrobe to conceal them all. The three of us sew until our backs are bowed, and all the while Tatiana bustles in and out to look in on our brother. "Aleksei must eat more," she insists, focusing her frustration on a row of diamonds. "I cannot understand it. His temperature is down, the swelling has stopped, but he is so weak and listless. I tell him he must get strong so we can all be together again, but nothing helps."

That's how it is with Tatiana. Sometimes she sees things simmering inside us before the bubbles even break our surfaces, but it's almost impossible for her to guess what's lit the fire beneath it all. Somehow, it's a dear trait in someone who's always so capable. Her face is so forlorn, I'd like to kiss her.

"I'll sit with him," I tell her. "You and Anastasia can manage the medicines for an hour or so."

"The Governess was right," I tell Aleksei. "You're looking much better."

He slouches down and glares at his pocket watch. "You don't have to pretend. I know it's all my fault."

I nod to Monsieur Gilliard, who quietly closes his copy of *Ivanhoe* and slips out of the room. "What's your fault, Alyosha?"

"If I was well, we'd all be together," he says into the striped ticking of his cot.

Oh, my poor little brother. I thought it would be something like this. "Baby, don't—" But he snatches his shoulder away before my hand even touches him and throws his watch into the blankets.

"You can't tell me that isn't true, Olga!" he shouts. "Everyone looks at me like I'm a clock, waiting to see how long before we can leave. What am I supposed to do? I can't make myself get better any quicker."

Down the corridor a door opens, and Tatiana's unmistakable footsteps batter the floor. "You're right," I tell my brother. "But listen to me," I demand, hastily straightening his blankets and wiping his tears, "even if it's true, it isn't your fault, do you hear me?" He nods, his passion suddenly snuffed. "*Khorosho.* Now you rest. I'm about to have my hands full with Tatiana, but I'll manage her. I promise. Take your watch, and don't say a word." My wink pulls a smile from Aleksei as the door bursts open, and I'm there to meet Tatiana at the threshold.

"What is going on?"

"Nothing." Linking my arm through hers, I give our faithful Governess just enough time to glimpse Aleksei in bed with his watch as usual, then spin her back into the corridor, pulling the door shut behind me. She reaches for the handle, but I step in front of it.

"Olga! What is it?"

"It's all right."

"I heard Aleksei shouting."

"He's fine, Tatya. Let him be." With a little nudging, the two of us end up sitting side by side on one of the trunks lining the corridor. "Tatya, sweetheart, you can't coax Aleksei with seeing Papa and Mama anymore," I tell her. "He knows better than any of us that we're all waiting for him, and feeling guilty and worried won't help."

She jolts as if my voice is made of electricity. "I never said—"

"It's nothing you've said, Tatya," I soothe. "It's how he feels. Do you remember what *Otets* Grigori telegraphed when Aleksei was so ill in Spala? 'Do not let the doctors bother him too much.' He was right. It only reminds Aleksei of how ill he is when we all hover over him. Let me look after him. Before you know it, you'll be flooded with arrangements to make for our trip to Ekaterinburg." Inside my chest, where there has been nothing but worry, a little smudge of energy kindles as I speak. "Please, Tatya, let me help. I can do this much."

Tatiana cocks her head at me. Her face relaxes, as if I've taken two weights from her shoulders. *Konechno, dushka.*

After that, I sit with Aleksei for hours every day, working jigsaw puzzles, playing cards, and telling stories. He's thin and brittle as a candle, but his eyes spark with brightness when I begin a new tale. Usually by the time I'm done, his plate is empty. Sometimes Tatiana lingers in the doorway, listening to the old Russian stories.

"One night as they feasted, Prince Vladimir's knight Sukhman made a boast that he could capture a wild swan and bring it back alive, without one trace of blood on its feathers," I recite. "But no matter how he hunted, Sukhman couldn't find a single duck or goose on the waters, much less a swan. 'I cannot go back without keeping my promise, or my prince will have me executed,' Sukhman said. 'I'll try my luck on the river Dneiper.'"

"Would he really execute Sukhman, just because he couldn't find a swan?" Aleksei asks.

"That's the way the story goes. When he reached its shore, the river Dneiper was muddy and listless. 'Mother Dneiper, what's happened to you?' Sukhman asked. 'A horde of heathen Tartars covers my far bank,' the river answered. 'Every night they build bridges to cross me, and every night I break them down. My strength has flowed away on my waters.' So Sukhman uprooted a young oak tree and demolished the Tartars, but not before their archers struck him three times. Undaunted, Sukhman pulled out the arrows and plastered the wounds with herbs and poppy flowers for the pain. 'And where is my white swan, Sukhman,' asked haughty Prince Vladimir when Sukhman returned to Kiev, 'without a drop of blood upon it?' Sukhman replied, 'My prince, my shining sun, I found no swan. Instead I destroyed an army of Tartars before they could cross Mother Dneiper and invade Kiev.' But Prince Vladimir would have no excuses, and tossed Sukhman into a dungeon while he sent a scout to the Dneiper. When the prince found out Sukhman had told the truth, he commanded his servants to free Sukhman and grant him gifts of land and gold. But Sukhman, offended by Prince Vladimir's lack of trust, left everything behind, riding away onto the open steppes. There, brave Sukhman removed the leaves from his wounds and his blood poured out to become a river, the river Sukhman."

"He's like me," Aleksei muses.

"How, Baby?"

"My blood could flow into a river too," he says, so matter of fact, it hurts.

About the only thing we have to look forward to is the mail. The letters we get from Maria make it sound as if they are safe and comfortable, but there are occasional lines that lodge like slivers in my thoughts.

We have a nasty surprise almost every day.

Such a shock after so many months of good treatment.

Each letter is numbered, so we can plainly see many aren't getting through to us at all. Either the post is falling apart along with everything else, or someone is deliberately keeping things from us. My mind squirms around such thoughts, but even when I forbid myself to consider the possibilities, my nerves refuse to let me forget. It isn't as if we don't have our own share of shocks right here in Tobolsk.

Tatiana motions from the doorway of Aleksei's room. Without a word, I turn my hand of *nain jaune* over to Nagorny and follow her to Papa's study. She shuts the door behind us, then slumps against the knob and cries softly into her handkerchief. The air in the room swirls. "Tatya, what is it?" My thoughts fly to our parents and Maria when she doesn't answer. I scan the room for a telegram or newspaper, but there's nothing, only Colonel Kobylinsky standing beside Papa's desk.

Tatiana clears her throat. "Colonel Kobylinsky has been informed that he is no longer in charge of the guards," she falters.

Everything inside me stops. "Who is?"

"A man called Rodionov, Your Highness," Kobylinsky says. The name makes him sneer. "A small fellow, round-shouldered like a beetle. The guards themselves are to be replaced as well. Latvians, I've heard."

"Rodionov was here with Yakovlev to inspect the house weeks ago," Tatiana explains.

A smother of panic blocks out my sister's voice. "Are we still going to Ekaterinburg?" I blurt.

"Rodionov and his men are in charge of your transfer as well, and I will not leave Tobolsk until you do," the colonel promises. "There is no reason Rodionov should not honor

Yakovlev's word and send you to your parents in Ekaterinburg. So far I have not been forbidden to enter the house. I
will visit as often as I can."

So many words, and not one of them *Yes*. While I swallow a ripple of nausea, Tatiana says, "Thank you, Colonel,"
and he's gone before I can press for more.

"Until this, I thought I could bear it," I tell her. But to
lose Kobylinsky when we're all alone?

"The colonel promised not to abandon us."

"But he has no power, Tatya. He's been depending on
the guards' decency for weeks now, and these men will all
be new."

"Olga, please!" she cries. "I cannot worry about any of
this until it happens. Even then I may not be able to fix it,
but I know for certain there is nothing to be done for it now.
God will give me the strength when the time comes. Until
then I do not dare ask for any more."

Her tears steal the wind from my lungs. I finger my St.
Nicholas medal and try to think like Papa: *Sudba*. "All right,
Tatya."

33

ANASTASIA NIKOLAEVNA

May 1918
Tobolsk

I will not be searched!" Nagorny bellows. The pen drops out of Olga's hand, splattering her letter to Mama. I'm out of my seat before I know it. I've never in my whole life heard Aleksei's *dyadka* shout like that.

"Shvybs, don't," Olga pleads, but I dart to the stairs to see what's going on.

"Then you will not leave this house," Rodionov is saying when I peep around the doorway.

Nagorny's voice sounds as if it's made of metal. "The tsarevich and his sisters have requested me to take two bunches of radishes and a scrap of a letter three lines long to the Botkin children. There is no cause for this sort of treatment."

"You forget you are under arrest, sailor," Rodionov retorts. He circles Nagorny like a dog getting ready to wet on a tree. "A grown man taking orders from a pampered lot of children, yet he has the nerve to defy the commandant. It's disgraceful."

Nagorny stares straight ahead. "A grown man taking out a political grudge on three frightened young women and a sick boy is a disgrace to his own conscience."

I gulp down something that might have turned into a laugh if I couldn't feel the anger radiating off the both of them like stovepipes. Someone should give Nagorny a medal, the way he stands up to Rodionov.

"Take your vegetables and get out of my sight," Rodionov growls. "You will submit to a search when you return, or you will not reenter this house."

Stinking swine. And it's not just Nagorny he torments. Every morning, Rodionov makes my sisters and me line up like schoolchildren in the ballroom for roll call. "Are you Anastasia Nikolaevna?" he asks day after day. "Olga Nikolaevna? Tatiana Nikolaevna?" He says my name as if it's something to be ashamed of. As long as I can remember I've mostly tried to ignore being an imperial highness, but this commandant makes me want to drape myself in ermine and diamonds and promenade across the courtyard out of plain old spite.

So the morning after the Radish Incident, I stand proud as a flagpole and answer him, "I am Grand Duchess Anastasia Nikolaevna." Olga twitches like I've stuck a fork into her, but beside me Tatiana straightens up until she's an eyebrow taller than Rodionov himself. When it's her turn she answers like me:

"I am Grand Duchess Tatiana Nikolaevna."

A swallow bulges down Rodionov's stubby neck before he slumps out.

"We have to be careful, you two," Olga says.

"Konechno, dushka," Tatiana soothes. "But I will not let him insult us. We may not be imperial highnesses, but Anastasia is right. We are still grand duchesses."

I feel like I should gloat or something, but as soon as I walk into our bedroom my spirits flump back down again. Our bedroom is so horribly lopsided without Mashka's cot next to mine. It's like having a compass with only three directions. When I'm working puzzles with Aleksei or out walking the dogs, I can usually manage to pretend Mashka's only sewing jewels in the other room or sitting inside with Mama. But in here there's no getting away from the fact that we've been zigzagged apart. It's all wrong. I don't care what Ekaterinburg is like. I can't wait to get out of here.

All day long, I'm like a bicycle wheel spinning and spinning without going anywhere. Olga nurses Aleksei while Tatiana does everything else. I do nothing at all but play with the dogs and tromp circles around the garden. What do I even know *how* to do except saw a log, knit a scarf, or crack a joke? The Big Pair must think being the family clown is great fun, but it's as boring and depressing and sad as everything else. When does the clown get to laugh, or cry, I'd like to know? Nobody ever thinks about that.

Only flinging myself through the air on the swing seems to help. I pump my legs so fiercely that when I jump off, I fall in a walloping heap on the ground. A laugh shakes out of me, and I roar and cackle until I nearly cry.

"Are you all right?"

"Huh?" I prop myself up on my elbows and find one of the new Red Guards leaning over me, rubbing at the back of his neck.

"May I help you up?"

He looks about as graceful as a stack of firewood, but I let him pull me up anyway.

"*Spasibo.* I don't know what gets into me sometimes," I say, brushing myself off. The two of us back away from each other without even thinking about it, like we have to get back to our own sides before anyone sees us being almost nice to each other. It makes me want to jump over the fence. Maybe next time I go swinging I'll try just that.

While someone sits with Aleksei, the other two of us get stuck sewing jewelry into our clothes. We've run out of buttons and hats to disguise them in, so Tatiana figured a way to sandwich rows of stones between two chemises, sealing them up like little tubes. There are so many, even Aleksei has to wear a chemise under his khaki field shirt.

"Boys don't wear corsets," he fusses when I take his in to try on.

"It's not a corset. It's just a double undershirt. Pretend you're a machine gunner at the front, and this is your ammunition belt. I bet it feels just like being wrapped up in bullets."

"I bet ammunition belts don't have lace all around the edges," he grumps, but he puts it on.

"I'm sick and tired of 'arranging medicines,'" I tell Tatiana when I tramp back into Mama's drawing room. "I feel stiff as a drainpipe every time I put my underwear on. What's eighteen pounds of stones divided by four people?"

"A sixteen-year-old should be able to figure that out all by herself," Tatiana teases.

"Bah. You know I never paid any attention to fractions or division. As if I needed to gain any more weight. Our underthings are so worn out, I don't know how they'll hold together anyway. I'd rather play on the swing than mess with this."

"Did you see what one of the new soldiers wrote on our swing?" Tatiana hisses. "No matter how bored I get, I will never sit on such filth."

"Don't be such a snob. A few scribbles aren't going to crawl under your dress. I don't care what they write on that swing. I think my eyeballs are going to turn square if I have to look at one more hand of *nain jaune* or game of dominoes."

Tatiana shakes her head. Fine. For once I feel as hopeless as she thinks I am.

"Forgive me, Your Highnesses, but I have a bit of news, and Tatiana Nikolaevna is occupied with the heir," Trupp says, interrupting our letter to Mama.

Olga perks right up. "A wire from Papa and Mama?"

"No." He twists his knobby hands tighter than a taffy puller. "I'm afraid Commandant Rodionov has forbidden doors on this floor to be shut or locked at night."

Olga goes perfectly green.

"Please don't worry. The men of the suite have worked out a schedule to keep watch outside the bedrooms. We will see that you are not disturbed."

Olga's forehead droops into her hands. Her shoulders jerk when the latch catches behind Trupp. Part of me thinks if I touch her, she might break, but she might fizzle down into a pool of nerves if I don't do something.

"What a stupid, swinish oaf!" I toss my pencil across my exercise book and sneak a glance at Olga. "Does Rodionov think we'll climb out the windows in the dead of night?"

All she'll say is, "Locks work two ways."

I'd like to reach down her throat with a pair of silver salad tongs when she leaves me dangling this way. Trouncing out for Aleksei's bedroom, I fling the words over my shoulder. "Do you always have to say half of what you mean?"

"Shvybs!" she calls behind me. "I just don't want you to have to worry the way Tatiana and I do."

I spin back, the heat under my collar almost choking me. "Well, it doesn't work! How dumb do you think I am? You two are always whispering with Monsieur Gilliard or Colonel Kobylinsky. Every time you open your mouths you eye each other sideways, and I can almost hear what you're *not* saying. You're the one who told me you'd rather know nothing at all than too much. Let me tell you, not enough is just as bad."

"I'm sorry, Shvybs. You're right." Just like that. "What do you want to know?"

I look her dead in the eye. "Are Maria and Papa and Mama all right?"

She gives me a queer stare. "*Konechno.* I promise you know as much as I do about what's happening in Ekaterinburg. Is that what you've been thinking all this time?"

I don't answer, but relief trickles all the way down to my boots. "So you're worried about us?"

"Yes." Olga speaks slowly, but I think it's because this time she's trying to decide *how* to tell me, instead of how much. "I don't trust Rodionov or his men. It isn't good for three young women to be left alone in times like this."

"Even with Nagorny, and Monsieur Gilliard, and all the rest of them?"

"Yes. Even so. They're good men, but they have no real power." Her eyes drape over me from top to bottom like a measuring tape. I try my best to look strong and brave. "Do you remember after the abdication, how the soldiers at Tsarskoe Selo shot the tame deer in the park before Papa came back home?" I nod. I'd almost been sick when I saw them. "I'm afraid we're not so different from those deer anymore." She looks at me like it hurts her. "Do you feel better?"

"Not exactly." But I don't think I feel worse.

Olga may not treat me like a dunce so much, but as usual, Tatiana still doesn't tell me anything about anything until she's decided it's more bother *not* to tell me. So when she says, "You should start packing your things, and Maria's, too," I end up being the one who sounds like an *idiotka.*

"For what?"

"For our transfer to Ekaterinburg. We leave in three days.

What did you think the servants and I have been arranging all this time?"

Of course I knew, but the way she says it, why bother explaining the difference between arranging and *going*? Alekcei still can't walk, but he can move around a little without oozing like an egg yolk. Apparently that's good enough for Dr. Derevenko.

Our people haul more trunks up from the storage sheds, and for a while it's just about possible to forget Maria's missing cot with the luggage strewn all over the place. Usually packing is like digging a hole—there's always more to go back in than what came out—but this time there's space left in almost every bag and suitcase. There are no diaries or letters, and most of our notepaper and film's been used up. Our dresses and underclothes have gotten thin and tired as the tissue paper we packed them in. When I take the shawls and pictures down from our side of the room, it looks like Mashka and I never lived here at all. I can't decide if that's better or worse.

"Do you think anything good can come out of all this?" I ask Tatiana.

"*Konechno*. We never know what the Lord has in store for us. Think of Auntie Ella. When that Red terrorist blew up Uncle Sergei, she founded her own convent. She and the sisters have done so much good for the sick and poor of Moscow. With God all things are possible."

I'd like to know what Uncle Sergei would think about that, but I know better than to ask Tatiana.

She pulls her head out of a trunk and eyes me. "Are you packed?"

"No."

"Then what are you doing in that windowsill? It is almost three o'clock."

"Watching for Maria's window-family." I should have thought of it sooner. Mashka wouldn't forget to tell them good-bye. "Look, it's Gleb!"

Dr. Botkin's son stands in the street waving up at me. I grin and salute like a Mishkoslavian bear-soldier. He takes off his cap and bows low. Like a whip crack, Rodionov is out in the street shouting, "Nobody is allowed to look in the windows of this house! Pass on, pass on!" He turns to the sentries. "Comrades, shoot everybody who so much as looks in this direction. Shoot to kill."

Of course that's just when the lady in the blue coat finally turns up with her boys. The look on their faces makes me wish I could sizzle that Rodionov with one glare. Hateful insect!

That night we have our last supper in Tobolsk. There are still two bottles of wine left, and we might as well drink them up. It's almost like a party, with the four of us and our tutors and everyone else. Tatiana fusses so much about every last thing—it is bad luck to hold the bottle from the bottom, or fill a glass being held in the air—that I don't know how we'll have time to drink a drop, much less two whole bottles. I couldn't care less, though. I don't even need the wine to feel tipsy at the thought of seeing Mashka and Papa and Mama again.

"What's that noise?" Olga asks.

"It sounds like a rat creeping down the hall."

"Anastasia Nikolaevna! Do you always have to be so crude?" Tatiana, of course.

"Well it does." I scritch my fingers over the tablecloth toward her. "Don't you remember how those nasty rats on the *Standart* used to scrabble in the corridors until we threw our shoes at them?"

"We don't have a shoe big enough for this rat," Olga whispers. "I think it's Rodionov."

"Quickly, ladies," Monsieur Gilliard says, "the wine! Under the tablecloth."

"The glasses!" Tatiana pops up like a waiter and starts us stuffing the wineglasses under the table.

When Rodionov pokes his head around the doorway, we're all staring at the table as solemnly as if we've got Bibles lying open in front of us instead of veal and macaroni. I don't dare look up, but I can feel him standing behind us. A squeak leaks out of Tatiana, and she claps a napkin over her mouth. Before I can get ahold of myself, my eyes pop up and catch Monsieur Gilliard's long mustache wiggling like a rabbit's nose. Next thing I know, I'm trying so hard to swallow a laugh it probably looks like I'm gagging. Then, *bang!* Mr. Gibbes lets out a whoop like a schoolboy, and we all go to pieces. Olga practically slides down her chair like a smear of butter, she's laughing so hard.

We kick up such a rumpus, I don't even hear Rodionov slink back down the hall. Good riddance.

34

MARIA NIKOLAEVNA

Spring 1918
Ekaterinburg

*E*lectric streetcars clatter by just before the bells sound matins from the cathedral across the square. Lying in my cot, the chimes make my ribs rumble, but beyond the fence all I can see are the onion domes with their crosses on top. Today I'll write a real letter to my sisters, I promise myself, and make sure to tell them God hasn't abandoned us.

Before we've dressed, there's music out in the street, mixed with the sound of banners flapping in the breeze. Mama scratches her lucky swastika sign into the window frame while Papa hoists himself up to the highest pane for a look. "Can't see a thing," he grumbles. "The palisade is so close to the house, it's like looking into another room instead of the outdoors."

If the view is terrible, at least this room is pretty, with irises and pansies painted above the striped yellow wallpaper.

It reminds me of the cabbage roses and butterflies Anastasia and I had along our ceiling back home.

"Perhaps the people are celebrating, Nicky. It's May Day on the Western calendar," Mama says, opening her diary. Warm air from the window ruffles its pages. "Maria, go and see if there's a thermometer in this house. It must be nearly twenty degrees outside already."

I hesitate in the doorway to the duty office. This room has two windows, and the fence only covers one of them. Below, people cluster in the street like they did in Tobolsk while a guard shouts, "Walk on, citizens, walk on! There's nothing to see here."

"If there's nothing to see, why can't we stand here?" one of them wants to know.

The room smells a little of liquor, even though there isn't a bottle in sight. Maybe it's Commandant Avdeev himself. Instead of answering my question, he shoos me away. "Tell your family and your people to assemble in the drawing room in twenty minutes for an outline of daily procedure. I will answer any questions following the briefing."

Commandant Avdeev's mustache is so neat, I can't help wondering if he pencils it on every morning. It wavers up and down like a thin brown caterpillar as he goes over the rules with his hands clasped behind his back. "Also, you will no longer be addressed by your former titles."

"What!" Mama says. "Why now?"

"The Revolution has swept away such vanities, Alexandra Feodorovna." He says "revolution" as if it begins with a capital

R. "You are now in the hands of genuine revolutionaries."

Mama turns to Papa and says in English, "This is absurd."

"No foreign languages are permitted in the presence of myself or the guards," Avdeev adds.

Mama's lips go white. I think she'd like to crush this commandant like a cigarette under her shoe. My stomach teeters like a tightrope walker. How will I calm her after this?

"There are two guard posts inside the house," Avdeev continues. "One at the head of the main stairs leading down to the street, and another behind that, in the hallway containing the lavatory and the staircase to the garden. If you wish to leave your quarters and enter an area where guards are stationed, you are required to ring first. The bourgeois system of bells formerly used to communicate with servants has been modified for that purpose. In addition to the sentries outside the palisade, there are also guards posted in the garden, on the balcony, and at the corner of the house below your bedroom window. Machine guns have been stationed in the attic, the guards' quarters downstairs, and on the balcony."

Suddenly I can't swallow, but Mama doesn't even blink. "We must make arrangements to attend regular *Obednya* services as well as the High Holy Days," she interrupts. "Our transfer has already deprived us of celebrating Palm Sunday. Tomorrow is Great and Holy Thursday."

"You may file a request with the Central Executive Committee for a priest to serve *Obednitsa* in the drawing room, but you will not be permitted to attend services outside this house."

Mama stamps her cane on the floor. "Why not?"

Even I'm frightened of her when she gets this way. Not Avdeev. "Because, Alexandra Feodorovna, this is a prison regime."

"And what about exercise?" It's the first thing Papa's said. "We are accustomed to walking outdoors twice daily."

"Starting tomorrow, you will be allowed one hour for your customary morning and afternoon walks in the garden. Today I cannot permit you to go outside. There are demonstrations in the streets for International Workers' Day. In the meantime, you may unpack your hand luggage and arrange the rooms as you see fit. The remainder of your baggage is expected tomorrow. If you have further concerns, my office is at the northeast corner."

Mama goes straight to bed with a sick headache after that. I stumble through a few pages from *The Great in the Small* until she drifts into a doze, then slip away to get acquainted with the house.

Almost all the doors at the back of the house are locked, leaving four rooms for the three of us to share with Dr. Botkin, Nyuta, and Sednev. Five if I count the doorless dressing room leading into our bedroom. Avdeev's office is off the drawing room, between our quarters and the sentry posts. Outside the duty office there's a funny little passage— too wide to be a corridor and too small to be a room—with an inside window cut right into the wall so you can see who's posted in the back hall where the lavatory and stairs to the courtyard and guards' quarters are.

Even including the locked rooms, it's much smaller than

the governor's mansion in Tobolsk, but prettier and cozier, too, with fancy wallpaper, wainscoting beaded with gilt, and carved moldings like thick braids of icing. My favorite chandelier is made of pink frosted Venetian glass, blown in the shape of lilies. There's a piano, and the furniture has velvet and damask upholstery. Only the linoleum in the water closet is a little shabby where the copper pipes leak onto the floor.

Best of all, when I look around I can tell people really lived in this house, and not just because so many of their books and plants and things are still here. It's different from Tobolsk, where everything was stripped and cleaned and remade in a big hurry for us to move in. A house that someone's decorated just the way they like it, even if it's someone else's house, is so much nicer. Even the air smells gently of other people's tea and perfume and soap.

"Don't I know you?" I ask before the new deputy commandant can introduce himself. I put down my tea and go right up to him. A tiny scar under his nose tickles my memory. "I do—you're from the Crimea! Papa, look at him. He was in the army, do you remember?"

"My name is Ukraintsev," the man says, "and you're right, I'm from Gagra. I served as a beater to your brother, Mikhail Alexandrovich, on hunting trips at Livadia," he tells Papa, "and also played with your sister as a small boy."

With a squeal, I practically pounce on him. "You know Uncle Misha and Auntie Olga? Did you know she had a baby of her own last summer? A little boy called Tikhon.

We've never seen him, but he must be just gorgeous, don't you think? I'm dying to meet him. We haven't been to the Crimea for nearly two years. I miss it dreadfully! How long has it been since you were at Livadia?"

Ukraintsev looks as bewildered as if he's stepped into a puddle and sunk in up to his shoulders. Papa and Mama just chuckle and shake their heads at me.

"Please sit down," Papa says. "Tell us about yourself. If there is one thing our Maria likes better than bowling a man over with questions, it's hearing the answers."

Next morning I sniff at the air in the dining room. "It smells of tobacco, doesn't it?"

Papa wrinkles his nose. "Cheap tobacco at that."

Mama holds her handkerchief to her face. "Do you want one of your Christmas sachets?" I ask her. "Or your heart drops?" She waves me away.

"I'm sorry, Your Majesties, but there is no hot water for tea this morning," Nyuta says. "The guards drained the samovar for themselves."

"Outrageous," Mama sputters at Avdeev when he comes in to apologize. "Men! Wandering in our rooms!"

"This will not be repeated," he promises. "Only myself and my three senior aides are permitted to enter your rooms at any time. I will order a separate samovar for the guards myself this afternoon."

I don't think Mama is impressed, but maybe she's only too offended to say any more.

That afternoon when our belongings arrive, they take us into the hallway by the lavatory and search through every last thing. I have nothing to be ashamed of in my bags, but I back up to the wall like a naughty child anyway. Papa paces along the banister, muttering. Next to me, Mama trembles and fidgets with the lace on her cuffs. If Tatiana were here, she'd know right away if Mama is nervous or angry. I link my arm through hers the way Papa does sometimes, hoping it will calm her. And me, too, if I'm going to tell the truth.

Our bags are a mess, even before the guards rummage inside. The roads shook everything so horridly, the papers we used as wrapping are almost destroyed. Even the tobacco has jostled out of Papa's good cigarettes. Strangely enough, not one bit of the glass and porcelain we packed has broken.

"I don't see the reason for this—this *search*," Mama spits as the men open up her valise. "It's an insult. Mr. Kerensky would never have subjected us to this. Compared to you Bolsheviks, he was a revolutionary and a gentleman."

One of Avdeev's assistants, Comrade Didkovsky, shakes his head and smiles into the bag he's examining. He must think my mama is a silly woman. Last of all they go through Mama's traveling pharmacy and open every vial. Papa's voice makes me jump. "Until now, we have dealt with decent people!"

"Remember, you are all under investigation and arrest," Didkovsky barks back.

The whole time, Avdeev keeps his hands behind his back, just nodding or shaking his head at the objects his assistants fish out. They take away all sorts of things—my camera and film, Papa's ceremonial daggers and swords, all our binoculars—then demand to know how much money we've brought. Papa and Mama don't have a kopek between them, and I have to hand over my seventeen rubles and sign for them.

After that, everything is routine. At eight thirty we have to be ready for inspection so Avdeev and his aides can make sure we're all here. Once in a while the commandant is a little tipsy, but we all pretend not to notice, even the guards. For breakfast there is always tea and black bread, and sometimes cocoa, fruit, oatmeal, or pastries. Still no butter or coffee. Our other meals come from the soviet canteen downtown. It's on the dull side, mostly soup and fish or cutlets, but tasty and plentiful, as Papa says, and sometimes I trade smiles with the delivery women.

In between meals and walks outside, we read, sew, play cards, and write letters. No matter what we do, we're really just waiting. Waiting for the next meal, or the next walk, or most of all, for the next letter. I write pages and pages to my sisters, leaving space for Papa and Mama's little notes at the bottom, but we get no reply.

At first we're allowed two hours outdoors a day, then one, but since the garden is so tiny it hardly matters much. Papa paces it off at just forty steps square, and it's full of rubbish. The sentries in the garden and on the balcony carry revolvers and hand grenades along with their rifles. After a few days, they don't frighten me at all. I sit with Mama all day long, but if I want to walk outside I have to leave her alone sometimes. Secretly, I'm glad. The delegations who show up from the Ural Regional Soviet to watch us would make her temper crackle like dynamite.

It's bad enough when she has to go past the duty office and the two sentries to get to the toilet, even though there's a door directly across from the lavatory that must lead straight into one of the locked rooms in our quarters. Just like on the train to Tobolsk, Mama doesn't go more than twice a day if she can help it, and she never rings first. "I would as soon bark like a dog at the door than ring that bell," she tells Avdeev when he objects.

Every time I have to go, I look through the window in the passage outside the commandant's office to see who's on duty first. It seems silly, stationing a man out there with a rifle and bayonet, as if he's keeping watch over the toilet. Some of them fidget and squirm so much, their boots creak. You'd think they'd never seen anyone walk into a water closet before. If they're embarrassed now, Anastasia will mortify them when she arrives, poor things. Sometimes they even fall asleep at their posts. A few glare at me, with cigarettes drooping out of their lips like lolling tongues. Whenever one of those men are on duty, I wait for a shift change before I ring the bell.

Every day is the same. Not one thing has happened that couldn't have waited for Aleksei to be well. Nothing has happened at all! Papa fills hours with books and cigarettes and chin-ups while Mama frets all day long about Aleksei. Missing my sisters and brother takes up so much of me, I hardly know what to do for her. A puppy wagging its tail from morning to night would be as much use as I am. I read and sew with her, and try to arrange her hair the way Tatiana does, but I don't have the knack. Mama's heart isn't in it anyway. Now and then she'll smile or pat my arm, and I'm the one who's supposed to be comforting her. The only time she seems happy is at night, after she's torn another day off the calendar on our bedroom wall. In the dark sometimes, I hear her giggle like a girl at the tickle of Papa's beard as they kiss good night. *Good night, Nastya,* I say inside my head every night. *Sleep tight.*

But things aren't all bad. We have Ukraintsev to chat with, and the chief of the guards, a man called Glarner, is friendly too. If no one is looking, they'll take letters from us and tuck them into their cuffs to mail in private. Papa even invites Glarner into the drawing room sometimes to play bezique with us. One evening he can hardly keep his eyes open.

"What is it, man?" Papa finally asks when Glarner's hand of cards droops and waves like a wilted little fan.

"My apologies, Your Maj—Citizen Romanov." He yawns wide as a bear crawling out of its cave. "I was up most of the night."

"Was there danger in the city?" Mama asks.

"No, Ma'am." He grins. "I was dancing at a ball."

"A ball!" I cry. "Oh, tell me all about it, please! What are the ladies wearing now? My sister Tatiana will be so eager to know. Did you take any pictures? Are there any new dances? My sisters and I haven't had a dance lesson in simply ages."

He stands up and brushes off his uniform. "With your permission," he says to Papa.

Papa glances at Mama. She nods, and Papa says, "Certainly."

Glarner offers me his hand. "May I have this dance?"

My fingers quiver and my feet are clumsy as a lame pony's after so many months of plodding behind fences. We have no music, so Glarner hums, "*Rrrum* pa-pa-daa, *rrrum* pa-pa-daa," as he sweeps me around the room. I make an awful mess of it, but in the end I can feel my own smile shining like someone's brushed the dust off me.

Papa and Mama clap as Glarner bows to me, and they look brighter too. After all the time I've turned my head inside out trying to comfort Mama, this seems to have done us all more good than anything.

Finally, a few days after Easter, Ukraintsev himself hands us a telegram from Olga: *Thanks letter. All well. Little One already been in garden. We are writing.*

Mama cries, she's so relieved. Seeing her tears makes me feel like I can breathe again.

The next day Ukrainstev is gone, and a man called Moshkin is in his place. He's nice-looking, with dark brows and lashes as lush as a lady's, but awfully crude. He probably spent half his life tracking mud across his mama's kitchen floor and then batting those gorgeous eyes to dodge a scolding.

After Commandant Avdeev goes home and Moshkin takes over the night shift, we hear a woman's voice giggling behind the office walls. It sounds like champagne bubbles. I wouldn't want to be alone with Moshkin, but that doesn't stop me from blushing and chewing my lips to keep from giggling to myself while Mama scoffs and huffs over her hand of bezique.

Along with Moshkin comes a new set of guards. Papa
and I watch them from the window. They're scruffy-looking,
but it doesn't matter much. They only last a few days before
a third set shows up—recruits from a nearby factory. Then
Glarner disappears. "Relieved of his duties," Moshkin says
with a wink.

The day after that, we wake up to find an old man painting the windows over with whitewash from the outside. I
follow him from room to room, watching the paint lap him
up with every brushstroke. He never once looks through the
windows, only at them, like they're a wall between us even
without the paint. By the time he's done, it feels like we live
in a giant glass of milk. Next, Avdeev seals all the windows
from the inside.

"We can't even see the thermometer," Mama complains,
shaming Avdeev into going outside to scratch away a narrow
gap in the paint so we can read the temperature again. Once
he's done, the only window we can open is the little *fortochka*
pane near the very top of our bedroom window. Mama and
I can't wear our own perfume indoors without sneezing. Dr.
Botkin stops putting on his cologne, but a hot day makes it
rise out of his clothes like steam.

"What's this?" Papa asks as Avdeev sets down a parcel on the
breakfast table after morning inspection.

Avdeev looks at the parcel, then at Papa. His eyebrows
climb up his forehead the way Anastasia's do when I've said
something stupid. "A package," he says, and walks out, shaking his head.

It's barely been one day since the whitewash man came, and already we're so shocked to see something from outside the fence, it's like we've forgotten the world doesn't end at our windowsills.

"It's from your sister," Papa tells Mama.

"Auntie Ella?" My own darling godmother! Oh, I could just hug it! "How did she know where to send it?"

Mama almost smiles. "Open it, Maria."

"Coffee, chocolate, and hard-boiled eggs!" The scent makes my eyes go all teary, like I'm bent over a box of onions. "It smells like home," I sniffle. But it's more than that. It smells like running arm in arm through the corridors with Anastasia, waving at officers and sailors. It smells like the last day before everything fell apart.

At night Moshkin brings his friends from the factory to the house to show off. The first few days we only catch them peeking through the window by the second sentry post, but before long they take to gathering in Avdeev's office. "Carousing," Mama calls it. One evening they barge right into our rooms and push the piano into the duty office so they can sing revolutionary songs. When he drinks, Moshkin's voice gets so loud and slippery it slides right under the door.

"Nikolashka himself pisses behind that door," Moshkin brags. "Go on, boys—don't be shy. You can tell all your friends you've used the same toilet as the ex-tsar!"

Papa's beard twitches like someone's torn a whisker from his chin, but he doesn't say a word.

"At least Avdeev has the decency to do his drinking at home," Mama huffs.

"Did you know almost half a dozen of the new men are younger than I am? Two are barely Anastasia's age. One of them they call Kerensky, because his name is Alexander Feodorovich. He has the sweetest face. I think he's the youngest of all. Ivan Cherepanov reminds me of the men in the Fourth Regiment. He's older than almost all the other guards, and came here to help earn money for his great big family. And did you know there's even one man named Romanov, just like us. Isn't that funny?"

Mama snips a thread with her teeth. "You shouldn't talk so much with these guards, darling. It isn't proper."

I'm always being scolded for saying too much to the guards. I don't know why. Mama talked with Ukraintsev for hours, and most of the new guards aren't even as old as Olga. They're factory workers, not real soldiers at all. But I promised Tatiana I'd look after Mama, not annoy her, so I hush.

Since Mama never goes outside and Papa never tattles, she doesn't know how often I chat with the sentries in the garden. That's one good thing about locked doors and white-washed windows.

"I've heard one of the men is Jewish," I tell the one called Filipp Proskuryakov. "Is that true?"

"Yes. He's a member of the Bolshevik Party too."

"Oh. Well, I guess I won't be talking to him, then. Too bad. I've never really known a Jew before." I wish Anastasia was here. Proskuryakov is a bit of a hooligan. I bet the two of them would get along famously.

He glances at his watch. Our time is almost up, but I don't want to go back into those same five rooms for the rest of the day. "I'll tell you a secret about Ivan Kleshchev if you let us walk a little longer." Proskuryakov raises an eyebrow. He's fascinated by Papa, and trades with the others to take one of the posts in the garden when we exercise. Papa loves to walk, so what's the harm in a little bribe to make all three of us happier? "He's almost exactly my big sister Tatiana's age," I whisper, "but Ivan's mama is the one who signed him up for guard duty. Can you imagine?" Filipp snorts, and Papa and I get to dash around the garden three more times before they shoo us indoors.

On 8 May, Avdeev unlocks three more rooms and hands over the keys to Papa. "The remainder of the imperial party is expected," he tells us. It takes me a moment to realize he means Anastasia, Aleksei, and the Big Pair are coming at last. All day long I linger in the passage outside the duty office, hoping to hear or see something.

But for three days, nothing. No news, and no arrivals. Avdeev won't even tell us what day they left Tobolsk. By the second morning I was so anxious, I ate up all my chocolate from Auntie Ella's package, and a little bit of Mama's share too. Not even the smell of the coffee could calm me.

Where can they be?

35

OLGA NIKOLAEVNA

May 1918
Tobolsk

𝒴our Highness," Colonel Kobylinsky says, his voice so low I almost have to crouch to hear it, "I must ask you to give me your pistol before you depart for Ekaterinburg."

Shock blasts through me. I can feel the color wash from my face. I have no chance of denying it. "How long have you known?"

"Your father confided in me back at Tsarskoe Selo, after I returned the heir's toy rifle. Thank God he did." A glaze of sweat moistens his face, beading on his upper lip. The colonel's eyes flicker over me, but he can't hold my gaze. Instead he studies the polished desktop as if he's trying to piece together all those tiny glances. "I don't want to alarm you, but yesterday Rodionov had the nuns and priest who came for vespers searched in a most . . . indecent manner before they entered the house for services."

Disgust crawls over me like flies on the rubbish pile.

"Forgive me, but if Rodionov . . ." He grimaces and begins again. "If they discover you are carrying that gun, nothing short of your lives will be in danger."

Christ have mercy. I have no choice. The colonel looks aside as I raise my skirt and fish the pearl-handled gun from my boot. After nearly a year, I feel naked as a newborn without that pistol nestled up against my ankle. From this minute, the guards' eyes will feel like hands on me. No matter what awaits us in Ekaterinburg, I cannot wait to get out from under Rodionov.

"I wish I knew what's made the Bolsheviks angry enough with my family to take it out on the innocent people who come to comfort us." Guilt burns my eyes and throat like a swallow of vodka. I'm the one who requested permission for vespers to be said. All I wanted was some assurance of God's blessing for tomorrow's departure. Now the thought of what it cost the clergy to bring me that solace blots everything else out.

"These are troubled times." Colonel Kobylinsky lifts his cap and pushes back his hair with a sigh. The blaze of white along his temple looks broader than I remember. "Everywhere I look, I see men drunk on chaos."

My country is going to pieces all around me and I'm hardly allowed to watch, much less help. "Would the Reds stop dragging us by the scruff of the neck if they knew we love Russia just as much as they do?"

He opens his hands, too defeated to shrug. "I wish I knew. But there is another man, Khokhryakov, managing your journey along with Rodionov. He seems to be a decent sort. If you have any trouble, go to him. And may God go with you all."

"Thank you, Colonel." I wait until he shuts the door, then put my head down on Papa's desk and cry.

Eager as we are to leave, my sisters and I hesitate in the doorway until Nagorny goes first, carrying Aleksei. Two rows of armed Latvians line the steps down to the carriage in front of the house. In spite of Rodionov's shameful treatment of the clergy, it's the archbishop who's loaned his own carriage for our brother to ride to the riverbank.

At the dock Aleksei points at the crates and asks Rodionov, "Why are you taking those things? They don't belong to us—they belong to other people." Everything from the house is scattered over the deck of the *Rus*, from our luggage and the crates from the storage sheds to the governor's own furniture. It took Rodionov's men six hours to load it all.

"The master is gone. It is all ours," the commandant replies. His tone makes me wish I were packed up tight in a crate instead of standing on the dock with the wind ruffling my skirt. Even the archbishop's horse and carriage are led on board. Khokhryakov watches without protest.

"Darlings!" a voice cries, and suddenly Isa Buxhoeveden's throwing her arms around us. For a moment I feel protected again. It's such a relief to see a familiar face, I could weep.

While Tatiana goes to situate Aleksei into his cabin and Anastasia romps with the dogs on deck, Isa and I settle down on a bench along the rail. Before we've had a chance to do more than cross our ankles, a guard positions himself at the end of our bench. *"Russki,"* he growls at us when I switch to English.

Even with the soldier in earshot, I tell Isa everything I can about the last eight months, sliding in a mouthful of English or French here and there when the guard's attention seems to wander. In bits and pieces, I make her understand about Rodionov's daily roll calls, the humiliation of the clergy, and even the jewels we're carrying.

"You poor, brave things," Isa says. "It's no wonder you're looking so tired and pale."

"Tatiana and I have been keeping up a brave face, for Papa and Mama as much as the little ones. I think that tires me more than anything."

"I don't trust these men in the least. I was roughly searched myself when Commissar Yakovlev arrived in town. Almost the whole time I sat shivering in my nightgown while they rifled through my things. They even made me brush my hair to prove I wasn't hiding anything in it. And today, when I went below to put my luggage in my cabin, there were soldiers in my dressing room! It took a good deal of complaining to have them dislodged. If I were you, I wouldn't undress tonight."

I nod, feeling as though I've swallowed a bottle of thick black ink.

Before I can even think about how to warn my sisters not to undress, Rodionov shuts Aleksei in his cabin and locks the door.

Nagorny bangs from the inside. "A sick boy—he can't even get out to the lavatory!"

"He can't walk anyway," Rodionov retorts. "Let him use the chamber pot."

Nagorny shouts and swears, demanding that at least Dr. Derevenko should be allowed in and out.

"I've had enough of your imperial insolence," Rodionov yells back, and stalks down the passage, locking one door after another until all our men are trapped in their rooms. At our cabin, he stops. "You are still under arrest," he informs my sisters and me. "As in Tobolsk, your doors will stand open at all times."

God in heaven! Trapped on a steamer swarming with guards, and all our men locked away in their own cabins? The jewels sewn into my underthings cling to my ribs like strips of hot metal.

I don't have to say a word to Tatiana and Anastasia—not one of us will consider undressing with that door hanging open. I think of the poor nuns and priest, of the soldiers inspecting Isa's room right down to her hair, and I know I cannot let Rodionov's guards near us. If we're discovered hiding these jewels, God only knows what will happen.

As the night wears on, laughter and gunfire echo from the decks above. Between the ringing of boot heels come seagulls' squalls punctuated by limp thuds over our heads. When the machine gun rattles, it startles the three of us so, we all shriek and then giggle sheepishly at one another. Our laughter sounds as out of place as the gunfire, but it will splinter us if we hold it in.

Khokhryakov's voice carries down the passage, "Don't be afraid, Aleksei Nikolaevich. The men are only shooting at birds."

Why doesn't he come to reassure my sisters and me, too?

Sentries pass before our open door, but they are not the men of our household like they were in Tobolsk. I can't stop thinking of how Rodionov told Aleksei, *The master is gone. It is all ours.* I have a feeling that if they searched us, they might not stop at our layer of jewels.

My back straightens. Whatever these men might think they are entitled to, I will not let them take it from my sisters. I wish to God I hadn't let Colonel Kobylinsky convince me to leave my little gun behind in Tobolsk. What good it would have done against so many rifles, bayonets, and hand grenades, I don't know, but it made me feel I had some speck of control over my own fate.

"Go to sleep, you two," I tell Tatiana and Anastasia. "I'm going to sit up awhile and read." I prop a pillow against a chair, lay my copy of *L'Aiglon* on the table, and hide my trembling hands in my lap. Thinking of the chat Mr. Gibbes and I could have about the irony of an ex-tsar's daughter reading a drama about the son of Napoleon brings on a small smile to help put my sisters at ease. As slight a man as he is, even Mr. Gibbes would be a comfort now.

Once Tatiana and Anastasia surrender to sleep, I turn my chair to face the passage. Within a few minutes, Ortipo and little Jemmy pad out of my sisters' bunks to take up posts on either side of the door frame. Each time a soldier approaches our cabin, the dogs' low growls warn me.

Fixing my gaze, I meet the eyes of every man who passes. Forcing them to see me, making sure they know I'm watching, is all the defense I have.

Whether I turn my mind toward the future or the past, my thoughts give me no more peace than the guards. I cannot read my books about Napoleon and the French Revolution and pretend not to know how it came to this. Anger doesn't grow this thick and fast without soil rich enough to root in. For over twenty years my parents carried the fate of an entire nation in their hands. Now, we seven are in the hands of the Russian people. For all Papa and Mama's good intentions, we are paying the price for whatever they did to cost their subjects' happiness.

But what could they have done, my gentle papa and my sick mama, to make men desperate enough to organize mutinies and throw bombs? Those revolutionaries back in Petrograd, the ones Mama called hooligans, must have been trying to make their voices heard in the only way they knew how. If I thought it would make someone see what we're enduring on this very ship, I would light a bomb myself.

The evil in the world now will be stronger still before this is all over, Papa said. *It is not evil that conquers evil, but love.*

If Papa is right, I do not want to be part of the evil. And if I can forgive Papa and Mama for their part in this, I must forgive our captors, too. Papa and Mama and Tatiana believe the revolutionaries must be forgiven for disrespecting the Romanov dynasty. It seems to me their real sin is disregarding our humanity. No matter what happens tonight, there is a part of me our jailers cannot touch. Papa has his meekness, Mama her pride, Tatiana her faith, and the Little Pair and Aleksei their innocence. I will hold on to my humanity. No matter what.

"*Dushka*, did you sit up all night?"

"I couldn't sleep." It's close enough to the truth—if Tatiana wants to understand, she will. "Let's go up on deck. The fresh air will do me good."

Out in the open, I doze against Isa's shoulder, letting the wind rinse my face until Khokhryakov slips on a ladder and lands sideways on his foot, right next to us. Bolshevik or not, I'm on the deck beside him before his pain seems to register. He steps back and winces. "I was a nurse," I explain. "Please, let me see it."

Khokhryakov glances over my shoulder. "It's nothing," he insists, and limps off.

Turning to Isa, I spot a group of Rodionov's Latvian guards loitering along the rail. "Poor fellow," I say loudly enough for them to hear. "His ankle will swell up like a baked potato if he keeps walking on it like that." Maybe spattering kindness with defiance isn't wise, but I'll take the risk if they might begin to think of us as anything other than the children of Bloody Nikolashka.

At the dock in Tyumen, Rodionov orders everyone into the main salon. Outside the window, a train looms along the riverbank.

"Buxhoeveden," Rodionov calls from the doorway. "Derevenko. Kharitonov. Trupp." One by one, our people are escorted out. The seams of my valise bite harder into my palms with each name he calls. Then it's our turn.

"Romanov: Aleksei Nikolaevich. Romanova: Olga Nikolaevna, Tatiana Nikolaevna, Anastasia Nikolaevna." Nagorny's name is not called, but the faithful *dyadka* lifts Aleksei from his chair and leads us past Rodionov without incident. Behind us, Monsieur Gilliard, Mr. Gibbes, their maids, and a few others still wait.

Along the railroad siding, people have gathered like a flock of crows to watch us pass. Some of the women throw flowers, but the guards shuffle and kick the blossoms from the platform. One by one, an armed soldier puts us into the second-class compartment. They examine our bags and make us turn out our pockets before we can board, but they don't touch us. Isa, Dr. Derevenko, and a few others are already in the rail car. A soldier shoves Monsieur Gilliard back as he tries to climb in next to Aleksei.

"*Nyet,*" he barks, gesturing toward the end of the train with his rifle. "You ride fourth class, with baggage, or not at all."

By the time we arrive in Ekaterinburg, a rain fine as a veil is falling. The train halts on a storage line, far from the station, with armed guards posted around it. Their rifle barrels shine in the drizzle. All night long the cold seeps into our rail carriage like whispers.

In the morning it pours of rain while our boxes and

crates are unloaded. People on the platform push and clamor to watch, their faces running like wax behind the wet windows. One box breaks open, spilling out half a dozen pairs of Papa's boots.

"I go barefoot, and the tsar has six pairs of boots?" a man shouts. "Death to the tyrant!"

They tear into another carton. "Mama's gowns," Tatiana whispers.

A man climbs on top of a crate and shakes one of Mama's dresses over the crowd. "Comrades! We work our lives away, and they turn our sweat into ball gowns? Now it's their turn!"

"Hang them! Drown them in the lake!"

The ugly words burn my eyes, nose, and throat, but Rodionov's men only laugh as the crowd works itself into a frenzy. Finally Khokhryakov elbows his way in and begins to clear the platform. Most of the crates go one way, but a few stay behind to be loaded onto droshkies.

"Where are they taking our things?" Anastasia asks.

"Where are they taking us?" I answer. Tatiana frowns and shakes her head at me.

"Well, why not?" I snap. "We're all thinking it." No one answers.

At ten o'clock Commandant Rodionov appears in our carriage with another man. "You four bring your luggage outside," he orders us. "The rest of you stay behind."

"Nagorny, please carry Aleksei Nikolaevich out first and settle him in the droshky," Tatiana says. "We will manage the bags."

The rest of us stare at one another once Nagorny goes

out with Aleksei's arms wrapped around his neck. My feet
have seized up like cement in my boots at the thought of
leaving Isa, our tutors, and Dr. Derevenko behind.

"What is the use of saying good-bye?" Tatiana asks in
her bright-side voice. "We will all be rejoicing together in
half an hour's time. Leaving a place in the rain is a good
omen, after all." Putting bags in our hands, she shoos Anastasia and me out ahead of her.

As always, two lines of sentries mark the path to the
covered droshkies. The mud rises thick as pudding over our
boots as we slosh toward the carriages. Ahead of us, Nagorny
tries to come help, but the soldiers push him back. When I
turn around, Tatiana's struggling with a big leather suitcase
and Ortipo under her arm. Monsieur Gilliard gets another
shove for his trouble when he steps out of his carriage to
lend a hand.

When the door opens and Papa and Mama and Maria are all
sitting there like a picture in a storybook, the sight splits me
open, and I cry at last.

36

ANASTASIA NIKOLAEVNA

May 1918
Ekaterinburg

My hug swoops Maria off *her* feet and twirls us across the room. When my head stops spinning, there's a sea of hugs and kisses and questions. I've never been so glad to feel Papa's beard on my cheek, or smell the tobacco on his clothes. Mama holds Aleksei on her lap like a giant china doll while Olga snuffles on Papa's shoulder, and Jemmy and Ortipo bark like mad. Tatiana just stands there, crossing herself with a wide, wet grin on her face. Even Dr. Botkin's cologne smells homey.

After we've squeezed and cried ourselves runny, I make Mashka show me the house. In five minutes, we've seen everything there is to see.

"Before, Papa and Mama and I shared the corner room, but now that you're all here, they can be alone again." I don't think I've ever seen Maria smirk in my whole life, but she's stifling one now. "You know . . . ?" she presses, her lips twitching like two fat worms on a hook.

My nose wrinkles up all by itself. "Of course I *know*," I tell her with a swat. "But I'm not going to stand around here thinking about it. I'm not that bored. Yet."

Just like in Tobolsk, our bedroom's right next to Papa and Mama's, except nobody can get into their room without marching straight though the middle of ours. At least it's prettier than Tobolsk, with flowered wallpaper in pink and green, two corner stoves, and even a painted screen like we used to have back home. Our camp beds are still at the station, so Maria gives up her cot for Aleksei, and we four sisters sleep on the floor, smothered in overcoats like puppies in a heap.

In the other room, Aleksei insists on climbing into bed without any help, and ends up knocking his knee. Again. And since there's no door between our room and Papa and Mama's, all night long we have to listen to Mama croon and dote while our brother moans.

By the next morning Aleksei's knee has swelled up badly enough to keep him in bed, and there's no one but Dr. Botkin to help look after him. Until this, I'd almost forgotten Nagorny, Dr. Derevenko, Monsieur Gilliard, Mr. Gibbes, Isa, and all the rest. Out of all the people on the train, only Chef Kharitonov and Leonka Sednev came in with us.

"Where is everybody?" I ask Olga. "I haven't even seen Joy since we left the train."

"*Bozhe moi.* Tatiana sent me out first. I didn't think of taking Joy's leash. Didn't anyone else bring him?"

"I had my hands full with Jemmy. Tatiana carried Ortipo."

"And Nagorny carried Aleksei."

Our shoulders slump like wilted cabbages. "Maybe one of our people has him. Nagorny, or Isa or someone."

"I hope so, Shvybs. But who knows where they are?"

Even with so many people missing, it's like a parade with everyone trooping through our bedroom with compresses, thermometers, and trays of food and tea. I'd like to charge them a toll. In the afternoon Dr. Derevenko appears out of nowhere with Commandant Avdeev trailing behind. My sisters and I cluster around him, eager for news of our people, but the doctor doesn't even look at us. A gnat would get more notice than we do.

Every time the crowd in the doorway thins, I can see our brother sitting there in Maria's cot like it's a striped throne and he's Tsar Aleksei II. "I bet he hurt his knee on purpose," I whisper to my sisters.

"If that's true, I'd like to take him across my own knee," Olga says.

"Olga!" Tatiana scolds. "How could you?"

"After what we went through for all those weeks because he was too sick to move? It isn't fair to play with his illness like that."

"The first time was not on purpose, Olga."

"I know it. But think of how Mama suffers. It's selfish of him."

"Mama doesn't seem to mind," I say. "She looks pretty pleased to have someone to fuss over." Tatiana's jaw falls open so far her teeth ought to drop out. "And the only good part so far is that Mama's hovered so much, Aleksei hasn't had a chance to notice his own dog is missing."

"Don't, Nastya," Maria begs. "Not on our first day all together again."

I shut my mouth, but what's the use of being all together again if everybody's going to set up camp around Aleksei's cot and never mind the rest of us?

Just then Mama bursts into tears and pushes past us into the dining room. My heart booms and we all four pop up and crane into the corner bedroom, but Aleksei's just as bewildered as anybody. Papa, the two doctors, and Avdeev shrug at one another.

Tatiana starts after Mama, then marches into Papa and Mama's room. "What happened?" she asks Dr. Botkin.

"A misunderstanding," Dr. Botkin says, leading Tatiana back out again. "Dr. Derevenko has been forbidden by the commandant to discuss anything but Aleksei Nikolaevich's health. When the empress asked about the rest of the people who accompanied you from Tobolsk, Dr. Derevenko drew his finger across his throat to show that he couldn't speak of them. Her Majesty took it as a signal that they had all been killed."

"The poor darling," Tatiana cries. "Please, Evgeni Sergeevich, you stay with Aleksei. I will see to Mama."

And I'll sit here, just like always.

"We're not really supposed to talk with the guards, but nobody cares," Maria tells me on my first walk in the garden, "especially out here. Well, nobody except for Mama minds. Watch." Mashka links her elbow through mine and promenades me straight under two sentries' noses. "Have you met my sister? This is Anastasia Nikolaevna."

"Chieftain of All Firemen," I add.

One guard's Adam's apple bobs as if he's swallowed his tongue. "You don't fool me with your fine words," the other says with a wink and a voice that sounds like Mr. Gibbes acting in a play. "Move along!"

Mashka tugs me away, giggling like a fiend, until we flop into a hammock. Behind us, the men chuckle together. "What's so funny?"

"There's a guard named Sadchikov who really talks like that, but he's no older than Tatiana, and not even a Bolshevik. Some of the others make fun of him behind his back if none of the Party men are on duty."

"What's he doing here if he isn't a Bolshie?"

"I don't know. I don't think even half the guards are Party members."

I twist onto my belly and let my fingers drag back and forth through the scruffy grass. "What do you *do* all day?" I ask Maria. "I'm bored stiff already."

"Not much. It was worse before all of you got here. At least I've got someone to really talk to now. And don't tell anyone, but I'm glad Tatiana's here to take care of Mama again. It was like . . . like looking after a baby who wouldn't cry."

"What's that supposed to mean?"

"Tatiana always makes everything right, even before I

know anything's wrong. I knew Mama was miserable, but she wouldn't admit it. How do you comfort someone like that? And all the time I knew if Tatiana were here, she'd be bustling and doting like a proper nanny."

"Sometimes I think the way Tatiana acts only reminds Mama and Aleksei that they're sick or unhappy. I hate it when she buzzes over me that way. It's so . . . *nosy*. I'd much rather have you or Olga when I'm mopey or ill."

"Truly?" She blushes like a rose. I missed her so much. The pair of us are like salt and sugar: such different flavors, but so close in every other way you could never sort us apart once we're together.

"I don't know how you stood it in this place without us. It's so dreary with that murky-looking paint smeared across the windows. It's as much fun as living in a jar with the lid screwed on. I'd have gone crazy all by myself."

"It was hard after Deputy Ukraintsev left. He was such a nice man. Mama even invited him in for tea and bezique. I don't understand why they won't let us have friends anymore."

"Probably afraid we'd escape. Kobylinsky and the Fourth Regiment would have let us, I'll bet."

"What difference would it make if we did? Papa hasn't been tsar in over a year. Why can't we just be left alone to live as we please?"

I'm too chicken to admit it even to Mashka, but the minute I saw those blotted-out, nailed-down windows and the padlock on the dining room shutters, I caught myself wondering why they don't just put us in jail.

That evening there's some kind of ruckus in the commandant's office. Maria and I take turns pretending to need the
lavatory so we can ring the bell and put our ear to Avdeev's
door on the way past. "I thought I heard Nagorny's voice,
and someone else, too," Maria says.

"I only heard barking," I report when I come back.

"Probably that vulgar Moshkin," Tatiana says.

"No, silly, real barking. I think it was Joy."

"Joy!"

"Enough guessing," Tatiana decides, throwing down her
mending. "I will find out for myself."

"Well, tra-la-la. And good luck to her too," I tell Mashka.

"Avdeev is questioning Nagorny and Trupp," Tatiana
announces when she gets back. "They have been in there for
over an hour."

I stand there like Peter Pan with my hands on my hips.
"How do *you* know?"

"I spoke to the sentry in the vestibule," she says, brushing
by me.

"You?"

"You make it sound as if we exchanged vows. I asked a
question and he answered. Much more quickly than all your
sneaking, too."

"Did you smile?" I tease, but Tatiana won't look at me.

"I was no more pleasant than I needed to be."

Ha! Maybe Mashka's got competition!

Sure enough, after another hour, Avdeev turns our men
loose and Joy comes tearing through the house, straight to

Aleksei's cot. He feeds that dog so many scraps from his supper tray, Joy gets indigestion and stinks up half the house. Avdeev's face bends at the smell, but he still won't let us open one of our windows. He just shuts himself into his office to hog his own two whole windows' worth of fresh air.

Every morning we have prayers and a Bible reading, then Avdeev comes in for inspection. Sometimes other people come with him, and Papa mentions the "inadequate ventilation" to anyone who'll listen. It's so close in here, I swear I can smell Papa sweating by his second chin-up of the day.

The most excitement we get those first few days is when Avdeev and his men inspect the rest of our things from Tobolsk. They're nosy as old ladies, shaking our books by the bindings and fanning through our photograph albums. The way they raise their eyebrows and point at some of the pictures, it makes me glad I burned up my letters and diaries. After all their poking around, only the "necessary trunks" are brought into our quarters. Everything else stays in the storage shed outside. "If there is something you require from your trunks, you may submit a request for a guard to accompany you to the shed," Avdeev says.

"What makes them think they know what is necessary?" Tatiana wants to know. "*Konechno*, we can do without tablecloths, but there is not enough of the Ipatievs' silverware to go round."

The servants volunteered to eat separately, but Papa won't have it. Everyone who's come this far will dine as family, he says.

"I'd like to know which photos made them all whispery," Maria says, turning the pages of her album.

"Easy," I tell her. "For starters, how about the ones of Papa's naked backside, from when he'd go skinny-dipping at Livadia?"

"Or the ones of us with Mama and *Otets* Grigori," Olga says. And that's the end of *that* conversation.

"Who was that man with Dr. Derevenko?" I ask Tatiana when she comes out of Aleksei's room.

"The dark one?"

"Who else?" It's not as if we've had visitors breezing through all day.

"His name is Yurovsky. He must have been a doctor."

"I don't think I've ever seen a doctor in a black leather coat," I press, keeping my eye on Olga. She's my best thermometer for trouble. "Black coat, black hair, black beard. But no black *bag*." That makes Olga's high forehead crinkle. Tatiana doesn't even blink. Or answer. "Last time a dark gentleman like that arrived, we got split up like a loaf of black bread," I insist.

"He examined Aleksei's leg very carefully." Tatiana says the last two words like they're sentences all by themselves. "Why do you ask if my answers never suit you?"

I stretch out my neck and make my voice as haughty as hers. "If anyone would let me into the room, I would not. Have. To. Ask."

"What use would you have been? You are not a nurse, and there is no need for a crowd round Aleksei's cot."

I flop onto Mama's wicker wheelchair and spin myself in circles until Tatiana leaves. I can just about hear her throwing her hands in the air.

How should I know what use I'd be? I never have a chance to do anything except play up. Court jester, that's me. Too bad nothing feels funny anymore. This place already makes me edgy, like all my bounce and spring's been scraped away. I know perfectly well I'm an obnoxious little pig when I act like this, but I can't help it. Every time Tatiana tries to pull me her way, I wrench everything up like a bockety wheel.

"No one could mistake our Tatiana for anything but the daughter of a tsar," Olga says. A smirk leaks through my pout. Olga's knack for saying more than the words mean isn't always so irritating—as long as she's aiming at someone else.

"She's about as much fun as a nun," I grouse, kicking at the footrests.

"You shouldn't say that, Shvybs. Auntie Ella is a nun. Think of all the eggs and milk the nuns in Tobolsk brought us. The sisters everywhere have been nothing but a comfort to us."

Olga hardly ever sounds like a rule book, so her voice doesn't jab at me the way Tatiana's does, even when she's giving me a talking-to. I know Olga's right, but that doesn't stop me from thinking it'd be nice if *my* sisters were always such a comfort.

"Eighty-seven rubles," a man called Beloborodov announces at morning inspection. The number doesn't mean a thing to me, but he holds the receipt as if it's jumping with fleas. "The charges have been high before, but with six extra people, the Ural Regional Soviet has declared this week's laundry bill astronomical." He turns to my sisters and me. "If you insist on changing your sheets each and every morning, I suggest you busy yourselves with helping the maid wash your linens. Only clothing may be sent out from now on. After all, a little work never hurt anybody."

He should talk! Doesn't this Beloborodov know Avdeev's the one who won't let us saw wood in the yard like we did in Tobolsk, or allow our tutors in for lessons, or even use our cameras? The lunk took our gramophone, too, and looked the other way after Moshkin pushed the piano into the duty office. What does Belo-whoever think we should be doing all day long, turning Aleksei's toy soldiers into shells for the Red Army? The oily way he remarks about working, like we four still sleep in cradles lined with satin, I bet he'd love to think he's forcing us to sleep on bug-bitten sheets rather than do a bit of common labor.

"We can do our linens as well as anybody," I announce. He may be the chairman of the Ural Regional Soviet, but he's hardly much older than Olga. I'd like to tell him maybe Papa's monogrammed underwear will stop disappearing if we do our own wash, but Tatiana's hand around my wrist stops me.

"We will need instructions, please," she informs the chairman. "Our Nyuta is a lady's maid, not a laundress."

Ha! That stumps Avdeev for days. He goes to the public library, the bookshops, and even the local labor union looking for instructions and can't find a thing. And what does he end up bringing us instead of books? A man! "This is Andreev, Comrade Laundry Teacher to the House of Special Purpose." And they turn up their nose at our titles? Honestly!

"We should have told Commandant Avdeev that Monsieur Gilliard knows how to wash clothes," Maria says. "Maybe they would have let him in."

"But they wouldn't have let him talk about anything but soap and towels," I retort.

Laundry is damp, steamy work, but I don't mind it. Maria's hopeless with the washing—she can't carry a load of sheets to the kitchen without tripping over them. But she keeps at it. At least she's strong enough to help lug the big pots and masses of dripping linens around. "When I have a family of my own, I'll have to know how to wash clothes," she says.

At least with the laundry, I know there'll be something for me to do every day. Maybe I *will* be able to stand it here. Just barely.

37

TATIANA NIKOLAEVNA

May 1918
Ekaterinburg

"Mama?" Aleksei calls from his bedroom. "Mama!" I drop a stitch and a sigh. Nearly fourteen years old, he should know better than to shout like that while Mama is finally resting, especially with his *dyadka* on duty. But Aleksei keeps calling until I finish the row and lay my knitting aside.

What do I find in the back bedroom but my brother with his good leg dangling out of his cot and Leonka the kitchen boy holding Mama's wheelchair at the ready.

"Aleksei Nikolaevich, get back into that bed this instant!" Both of them look up at me, frightened as rabbits. Leonka wipes a cuff along both sides of his long, pale nose as if he has been crying. Maybe I am the bossy one, but even I am not imposing enough to make my brother and his companion so tearful in one sentence. "What is it?" I ask as I help Aleksei ease back into the cot without bumping his bad knee. "And where is Nagorny?"

"Leonka says they're taking his uncle away, and my *dyadka*, too!"

"What?" I whirl to Leonka. "Who is?"

"Commandant Avdeev. He took Uncle Vanya and sailor Nagorny out through the kitchen and into the duty office. Now they're both gone."

Aleksei's room sways as though a beam has been sawed from under me. Christ have mercy!

"Leonka, go tell the tsar and the empress what is happening, then come right back here and sit with Aleksei Nikolaevich. Aleksei, stay put, and do not move that leg again, do you hear me? We will have this straightened out immediately."

"Citizens Nagorny and Sednev have been taken to the District Committee for questioning." The way the commandant leans back in his chair without even the courtesy to stand in Papa's presence stokes my temper even higher.

"Why?" I demand. "For how long?"

"I cannot say."

"Cannot or will not?"

Papa puts a gentle hand on my shoulder. His thumb travels back and forth across my shoulder blade, and I know without looking that his other hand is stroking his beard. "And what of the rest of our people?" he asks.

Avdeev shrugs. "I have no news."

"If the tsarevich cannot have his *dyadka*, you must let one of the others in," I insist. "Monsieur Gilliard or Mr. Gibbes. His condition requires round-the-clock care."

"Dr. Botkin is at your disposal twenty-four hours a day. Dr. Derevenko's visits will also continue daily so long as you follow the regulations. I fail to see how sailor Nagorny's absence constitutes a lack of medical attention."

I will not shout, but my throat has tightened so I have to thrust each word out. "Dr. Botkin is the empress's personal physician. He is not experienced in tending the tsarevich's condition."

"Yet these tutors are?" Avdeev interrupts.

"You do not understand!"

"We agree, at last." Avdeev puts up his hand before I can reply. "I am following the orders of the Ural Regional Soviet. If you take issue with your treatment, you are free to petition the Central Executive Committee."

"Come, daughter," Papa says, easing me backward through the doorway. "*Tak i byt.*"

Frustration propels me across our bedroom, pacing like Mama before she left Tobolsk. "Petitions! Avdeev wants us to write petitions while Alyosha lies sick without his *dyadka*, Gilliard, Gibbes, or even Kolya, the poor darling. And Leonka! A boy of fourteen, stranded in the Urals without a sliver of family. How can they be so cruel to a pair of youngsters?" My words rush after one another like train carriages. "This must be that hateful Rodionov's doing. He never liked Nagorny. They think they can humiliate us and wear us down by stealing our people away." I pause to capture a breath and catch Olga fidgeting. "What is it? Olga, tell me."

"Look who's left besides Nyuta and Leonka. The youngest man is Chef Kharitonov, and he's almost twenty years older than Sednev and Nagorny. Dr. Botkin's kidneys are turning him into an old man before our eyes. Trupp is another decade beyond that. Out of all the loyal people who followed us, they've shaved us down to the five weakest."

My fury retreats, leaving me motionless. "What do you think they mean to do with us?"

"I don't know. Maybe just wear us down, like you said, but I don't like the feel of this place, Tatya. Tobolsk was never like this, even at the end with Rodionov. Why did they paint the windows over when they'd already built a fence too high to see past? Why won't they let Dr. Derevenko speak to us about anything but Aleksei's leg, even in Russian?"

I shake my head. Trying to comprehend why they do these things only makes them loom larger in my mind.

". . . for at a loss for any defense, this prayer do we sinners offer Thee as Master; have mercy on—"

A *pop* sounds from the street below, then a *chock* rattles the windowpane, halting our evening devotions. Our eyes fly open all at once. Beside me, Olga's hand hovers over her breastbone, frozen in the middle of crossing herself.

"Nicky, what was that?"

"It sounded like a rifle," Papa says. "Keep away from the window," he orders the Little Pair, already scrambling up from their knees to investigate.

A few moments later Avdeev puts his head through the door. "Did you hear anything?" he asks. "Is everyone well?"

"We heard a shot," Papa answers.

"One of the sentries outside fired his rifle into the window frame," Avdeev admits. "He claims he saw movement." Movement! With six of us on our knees and Aleksei in his cot? As if to prove the point, not one of us budges. "I apologize for the disturbance," Avdeev says, and slinks out.

"Clumsy lout!" I spit. "How could he see anything through those fogged-up panes?"

"Probably just fooling about with his rifle," Papa says, patting Mama and Olga at the same time. "All sentries do."

The next day thirty new men join the detachment guarding us.

"They're mostly from the Zlokazov factory in town," Maria says. "It's where Avdeev worked."

"How do you know?"

Maria shrugs. "I asked one of them. He said he'd rather be here than at the front, and it pays better than the ironworks. Four hundred rubles a month, plus board."

Anastasia snorts. "I'd like to make four hundred rubles a month just by leaning on a rifle and smoking cigarettes."

"I don't want to think about thirty more factory men fooling with their weapons," Olga says. "I'm going to sit with Aleksei."

"Dr. Derevenko is with him now, putting a plaster of Paris splint on his knee."

"All the more reason to distract Aleksei."

"But what will you say in front of Avdeev?"

For an instant, a hint of our merry Olga surfaces. "Don't worry, Governess. I won't speak any foreign languages—just read good Russian stories."

Restless, I wind idly through the house. Before the front windows, I let my hands drift across the panes, trying to cast a shadow on the carpet. As the clouds break and gather the glass glows and dims, but no light ever seems to penetrate the whitewash. Blacked-out windows would have been more bearable than this teasing, weakhearted sunlight.

"Tatiana Nikolaevna? Is there something you need?" Behind me, Dr. Botkin looks up from the desk in the study, straightening his tie and glasses all at once.

"*Nyet, spasibo*, Evgeni Sergeevich." My empty hands seem conspicuous, so I flatten them at my sides. "Is there . . . is there anything I may help you with?"

"Thank you, but I'm only writing a petition to the Central Executive Committee to allow Monsieur Gilliard or Mr. Gibbes into the house in place of Nagorny."

"A petition?" With a tingle, my pulse wakens my fingertips. "Will you show me how to write one? I would like to make a request as well."

He stands and offers me the chair. "*Konechno.*"

Day by day Aleksei's swelling goes down while the palisade separating us from the street sprouts higher, turning our rooms murkier yet. "It looks perfectly horrid out there," I tell Mama and Aleksei after my walk in the garden. "The planks are ragged as railroad ties. Even if we could look out the windows, I doubt we would be able to see the cathedral's crosses anymore." I crouch down alongside the arm of Mama's chair. "Mama, I wish you would come out into the garden with us."

Her smile pulls down the corners of her eyes as if it pains her. "My rubbery old heart. And those stairs are no good for my sciatica. With Nagorny gone someone must stay in with Baby."

"I could do that. I worry about you, staying cooped up indoors for so long."

She pets my cheek with the back of her fingers. "I know, darling. I wish I could be like other mothers. But this is God's cross, and we all must bear it."

Pressing back a sigh, I nod and kiss her hand before joining my sisters in the drawing room. I have half a mind to ask Anastasia to put on one of her canine pantomimes for me, but the moment I sit down the Little Pair pop up and head toward the duty office.

"Where are you two going?"

"Shift change," Anastasia says, pointing her wristwatch toward me. "We're going to go see who's on duty at the top of the stairs. You can come if you want." Anastasia keeps her face flat as a canvas while Maria giggles.

"No, thank you," I tell them, smiling a little in spite of myself as they scurry off.

"How is she?" Olga asks, nodding toward Mama's room.

"The same."

"I'll sit awhile with her."

My mind calls out, *Sit with me!* Instead I tell Olga, "You might try reading *Stories for the Convalescent.* Averchenko's stories always make her laugh. And her heart drops are on the nightstand."

Left only with my darning for company, my emotions fray until my throat turns hot and small, and I have to rip my stitches out one after another. I never meant to make Mama think I wish she were different. I only want her to be healthy, and this house is no place for that.

Back home, Mama's lilac boudoir almost always had the windows thrown wide open to the imperial park. I could have stood on Papa's shoulders and still not reached the top of those windows. Even when she spent days at a time on her chaise behind a silk screen, wide planters full of palms, lilacs, and roses freshened the room. Sealed up in this house, the air itself tastes dingy. She is thinner than in Tobolsk too, and hardly eats anything the women bring from the soviet soup kitchen in town. When Kharitonov or Leonka boil vermicelli for her on the alcohol stove, Mama only picks at that. Just the smell of the warming food makes her blanch. No matter how I explain the situation to Commandant Avdeev, he refuses to unseal the kitchen window one centimeter.

The next day Mama has a sick headache and cannot leave her room, much less go outdoors. All day long she lies in bed with her eyes closed, even when I ask Kharitonov and Trupp to carry Aleksei's cot into her bedroom for company. Outside, the workmen hammer at the fence, drowning out the sound of my reading until I grow fed up enough to march to the duty office myself.

"Must they hammer all day long?" I ask Avdeev. "The empress is unwell with a headache and cannot rest."

Avdeev exhales through his nose and lays his pen across his stationery as if it is a great effort. In the space where a monogram should be, it reads HOUSE OF SPECIAL PURPOSE in red lettering. He glances at the sofa, where one of his aides lounges with a newspaper. The man's boots look suspiciously like a pair of Papa's. "You complain that the rooms are too stuffy, and you complain when we take measures to allow you to open a window. Do you or don't you want fresh air?"

My heart begins to pound harder than the workmen's tools, but I hold my voice steady. "We have requested many times that a window be opened. A single *fortochka* is not enough ventilation."

"Well then, you will have to put up with the hammering. Not one window will be unsealed until the fence has been properly extended."

If I were not the second eldest daughter of an emperor, I would stamp my foot. "When will our people be returned to us?" I ask instead.

Avdeev turns back to his desk. "I have no news."

"Thank you, Mr. Commissar." Only a grunt in return.

While my temper calms, I stand in the doorway between our room and Mama's, watching her agitated breaths and the way her eyelids flutter under the compress. I wish I knew whether Mama is truly ailing, or worn down with worry like Olga. She is so sensitive, perhaps my pleading yesterday made her ill.

Mama is so brave and capable in a crisis, yet so fragile without a cause to demand her strength. It amazes me, and God forgive me, but it frustrates me too, the way her aches and pains evaporate in the presence of anyone suffering worse than she is. A crisis with Aleksei, a charity bazaar, nursing in the lazaret, all of it can carry her above her own pain. Sometimes I think she can be healthy for anyone but herself.

But if that were true, she would be strong for me, too. Mama's love is as constant as the baptismal cross round my neck, yet I can hardly remember a time without wishing I could also be worthy of her strength.

When I was a little girl, I sent Mama notes nearly every day she was too ill to leave her sofa. Each time, I wrote to her how I prayed to Christ for her health, and how much I wished we could be together, even just for tea, but it was never enough. When one of us is sick, she devotes whole days and nights to tending us, but by the time we are well again it is Mama who needs weeks to recover. It only makes it harder to get well, knowing what our comfort costs her.

The next day Mama is enough improved that she comes to the dining room to eat with us, but by the end of dinner it sounds as if someone is battering the piano in the duty office with knives and forks.

Mama rubs her temples. "Tatiana, go ask the men to be quieter, please. I'm going back to bed."

Men I do not recognize crowd Avdeev's office, all sprawled about as if they own the place. Probably more of Moshkin's vulgar "comrades."

"Perhaps you would like to join us?" Moshkin asks before I open my mouth. "Do you know the words to 'The Workers'

Marseillaise'?" He gestures to the man at the piano. "Come on, boys, let's teach the tsar's daughter our new anthem!"

Arise, arise, working people!
Arise against the enemies, hungry brother!
Sound the cry of the people's vengeance!
Forward!

I turn on my heel and leave the filthy brutes behind. They will not see me even think about crying. Avdeev will hear about this tomorrow, even if he does nothing about it.

38

MARIA NIKOLAEVNA

May 1918
Ekaterinburg

Papa shuffles the bezique deck loudly as machine-gun fire. "This prison regime!" he complains. "It's unbearable, being penned up on a fine evening."

Out of nowhere, there's a sound like an ax biting into wood—*thock!*—and before Mama can finish saying "Nicky?" Tatiana comes running from the bedrooms.

"Did you hear that? Our bedroom floor jolted under my feet. It must have been a shot from the cellar."

A bullet! Without even thinking about it, my feet snap up from the floor and bury themselves between the sofa and my backside. Anastasia smirks at me, but I don't care. Both of us know perfectly well I'm not as brave as she is. Olga's already crying.

"Christ have mercy," Mama gasps. "Is Baby all right?"

"He did not even wake up, *slava Bogu*," Tatiana says. "*Dushka*," she tells Olga, "no one is hurt."

Just then Avdeev comes rushing in from the other direction and sees Olga hiccuping on Tatiana's shoulder. "Is anyone injured?"

"No, and no thanks to you," Mama snaps. "What's happened now?"

Avdeev blanches. I'm not exactly sorry for him, but I know how it feels to stand in front of Mama when she's like this. "Comrade Dobrynin accidentally fired a shot into the cellar ceiling while setting the bolt on his rifle. Did the bullet penetrate the floor?"

"See for yourself," Tatiana tells him.

It's silly of me, but when I finally coax myself into leaving the sofa, I rush to our bedroom on tiptoe, hugging the walls as if the floor is a fishpond full of sharks. If I wasn't sure Anastasia would tease me for days, I'd snug my cot up to the wall, too.

"We would like to be permitted to open a window," Papa reminds Avdeev at morning inspection as if everything is business as usual. It's not even nine o'clock, and the house already smells of cologne, damp tea leaves, dog, and last night's cutlets.

"Your request is denied, Citizen Romanov. My orders from the Ural Regional Soviet regarding windows have not changed. However, the Central Executive Committee is procuring supplies and workers to erect a second palisade around the entire property. When it is complete, the Committee for the Examination of the Question of Windows in the House of Special Purpose will reconsider its ruling on ventilation. Until such time, all windows will remain closed."

My sisters and I mope together. "'Committee for the Examination of the Question of Windows in the House of Special Purpose,'" Tatiana mocks. "I used to think Avdeev was joking when he spoke like that. How absurd. No one has the power to do anything without half of Russia approving it first."

I lean my head against the whitewashed pane. "Do you think the potted plants back home ever felt like this?"

Anastasia gives me her cuckoo-face. "What?"

"I always thought it was funny, the way their leaves turned toward the windows every day. Now it makes me sad to think about them stretching toward the outside."

Olga's lips tuck themselves over her teeth. I don't know why, but I wish I hadn't said that. "I'm going to go read with Aleksei," she says.

"That's all Olga ever does anymore," Anastasia complains. "Books, Aleksei, and Mama are her new best friends. She's butting in on your territory, Tatiana."

"Leave her be. If it makes Olga feel better to sit with Mama and Aleksei, I will find something different to do."

I wait to hear the door to Aleksei's bedroom close before I ask. "Tatya? You talk about her like she's sick."

Tatiana's lip trembles, and she nods. "I know, Mashka. It reminds me of the lazaret. Olga may not be ill, but I am afraid she is far from well."

"Whatever *that* means."

Anastasia's right. I don't think Tatiana knows quite what she means either, but now that she's said it, none of us can pretend we haven't noticed anymore.

By the end of May Aleksei is well enough that Mama lets me carry him outside. Propped in Mama's wheelchair, he can sit in the sun on the front steps with Mama, Tatiana, and Joy now that one side of the new palisade is finished.

The rest of us watch the last palings go up around the back garden, boxing in everything, even the fence that's been standing since Papa and Mama and I arrived. One by one, the long planks lean up out of nowhere, like soldiers standing to attention. From down here we won't be able to see a single thing when it's done, not even the tops of the trees in the neighboring yards. At least the lilacs are inside the fence.

Up on the balcony, one of the guards leans over the garden with his forearms propped across the railing and a book in his hands. Even from across the yard, I can see the binding is leather, not cheap paper.

"What are you squinting at, Mashka?" Olga asks.

I point. "Isn't that one of our books?"

She follows my finger. I can tell by her face that I'm right.

"Never mind," Tatiana says from behind me. "Mama needs you. Aleksei's squirming in the wheelchair."

"Baby, do you want Maria to carry you back inside?" Mama's asking. Joy nudges at my hand as if he doesn't want me to wait for my brother to answer.

Aleksei shakes his head, biting his lip. Our eyes all turn toward his knee. "It hurts," he admits, so I lift him up like a bundle of laundry and carry him straight to bed to wait for the doctor.

Dr. Derevenko frowns at his measuring tape. "The swelling has increased again. Probably from dressing and moving about. I'll have to put on another splint."

"I should have known better," Mama moans in English.

"Alexandra Feodorovna," Avdeev snaps. "Speaking German is not permitted in the presence of the guards. This is your second warning. If you persist in ignoring the regulations, the doctor will not be admitted at all."

Mama goes white, and I know Tatiana wants to correct Avdeev for not knowing the difference between English and German, but not one of us says another word, not even in Russian. With Monsieur Gilliard, Mr. Gibbes, and his *dyadka* all gone, the thought of Aleksei losing Dr. Derevenko makes my mouth turn to paste.

Just as we feared, Dr. Derevenko doesn't come the next day, or the day after that. Finally on Saturday Avdeev tells us Dr. Derevenko's house is under quarantine for scarlet fever, so he can't come until Thursday!

"I don't see what difference it would make," Anastasia complains. "We might as well have scarlet fever for all we thrash about in this heat."

It's true. Everyone gets so hot and antsy in between our walks outside, I'm afraid we're going to spark against each other like kindling.

Avdeev has nothing to say about what's going on, and he

doesn't give us any newspapers, either, not even when Papa's hemorrhoids leave him stranded in bed for two days straight. Tatiana reads aloud to us from *The Crusaders* for hours at a time, and it's all we can do to pay attention.

My eyes fly open in the dark, my body tensed for another blast, but my ears ring with silence. If the windowpanes weren't rattling as hard as my heart, I could make believe I dreamed that sound. On the other side of the room, Tatiana and Olga's voices whisper prayers. I don't know if it's Jemmy or Anastasia I hear panting. For the first time since our cots arrived, I wish my sisters and I were all piled together on the floor again. Outside, there's a little bit of scuffling and some voices. Then nothing, except the sound of nobody sleeping.

First thing Sunday morning Dr. Botkin goes straight to Avdeev's office to find out what happened. There isn't much for the doctor to do anymore, except give Mama her heart drops and try to convince Avdeev to be decent to us. "Only a hand grenade, Your Majesty," Dr. Botkin tells Papa. "A careless guard posted at the attic window dropped his grenade into the garden. No damages or injuries."

"The garden's such a wreck, we won't even be able to tell where it fell," Anastasia grumps.

"A careless guard at the attic post," Papa repeats. "Isn't that where one of the machine guns is stationed?"

Dr. Botkin nods.

Papa doesn't have to say another word. We all know what he's thinking. Suddenly I don't want my breakfast anymore, and go ring for the lavatory instead.

My hand is on the doorknob to the vestibule when Dr. Derevenko's voice comes up the main stairwell. I almost don't recognize him, it's been so long since we've heard him speak at all, much less about anything except splints and thermometers.

"There are rumors afloat in town that Aleksei Nikolaevich died of fright in the night and was buried at dawn," he calls to the sentry at the top of the stairs.

"Rubbish," Comrade Sidorov's voice answers. "Get out of here—you're under quarantine. You'll see for yourself on Thursday."

Thank goodness it wasn't Olga waiting by the door instead of me. I'm not terribly clever the way she is, but even I know things can't be good in town if our doctor is as nervous outside the fence as we are behind it.

Early the next morning, a whiff of fresh air wakes my nose so softly I'm sure I'm dreaming all over again. One by one, we creep from our cots and tip up our chins to follow the scent into Papa and Mama's bedroom.

Papa points at the tiny rectangle set into the window facing the lane. "The wind was so strong last night, it blew straight in through the *fortochka*." Barefoot in our white nightgowns, the four of us stretch our necks like swans to breathe it in.

"Happy birthday, Tatya!" I cry, and lift her to her toes in a massive hug.

"This is the best present of all," she says.

I don't know what there is about fresh air inside a house, but just that trickle of breeze is enough to make it smell so much better even than the outdoors. The scent winds itself like a ribbon all the way from Papa and Mama's corner bedroom into the stuffy drawing room and study. Without even thinking about it, my sisters and I sing folk songs and hymns as we dress and strip the sheets for the wash.

On top of that, thirteen new guards arrive and start duty indoors. Mama would scold if she caught me with my nose pressed against the window to the corridor, but it's like a present for me, having new faces to learn.

"Mr. Commandant, I would like to get something from the storage shed, please."

"What?"

"I said—"

"I heard you. What item?"

Stupid. I'd like to turn myself inside out. This was all Anastasia's idea. Somehow she thought I'd be the best one to do the asking. "Some photo albums and paints?" Avdeev looks at me as if I should have more to say. "If we can't take new photographs, my sisters thought maybe we could try coloring the old ones. To pass the time?"

"Fine, fine. Wait here." After a minute, he comes back with one of the new guards. "Comrade Skorokhodov will accompany you to the shed. Albums are permitted, but no camera equipment," he reminds the young man.

Out in the shed, some of our crates and suitcases are already lying open. "I'm sorry, I don't know which one it is. Things are mixed up since I was here last." Skorokhodov shrugs, so I sort through the luggage as best I can. It's hard to tell with everything in such a jumble, but it seems like little things are missing here and there. The albums and paints are easy, but the paintbrushes I can't seem to find anywhere. Some of Papa's uniforms have blank spots where fancy buttons and trim should be, and there's a whole stack of linens with the monograms torn out. I hold up a handful of ribbons from one of Tatiana's bags. "I didn't ask for extra hair ribbons, but do you think it's all right if I bring them to surprise my sister? It's her birthday, and our hair is getting awfully long again."

Skorokhodov looks over his shoulder, then back at me. "What happened to your hair?"

"Measles. This time last year, we were all bald as babies."

"Put them in your pocket," he says. I smile and fumble around my armload of albums. "May I hold some of those for you while you search?"

"*Da, spasibo.*" The pile reaches nearly from Skorokhodov's elbow to his chin. He stares down at the golden double-headed eagle stamped on the top cover. "You can look at the pictures if you like," I tell him. "I don't mind." He blushes so hard, you'd think I told him he could peek under my skirt.

Somehow I manage not to giggle, and turn back to my search without embarrassing him any more. Not even when I hear the album's leather binding creak.

Out in the square, people shout and march in front of the house, but we can't hear what they're saying. All I'm sure of is they're angry. Every time I turn to the windows, I feel like a goldfish bumping up against the walls of its bowl. I know I can't see out, but I can't help it. When Dr. Derevenko comes at last, it makes my throat ache with frustration to know he's walked right past all that commotion to get here and can't say a word about it. The way his kind old teddy-bear face sags, I think he feels the same way.

"What's going on out there?" I ask one of the guards in the yard, but he straightens his chin and stares past me. Oh, this awful fence! If we try to peek between the planks or tip-toe near a knothole, the guards bark at us—*Nelzya!*—even though there's another whole fence beyond the one we can see from the inside.

"Forbidden, forbidden. *Every*thing is forbidden now," Anastasia grumps.

"Something's changed," I tell Tatiana inside. "When I talk to the guards, they shuffle and look everywhere at once, as if they expect someone to sneak up on us."

"Mama has told you over and over, Maria. You should not be speaking to them in the first place."

"I don't know why you won't. I think you'd like Anatoly Yakimovich. He's a third-year seminary student. He even refused to join the Bolshevik Party."

"A third-year seminary student should know better than to earn his daily bread holding a family captive."

"Tatya," I beg, "some of them are friendly."

"That may be, but there is a long way between friendly and friendship. They are stealing from us. *Slava Bogu*, the crates of Mama and Papa's old letters and diaries have not been disturbed, but Mama's panoramic camera is missing from the shed."

"But we don't know which of them took it."

"*Konechno.* That is exactly my point."

"All right, already," Anastasia says. "So you're right. But listen, Governess. If the guards won't even talk to Mashka, there's got to be something fishy going on."

Tatiana looks up at the windowpane as if she can see through the whitewash. "Mama said the sentry outside has fidgeted terribly the last few nights. She has hardly slept for all his noise."

Now I'm right, and I don't like the way it feels one bit.

"Do you think God really cares how our icons are arranged?" Anastasia whispers so Mama and the Big Pair can't hear. "It's been nearly an hour."

"What else can we do? Avdeev said there'd be a priest for the Feast of the Ascension. *Otets* Storozhev should be here any minute."

"They might as well do a jigsaw puzzle instead, the way they keep moving things around."

"We've done all our jigsaw puzzles," I remind her. "Twice."

"Maybe we should mix them all together and see if we can't make one big picture."

Avdeev's voice breaks up our little huddle. "No priest could come," he announces. "It's such a big holiday." His upper lip wriggles as if his bristly little mustache tickles him.

"What priest is too busy to minister to oppressed captives on the Feast of the Ascension?" Mama demands. "Didn't you tell them who we are?"

Anastasia nudges me. "I'll bet you our dear commandant

drank too much last night and forgot to make the request."

Sadly we take our icons down and fold up the embroidered throw we use for an altar cloth. I tell myself I don't mind, but Mama and the Big Pair are so disappointed, it makes my nose tingle and my eyes smart just to look at them.

"You take the first walk," I tell the Big Pair. "I'll sit with Mama."

Avdeev interrupts. "You will not be allowed out today."

"Why?" Papa wants to know, but Avdeev won't say.

In the evening he comes back again. "There has been an anarchist attempt to take over one of the ironworks. We have reason to believe they may attack the town as well. It may be necessary to evacuate. Please pack quietly, so as not to arouse suspicion in the guards."

Papa twists his cigarette across his thumb. "And what of our people, Nagorny and Sednev?"

Is it my imagination, or does Avdeev roll his eyes? "Arrangements will be made for them to join you later if evacuation becomes necessary."

"Very well," Papa says. "But two of our crates, 'NA Thirteen' and 'AF Nine,' cannot be left behind with the men pilfering from the shed."

"I can make no promises about luggage in this situation," Avdeev replies. "The Ural Regional Soviet is not concerned with the safety of your belongings."

"That much is abundantly clear," Mama says behind his back.

"Papa, where will they take us?"

He takes a long drag on his cigarette before answering me. "Moscow, perhaps? And then to England, if God wills it."

That night and all the next day we live like a camp, dipping in and out of our valises every time we change clothes and pretending as if everything's normal when we go out in the yard.

I wait until we're past the guards to ask Olga, "Do you think they'll take us away?"

"If they can't get the anarchists under control, they'll have to."

"I mean like Nagorny and Sednev. Take us away and never tell Papa and Mama what's become of us?"

She takes so long to answer, I have time to notice one of the new guards smiling as we pass by the balcony. I think his name is Ivan, but there have been so many Ivans already! Anyway, I can't tell for sure if he's smiling at me, or just cracking a sunflower seed between his teeth.

When Olga finally says, "I don't know, Mashka," it blots that smile right out of my head.

"But you always know. You're the smartest."

"No, I'm not. Sometimes I see things coming, but not until it's too late to turn back. I wonder and worry until I wear holes in my thoughts. I don't think I've had a good, fresh thought in ages. Anastasia is the clever one."

"I don't see how. She's awful at lessons."

"And lazy, too," Olga agrees. "But when she wants to be, she's sharp and bright as a tack. I can put the pieces together when they're laid before me, but Anastasia is the one who could invent the puzzle itself—if she ever bothered to try."

"Which one am I?"

"The dearest one." She takes my hand. Her fingers are

so cold, even in the sunshine. "Sometimes I think you're the only one who might come through all of this without it really touching you."

I stop and stare at her. "But it does touch me! It presses on me all day long."

Olga stops too and gives me a tender look, fingering the curls on my forehead. "Only bruises, Mashka. You'll be the same darling girl, without bearing a grudge or a scar. It's too late for me, but you're the one with the golden heart. You are the one I never worry about, and I don't know how we'd get along without you ever again."

My heart reaches right up into my throat until I can only blink. I want to ask her what makes her so awfully sad and worried, but I'm too shy, or maybe only too scared. "I'm glad you need me now," I say instead, and reach my arm around Olga's waist to cuddle against her as we walk. "I remember when I was a little girl, before Anastasia was even old enough to play with. You and Tatiana built a playhouse out of chairs and blankets and wouldn't let me in. You said you already had a mama and a baby inside, and you didn't need anyone but a footman. I sobbed like anything."

Olga nods. "I remember. And then you dried your eyes and came knocking at our door. 'I'm the auntie,' you said, 'and I've bought presents for everyone.' Tatya and I could have cried, we were so ashamed. Even then, you were the sweetest blossom of the whole family."

I can't say anything after that, but I hold Olga's hand until it's every bit as warm as mine.

39

ANASTASIA NIKOLAEVNA

June 1918
Ekaterinburg

*A*fter we've been living like gypsies all day and all night, Avdeev calls the whole thing off. "The anarchists have been captured. You will remain in Ekaterinburg for at least a few more days," he announces, his words running together a little. "Sednev and the sailor Nagorny will likely rejoin you on Sunday. Also, Dr. Derevenko has made arrangements with the Notovikh"—he shakes his head and tries again—"the Novotikhvinsky convent for milk and eggs to be delivered."

"Promises," Olga says. "That's all we get anymore."

I don't believe Avdeev any more than Olga does, especially when he's tipsy, but the way she says it makes me want to stick a hatpin in her. Anything to yank her out of her never-ending slump. I used to wonder what I'd do when we got out of here. Watching her, I keep catching myself wondering *if* we'll get out of here.

But the next morning we have milk and eggs just as Avdeev said. Papa downs his first glass without a breath and comes up for air with little beads of white dripping from his mustache. There's enough provisions for Kharitonov to fix everybody's meals in the kitchen instead of just boiling Mama's macaroni while the rest of us wait for our dinner from the canteen. Mama hides behind her handkerchief and complains about the alcohol stove making it hotter, and how it smells of kitchen everywhere.

She's right about the smells and the heat, but Maria and I don't mind. The nuns never come late, so we wait in the dining room for them to smile at us as they carry the stuff through to the kitchen. After breakfast on Sunday, Maria and I nose through the boxes of food as if we expect to find Nagorny and Sednev tucked in between the beets and cutlets.

The day before my birthday, four men come strutting in with their hands behind their backs as if they've been taking lessons from Avdeev. They look into each room like they're thinking about buying it.

"So this is the new Russian government?" Mama jeers. "Four men sent to decide whether or not one window may be opened. Preposterous."

"They were up to something," Tatiana says. "Did you see the way they pretended not to look at anything at all? It felt like we were the ones being inventoried."

I don't care. It's horridly hot—hot as teacups—and thinking makes it hotter. Even through those frosted windows, the sun bakes us like soggy pastries all day long. When we go outside, sometimes I can't believe how cool the summer air can feel.

Tatiana snaps the newspaper shut. "Where do they come up with this rubbish?"

According to the latest rumor, Papa's been killed by a soldier in the Red Army. It's ridiculous, but none of us laughs. No wonder Avdeev's been holding the papers back.

"Is that why those men were here two days ago?" Maria asks. We look at her like one of the dogs has sat up and quoted Pushkin.

Olga nods slowly. "I think you're right, Mashka." The look on her face as she thinks it over makes something between my stomach and my throat clamp up. "It's no good for us if a newspaper story can make Moscow nervous enough to send four men to make sure we're still here."

My voice squeaks a little. "Do you think it could really happen?"

"I don't know. But Moscow must have reason to worry."

Maria sputters like a windup toy. "The Reds are supposed to be guarding us, aren't they? Why would one of them want to kill Papa? They already have us."

"If Olga is right, then we may not be able to trust our own guards, Mashka. You have to be careful who you speak to, and what you tell them." Tatiana may be bossy, but I'd rather hear bad news from her than Olga. She has a knack for telling it without scaring us. It's like she bites the fuse off the words before she lets them out of her mouth.

"Why does Olga always say 'Moscow' when she talks about the government?" Maria asks.

"I don't know. What's the difference?"

"She makes it sound like there's a machine cranking out decisions in an office somewhere. Like it isn't people deciding what happens to us. Do you think everyone talked about Papa like that when he was tsar? 'Petrograd says this and that'? It wasn't Petrograd, it was Papa, just like it isn't Moscow, it's Lenin. He's a man too, maybe even with a family. How do you like being called 'the prisoners'?"

I don't like it one bit, but that's what we are.

On Tatiana's birthday we feasted on a scrap of a breeze from Papa and Mama's bedroom window. For *my* birthday, we learn how to bake bread. The idea of having something new to do is so delicious, I don't even care how stinging hot the kitchen gets. Chef Kharitonov shows us how to measure warm water, oil, and yeast, and we all crowd around the bowl to watch it bubble up. "Look at it." I poke at the foamy goo. "It's just like a nasty hanky in there."

"Anastasia Nikolaevna, you will never change!" Tatiana's eyes roll like a pair of marbles, but today her voice feels like a tickle instead of the usual scratch.

I fold my arms, stand up straight as an imperial soldier at a review, and give her my best grin. "Oh, won't I?"

All three of my sisters cock their heads at me. Tatiana steps back to take in the full picture. How far inside me can she see? A moment, and her smile curls like a streamer.

"You may become a passable grown-up yet," she admits, then bats a smudge of flour from my nose. "But promise me you will always be our *shvybzik*."

Something inside me bubbles up even faster than yeast. "I promise."

For the first time in ages, we all go outside for our walk, even Mama. There's hardly enough room in the garden for the six of us plus Aleksei's wheelchair, so we troop in circles like a line of elephants while Mama and Aleksei crowd under the lilac. All I want to do is go inside and watch the bread dough rise. Imagine!

"Let me knead it," I beg my sisters when the dough's puffed up like a big pale mushroom. "It's my birthday— I want to make it for you all by myself. We'll have bread instead of birthday cake." My short hair clings to my neck and forehead as I smash and flip the dough. I have to keep stopping to mop my face against my elbow. I'll be lucky if the whole thing doesn't taste like sliced sweat when I'm done.

All afternoon the whole house smells of baking bread, and for once Mama doesn't turn green behind her handkerchief.

"Not bad," Papa says at dinner.

"Excellent bread," Mama proclaims, and I'm prouder of that loaf than any trick I've played, or joke I've told.

40

OLGA NIKOLAEVNA

7 June 1918
Ekaterinburg

"Mama is not going outside today." Tatiana fans Ortipo with a page torn from the wall calendar in Papa and Mama's room. "One of us must stay in with her."

Anastasia groans. "What a surprise. Whose turn is it?"

Tatiana points the limp square of paper at her. "Yours."

"Not again! I'll suffocate in here, or burst into flames—I broke a sweat the minute I stepped out of the bath."

"It's just as hot outside as in," Maria says. "Even the lilacs are too wilted to hold their heads up, poor things."

The heat in my sisters' voices makes the motionless air thicken like syrup around me. "I'll sit with Mama."

Maria's face falls. "You're always with Mama or Aleksei. We never see you anymore."

"Sweetheart Mashka, you can't be lonely for me in a

house this small. We practically bump into each other all day long."

"Maria could bump into someone at midnight in Red Square," Anastasia snaps.

"Stop your ugliness and leave Maria be," Tatiana chides, then turns to me. "You should get more fresh air and some sunshine, *dushka*. Only Aleksei is paler than you now. I would rather stay indoors myself than see you cooped up again."

Even though Maria and Tatiana are right, I can't tell them why. Maybe I'm threading things together that have nothing to do with one other, but I've read about the French Revolution, how King Louis XVI and Marie Antoinette lost their heads at the hands of their own people. Even the ten-year-old dauphin died alone in prison.

Only the daughter escaped.

"Hold my place, darling." Mama hands me her copy of *Spiritual Readings*. "I'm going to the water closet." She comes back breathless with a flush scattered over her cheeks. My shoulders clench, bracing for a tirade about some new limerick about Papa on the wall, or a remark from one of Moshkin's sentries.

"A letter," she whispers instead, patting her bodice. Paper crinkles softly beneath the graying lace. "One of the guards passed it to me in the passage outside the duty office."

"Who is it from?" Thoughts of Isa, Monsieur Gilliard, or our relatives in the Crimea carousel through my mind.

"I don't know. It was folded and rolled up tight as a medicine vial. I had to loosen the creases just to smooth it inside my dress. What I glimpsed was written in French."

Before I have time to wonder, Chef Kharitonov comes in with two glasses of tea on a tray. We puzzle at him, bringing tea at this hour, and in this heat. Trupp is always the one to serve, but as Kharitonov leans down to offer Mama a glass he whispers, "One of them found it hidden in the cork of a bottle of milk from the convent, Your Majesty."

We seven cluster in the farthest corner of Aleksei's room while Leonka Sednev toys with the dogs outside the commandant's office, coaxing them to yip. Trupp and Kharitonov stand guard in the drawing room and dining room.

"In the cork of a milk bottle, Kharitonov said?" Papa asks, marveling at the size. Creases cover the paper like a tiny checkerboard.

"Imagine a nun folding that all up and jamming it into a milk bottle," Anastasia says. "It's like something out of Sherlock Holmes."

"It must be against the law to sneak something like this in to us," Maria whispers. "A nun wouldn't break the law, would she, Papa?"

"God's law and the Bolsheviks' are not the same," Tatiana replies.

"'Your friends sleep no longer,'" Mama reads in French, "'and hope that the hour so long awaited has come.'"

Anastasia squeals. "It even *sounds* like a detective story!"

My eyebrows crimp. "The French doesn't seem right." It's correct, but something is off.

"It should be *Votre Majesté*, not *vous*," Tatiana says, but no one's interested.

Mama glows. "Didn't I tell you there were good Russian men waiting to save us?"

The rest of the note reads in red ink:

> *The army of Slavic friends is less than 80 kilometers*
> *from Ekaterinburg. The soldiers of the Red Army*
> *cannot effectively resist. Be attentive to any movement*
> *from the outside; wait and hope. But at the same time,*
> *I beg you, be careful, because the Bolsheviks, before*
> *being <u>vanquished, represent real and serious danger</u>*
> *<u>for you</u>. Be ready at every hour, day and night. Make*
> *a drawing of your two bedrooms, the position of the*
> *furniture, the beds. Write the hour that you all go to*
> *bed. One of you must not sleep between 2:00 and 3:00*
> *on all the following nights. You must give your answer*
> *in <u>writing</u> to the same soldier who transmits this note*
> *to you, <u>but do not say a single word</u>.*
>
> *From someone who is ready to die for you,*
> *Officer of the Russian Army*

Escape! The very idea makes my blood buzz in my ears. Could we truly? "Are we going to answer?"

"*Konechno*, it would be rude not to reply," Tatiana says. As if this message is no more dangerous than an invitation to a party.

"May I suggest that Your Majesties allow someone

else to write the reply?" Dr. Botkin asks before I can think how to say it myself. "If the Bolsheviks were to discover a smuggled correspondence, in your handwriting . . ."

Tatiana pats her pockets for a pencil. "Evgeni Sergeevich is right. Let me."

I swoop the paper from Papa's hand. "Tatya, darling, it has to be legible." Her cheeks color, but she hands over the pencil. If it weren't a fact as much as an excuse, I might feel guilty for embarrassing my sister—the real truth is, I want to be the one to write the reply.

Having the pencil in my hand, knowing I will be the one charting our path across the page—the thought alone makes me feel solid again, as if I'm finally connected to what's happening to me.

12 June 1918

The very day after we send our first reply, Avdeev orders two guards in to unseal a window in the corner bedroom.

All at once, the street sounds have sharp edges again. Just breathing is like biting into a peach straight from the tree in Livadia instead of one that's been sliced and laid on a plate in Petrograd. And the coincidence of it—as if God himself has been reading the officer's concerns over our shoulder:

> One of your windows must be unglued so that you
> can open it at the right time. Indicate which window,
> please. The fact that the little tsarevich cannot walk

*complicates matters, but we have taken that into
account, and I don't think it will be too great an
inconvenience. Write if you need two people to carry
him in their arms or one of you can take care of that.
If you know the exact time in advance, is it possible to
make sure the little one will be asleep for one or two
hours before?*

*The doctor must give his opinion, but in case of need
we can provide something for that.*

"What do they mean?" Aleksei asks. "Why should I be
asleep?"

"Nicky, do they mean to drug Baby?" Mama wonders.

"I'm not a baby!" Aleksei yelps. "Why should I have to
sleep through it all? I won't make any noise."

Tatiana's voice hisses through the air like an arrow. "Then
start practicing this minute! The commandant will hear you
before we even have the plan."

While Dr. Botkin reasons with Aleksei, I write about
the guards inside the house, that they're armed with rifles,
revolvers, and bombs, how Avdeev and his three aides can
come into our rooms whenever they please. There are three
machine-gun posts—that we know of—and fifty more
guards lodged across the street. I beg them not to forget
about Dr. Botkin, Nyuta, Trupp, Kharitonov, and young
Leonka, who have followed us back and forth across Russia
for almost a year. I tell them about Nagorny and Sednev,
still held somewhere in the city, and Dr. Derevenko. There
are the bells at each sentry post to consider, and our things

in the storage shed. Papa's diaries are still in there, a whole crate of them, and Mama's letters, too.

"Please, Your Majesties, do not worry about me, nor the other men," Dr. Botkin implores. "It will be much easier to get the seven of you with the maid and kitchen boy."

"I will not hear of it, Evgeni Sergeevich," Papa says. "We will not leave our people behind. Not after all your loyalty."

"I have been bedridden for three days with these kidneys," he pleads. "I am in no better condition for travel than the tsarevich—worse, perhaps. Please, do not miss your chance to escape on my account."

I'd like to shake the both of them, though I know neither will budge. "I will tell them what you said, Evgeni Sergeevich. And I will tell them what Papa said as well, about leaving our people behind. It's out of our hands, but they will know how both of you feel."

As I write, my skin prickles as if the air is charged, like the moments before a thunderstorm. Less than eighty kilometers, the officer said, and that was days ago. No matter whether this officer's plot is successful, something is going to happen. Soon.

41

TATIANA NIKOLAEVNA

12 June 1918
Ekaterinburg

*E*verything must appear just as usual. It does not seem possible with all of us practically crackling at the effort of appearing ordinary, but so far the guards have not given off a whiff of suspicion. Even Dr. Botkin, stricken with kidney pains for days at a time, refuses to moan for fear of calling attention to our rooms.

Yet when Papa complains to Avdeev, it sounds tired as an old play. "Your men are stealing from us."

"If you have complaints, you are free to petition the Central Executive Committee."

"Moshkin's girlfriends are probably parading round the city under our own parasols!" I add for good measure. Mama looks at me as though I have been cheeky as Anastasia. My body buzzes with the reprimand, even though she has not said a word.

If I could see anything but fence boards outside our window, maybe it would keep the tension in this house from twisting tight as a tourniquet. Walking outside is not enough, not when we can only turn circles in the yard like tigers in a cage. Even requesting our usual favors from Avdeev seems absurd, but I am the one who asks for things, and I must keep up the charade. The guards probably think I am as big a flirt as Maria, the way I linger in the doorway each day. For me, it is only another sort of idleness. With Mama on her feet again and the details of our escape out of my reach, I hardly know what else to do with myself.

"What does it say about me, if I am only content when others are suffering?" I ask Olga.

"That isn't true, Tatya."

"It is. That first day we arrived, I thanked God we were all together again, but the moment I thought of what I would do with myself in this place, I could have begged Him to send us back to Tobolsk. There was no household to manage, Aleksei was on the mend, and Maria had taken care of Mama. It was almost a relief when Aleksei bumped his knee that night."

"Tatya, sweetheart, don't. You'll wear yourself out."

The tremor in Olga's voice doubles the guilt already simmering inside me. Why do I have such wicked thoughts? I could be in a hospital nursing soldiers, doing good, useful work. Instead I sit in this house all day, wishing my family ill so I will have something to occupy myself. I would rather be sick in my own bed than think such terrible things.

13 June 1918

Nearly a week after his first letter, the officer finally lets us in on his plan:

> *As of now it is like this: once the signal comes, you close and barricade with furniture the door that separates you from the guards, who will be blocked and terror-stricken inside the house. With a rope especially made for that purpose, you climb out through the window—we will be waiting for you at the bottom. The rest is not difficult; there are many means of transportation and the hiding place is as good as ever. The big question is getting the little one down: is it possible. Answer after thinking carefully. In any case, the father, the mother, and the son come down first; the girls and then the doctor follow them.*
> *An officer*

Papa first, then Mama, Aleksei, and finally "the girls," he says. I have never chafed at my position the way Anastasia does, but being placed in a lump at the bottom of the list pricks at me like a syringe under my skin. Papa would never put his own safety before ours, yet there is no question whom this officer values most.

Looking up at our windows from the yard, I ask Olga, "What do you think?"

"This will never work. Never mind getting Aleksei down without Nagorny's help, can you picture Mama dangling from a rope over the street?" *Konechno*, Olga is right, but something in the way she says so jerks my exasperation straight to the surface.

"It must work," I insist.

She gives me a look my face recognizes instantly, even though I have never seen it myself: It is the expression I so often aim at Anastasia. No wonder my little sister scowls back at me so fiercely. "How many times has Mama even walked down the stairs to the garden?" Olga continues. "And what about Dr. Botkin and old Trupp? I'm not sure I could do it myself. What about the rope? We can't very well petition the Central Executive Committee for one."

"If the officer is willing to risk his life, we must try."

"His life is his own business—I don't see why he should chance ours as well."

"You have written him yourself at least twice that no risk should be taken unless he is absolutely sure of the result, and both times he has given his word."

"How can he be sure? There's risk in everything, even carrying Aleksei down the stairs."

I have no answer. "*Dushka*," I ask instead, "you make it sound as if you would rather stay here."

Olga wipes the perspiration from her temples. "I don't know which is more dangerous, remaining here or risking escape. All I know for certain is I'm tired of other people deciding what will happen to us."

"You must not speak a word of the officer's plan near the guards or the commandant," I tell Leonka. "Do you understand?"

"*Konechno*, Tatiana Nikolaevna. But what about my uncle Vanya?"

"The emperor is doing everything he can to insist on the safety of all our people." Leonka peers at me with his small, deep eyes until I realize I am speaking to a child, not a minister of the court. A child who has shown more bravery and loyalty than half of Russia these last weeks. I put my two hands on his shoulders. The coarse gray fabric has gone almost as thin as the silver tissue our court gowns were made of. "My papa will not let the officer leave your uncle behind, if he can help it."

"What about the dogs?" Anastasia wants to know.

I spin round. "What?"

"When the officer comes, how will we get them down?"

Bozhe moi, the dogs! How could I have overlooked my fat Ortipo, little Jemmy, and Aleksei's Joy? My mind gropes for a way to fill this gap in our plan. Perhaps if we had sacks to lower them in, but so far we do not even have a rope for ourselves. My face must tell Anastasia all she needs to know.

"I'm putting Jemmy in my blouse."

"Anastasia, we must not complicate things."

Her arms tighten round the poor thing until the tip of Jemmy's tongue peeps out. "I'm putting Jemmy in my blouse," she insists, and I know there is no use arguing unless I want a shouting match.

Kneeling, I clap for my Ortipo to come, then heft her into my lap. Nosing through the rubbish has made her potbellied as a pumpkin. Joy is even larger. My chest cinches with guilt. We cannot carry them. Not with Mama and Aleksei already needing so much help.

"Maybe one of the better guards would look after them," Anastasia says. "Maria would know who to ask."

"No! We cannot risk saying a word to any of them, not before we escape." I smooth the wrinkles on Ortipo's stubby snout, rub her pointed ears between my fingers. Her black eyes close, her sides heaving with blissful pants. I can hardly swallow, much less speak. "Nastya, *dushka*, would you please write a pair of notes for me to tuck under their collars?"

"In my very best penmanship," Anastasia says, so solemnly I have to bury my face in Ortipo's neck to hide my tears.

By midnight, nine of us sit dressed and ready in Mama and Papa's room, waiting for the officer's signal, whatever it may be. In the adjoining room my sisters and I share, Dr. Botkin, Trupp, and Chef Kharitonov wait, ready to bar the door with furniture. Sheathed in our jewel-lined chemises, Olga, Anastasia, Aleksei, and I can only dream of slumping into a doze like Mashka. Again and again, my fingers check that Anastasia's note is wrapped securely round Ortipo's collar.

The dark is too deep to see anything except the glow from Papa's cigarettes, but I can hear the ticking of all our wristwatches. In time with them, my mind ticks off all the sounds we have heard outside in the night since we arrived here: bells at the sentry posts, shots in the cellar, hand grenades in the garden, guards talking under our windows. How will we recognize the officer's signal if it comes?

Beside me Olga whispers, "I wish I could see the future, so I'd know what to hope for tonight."

"No one can know the future, *dorogaya*." Even in the darkness, she cannot hide her trembling. I take her hand in mine and spread it open, tracing the lines of her palm. "Do you remember back at the lazaret, when we had our palms read?"

"*Konechno.* The fortune-teller said I would live to be an old virgin. Better me than Mashka, I suppose. I don't remember yours, Tatya."

"My lifeline swerved so abruptly to the right, she did not know what to make of it." My sister turns our hands, searching with her fingertips for the crooked furrow on mine, then brings the back of my hand to her cheek to feel the gentle pull of her smile. I lean in. Together we wait and wonder until dawn, with nothing but God to comfort us.

42

MARIA NIKOLAEVNA

14 June 1918
Ekaterinburg

*P*sst!" The whisper zings across the hall, just as I'm about to go into the water closet. "Maria Nikolaevna." One of the guards peeps through the door from the kitchen. It's the one who let me bring the hair ribbons from the shed two weeks ago. He jerks his head the tiniest bit to motion me inside, then disappears like a turtle.

Maybe the officer sent another letter?

I use the toilet, then stand nibbling at my little fingernail to think how to get into the kitchen without attracting attention. With the guards in the hall, there's no way but winding through the whole house to the other door.

"I think I'll have a glass of cold water," I announce on my way across the drawing room.

"Don't be long," Anastasia calls. "Leonka and I are preparing the best canine pantomime ever, just for you."

In the kitchen, the young man bounces from toe to toe with his hands behind his back. We look at each other, not saying a thing.

"Has there been, that is, do you have something to say?" I ask.

"My name is Ivan Skorokhodov, and, I—I wanted to wish you a very happy birthday, Maria Nikolaevna."

I squeal, "My birthday!" then clap my hands over my mouth. "But we've almost all had birthdays here already. Why me?" I whisper.

He cocks his head at me like I've said something stupid. "Well, you're our favorite. My comrades and me."

"Me? But Tatiana is so much prettier, and Olga and Anastasia are the clever ones. Everyone knows that. I'm no one special."

"You are. The way you talk to us. You're like any of us, a real Russian girl."

My heart swishes like a fishtail in my chest. "We're all just Russian girls. Olga wouldn't even marry the crown prince of Romania because it meant leaving Russia."

"One of my comrades wants to rescue you," Ivan blurts. "He's said he'd like to marry you."

"Marry me?" Every inch of my skin seems to lift, like there's a thousand tiny wings rising inside me. I can't feel the floor under my feet or my tongue in my mouth, but my lips say, "Who? Who is it?"

Ivan shakes his head and stutters at the floor. "I can't say. I mean I shouldn't have said anything at all. The Party men would be furious if they heard such talk. But please, I made you this, on behalf of my comrades." He holds out his hands and offers me a brownish something, about the size of a saucer.

A cake. It's bumpy and lopsided, and there's no frosting or candles, but still—a cake!

"Where did you get enough sugar?" I whisper. "I hope your family didn't have to go without! I couldn't eat it if they had."

"Taste it before you worry too much about that."

"How did you ever get it in here?" I ask him, breaking off a big bite.

"Wrapped in paper and hidden under my hat. How is it?"

I've stopped chewing. It's not quite awful, but close—a bit like a mouthful of sweet talcum. When I open my mouth to try to say something nice, a dry spray of flour shoots out instead.

"Is it that bad?" Ivan takes a bite himself. He makes the most dreadful face, and I giggle so hard I know I'd wet myself if I hadn't just been to the toilet.

"You should see yourself. Even Anastasia's never pulled a face like that!"

"Why is this door unlocked?" The door swings open from the corridor, boots rapping across the floor. "What is all this?"

"Commissar Goloshchekin," Ivan coughs over the crumbs in his throat. It's the same man who sneered at Papa and Mama and me the very first time we walked into this house, the one with the drooping mustache who called Papa "Citizen Romanov." Beside him is Chairman Beloborodov.

"In the first place, your shift ended some time ago," Beloborodov says, "and in the second place you are not authorized to be in the prisoners' quarters." Ivan swallows so hard his collar pinches at his neck. "Citizen Romanova, please return to your living quarters immediately."

Withering with guilt, I scurry out, coughing at the flour coating my throat until my eyes stream. Once the tears start, I can't stop them, not even when my snuffling brings Tatiana into the dining room to investigate.

"Maria, what is it? What happened, *dorogaya*?"

"I was in the kitchen, with one of the guards. He signaled me when I came out of the water closet."

My sister trundles me straight into our bedroom and shuts the door. Out in the drawing room, I can hear Anastasia and Leonka's dog-circus rehearsal. "Has there been another message from the officer?" Tatiana whispers.

"No, nothing like that. He—Ivan, he brought me a cake. For my birthday. But Chairman Beloborodov and Commissar Goloshchekin came in and found us together."

Mama appears in the doorway, looking at me like Ivan and I were caught cuddling in the broom closet. "Did you tell this guard about the officer?"

I gulp. "*Nyet*, Mama. *Konechno, nyet.*" I didn't, did I? My head feels like it's sloshing full of water.

"Thank God," Mama says, crossing herself. "Maria, I forbid you to speak with those guards until this is all over. I won't have you endangering the officer's chances with your chatter. Do you understand?"

I nod, too twisted up with shame to speak.

"Very well. Do not leave this room until you've gotten control of yourself. But be quiet about it—Aleksei is sleeping, and there's enough noise already with Anastasia and Leonka provoking the dogs."

That's my fault too. And now Anastasia will be in trouble on top of everything else, all because of my birthday. Curled up in my cot, I cry and cry, but nobody understands why. I don't really understand myself, until Olga tries to comfort me.

"Mashka, sweetheart, don't," she soothes, combing my curls with her fingers. "The officer's plan is so risky, it might not work anyway."

My belly goes cold, remembering what the officer's last letter said about the guards being blocked and terror-stricken inside the house when the signal comes. After what Ivan told me about his comrades, how can I let the officer's plan put the guards in danger too? If we escape, what will the Central Executive Committee do to him, and the others? "We're putting everyone in danger," I hiccup. "The guards, too. . . ."

She looks at me hard, but it's not the same kind of hardness Mama has. "Birthday cake or not, they're stealing from us, Maria. You saw one of them reading one of our books in plain view yourself."

"You cannot overlook the insulting rubbish they have scrawled inside the water closet either," Tatiana adds.

"Tatya, Ivan's the same one who let me bring hair ribbons from the shed," I beg. "Some of the others have been smuggling our letters for weeks, and they let Papa hang the hammocks in the yard for us to play in. Even Commandant

Avdeev bought us a samovar with his own money."

"I would rather have freedom than hair ribbons. A few small kindnesses do not balance against their other sins."

"They're only trying to earn enough to feed their families!"

"By holding ours captive."

My chin quivers, and Tatiana sighs. "The return for good in this world is often evil, *dushka*. Look at us. What have we done to deserve being locked up this way?"

I turn on my side, talking more to Anastasia's dear little painting of Tikhon that's pinned to my headboard than to my sisters. "I remember how when you were all sick with measles, and that awful mob was marching on Tsarskoe Selo, Mama and I had to go out in the snow to speak to the soldiers. She begged every one of them not to shed any blood on our account. Why is it different now?"

No one answers. After a little while, I hear half whispers and catch a glimpse of Olga's hands moving above me. There's footsteps, and I know by the way the door shuts that Tatiana's gone out.

It's quiet for so long, I start to think Olga left too, until she leans her cheek against the ticking of my cot and strokes my arm, soft as the painted butterflies that ringed my bedroom back home.

"Maria, what you said about the guards—it reminded me of something Papa told me when the soldiers' committee in Tobolsk took away his epaulets. 'The evil in the world now will be stronger still before this is all over,' he said, 'but it is not evil that conquers evil, but love.' Of all of us, you're the one who remembers that best, sweetheart Mashka."

It's so hot I can hardly feel myself blush, but suddenly I can breathe again. "What about what Tatiana said? That the return for good is evil?"

"That may be the way of the world these days, but I can't make myself believe it's how God wants us to be. Life has ways of testing us." She smiles, almost dreamily, sweeping away my tears with her thumbs. "You may be the only one of us who will pass this test without even trying. Try not to worry. I'll talk to Dr. Botkin. If anyone can make Papa and Mama see reason, it's him. Happy birthday, angel Mashka."

With a kiss, she's gone.

I lie still, thinking about everything Olga's said, and what she told me before, that I'm the one who won't be changed by all this. Is that something good, if all of Russia has changed around us, but I'm still the same old Mashka?

43

OLGA NIKOLAEVNA

15 June 1918
Ekaterinburg

*W*hat would the Bolsheviks do to us if they discovered these letters?"

Dr. Botkin lifts his glasses the width of a fingernail, resettling them across the bridge of his nose. "I don't know, Olga Nikolaevna. But if they are looking for a reason to do something, evidence that we are plotting to escape would be a more than sufficient excuse."

His words tarnish my hopes, but I'm glad someone's said it. Every morning those same worries stir before I wake, stretching my nerves taut as the strings on Aleksei's balalaika. All day long the slightest twinge sets me vibrating, until I'm exhausted with the effort of keeping still. Even hearing bad news feels better than imagining this place closing like a fist around us over and over.

"Then do you think we're safe here?"

"The closer the Whites come, the harder that becomes to judge. You know how to play chess, I trust?"

"*Konechno.* Papa taught me, and I played with the soldiers at the lazaret sometimes."

"*Otlichno.* You know then, the quickest way to cripple your opponent's offensive?"

"Capture his queen. Or at least force him to defend it."

"Precisely. And many players will sacrifice any number of lesser pieces to spare their queen from harm. That is what your family means to the Whites. As long as the Reds have control over you, they have power over the Monarchists. The emperor is as valuable as a queen on a chessboard, and that is a fine incentive for the Bolsheviks to keep you all safe and well."

I nod as the tiny muscles at the corners of my lips and eyes relax.

"But," Dr. Botkin holds up a finger, "remember that the most clever player of all will sometimes sacrifice his own queen, drawing his opponent into a trap to win the game. And as long as we are in their hands, that is what the Reds can do to the Whites. Deposed or not, you are still the imperial family." The doctor turns his palms up, peering at me through his gold-rimmed eyeglasses. "The question is, which kind of players are the Bolsheviks?"

A shiver runs through me—as if I'm a book having its pages ruffled. "And my sisters and I, we're pawns in all this, aren't we?" I don't ask him what it might mean to the Reds if they knew I have written the replies to the officer.

"I sincerely hope so, Olga Nikolaevna."

Neither of us mentions Aleksei. Dr. Botkin probably knows better than I how the people shrieked with glee in the streets of Petrograd after Papa abdicated, toppling crowns, scepters, and double-headed imperial eagles from park monuments and chipping the emblems of autocracy from storefronts. Each morning I look across the table at my parents and my brother and wonder, will the revolutionaries be content to destroy only portraits and statues? There may be no greater symbol of autocracy left but my papa and his son—my brother, the boy who should have been Tsar Aleksei II.

"Sometimes I think I'm the only one who frets over these things," I admit. "Tatiana is too practical to concern herself with mights and maybes or ponder imaginary games of chess. I know what she would tell me: 'We are in God's hands, *dushka*.'" The doctor smiles fondly, nodding. "Papa's the same. No matter what happens, it's *'Tak i byt.'* I wish I could say, 'So be it' and be content, but even my prayers don't calm my mind anymore." Mama would never understand that. If I confessed my worries, her tongue would fly at me faster than a Cossack's whip. My fingers rub at a spot above my left elbow, as though I could smooth the unease from my skin. "God is still my greatest comfort, but God does not have to answer the officer's letters."

With an expression caught between a wince and a smile, Dr. Botkin shows me he understands. "Despite his reassurances, the officer's plan is fraught with perils."

"And not only for us."

"I have tried to convince the emperor not to trouble himself about myself nor the other men."

"Papa will never consent to leave you, Evgeni Sergeevich. You know that as well as I do. It's the guards. Maria doesn't think it's fair to threaten their safety either."

"Ah. Maria the tenderhearted," he says, studying his clasped hands. I know he's aware of what happened, but even in this cramped place, Dr. Botkin is too diplomatic to say so.

"Some of them have been good to us." No answer. Have I stepped too far? "What do you think, Doctor?"

"I think, given the physical demands of the officer's plan, Maria Nikolaevna's concern for the guards is beside the point."

"You believe it's too risky for Mama and Aleksei?"

"Yes. That is my medical opinion. Unfortunately, neither Alexandra Feodorovna nor Aleksei Nikolaevich like to be told they cannot do a thing once they have set their minds to it. I don't like to think about what would happen if the escape is attempted and fails."

The father, the mother, and the son come down first; the girls and then the doctor follow them.

I picture Papa, his arms strong from his thousands of chin-ups and hours of splitting wood, descending the rope cleanly as a monkey. Then Mama. No matter how I try, I can't imagine her putting one foot over the windowsill. Even if her body had the power, Mama's heart would never let her leave before Aleksei. And then? Would the officer let Papa climb back to us instead of whisking him away? Or would the guards' machine guns find him first? Fear thrashes like an eel down my throat at the thought.

We can't be split up. Not again. Mama won't survive

another choice between Papa and Aleksei. If anything goes wrong, my brother will take up the blame like a cross all over again. Better to take our chances here than risk any of it.

"And if we continue receiving news from the officer— even without attempting an escape?"

Dr. Botkin shakes his head.

My spirits lift and fall all at once, as if a bird has flown from my shoulder. Before this moment, I never realized hope had weight, that letting go could bring a relief of its own.

In our hearts, I'm sure each one of us has known all along that the officer's plan is impossible. It falls to me to make my family see. This final reply must satisfy every one of them, even the Bolsheviks and the officer.

"I will write the reply, Evgeni Sergeevich. Myself."

> *We do not want to, nor can we, escape. We can only be carried off by force, just as it was force that was used to carry us from Tobolsk. Thus, do not count on any active help from us. The commandant has many aides; they change often and have become worried. They guard our imprisonment and our lives conscientiously and are kind to us. We do not want them to suffer because of us, nor you for us; in the name of God, avoid bloodshed above all. Coming down from the window without a ladder is completely impossible. Even once we are down, we are still in great danger because of the open window of the commandant's bedroom and the machine gun downstairs, where one enters from the inner courtyard. Give up, then, on the idea of carrying us off.*

One by one, my family reads my letter and passes it on. Papa crosses himself. *"Sudba."*

Maria doesn't dare smile, but the gratitude in her eyes when she looks at me glows like an icon of the Holy Mother.

Mama frowns, pointing at the last line. "The officer knows more than we do about conditions outside. If he sees a chance to save us from danger, why should we discourage him from carrying us off?"

I nod, crossing out one line and adding another: *If you watch us, you can always come save us in case of real and imminent danger.* I won't pry my mama's last hopes from her. As though it were her idea from the start, Mama points out a handful of words for me to underline—*escape, carried off, any active help, worried*—before nodding her consent at last.

Even as I hand the letter back to Papa, I know our fate is no more certain than it was before. But the opposite of certainty is not doubt. It is faith. Such a fragile thing in comparison, but so much lighter, and gentler, too. I touch my fingers to my St. Nicholas medal.

Tak i byt.

44

ANASTASIA NIKOLAEVNA

16 June 1918
Ekaterinburg

*J*ust like that, we're supposed to go from playing innocent to pretending as if nothing ever happened? What
pig and filth!"

Olga watches me balance a treat on the end of Joy's nose.
"It never would have worked, Shvybs."

Out of nowhere, I go off like a popgun. "I know it!"

Joy cowers and the tidbit falls. I sigh and lean into his
neck, smearing the rim of sweat from my forehead against
his curly ears. "At least with the officer, my *thoughts* could
get outside the fence once in a while. Giving up on all that's
draining the flavor out of everything, and this place was
already dull as potato peelings the second we got here."

If either one of us says one more thing about it, I'll cry,
so I straighten up and start all over with Joy and the treat. I
don't know how Olga knows, but she does.

"Why don't you teach Ortipo and Jemmy to do that too?"

"I tried. Their noses are too stubby."

"Like my humble snub?"

I peer up at her. She can't be smiling. Not Olga. And she isn't, not quite, but she *is* teasing, for the first time since I don't know when. Right this minute, it feels better than a hug. "Exactly. Besides, I can't crouch down right with these dratted 'medicines' running from my armpits to my belly button."

"Where is everyone?" Chairman Beloborodov stands right in the middle of our drawing room as if he owns the place. I didn't even hear the door. Joy grumbles, like he wants to bark without moving his nose.

"At this hour?" Tatiana answers, appearing just as suddenly from the dining room. "Preparing for bed."

I check my watch. Only nine thirty. Plenty of times we don't go to bed until after eleven, but Tatiana never misses a chance to rub a Bolshie's nose in his own rudeness.

"I must see everyone at once."

It takes Mama a good fifteen minutes to show her face, while my stomach hops up and down, eager for whatever news Beloborodov has that's important enough for everybody from Papa to Leonka to hear. But the military commissar only looks over the lot of us like we're an imperial tea service for twelve, and he expected to find the lid to the sugar bowl missing. Next to me, Mashka shrivels like a burnt sausage when he turns her way.

"Thank you very much. From now on, Comrade Avdeev will conduct such an inspection morning and evening."

"Why?" Mama wants to know. She frowns like she'll take this Bolshie whippersnapper over her knee if he doesn't behave.

His excuse? To make sure we're all here.

"As if one of us might have hopped the fences or strolled out the front door without them noticing!" I gripe at Maria. "Don't they know they've missed their chance?"

21 June 1918

"This is Comrade Yurovsky," Commissar Goloshchekin announces, barging in on our lunch. We all put down our forks and look over the new Bolshie. "He will replace Avdeev as commandant. Comrade Nikulin takes the place of Moshkin." Nobody says why.

As soon as I see his black leather jacket I recognize Yurovsky. He's the very same man who came weeks ago to examine Aleksei. "I *told* Tatiana he wasn't a doctor," I whisper to Mashka.

An hour later Yurovsky is back with an empty box tucked under his elbow. Nikulin follows with a ledger. "I understand there was an unpleasant incident in the house, and that the previous guard stole some of your belongings," the new commandant says. "I must ask you to remove all your jewelry to avoid unnecessary temptation." I look at my sisters. Jewels line our underthings like the stripes on a chipmunk's back. It's a good thing Mashka's not wearing any—she'd melt of guilt right on the spot. Only Tatiana looks like the thought hasn't even crossed her mind.

Nobody says a thing, then Papa takes a gold cigarette

case from his pocket, empties out the last of his smokes, and hands it over.

We strip off earrings, necklaces, and brooches. Nikulin writes every piece down in his ledger. Papa's wedding ring won't budge from his finger. Mama takes off all but a few gold bangles. Yurovsky points at them with a pen. "Everything, please."

"I have had these bracelets since I was eleven years old." She doesn't even look at him. "They were a gift from my uncle Leopold, the Duke of Albany. Anyway, they're too tight."

"I must have everything, Alexandra Feodorovna. Please give me your arm."

Mama snaps her head around at him like he's said something dirty.

"Allow me," Papa says, and starts to waggle the bracelets down Mama's wrist. Even when she folds her thumb under her fingers, her skin bunches up like an elephant's ankle as Papa tries to coax the bands over her hand. Mama splutters the whole time.

"Ridiculous. No one is going to steal them if they won't come off. Ouch!"

Nikulin taps his pen on the ledger, like Monsieur Gilliard used to while I worked a foul math problem.

"All right," Yurovsky says. "Enough."

"I would request that my son be allowed to keep his watch," Papa says. "Otherwise he is bored."

"Very well." Yurovsky glances at my sisters and me. We each have a gold bangle bracelet left. Papa and Mama gave them to us when we were little girls. "Too tight?" We all nod.

He looks at Tatiana, the thinnest one of us. "Even yours?" She slides the bracelet down her arm, but her thumb juts out into its way. "Never mind. You may keep them."

"Ox Commandant," Papa mutters as the duty office door closes.

Later, when we walk outside, Yurovsky's standing along the fence. If any of the guards speak to us, he shouts at them, *"Nelzya!"* Even when things are different around here, they're the same.

Aleksei sits up in his cot, directing Leonka to set up their next miniature battle formation while I brush my hair at the windowsill.

"Watch every movement from this window," someone orders the night sentry at the corner of the house.

"Is that the new commandant?" Aleksei asks.

I put down my hairbrush and lean out a little ways to see.

"You there!" The sentry points up at me with his rifle. "Get out of that window. *Nelzya!*"

I don't even blink, just slink off the sill into a scowly pile on the floor. Being forbidden isn't even interesting anymore.

"Nastya?" Aleksei asks. "What's the matter with you?"

I could kick myself square in the teeth for acting like such a milksop. "That's what I was thinking. Somebody waves a gun at my face and all I do is pout?"

He holds up one of the foil-wrapped party crackers his lead army uses for artillery. "I dare you to pop this over his head. It's my last one."

"I may be bored, but I'm not crazy. You want me to get

my nose shot off? He hears that and the dummy'll think we're firing at him."

"It's just a noisemaker. Mama wouldn't let me pop them indoors if they were real firecrackers."

"*Nyet.*"

"Then I dare you to make a face at him." I pick at my nightdress. "Or aren't you the Chieftain of All Firemen any-more?" he wheedles.

That does it.

I brush all my hair forward so it covers my face like a bandit's mask, then creep to the window on my hands and knees.

Just as my nose clears the sill, *bang!*

Gunpowder singes my nostrils. I somersault backward, right into Leonka. And then? Nothing. Leonka only stares sheepishly down at me, a shredded bit of green foil in each hand. A gold paper crown dangles from one end of the spent cracker he popped over *my* head instead of the guard's. "Alyosha made me." He presses his wide, skinny lips together so tight, they disappear.

From his cot, Aleksei snorts and squeals with laughter.

I snatch the paper crown and use it to bat every last soldier off his bed tray. "You little swine! If you weren't sick I'd tip your whole cot over!"

"Nastya, don't be mad," he begs as I go blazing out of the room. "It's just a joke—you're not bored anymore, are you?"

"Idiot!" Let him think I'm angry. I'm trembling right down to my toenails, but I'd sooner swallow a mouthful of bullets than admit the truth: I'm scared.

For a second, I'd *believed* that sentry took a shot at me.

45

MARIA NIKOLAEVNA

25 June 1918
Ekaterinburg

I ring the bell for the lavatory and wait. When the door opens, a guard I've never seen before lets me through the vestibule and into the hall. A second unfamiliar face is stationed there. I know Mama's waiting for me to read to her, but the sight stops me in the doorway. One of them *ahems*.

Finally I remember my manners and say hello. *"Zdorovo, okhrannik."*

No answer.

When I come back out to wash my hands and return to our quarters I want to say *spasibo* like I always do, but a funny flat feeling in my middle tells me I've already said more than I'm supposed to.

"They behave like real guards," I tell Anastasia as soon as she comes in from the morning walk, "like the jailers in

The Count of Monte Cristo. They look at you like you're not even there."

"The ones in the garden, too. I'd almost rather be ogled than that."

Letts, Papa calls them. "Mostly Latvians, though Olga recognized one of them outside this morning," he tells Mama at lunch. "He'd been one of our grenadiers, a man by the name of Kabanov I met once during a review. The Ox Commandant spoke German to order the fellow not to speak to us."

It sounds almost like the first time I saw Ukraintsev. I look across the table at my sister. Olga only stirs sour cream into her borscht and rubs her thumb along the edge of the table. Why didn't she tell me anything about Kabanov?

28 June 1918

All kinds of banging and clanking from Papa and Mama's bedroom brings me running to check on Aleksei. The bars of shadow stretched across his cot stop me before I see the iron ones over the open window. Outside, one workman braces a grate against the plaster while another hammers it into place. Because of me? The way Mama and Olga look at me, I can't help wondering.

I watch from the doorway without saying a word. When Mama asks me to sit with Aleksei so they can "arrange medicines," I only nod and take Olga's chair.

"Papa said the Ox Commandant's forbidden any more cream deliveries, and there's only going to be enough meat for soup this week," Aleksei tells me.

My eyes follow the ladder of stripes across his nightshirt, too ashamed to look at my brother or the window.

He tries again. "I'm going to have a real bath today, my first since Tobolsk. And I can stand up again, except only on one foot."

That must be why Mama looked so happy before. Before the grate. My heart wants me to smile, but my face hardly follows. "I'm glad, Alyosha. You're getting heavier to carry now too." My voice doesn't sound glad at all. No matter what I try to say these last few days, it comes out sounding like *I'm sorry.*

"It isn't just you," Aleksei says after another minute or two. "Everybody's glum. Papa's quit writing in his diary every night, and Mama doesn't even bother to tear the days off the calendar anymore."

News like this should make me feel something. Scared or unsettled, maybe. Even when he's sick, Papa asks Mama to fill in his diary for him.

Outside, the sounds of marching men drift over the fence. There's no way to tell the difference by listening, but I suppose since they're not storming our gates they must be Reds.

Suddenly Aleksei reaches into his pillowcase and brings out something smaller than one of Mama's pearl earrings, wrapped in a twist of limp pink paper. "Here."

The tender smell of it caresses my memory before I realize what I'm looking at. "Oh," I exhale. "Isn't this one of the pastilles from Anya's Christmas parcel?"

He nods. "Papa gave it to me, after Anastasia gave it to him."

And before all that, it must have been mine. I'm the only one who didn't eat my share that first day, because I wanted to save them for Anastasia's Christmas present. "But it's yours now, Sunbeam. You haven't had candy in ages."

He shakes his head. "Take it. If I eat it, it'll be gone, and no fun to think about anymore. I know it's the last one, so I can't. Getting it was more fun than having it."

Breathing the dusty strawberry sugar, I know just what he means. Maybe there wouldn't be new guards and bars on the windows if Ivan and I hadn't gotten caught laughing together over a bite of cake, but I wouldn't trade that moment for anything. It was so wonderful, talking to someone new, someone who seemed interested, instead of just gawking. Olga's the thinker, Tatiana's the beauty, and Anastasia's the clown, but Ivan picked me instead of any of them.

I turn the pastille over in my hand, smiling to think how one tiny morsel has traveled from pocket to pocket, brightening so many moments. And I started it all.

If such a little button of candy can survive all the way from Petrograd to Siberia and back, why shouldn't I? Maybe it isn't too much to want a life with sweetness and even a little spice.

Before the revolution, I was just a little girl dreaming. I wonder, if a Red Guard is willing to bring me a birthday cake, maybe I really can marry an ordinary young man and have masses of children like anyone else. Imagine, one of the men hired to hold us prisoner looked at me and saw a girl he wanted to take home to his mama. Me! Citizen Romanova, with my very own house and family. The thought makes my skin shiver like I've been kissed. Auntie Olga divorced a duke, married an everyday captain, and ended up having her little Tikhon right in the middle of all this mess, and she's as much a grand duchess as I am. Imagine having your very first baby during a revolution! Oh, I wish I could see them.

"It helped, didn't it?" Aleksei asks, proud of himself in a soft way I've never seen before. My heart bulges with so many things, I can't squeeze a breath past it to answer him. "I knew it would, Mashka."

I pull him close to me, so glad he's ours, and hope maybe one day I'll be lucky enough to have a house full of such gentle boys as my golden-hearted brother.

My sisters think I don't know about the risks. How could I not? All my life I've watched the way Mama suffers over her darling Sunbeam. But to have a family of my own, a family like ours? I don't even have to think about that.

I know that is worth the risk.

46

ANASTASIA NIKOLAEVNA

1 July 1918
Ekaterinburg

For *Obednitsa,* Yurovsky stands in the far corner just like Avdeev did, watching while Tatiana settles Aleksei's wheelchair beside Mama and the rest of us line up in our usual spots. I wonder if the Ox Commandant ever goes to church himself, or if he thinks just looking at a service is enough.

The way *Otets* Storozhev and his deacon try not to stare at us, I can tell how dreadfully worn out we must still look from sitting up all those nights, especially Aleksei and Olga. Even my clothes feel tired. *Obednitsa* always perks us up, at least.

As soon as the service starts, everything seems almost normal. Then out of nowhere the deacon begins to *sing* the words to the prayer, Who Resteth with the Saints. Bewildered, *Otets* Storozhev joins the chant, and the sound of their voices makes the hair on my arms prickle with electricity. As if someone's whispered in all our ears at once, every last one of us but Aleksei in his wheelchair and Yurovsky in his corner go down on our knees. It isn't the right time to kneel or to sing, but it *feels* right, like there's something bigger in the room than just the music.

At the end of the service, each of us kisses the cross like always. On the way out, Olga whispers, *"Spasibo,"* as the priest passes in front of us.

Only after the priest and deacon are gone do I realize that for the first time since I can remember, not one of *us* sang through the whole service.

2 *July 1918*

"Mashka, Olga, Tatiana! There are four women in the house!"

"What?"

"Visitors?"

"They've come to wash the floors."

When the washerwomen get to our room, they stand in the doorway with their buckets and rags like they're waiting to be invited in. Tatiana does the honors.

"My name is Tatiana Nikolaevna, and my sisters are Olga, Maria, and Anastasia."

The four of them curtsy so low, their buckets almost clang on the floor.

"You don't have to do that for us," Olga says. "Please, tell us your names."

They're Varvara, Evdokiya, Mariya, and Nadezhda.

"From the Union of Professional Housemaids," the fat one called Evdokiya explains.

I elbow my sisters. "We should have a union! They're all the rage nowadays. We can be the Union of Professional Ex–Grand Duchesses. UPEGD. It sounds so much more official than OTMA." I turn back to the solemn line of women. "Promise you'll call us if you need experts to walk circles around your garden twice a day, won't you? Or we're perfectly divine at sitting around looking bored."

For a moment, all seven of them stare at me like I'm a trout in a samovar.

"Stop teasing." Tatiana swats at my backside. "Let us help you move the cots," she tells the women. "We have the knack. They might fold up on you otherwise."

They blink at our four cots like they're covered in velvet polka dots instead of plain old blue ticking. "These are your beds?"

"Since we were little girls," Olga explains. "They've come with us all the way from Petrograd."

"Do you have children?" Mashka interrupts.

"Don't let them near our Maria if you do," I tell them. "It's been so long since she's seen a baby, she'd squeeze it until it pops like a bonbon."

"My boys are away, fighting," says Nadezhda.

"I have a sweetheart in the army," the other Mariya admits, and she and Mashka link up like magnets.

I roll up my sleeves. "This'll go heaps quicker if you let us help scrub."

Varvara looks properly horrified at first, but all four of

us get right down on our hands and knees beside our visitors and dip into their buckets with cloths and brushes, even the Governess. "We have always helped our maids with the chores," Tatiana assures Varvara.

Once the union women figure out scrub water won't melt my sisters and me like the Witch of the West, the eight of us chatter and splatter like a flock of ducks in the golden fountains at Peterhof. Before we've gotten halfway across the floor, Yurovsky points his weaselly beard through the doorway, snuffing out our talk with one glare. He swipes his eyes like a rag over the whole room, then goes back across the dining room toward the duty office. Disgusted, I drop my brush into Evdokiya's bucket and tromp to the doorway, exactly in rhythm with the commandant's steps.

Tatiana hisses, "Anastasia!" but I wave my hand at her to shut up. When I'm sure Yurovsky's not going to turn around, I cram my fingers into my eyes, nose, and mouth, stretch my face into the awfullest grimace I can manage, and waggle my tongue at his back.

Maria snorts. "You look just like a Pekingese."

"We call him the Ox Commandant," I whisper to Evdokiya. "He's such a bore."

"You should have seen the floors in the Popov house across the street where those men of his are lodging," Evdokiya says, shaking her head. "Thousands of sunflower seeds all over the place. We had to scrape and scrub the leavings from their dirty boots. Not much better in the basement of this house either. I think there are women staying down there with the guards."

We keep our voices quiet so the commandant won't snoop, but the talk feels brighter. Maybe this is what it would have been like if we'd ever been able to make friends with regular people. Sharing jokes and secrets with more than just my sisters.

"Hey, you there, peasant urchin," Olga calls to Tatiana when it's time to scoot the cots back into place. "Move that bed faster!"

"*Otlichno*," Evdokiya says when we're done, "and in half the time. I proclaim you all honorary members of the Union of Professional Housemaids." My chest puffs up like a rooster's. If they made badges for this, I'd wear one as proudly as Aleksei's St. George medal.

"Your nails are all chipped and dirty," Varvara says, pointing.

"Oh, who cares?" I spread my fingers out like a duck's webbed feet and grin at the grime. "Nobody but Mama, and we've got nothing else to do all day but file and buff them."

For the first time, Varvara laughs, then looks at the painted-over windows and bites her lip. "You know, you're nothing like we expected."

"*Spasibo,*" I tell her, and her smile comes back. "I'll make a mess so big you'll all be ordered back tomorrow."

"I hope it's not too hard for you here," Evdokiya whispers. My throat closes up, but I square my shoulders and shake my head.

After they've gone, I look at the way the floor shines and think of how those women gaped at me when I said we'd help clean, and Yurovsky when he saw us down on our hands and knees, chatting with his workers. There isn't much more delicious than taking people by surprise. Maybe when I was little, it was just to shock the stiff-faced courtiers. But now it really means something to be able to show these Bolsheviks we're not what they think. I may be a grand duchess, but I can be useful as a cook pot if I want to. I know how to bake bread and do the washing. I can knit, and paint and draw. And now I can scrub floors as well as any housemaid.

When I get out of here, I want to be able to stand on my own two feet. Whatever I do with myself, I don't want people to look at my work and say, "Not bad . . . for a grand duchess."

Because no matter what the Bolsheviks say or do, I *am* a grand duchess. My papa was the tsar of all the Russias, and that's nothing to sneeze at. That's how I was born and that's how I'll die, no matter who's in charge of this country when I'm old and gray. But I'm more than just that. This hateful revolution means I can be anything I want, instead of a frill on some grand duke's sleeve. Auntie Ella is a nun. Auntie Olga is an artist. My big sisters are nurses, and my Mashka is a darling. Aunt Miechen is a sour old goat.

I am Grand Duchess Anastasia Nikolaevna, Chieftain of All Firemen, and I will not let history overlook me.

47

TATIANA NIKOLAEVNA

3 July 1918
Ekaterinburg

Outside, soldiers choke the city's streets, rattling the panes of our whitewashed windows day and night with the crackle of gunfire. Inside, none of it pierces our routine.

"Mama, I could read to you in the shade while the others walk."

"Not today. It's too much in this heat."

"Then shall I read from one of *Gospodin* Ipatiev's books for a change?"

"No, darling. We'll go on with the prophets."

A sigh withers my chest.

Together, Mama and I read from the book of Obadiah while the others have their walk: "Though thou shalt exalt thyself as the eagle and though thou shalt set thy nest among the stars, thence will I bring thee down, saith the Lord."

The words make me shiver, but in a different way from

our last *Obednitsa*. All my life, I lived under flags emblazoned with the double-headed imperial eagle. Our dinner
napkins were woven through with the design, our books and
photo albums stamped with it.

And now look at us, strained with confinement and
grateful for the tiniest favors. Yet twinges of unease accompany even the comforts of *Obednitsa* and the open window;
the more requests Yurovsky honors, the more I find myself
remembering the lazaret, and how we used to indulge the
patients whose wounds were beyond us.

All evening the dogs whine and pace as one boom after
another sends tremors through the plaster and floorboards.
Surely there are wounded men at the other end of those
sounds. Useless as it is with the Bolshies in command, I pray
to God that I might be allowed out of this house to nurse
them.

"I would not even look at their uniforms," I confess to
Olga. "Red or White makes no difference to me. What
would Mama think of that?" I glance through the doorways
to where Mama and Papa sit over another hand of bezique.

"Does it matter, Tatya?"

I have to think a long time about that. There are so many
ways I want to be like my mama: pious, loyal, industrious,
courageous. And yet I want to live on more than just the
edges and extremes of life. "It has always mattered what
Mama and Papa thought. Since I was a little girl I have tried
to do right in their eyes. But if they had done everything
right, would we be here now?" It is so wicked of me to doubt

them; my papa the tsar is God's own anointed. "Yet we are all Russians, even the Reds, and Christ said we should love our enemies as ourselves."

"Do you think Papa and Mama have truly forgiven their enemies, Tatya? With their hearts, I mean, not just their voices."

I know what she means. Our parents have been so meek and humble, but if I still worry what Mama would think of my wishing to nurse the Reds, there is no ignoring my doubts.

I shake my head. "Papa, perhaps. I wonder sometimes if he has forgiven, or only given up. But I know Mama thinks she is right and the Bolsheviks are wrong."

"You can forgive someone and still think they're wrong, Tatya."

"But am I any better, if I am only willing to nurse the Reds to soothe myself?"

"I don't think Christ meant for us to be perfect on the first try. For now it's enough that you're willing. Wanting and caring can come only after that."

My sister's words crumble some of the brittleness in my chest like the dried paste in our old photo albums. I take a good, round breath, smiling at the sudden stretch of my lungs. "How did you get to be so wise, *dushka*?"

Before Olga can answer, Yurovsky barges into the drawing room. "You," he says, pointing at Leonka, "gather your things and come with me. Your uncle wants to take you home."

My body jolts as if an icicle has been rammed down my spine. I do not believe him for an instant. Sednev and Nagorny have been gone for weeks filled with nothing but promises, and now this? One by one, they have stripped away our position, our freedom, and even our friends. But to whisk away the playmate of a sick little boy!

I charge after Yurovsky into the duty office, vibrating with outrage. He makes no concessions, yet each time he refuses, something deeper than indignation surges inside me at the opportunity to shout and complain. My heart gallops like a cavalry regiment, the force of it thrilling me to the ends of my fingers. All at once I hardly care anymore what Yurovsky says about Leonka. With that realization, selfishness stuns me to silence.

Far down inside me, a sob breaks loose and forces its way up the back of my throat like a fist.

"Thank you, Mr. Commandant," I choke, and flee to my bedroom, where I clutch at Ortipo, too ashamed to answer Olga's concern.

Only Anastasia's voice reaches through my tears. "What's going on now?"

"Tatiana is upset," Olga says.

"Anybody can see that much. Honestly." She plops down beside me. "What is it, Tatya?"

"Everything is so wrong here, and there is nothing I can do to mend it," I wail. "And now with Leonka gone, Aleksei is sure to be miserable! How do I fix that? Everyone is aching somehow, but there is not one wound I can put a bandage on."

"Well, of course not. Who expects you to?"

"But I have always been the one to fix things," I whimper. "I am the Governess."

Anastasia laughs and shakes her head at me. "Look around you, silly. Nothing is the same anymore. The former tsar of all the Russias is in the drawing room reading *War and Peace* with his feet up, and the doctor is moaning in his bed. Besides, we got here by doing the same old thing for the last three hundred years, didn't we, Olga?"

Olga's eyes moisten with pride. She nods at Anastasia, who is suddenly not a *shvybzik* anymore. It tears at me all over again to see the change in our youngest sister.

"Tatya?" Anastasia whispers. Her eyes are so big. I must be frightening her terribly with my hysterics. "Tatya, it's all right. You can't mend everything. You shouldn't even try if this is how it makes you feel. And anyway, there's one thing you can fix—Mama sent me to ask you to give Dr. Botkin his morphine injection. His kidneys are killing him."

It is as if Anastasia has ripped a scab from my thoughts. The place beneath it is tender yet, but as she takes me by the hand and pulls me along behind her, the feel of fresh air on new skin takes my breath away.

My baby sister is right. There are so many things I cannot mend. But that does not mean I can do nothing. There is so much suffering in the world, I must provide whatever small comfort I can. Even if it is only to myself.

Tomorrow will be different. Of that much I am certain.

48

OLGA NIKOLAEVNA

4 July 1918
Ekaterinburg

A knock wakens me, a slice of light opening like a jack-knife across our bedroom. Dr. Botkin's face appears in the crack. His round glasses glint like silver rubles as his fingers fumble to unrumple his tie. Before I can wonder why he is knocking at this hour, the thought of our dear doctor sleeping in his tie and collar stretches my yawn into a smile.

"Forgive me," he says, a little louder than a whisper, "but the commandant has asked us to prepare to move to the cellar for safety. Shooting in the city, he says."

"What time is it?" Tatiana asks, her voice clear in the dark. Anastasia yawns. Maria snores softly and doesn't budge.

"Almost one thirty." The boom of artillery echoes inside the hollow of my lungs. "Yurovsky insists there is no reason for alarm, but it may be necessary to evacuate if the conflict escalates. He asks that you please dress promptly and gather in the drawing room. No bags—our luggage will follow in the event of evacuation."

"Thank you, Evgeni Sergeevich," Tatiana says. "I will inform the tsar and the empress. Will you please see that Nyuta and the others are ready?"

"Konechno." The door closes, and it's dark again.

From the next room, the thump of Mama's cane on the floor stirs Tatiana from her cot. While Anastasia and I rub our eyes and fumble out of our sheets, Tatiana dresses and washes deftly in the dark. "I am going to help Mama and Aleksei. Remember to take your medicines." I fancy I can hear her eyebrow rising with emphasis.

"All right, Tatya."

She murmurs a moment over Maria, still a solid lump in her cot, then switches on the bedside lamp before slipping through the doorway. The light whispers over our icons and picture frames.

Together, Anastasia and I help each other into our jewel-lined chemises. "Let Mashka wear mine," she fusses. "I'm sick to death of this heavy old thing."

"You must still be dreaming if you think Mashka could ever squeeze into your chemise," I tease. "Someday you may be glad to have this—these jewels are all the money we've got left in the world. If we really do get out of here, we'll need it."

She yawns wide, showing her teeth like a cat. "Why couldn't there have been shooting in the streets *before* we went to bed?"

Papa carries Aleksei. Mama leans on her cane. Behind them I lead my sisters all in a row—OTMA—just like the old days of court processions and presentations. My sisters and I each have a few little things, cushions and purses and trinkets, though Yurovsky frowns when he sees them. Even Tatiana has brought Mama's favorite rose-leaf pillow instead of anything of her own. Dr. Botkin, Nyuta, Chef Kharitonov, and Trupp all follow a few steps behind. Stitched deep inside the cushion Nyuta carries is a box filled with diamonds wrapped in wadding—the last of our jewels.

Across the house and down a flight of stairs we file, just as if we were going for our daily walk in the garden. Dangling from Papa's arms, Aleksei's body swings like a pendulum all the way down the steps. When he reaches the door, Papa turns to smile at us. "It looks like we're getting out of here." A Fiat idles inside the gate, its nose already pointed toward the street. There are no seats in back, but the lorry's bed is large enough to carry all eleven of us away from here, if it comes to that.

In the courtyard beyond, the air sweeps over me as if the night has let out a sigh at the sight of us. Suddenly I can't remember the last time I was outdoors after dark, and my skin seems to gasp with relief. Ahead of me in the moonlight, wisps of Mama's disheveled hair stand out like a halo of spider's silk.

After only a few breaths of night, we snake back into the house through another door, down another short flight of steps. On the landing, a stuffed bear and two cubs watch us pass with their glass eyes. One by one, Mama and my sisters and I cross ourselves as we pass. "Poor things," Maria murmurs behind me. At the bottom, I've counted twenty-three steps to the basement—one for each year of my life, though my birthday isn't until November.

Yurovsky leads us across the sunflower seed-scattered floors of the guards' quarters to a bare room behind a set of paneled double doors on the far side of the cellar. I'm not certain until I find the bullet hole in the ceiling—we're directly below the room my sisters and I share upstairs. Finely striped yellow paper covers the walls, but the only light comes from a bare bulb dangling above us. Overhead, the swoop of curved plaster crowned with a beaded burgundy frieze reminds me a little of the cove-ceilinged basement rooms back home in Tsarskoe Selo. There's an arched window, and another set of paneled double doors across from us. It's almost attractive in here, for a cellar. I wonder why they haven't used it, instead of crowding all the guards into the other chambers.

Mama takes in the empty room all at once and swivels on her cane to face Yurovksy. "Why are there no chairs?" she asks, gesturing to Aleksei, stranded in Papa's arms. "Is it forbidden to sit?"

The commandant says nothing, but returns with two bentwood chairs like the ones my sisters and I keep at the end of our cots. He places them below the lightbulb. Papa eases Aleksei into one, and Mama sits down beside him. Tatiana takes her usual place behind Mama, slipping the rose-leaf cushion against Mama's back before resting her hands protectively on the back of the chair. Maria, Anastasia, and I cluster nearby. Yurovsky shuts the door, and the faint smell of Dr. Botkin's cologne slowly veils the back of the room. There is nothing to do but wait.

In spite of the tremor of excitement beneath my ribs, one yawn after another finds its way down my throat. Maria and I lean against the wall; a nudge now and then keeps her from dozing off. My ears perk up when footsteps tap along the linoleum-covered corridor—the sound of boots, close together and out of sync, like a pack of clumsily shuffled cards. They gather outside the double doors, then stop. Why so many, and what are they waiting for?

Beside me, Jemmy peeps out from the purse in Anastasia's arms, panting and trembling the way she does before a storm. If the poor sweetheart weren't so frightened, I'd have to scold Anastasia for sneaking her down here. "Probably the artillery rumbling," I whisper.

Out in the courtyard, the lorry's engine revs and backfires. I flinch like Jemmy, startling Maria awake again, then smile at myself. It's been almost three months since I rode in a motorcar. The wind in my face, the road bumping under us, the stars overhead as my sisters and I jostle together— for those few moments, I wouldn't even think about where they're taking us. It won't be long now.

The paneled door opens and Yurovsky steps inside, his hands fisted in his coat pockets. Behind him, nine men file in, forming two lines before us—four hunched in front, six with their backs to the door. Only a few faces are familiar. Curiosity whirs in the space between us.

"Please stand," the commandant says.

Our sleepiness falls away. Mama glares at Yurovsky,

levering herself up on her cane. Beside me, Maria inches back as Papa takes a step forward, placing himself in front of Aleksei. There's not a word as we face each other, but the air feels charged, metallic. My skin buzzes like a thousand thoughts as I begin to realize that my body senses something my brain can't grasp.

All their hands are behind their backs.

With a flash of motion that severs my thoughts, Yurovsky pulls a scrap of paper from the breast pocket of his leather jacket and reads:

"In view of the fact that your relatives continue their offensive against Soviet Russia, the Presidium of the Ural Regional Soviet has decided to sentence you to death."

A flurry of panic erupts around me, but nothing penetrates. Only a haze of sounds brushes against me. Yelps from Mama, my sisters. Papa turning back to Yurovsky, his mouth moving. *What? I can't understand you. Read it again, please.* Yurovsky's voice once more, like a needle on a gramophone. Papa, still asking, *What? What?*

Another flash—Yurovsky and his squad answering with open fire.

I cross myself and close my eyes.

Where we go next, we go together.

EPILOGUE

To maximize efficiency in the small space of the cellar, each of the ten executioners had been assigned a specific victim to dispatch. In the passion of the moment, however, nearly all of them first took aim at their former emperor, collapsing Nicholas II almost instantly in the barrage. Dr. Botkin, Kharitonov, and Trupp also fell in the first volley, struck down by straying gunfire. Behind the tsar, Alexandra had not quite finished making the sign of the cross when a shot to the head toppled the empress to the floor.

Smoke, plaster dust, and gunpowder already filled the crowded room, obscuring all but the victims' legs and choking the executioners' lungs as they fired into the haze. Some of the killers lurched from the room, coughing and vomiting while screams and sobs ricocheted inside.

All five of the imperial children were still alive.

One of the girls, probably Maria, had broken away during the first volley and lay wounded in a corner by the locked storeroom doors. The other three sisters huddled together in the opposite corner while a man called Ermakov attacked Aleksei with bullets and bayonet. Despite the Bolshevik's brutality, the thirteen-year-old boy, it seemed, would not die. Unknown to his murderers, the jewels hidden under Aleksei's khaki tunic apparently blunted Ermakov's shots and blows until Yurovsky dispatched the tsarevich with two shots to the head.

Next, the two men advanced on the grand duchesses.

Anastasia somehow fled to Maria's corner, leaving the Big Pair to face Ermakov and Yurovsky. First Tatiana, then Olga fell to point-blank head wounds, though some of the killers would testify that their bullets initially bounced off the girls' torsos "like hail." Turning to the opposite corner, Ermakov attacked Maria and Anastasia with his bayonet, but again, the jeweled chemises seemed to protect at least one of the girls until Ermakov finally gave up and finished them both off with his Mauser.

The maid Anna "Nyuta" Demidova, who at some point fainted near the Little Pair, was the last to die—yet another victim of Ermakov's savage bayonet.

Almost from that moment, rumors of survival began to surface—perhaps because the burial of the imperial family spiraled into a grisly two-day farce involving mechanical breakdowns, drunken Bolsheviks, multiple grave sites, and nosy peasants. Some accounts say that one of the younger grand duchesses showed signs of life after Yurovsky and another man checked the scattered bodies for pulses. Another reports that Maria or Anastasia suddenly sat up screaming as she was being hauled from the cellar to the waiting truck. At one point the Fiat loaded with bodies became mired in the swampy forest outside Ekaterinburg, forcing Yurovsky to leave the victims' remains behind to scout ahead for the mine shaft where he intended to dump the imperial corpses.

Throughout the ordeal, the executioners were tantalized by the discovery of yet more diamonds, pearls, and loops of gold wire peeping from their victims' torn clothing. Only

Yurovsky's threats to search and shoot anyone found guilty of theft kept the men from succumbing to temptation. By the time the burial was complete, Yurovsky's desk stood heaped with valuables collected from the corpses. The diamonds alone weighed eighteen pounds. Everything deemed of value—diaries, letters, and photograph albums as well as jewelry—was shipped to Moscow. What remained of the Romanovs' possessions were pilfered by the guards, burned in the stove, or tossed down the latrine pit.

Strangely, Yurovsky's own accounts of the murders state that he first attempted to burn two of the bodies, then gave up and buried the remaining nine together. For years, it seemed as if this might have been only a cover-up to disguise the disappearance of two of the victims, although the only corpse found during the White Army's investigation was that of a small dog, believed to be Anastasia's Jemmy. In short, the story of the Romanovs' murder is riddled with gaps that opportunistic pretenders were eager to fill with tales of escape. The Bolsheviks themselves paved the way by initially refusing to report the murder of Alexandra and her daughters. Even the "officer letters" were a cruel hoax perpetrated by the Romanovs' guards to create a pretext for the execution.

The most famous claimant is, of course, Anna Anderson, an eccentric, charismatic woman who declared for six decades that she was Grand Duchess Anastasia Nikolaevna. (In fact, over two hundred people have pretended to be survivors of the Ekaterinburg massacre, most of them posing as Aleksei or Maria.) After her death, DNA tests plainly contradicted Anderson's claim, linking her to a family of Kashubian peasants instead of the Romanovs. Reluctant to give up hope, Anderson's staunchest supporters questioned the results on several grounds. Nevertheless, a second round of DNA tests in late 2010 upheld the original findings.

In 1991, when a group of Russians announced publicly that they had found the tsar's grave, only nine skeletons lay tangled in the pit: four servants and five members of the imperial family. Examination of the remains determined that Aleksei and one of his two youngest sisters were missing, prompting survival theories to flare once again despite the eventual DNA tests that would refute Anna Anderson's famous claim. Controversy also erupted over which of the four grand duchesses was missing—the Russian forensic team believes Maria's body is absent, while an American group sees Anastasia as the more likely candidate. (Individual DNA profiles for the grand duchesses do not exist, so identification of their remains hinges on factors like height, facial reconstruction, and skeletal development. Only Skeleton Number 3, with its prominent forehead, has been identified with any certainty as Olga Nikolaevna.) When the nine skeletons were finally buried in a state funeral at St. Petersburg's Fortress of St. Peter and St. Paul on July 17, 1998, the youngest sets of remains were interred below markers bearing the names Tatiana Nikolaevna and Anastasia Nikolaevna, though the dispute over the identities of Skeletons Number 5 and Number 6 has never been conclusively put to rest.

Then, in the summer of 2007, searchers unearthed a second shallow pit containing several dozen charred bone fragments, teeth, and a scrap of cloth similar to the sailor-style undergarments Aleksei favored. It now appears that Yurovsky's story about burning two bodies was not a ruse after all. DNA tests have shown these fragments are almost certainly the remains of the tsarevich Aleksei and his sister. The same series of tests also revealed that Skeleton Number 6, one of the three grand duchesses in the original grave, was indeed a carrier of type B hemophilia.

The Imperial Family, 1913 (Courtesy of Kelly Wright)

Maria, Tatiana, Anastasia, and Olga, 1914 (Marlene A. Eilers Koenig collection)

Tsar Nicholas II and his children at *Stavka*, 1916
(General collection, Beinecke Rare Book and Manuscript Library, Yale University)

The grand duchesses resting between tennis matches with an officer, 1914
(General collection, Beinecke Rare Book and Manuscript Library, Yale University)

The Big Pair working
in the lazaret, 1914
(General collection,
Beinecke Rare Book
and Manuscript
Library, Yale
University)

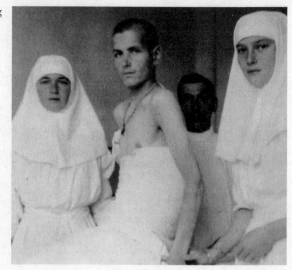

The Little Pair posing in the wards, 1914 (General collection,
Beinecke Rare Book and Manuscript Library, Yale University)

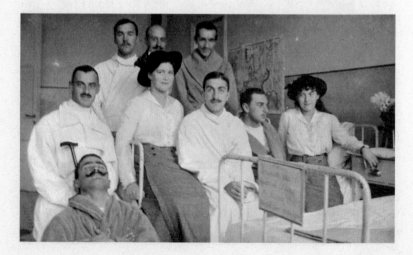

Tatiana, Anastasia, and Ortipo, photographed by Maria in June 1917 (Courtesy of Kori Lawrence)

Olga, Nicholas, Anastasia, and Tatiana on the greenhouse roof at Tobolsk, 1918 (General collection, Beinecke Rare Book and Manuscript Library, Yale University)

For over ninety years, studying the history of the last tsar and his family has been a murky, mine-filled proposition. Opinions vary widely, and tempers run high. Fans and historians alike argue over whether Tsar Nicholas II was a malleable despot or a mild-mannered daddy. Was Alexandra a hysterical religious fanatic or a painfully shy woman afflicted with anxiety disorders? Depending on who you ask, their five children might have been angels or hooligans. From violently anti-Semitic Soviet tracts to the moistly sentimental memoirs of friends and courtiers, there is plenty to sort and sift. Where the Romanovs' captivity and execution are concerned, myths and misremembrances sometimes snowball into outright lies, and contradictions abound.

Fortunately, the Bolsheviks preserved mountains of the imperial family's letters, diaries, and photographs, though the Soviets kept the archives sealed for decades. With the fall of the USSR, however, the personal documents of the last tsar's family began to trickle, then flood, from behind closed doors.

As often as possible, I relied on those documents and photographs, which number in the hundreds of thousands, to guide me. When that proved impossible, I turned to memoirs of the people who shared the Romanovs' final years, particularly favoring those who wrote down their impressions as events unfolded. Even then, the testimony of firsthand witnesses diverged time and again. What's an author to do?

In the end, I trusted my own collective impressions of my characters. Aside from the inevitable jiggling of the chronology inherent in fiction, I occasionally made choices to best serve my story, but only when the history itself provided no clear hints. Specifically:

OTMA and Politics

It is impossible to know how much the Romanov children understood about the revolution, or the danger their family faced under captivity. None of the grand duchesses' post-revolutionary diaries have survived, yet the fact that Maria and Anastasia burned their 1918 diaries before being transferred to Ekaterinburg perhaps speaks for itself. At the very least, the children were aware of the news headlines, and I don't believe they could have been immune to the tension mounting in the Ipatiev house in late June and early July. Even so, I have very likely portrayed them as more informed than they actually were. On the whole, their lives were sheltered, and their education lackluster. Their contemplation and experience of the world outside the imperial parks and palaces was limited. Captivity didn't change that fact. To some observers, the Little Pair seemed content and more or less oblivious in Tobolsk. Olga, however, has gained a reputation for being sensitive, insightful, and perceptive. Although I think that's an exaggeration and do not believe she was especially gifted, I have nonetheless made use of that view of Olga in service to my story. While there is some evidence to suggest that Olga and Tatiana were more aware of the family's peril than their younger siblings, I myself don't believe Olga had any reason to suspect they would all be executed.

Rasputin

Did he truly have healing powers? No one knows. Some scholars believe he used hypnosis to soothe the tsarevich, while others claim his "powers" were well-timed coincidences. Ultimately, it doesn't matter. A story told through the eyes of the imperial family can only show what the Romanovs themselves believed: that Grigori Rasputin healed Aleksei through the power of prayer. Traditionally, Rasputin has held a vivid reputation as a drinker and a womanizer. At the time of his murder, the majority of Russians believed he was a demon who possessed the empress, made vulgar public displays, and meddled in politics. Yet to the imperial family, he showed nothing but virtue. Which of these two extremes is closer to the truth? Again, for my story it doesn't matter—whether they were true or not, the gossip and rumors were enough to destroy Rasputin in the end, and with him, the Romanov dynasty.

Russian Nicknames

Although Russians consider it stiff and formal to call close friends and relations by given names, at first glance the family of Nicholas II seems to be an exception. While they had dozens of cloying pet names—Wify, Huzzy, Boysy, Sunny, Sunbeam, Baby, girlies, etc.—their letters and diaries show almost no trace of traditional Russian diminutives. Privately, Nicholas and Alexandra favored English nicknames for each other: Nicky and Alix rather than Kolya and Shura. As for the children, I've found a scant handful of letters in which the empress refers to three of her daughters as Olenka, Tatianochka, and Mashenka. Even the children addressed and signed their letters and notes among themselves with their given names—though once in a while Anastasia closed a letter with "Nastasya" or "Nastaska." Only Maria Nikolaevna stands out from the pattern for being routinely called Mashka by her sisters.

In spite of the documentary evidence, the Romanovs considered themselves quintessentially Russian, so chances are slim that they would have ignored this ingrained facet of Russian culture. The imperial children spoke Russian among themselves as well as with their father, so although I can't prove it, I believe it's almost certain they used the expected diminutives—Olya, Nastya, Alyosha—when speaking to one another. As a compromise, I reserved those nicknames for moments of tenderness or stress. I should also admit that Tanya is a far more common diminutive for Tatiana than Tatya. I chose Tatya because I like the sound of it, and because I do know that the imperial children addressed Tatiana Botkin as Tanya, and I wanted to avoid confusion.

In the west, Anastasia's nickname, Shvybzik, is commonly believed to mean "imp" in Russian. It doesn't. In fact, it means nothing at all in Russian. Instead, it seems the imperial family adopted a German word, *schwipsig* (meaning "tipsy"), to describe their impish prankster, altering the pronunciation in the process.

FOR MORE INFORMATION

ONLINE

Alexander Palace Time Machine
The world's preeminent Romanov website—a treasure trove of photos, letters, books, articles, and more.
http://www.alexanderpalace.org/palace/mainpage.html

Frozentears
A media-rich memorial to the last imperial family.
www.frozentears.org

Livadia.org
A tribute to the Romanov children, featuring scrapbook-style biographies and photo albums of each grand duchess.
www.Livadia.org

Romanov Memorial
A virtual tour of the Ipatiev house.
http://www.romanov-memorial.com

Yale Beinecke Albums
Browse six of Anna Vyrubova's personal photo albums, loaded with candid snapshots of the grand duchesses and their family.
http://beinecke.library.yale.edu/dl_crosscollex/romanov_album.htm

BOOKS & FILMS

Hundreds of books and documentaries have been produced about the Romanovs; these are especially good starting points:

Anastasia's Album, by Hugh Brewster

Last Days of the Romanovs, by Helen Rappaport

A Lifelong Passion, edited by Andrei Maylunas and Sergei Mironenko

Nicholas and Alexandra, by Robert K. Massie

Tsar: The Lost World of Nicholas and Alexandra, by Peter Kurth

Last of the Czars. Produced by Discovery Networks, in association with Brooks Associates Limited, 1996.

Russia's Last Tsar. National Geographic Video, distributed by Time Warner, Inc., 1995.

Visit the Alexander Palace Time Machine's Bookfinder (http://www.alexanderpalace.org/palace/book_finder.html) for information on dozens more current and out-of-print Romanov titles.

SELECTED BIBLIOGRAPHY

BOOKS

Alekseyev, Veniamin Vasillievich. *Last Act of a Tragedy: New Documents about the Execution of the Last Russian Emperor Nicholas II*. Ekaterinburg, Russia: Urals Branch of Russian Academy of Sciences, 1996.

Alexandrov, Victor. *End of the Romanovs*. New York: Little, Brown, 1966.

Alfer'ev, E. E. *Pis'ma Tsarskoi Sem'i iz Zatocheniya*. Jordanville, NY: Holy Trinity Monastery, 1974.

Baker, Raegan. *The Diary of Grand Duchess Olga Nicholaievna 1913*. Pickering, Ontario: Gilbert's Royal Books, 2008.

Bardovskaya, Larisa. *Tsarskoe Selo: The Imperial Summer Residence*. St. Petersburg: Alfa-Color Art Press, 2005.

Barkovets, Olga, and Aleksandr Krylov. *Tsesarevich*. Moscow: Vagrius, 1998.

Barkovets, Olga, and Valentina Tenikhina. *Nicholas II: The Imperial Family*. St. Petersburg: Abris, 2004.

Bokhanov, Alexander, Manfred Knodt, Vladimir Oustimenko, Zinaida Peregudova, and Lyubov Tyutunnik. *The Romanovs: Love, Power and Tragedy*. London: Leppi Publications, 1993.

Botkin, Gleb. *Lost Tales: Stories for the Tsar's Children*. New York: Villard Books, 1996.

———. *The Real Romanovs*. New York: Fleming H. Revell, 1931.

Brewster, Hugh. *Anastasia's Album*. London: Little, Brown, 1996.

Buxhoeveden, Baroness Sophie. *The Life and Tragedy of Alexandra Feodorovna, Empress of Russia*. London: Longmans, Green, 1928.

Bykov, Paul. *The Last Days of Tsardom*. London: Martin Lawrence, 1934.

Dehn, Lili. *The Real Tsaritsa*. London: Thornton, Butterworth, 1922.

Diterikhs, M. K. *Ubiistvo Tsarskoi Sem'i*. Moscow: Veche, 2008.

Eagar, Margaret. *Six Years at the Russian Court*. London: Hurst & Blackett, 1906.

Esmond, H. V. *In and Out of a Punt: A Duologue*. London: Samuel French, Ltd., 1902.

Eugénie de Grèce. *Le Tsarévitch: Enfant Martyr*. Paris: Perrin, 1990.

Fomin, Sergei. *Skorbnyi Angel*. St. Petersburg: Obshchestvo Svyatitelya Vasiliya Velikogo, 2005.

Fuhrmann, Joseph T. *The Complete Wartime Correspondence of Tsar Nicholas II and the Empress Alexandra, April 1914–March 1917*. Westport, CT: Greenwood, 1999.

———. *Rasputin: A Life*. New York: Praeger, 1990.

Gilliard, Pierre. *Thirteen Years at the Russian Court*. New York: George H. Doran, 1921.

Ginsburg, Mirra. *How Wilka Went to Sea and Other Tales from West of the Urals*. New York: Crown, 1975.

Grabbe, Alexander Graf. *The Private World of the Last Tsar*. Boston: Little Brown, 1984.

Grattan, H. P. *Packing Up: Farce in One Act*. London: Samuel French, Ltd., 1904.

Halliburton, Richard. *Seven League Boots*. Indianapolis: The Bobbs-Merrill Company, 1935.

Khrustalev, V. M. *Dnevniki Nikolaya II i Imperatritsy Aleksandry Fedorovny: 1917–1918*. Moscow: Vagrius, 2008.

King, Greg. *The Court of the Last Tsar: Pomp, Power and Pageantry in the Reign of Nicholas II*. Hoboken, NJ: John Wiley & Sons, 2006.

———. *The Last Empress: The Life and Times of Alexandra Feodorovna, Empress of Russia*. New York: Carol, 1994.

King, Greg, and Penny Wilson. *The Fate of the Romanovs*. Hoboken, NJ: John Wiley & Sons, 2003.

Kozlov, Vladimir. *Dnevniki Imperatora Nikolaya II*. Moscow: Orbita, 1991.

Kozlov, Vladimir, and Vladimir Khrustalëv, eds. *The Last Diary of Tsaritsa Alexandra*. New Haven, CT: Yale University Press, 1997.

Kurth, Peter. *Tsar: The Lost World of Nicholas and Alexandra*. London: Little, Brown, 1995.

Lieven, Dominic. *Nicholas II: Twilight of the Empire*. New York: St. Martin's Press, 1994.

Lyons, Marvin. *Nicholas II: The Last Tsar*. New York: St. Martin's Press, 1974.

Massie, Robert K. *Nicholas and Alexandra*. New York: Scribner, 1967.

———. *The Romanovs: The Final Chapter*. New York: Random House, 1995.

Massie, Robert K., and Marilyn Swezey. *The Romanov Family Album*. New York: Vendome Press, 1982.

Maylunas, Andrei, and Sergei Mironenko. *A Lifelong Passion: Nicholas and Alexandra: Their Own Story*. London: Weidenfeld & Nicolson, 1996.

McLees, Nectaria. *Divnyi Svet*. Moscow: Russkiy Palomnik, 1998.

Mel'nik-Botkina, Tat'yana. *Vospominaniya o Tsarskoi Sem'e*. Moscow: Zakharov, 2004.

Michael, Prince of Greece. *Nicholas and Alexandra: The Family Albums*. London: Tauris Parke Books, 1992.

Moynahan, Brian. *Rasputin: The Saint Who Sinned*. New York: Random House, 1997.

Nekrasov, Nikolai, and Juliet Soskice. *Poems by Nicholas Nekrasov*. London: Oxford University Press, 1936.

Nepein, I. G. *Pered Rasstrelom: Poslednie Pis'ma Tsarskoi Sem'i*. Omsk, Russia: Omskoe Knizhnoe Izdatel'stvo, 1992.

Pankratov, V. *S Tsarem v Tobolske*. New York: Slovo, 1990.

Radzinsky, Edvard. *The Last Tsar: The Life and Death of Nicholas II*. New York: Doubleday, 1992.

Rappaport, Helen. *Ekaterinburg: The Last Days of the Romanovs*. London: Hutchinson, 2008.

Rasputin, Maria, and Patte Barham. *Rasputin: The Man Behind the Myth*. Englewood Cliffs, NJ: Prentice-Hall, 1977.

Shelayev, Yuri, Elizabeth Shelayeva, and Nicholas Semenov. *Nicholas Romanov: Life and Death*. St. Petersburg: Liki Rossi, 2004.

Solodkoff, Alexander von. *The Jewel Album of Tsar Nicholas II and a Collection of Private Photographs of the Russian Imperial Family*. London: Ermitage, 1997.

Spéranski, Valentin. *La « Maison à destination spéciale»: La tragedie d'Ekaterinenbourg*. Paris: J Ferenczi & Fils, 1929.

Spiridovitch, Alexandre. *Les Dernières Années de la Cour de Tzarskoïë-Sélo*. Paris: Payot, 1928.

Steinberg, Mark D., and Vladimir M. Khrustalëv. *The Fall of the Romanovs*. New Haven, CT: Yale University Press, 1995.

Swezey, Marylin Pfeifer. *Nicholas and Alexandra: At Home with the Last Tsar and His Family*. Washington, DC: The American-Russian Cultural Cooperation Foundation, 2004.

Syroboyarskii, Aleksandr Vladimirovich. *Skorbnaya Pamyatka*. New York: privately printed, 1928.

Timms, Robert, ed. *Nicholas and Alexandra: The Last Imperial Family of Tsarist Russia*. New York: Harry N. Abrams, 1998.

Townend, Carol. *Royal Russia: The Private Albums of the Russian Imperial Family*. New York: St. Martin's Press, 1998.

Trewin, John C. *The House of Special Purpose: an Intimate Portrait of the Last Days of the Russian Imperial Family*. New York: Stein and Day, 1974.

Vasyutinskaya, E. F. *Na Detskoi Polovine*. Moscow: Pinakoteka, 2000.

Vorres, Ian. *Last Grand Duchess: The Memoirs of Grand Duchess Olga Alexandrovna*. New York: Scribner, 1965.

Vyrubova, Anna. *Memories of the Russian Court*. New York: Macmillan, 1923.

Warner, Elizabeth. *Heroes, Monsters and Other Worlds from Russian Mythology*. New York: Peter Bedrick, 1985.

Wilton, Robert. *The Last Days of the Romanovs (including depositions of Colonel Kobylinsky, Pierre Gilliard, Sidney Gibbes, Anatoly Yakimov, Pavel Medvedev, Philip Proskuriakov)*. London: Thornton Butterworth, 1920.

Wortman, Richard S. *Scenarios of Power: Myth and Ceremony in Russian Monarchy, Vol. 2*. Princeton, NJ: Princeton University Press, 2000.

Yermilova, Larissa. *The Last Tsar*. Bournemouth, UK: Parkstone Press/Planeta, 1996.

Zeepvat, Charlotte. *The Camera and the Tsars: A Romanov Family Album*. Gloucestershire, UK: Sutton, 2004.

———. *Romanov Autumn*. Gloucestershire, UK: Sutton, 2000.

Zhuk, Yu. A. *Ispoved' Tsareubiits*. Moscow: Veche, 2008.

Zvereva, Nina K. *Avgusteishie Sestry Miloserdiya*. Moscow: Veche, 2006

ARTICLES

Chebotareva, Valentina Ivanovna. "V Dvortsom Lazarete v Tsarskom Sele. Dnevnik: 14 Iyulya 1915–5 Yanvarya 1918." *Noviy Zhurnal* vol. 181(1990): 173–243; vol. 182(1990): 202–250.

Atlantis Magazine, Vol. 4, no. 5 (2003)

King, Greg, and Penny Wilson. "The Departure of the Imperial Family from Tsarskoe Selo." *Atlantis Magazine: In the Courts of Memory:* 12–31.

———. "The Murder of the Romanovs: An Annotated Bibliography." *Atlantis Magazine: In the Courts of Memory*: 110–140.

———. "The Officer Letters." *Atlantis Magazine: In the Courts of Memory*: 73–86.

———. "The Romanov Children." *Atlantis Magazine: In the Courts of Memory*: 6–10.

———. "The Timeline." *Atlantis Magazine: In the Courts of Memory*: 48–72.

ONLINE

Ashton, Janet. "The reign of the Empress? A re-evaluation of the war-time political role of Alexandra Feodorovna." http://www.directarticle.org/Alexandras_political_role. pdf/(Accessed November 7, 2009).

Benckendorff, Count Paul. *Last Days at Tsarskoe Selo*. London: William Heinemann, 1927. http://www.alexanderpalace.org/lastdays/.

Buchannan, Meriel. "Grand Duchess Olga Nicholaievna." http://www.alexanderpalace.org/ palace/olgabuchannan.html (accessed October 15, 2009).

Buxhoeveden, Baroness Sophie. *Left Behind: Fourteen Months in Siberia During the Revolution*. London: Longmans, Green, 1929. http://www.alexanderpalace.org/ leftbehind/.

Hanbury-Williams, John. *The Emperor Nicholas II As I Knew Him*. London: Arthur L. Humphreys, 1922. http://www.alexanderpalace.org/hanbury/.

Kerensky, Alexander. "The Imperial Family." http://www.angelfire.com/pa/
ImperialRussian/royalty/russia/kerensky.html (accessed July 4, 2009).

Mossolov, Alexander. *At the Court of the Last Tsar*. London: Methuen, 1935. http://www.
alexanderpalace.org/mossolov/.

Volkov, Alexei. *Souvenirs d'Alexis Volkov, Valet de Chambre de Tsarina Alexandra Feodorovna,
1910–1918*. Paris: Payot, 1928. http://www.alexanderpalace.org/volkov/
volkovmain.html (Translation by Robert Moshein, © 2004).

"Evening Prayers from the 'Jordanville' Prayer Book." http://www.orthodox.net/services/
evening-prayers.html (accessed December 27, 2009)

FILMS

Last of the Czars. Produced by Discovery Networks, in association with Brooks Associates
Limited, 1996.

Nikolai i Aleksandra. Castle Communications PLC/Eastern Light Productions, 1994.

Nicholas and Alexandra. Granada Television Limited, for A&E Television Networks, 1994.

Russia's Last Tsar. National Geographic Video, distributed by Time Warner, Inc., 1995.

ACKNOWLEDGMENTS

Robert Beaudoin, Bethanie Connors, Nemanja Djurasinovic, Catherine Hamel, Martha Nelson, Anne Nevala, Inga Sonnenfeld, and Svetlana Storozhenko served as volunteer translators of Russian, French, and German. Robert Moshein also shared his extensive translation of Spiridovitch's memoirs before the book became available in English.

A long list of people lent, traded, gifted, sold, photocopied, and/or hunted down rare books, films, and photos for my research: Elaine Duncan Achenbach, Helen Azar, Claire Chernikina, Nicola de Valeron, Judy and Rich Dugger, Kathleen Fannon, Harold and Phyllis Gass, Robert Gass, Robert Hall, Gayle Haynie, "Hikaru," Greg King, Sue Lorenzen, Laura Mabee, "Marialana," Charlotte and Gary Miller, Stacie Narlock, "Ortino," Inga Sonnenfeld, Svetlana Storozhenko, Penny Wilson, and Joanna Wrangham.

Bob Atchison, Raegan Baker, Claire Chernikina, George Hawkins, Greg King, Peter Kurth, and Helen Rappaport shared insight and tidbits of information not found in books.

Elaine Duncan Achenbach, Holly Daugherty, Laura Mabee, Maggie Patterson, and Janet Whitcomb read snippets of early drafts and reassured me I was on the right track; later Kristin Cashore, Simon Donoghue, and Kathe Koja offered substantial encouragement and critiques of various revisions. Bob Atchison, Greg King, Robert Moshein, Helen Rappaport, and Penny Wilson vetted the manuscript. Whatever errors remain are my own.

Finally, I'm especially grateful to Bob Atchison for founding the Alexander Palace Time Machine website and discussion board. When I discovered the site in 2005, I thought I knew plenty about the Romanovs, but in the last five years, my book collection has quadrupled and my knowledge of the imperial family has increased exponentially. The friends I've made and the resources I've been able to access because of the APTM provided a richness of detail and perspective I could not have found elsewhere.